In the Distance with You

ALSO BY CARLA GUELFENBEIN

The Rest Is Silence

In the DISTANCE *with* YOU

CARLA GUELFENBEIN

Translated from the Spanish by John Cullen

OTHER PRESS / NEW YORK

Production editor: Yvonne E. Cárdenas
Text designer: Jennifer Daddio
This book was set in Mrs. Eaves by Alpha Design and Composition of Pittsfield, NH

1 3 5 7 9 10 8 6 4 2

Printed in the United States of America on acid-free paper.
For information write to Other Press LLC,
267 Fifth Avenue, 6th Floor, New York, NY 10016.
Or visit our Web site: www.otherpress.com

LIBRARY OF CONGRESS CATALOGING-IN-PUBLICATION DATA

Names: Guelfenbein, Carla, 1959– author. | Cullen, John, 1942– translator.
Title: In the distance with you / Carla Guelfenbein ; translated from the Spanish
by John Cullen.
Other titles: Contigo en la distancia. English
Description: New York : Other Press, 2018.
Identifiers: LCCN 2017045135 (print) | LCCN 2017047616 (ebook) |
ISBN 9781590518717 (ebook) | ISBN 9781590518700 (hardcover)
Subjects: | BISAC: FICTION / Contemporary Women. | FICTION / Jewish. |
FICTION / Literary.
Classification: LCC PQ8098.417.U35 (ebook) | LCC PQ8098.417.U35 C6613 2018 (print) |
DDC 863/.7—dc23
LC record available at https://lccn.loc.gov/2017045135

Publisher's Note: This is a work of fiction. Names, characters,
places, and incidents either are the product of the
author's imagination or are used fictitiously.

For

ELIANA DOBRY

and

MICAELA AND SEBASTIÁN ALTAMIRANO

My Traveling Companions

Part

ONE

I.

DANIEL

Somewhere on the planet, there was someone responsible for your death. That certainty grew stronger as each day passed, bludgeoning my conscience, making itself unbearable. But who? Why? I never imagined the answer might be so close that I could turn around and meet myself.

I remember the moment when I ran across the neighborhood vagrant, right after I bought the bread for our breakfast. His eyes, at once wounded and menacing, came to rest on me. I quickened my pace while the jumbled mass of people around me, all of them in raincoats, walked past and disappeared into the morning fog. A group of kids crossed the avenue. The girls, wrapped in colorful scarves and speaking in low voices, shared their secrets as they walked, while the boys ran around shouting, pushing at one another like clumsy puppies. Their innocence increased the agitation that meeting the bum had produced in me. I couldn't know what I would know a few minutes later, I couldn't know what had happened to you during the night, or maybe at dawn.

Every morning before seeing you, I'd always wonder what sort of mood you'd be in. It was impossible to predict, governed by your dreams, by the intensity of the light and the temperature, by infinite layers of circumstances I never managed to figure out. Sometimes you talked to me incessantly, but at other times you would seem absorbed in listening to the sound of a world that existed inside you.

When I reached your door, Arthur sat down next to me with his customary papal dignity, while Charly feverishly wagged his tail. I was thinking I'd suggest going for one of our walks after breakfast.

In spite of your age, you walked at a fast, steady clip. Anyone who saw us from a certain distance would have found it difficult to imagine that you were more than fifty years older than me.

I remember a time, a few days after I became your neighbor, when I saw you at your front door, doing battle with the climbing plant that obstructed your passage. You told me the thing had grown overnight; you said its obstinate presence was an affront to your personal freedom. You talked about the plant as though it were a creature of flesh and blood, while at the same time you were trying to take it apart with a kitchen knife. I fetched my pruning shears and set about clearing the entrance, and after a while we fell into animated conversation. A few weeks back, I'd seen your picture in the newspaper. An important critic had praised your work in the *New York Times*, and the daily papers in our country had reprinted that review. Nevertheless, when I saw you in your yard, I was surprised by your height and your gray hair, which you wore gathered at the back of your neck. Time had failed to destroy your beauty. Your features must have been softer and more rounded once, but now angles were beginning to emerge—in your prominent nose, in your chin, in your cheekbones, in your lined forehead. Your long hands were like birds that had forgotten the art of flying. You were memorably vehement when you told me, sometime later, that you detested performing practical tasks and would have liked to have a wife like the ones the great creators had, the wives who took care of all mundane matters and shielded the artists from the banalities of life. After you told me that, I always tried, however clumsily and incompletely, to protect you. I found the world you lived in unfathomable. But at the same time, the light pouring out of the doors you left half open filled me with agitation and curiosity about what I couldn't see.

I dug around in my pocket for your house key and discovered I'd forgotten it. I rang the doorbell, but there was no response. I waited for a few seconds and tried again, and then again, more and more insistently. I remembered the bum's eyes, brutal and defeated at the same time; they stood out in my memory like a dissonant note in a music score. I turned and walked toward the left side of the yard, and Arthur, with his usual weary gait, followed me. The morning light on the gravel path was dazzlingly bright. Like the house, the yard was silent, bereft of all human presence. A violet was starting to put out its winter shoots. Little lives that you'd be sure to follow attentively, as you did every year. I took a look through one of the side windows. The stripes of filtered sunlight reinforced the darkness of the hall.

It took a few seconds for me to see you. You'd fallen to the foot of the staircase, where the light practically didn't reach. Your inert body lay like a toppled tree next to the standing lamp I'd given you for your last birthday. I ran to the patio in the back. The door to the kitchen was wide open. It looked as though someone had been there and—in too much of a hurry?—forgotten to close the door. *Who?* I wondered.

I crouched down beside you. Your hands were curled into claws, as if they'd been scratching invisible bodies before they surrendered. A pool of blood encircled your head. You also had a long scratch on one arm, a reddish streak that ran from your wrist to your elbow. Your nightgown was bunched up around your hips, and your pubis, smooth and white, showed between your open, elderly legs. I covered you as best I could with your nightgown, and only then did I grab you by the shoulders and shake you. "Vera! Vera!" I shouted.

You seemed so light, so fragile. Everything took on the appearance of a dream.

After that, things got blurry. Time started to pass in a different way, extending itself formlessly, darkly. I just remember that at some point after the ambulance arrived, I ignored orthodox procedure and lifted up your body myself, while the people around me begged me to calm down and let them do their work. I didn't want anyone to touch you, I didn't want anyone to feel the warmth your body was giving off. I didn't want anyone to hear your breathing fade away.

2.

EMILIA

"*I am you*. Don't ever forget that," Jérôme told me as we were saying our good-byes in Charles de Gaulle Airport.

He was the one who had urged me to travel. Alone, I would never have gathered enough strength to leave my cloistered state. Although the idea was unimaginable, we were to be married upon my return from my trip.

Through the big window in front of us, we could see the tails of the airplanes, which seemed to be hanging from the sky.

I am you.

Those were the words that united us. That had always united us and protected us from misfortune. Like a spell. I was him and he was me. We walked in silence to the boarding area and said good-bye without touching. The expression on his face was serene, assured. I couldn't betray the confidence he had in me. The day before, I had bid farewell to my parents in Grenoble, and Dr. Noiret, my psychiatrist, had medicated me so that I wouldn't suffer a panic attack.

Even so, I couldn't help saying for the *n*th time, "Jérôme, I don't know if I can do this."

"Sure you can, Emilia. Sure you can." He grazed my lips with an index finger to keep me from repeating what I'd said.

Huddled in my seat in the airplane, looking out of my little window at the bed of clouds, I fixed my imagination on Jérôme's small-featured face. He'd always been there. He was the human race, and nothing that lived beyond him existed for me. I thought about the life we'd made together, a life without wings but also without disasters. It's hard to settle for such a life. For such ordinariness. Extraordinary things are exciting, they call to us with their trumpets and their bright colors. But they're fragile. They break.

That was the understanding we'd always had, Jérôme and I. Nevertheless, now he was letting me go. He was letting me go, and at the same time binding me to him with his marriage proposal. Why did he do that? Why had he pushed me to go, encouraging me with his rosy predictions? Out of goodness. Yes, out of the goodness of his heart. But also—and this pointed thought pierced my consciousness—because we'd reached an impasse we had to move away from, we had to go somewhere else. We were both twenty-four, and when you're young, the present needs to be open to the sea of future possibilities that don't yet exist.

Opportunities you have to go out and look for.

I had got this far, holding on to his hand. But now he and our protected world, its edges frayed by wear and time, were disappearing below the clouds. Breathing cost me an effort. I asked for a glass of water. Before leaving, the sun began to grow larger. Its light ricocheted off something and came crashing through my little window with such intensity that I had to put on my sunglasses. I thought I could see the ocean, far down below. Fragments that looked like watery mirrors. If that was the sea, from this distance it didn't possess the violence that had frightened me as a little girl.

I remembered the sea at La Serena, the city in northern Chile where my mother was born. I'd gone there a few times when I was a girl. I saw the waves rising up, with their scaly texture. I saw my mother running to plunge into the heart of that wall of water and then sink under the explosion of a thousand backlit, glittering particles. I saw my father at my side, the two of us standing still on the sand, and me holding my breath, imagining that the giant whale had swallowed her forever. And at last I saw her dark head emerge from the far side of the explosion, and she waved her arms for us to see her at that distance, and we recognized, once again, her indomitable energy. Which was what had carried her so far from us so often. Far from my father's simultaneously vigilant and defeated gaze. It had been while she was on one of those forays outside the dominion of marriage that she had conceived me. They told me as soon as I could reason. My father wasn't my father.

They had been married for five years, and they both worked in the Nice Observatory. They'd intended to have children, but my father's semen lacked the density needed for procreation. For this reason and others that made themselves obvious to me with the passing years, my father, when my mother told him that she was pregnant by one of her student trainees, accepted the creature that was already floating in her belly.

These were, for me, the predominant images of that distant place where my mother was born and to which I was now headed. Images of her vanishing and then reappearing. Of my father's hand, next to mine but never touching me. Our smiles united in silence, corroborating the fact that no matter what our genetic composition might have been, he and I were stranded on the same shore.

Now those pieces of ocean looked tranquil, shut up in their own silence.

All things have another reality, I thought, and until then I had never seen it.

3.
DANIEL

The room was plunged in darkness. I stepped close to you and placed my fingers on your gray head. All around us, silence and heated air. The stillness was so deep that death seemed to be looming behind it. The plastic bracelet on your wrist bore your name. You had a cast on one leg, and another on one hand. Your arms were immobilized on both sides by countless tubes, which were in turn connected to the machines recording your vital signs. Beneath your closed eyelids, your eyes were pulsating. A ventilator supplied your oxygen.

The doctor had explained to me that besides various contusions, your fall had caused a severe closed-head trauma, with hemorrhaging in the cerebrum. In order to buy enough time for the swelling to go down, they had "put you to sleep." A euphemistic phrase that would have annoyed you. Inducing a coma was the only way of reducing cerebral activity to a minimum and keeping intracranial pressure under control. He explained himself exhaustively, your doctor. Nevertheless, when I asked him if you could hear me or perceive another person's presence at your side, he gave an ambiguous reply. "That's not something we can know with certainty," he told me. "But all the studies indicate that comatose patients lack perception."

"Vera," I said to you, and I couldn't go on.

I felt a weight on my chest when I imagined the possibility that you were there, behind the body lying under the bedcovers; that you were on the other side of life, trying to speak to me. I took your hand and squeezed it hard.

It had rained, and through the window of your hospital room I could see the reflections of the first streetlights glistening on the wet pavement.

A nurse knocked on your door and without waiting for a response came into the room. She was a woman in her thirties, short in stature and broad in the hips. Her face seemed to have the transitory firmness of a ripe fruit.

"You haven't eaten in hours," she said to me while making notes on a clipboard. "Why don't you go down to the cafeteria? Nothing's going to happen to the lady."

As I didn't answer, she stopped her work for a moment and looked at me. Then she took a step backward and adjusted her hair, which was done up in a bun. Her cheeks reddened. I could tell that she felt intimidated by me.

"It's good that you talk to her and keep her company. I'm sure she can hear you."

I would have liked to ask her to say more, but her flushed face made me abandon the idea.

"My name is Lucy. If you need something, all you have to do is press this little button."

When she went away, I sat in the chair next to your bed and dozed off.

At regular intervals, another nurse would come in to check your vital signs, and I would start awake. It was during one of those sudden returns to consciousness, sometime in the middle of that broken night, when I felt a pang of regret at knowing so little about you. About your origins, your family, your life. You'd had a husband and a son, Manuel Pérez and Julián, but you never talked about them. All I knew about your son was that he'd died of a lung disease at the age of thirty. The mystery you surrounded yourself with in order to face the world had resisted me too, despite our closeness.

After the news of your accident was made public, I couldn't help noticing that no one came forward and claimed to be a member of your family. Even though the grief of those who did show up—writers, poets, men and women of letters—was obvious, none of them seemed to have known you very well. The only person I contacted was your poet friend, Horacio Infante. I didn't have his number, but Gracia got it somehow. I had deduced from our conversations—even though you never stated it directly—that Infante meant a lot to you. On the telephone, his voice sounded shocked. I couldn't help noticing, however, that he never showed up at the hospital. I tried to speak to him again, but I was unable to get hold of him. I left my cell phone number on his voice mail and told him to call me if he wanted to know how you were doing. I learned from the papers that he'd returned to Paris, his place of residence, a few days after your accident.

While the first blue gleams of dawn began to tinge the darkness, I thought that under the wrapping of your body, your heart was beating, and that you were that heart. Even though you couldn't hear me, that was where you lived now. Secluded inside its walls, going on with your life, but in another form.

Confused by my sleepless night, I left the car at the hospital and returned home on foot, walking along the river. A pitiless light was growing in some corner of the mountains, showing itself above the snowy peaks and then crashing down onto the windowpanes.

When I reached our street, I saw the tramp asleep on some shapeless sacks. He was covered with a blanket, his back against the wall of a neighbor's house. For at least a year, he'd been prowling around the neighborhood, and we'd got used to his presence, his smell, the sound of the empty cans he carried slung over his shoulder, banging against one another as he walked. He was a tall fellow with a small, birdlike head, and behind his ravaged appearance you could just discern the elegant man he must have been. He had never asked us for food or money, and it was hard to be clear about whether he refrained because he lived in another world, or for dignity's sake.

Arrived home, I took off my clothes and snuggled up to Gracia. Her warm skin aroused my senses, but she was sleeping and didn't react to my attempts to make love to her.

I woke up a few hours later. My body ached all over. Gracia came out of the bathroom, wrapped in a towel from chest to knee. She went to the window and pulled the curtains wide open. I could see your house, with its wooden shingle roof and the vegetation that covered it. I thought that Arthur and Charly must be hungry. As soon as I got up, I would go over and feed them.

"Good morning," she said in that husky voice of hers.

Her eyes were red, as if she hadn't slept much or she'd been crying, and I was touched by the slight tremor in her chin.

Her skin, always sun-browned, looked even darker against the white towel. She sat in the middle of the bed with her legs crossed, gathering up her long, wet hair at the base of her neck. Gracia possessed indisputable self-confidence. I never asked you about that, but I know it's no virtue as far as you're concerned. You used to tell me that a creator's sole possessions were her fractures, her uncertainties, her questions and her idle pursuits, and the constant doubt about the ultimate reason why things are. Only through those cracks, you said, could something grow that had never been there before. But Gracia had no creative aspirations, and the self-assurance she displayed in all the areas of her life brought her ample benefits and rewards. She had studied engineering, but at twenty-two she'd begun to work in television. Now, fourteen years later, she was one of the news anchors on the most popular channel, and her energetic temperament entered the homes of millions of Chileans every day.

"I didn't hear you come home. Tell me about Vera," she asked. Her expression showed her distress.

"They're putting her into an induced coma. Given her age, the possibility that she won't wake up again is pretty high."

Gracia squeezed her eyes shut, as if an image had appeared before her pupils and wounded them. Then she shook her head from side to side, and droplets of water from her hair gleamed on the window. She gathered up her hair in a knot again and looked at the wall where she herself had framed the drawing of the facade for my museum project. It was a drawing that reminded me, every morning of every day, that one day not so long ago I had won an important prize, and maybe I still had hopes that the project would be built.

"That's very tough, what you're telling me," she said, embracing herself with both arms.

It had always been difficult for me to know what Gracia was feeling or thinking.

When I first met her, I longed to drown the feeling of distance that had hampered me ever since my childhood, to drown it in our love. It was you, Vera, who made me see how puerile that longing was. It was you who showed me that beneath our skin there's a private world with its own structures and its own landscapes, a world no one else can ever enter. Gracia never appreciated you. And you knew it. She blamed you, in part, for my "lazy days," as she called the long wait to begin construction on the museum. More than a year had passed, and the authorities still hadn't reached an agreement concerning the project. There was always someone trying to steer it forward, but also someone with more clout running it aground. Power struggles, different studies, other priorities. There was no lack of reasons to postpone it month after month. And in the meantime, I'd been left hanging.

Every day I got up thinking about some aspect of the design that could be improved, a new material, a steeper angle, a wider corridor, and no day passed without my opening the archives in my computer and adding or eliminating a detail. During that time, Vera, you were always there. By your side, I never felt anxious about the idle passage of the days. There were other things: our conversations, our walks, the discovery of the universe that surrounded you.

"It's horrible. I...," she said, and then she stopped.

"What?"

"Nothing, nothing. It's just that life changes so abruptly, so cruelly."

I imagined that Gracia might be referring to something else, something related to herself or to us. I wanted to ask her, but she'd already left the bed and disappeared into the depths of her closet. Things that matter, I thought, are too raw, too disturbing to be uttered. Too overwhelming. I slipped farther under the sheets and went back to sleep.

At ten that morning, I went down to the kitchen and made myself some coffee. A few minutes later, I was going through the little gate in the back of the yard, the one I'd built to connect our yard to yours. Winter had given us a gift, a day filled with light you couldn't see. A luminous, low-lying little cloud of dust was seeping around the vegetation. Arthur and Charly appeared between the bushes.

Arthur, with his customary calm, looked at me incuriously and sat down on the stone path, while Charly attached himself to my legs, sweeping the air with his tail.

From the beginning of our friendship, you had insisted that I could go in and out of your house whenever I pleased. For that purpose, you'd given me a copy of the key to the main entrance, and moreover you would leave your kitchen door unlocked. It was instantaneous trust that united us. You'd even shown me where you kept the key to your strongbox.

"If you ever have to open it one day, Daniel, take out everything you find inside and throw it into the trash. There's nothing worth anything, nothing but an old woman's knickknacks. And as for the papers, burn them. I don't want the dogs sniffing around my life after I die. Agreed?"

I didn't understand why you were entrusting me with such a personal mission. It was the first time that I thought about your family, about the people who used to be by your side and who for some reason had disappeared. One day you'd go too, and maybe that day wasn't so far off. Your presence in my life had changed me in a way that wasn't visible to others—except Gracia—and for that very reason was much deeper and more meaningful. You had deposited something inside me, and you'd asked me to keep it. There it had remained, and now that you weren't around, I was afraid it would gradually disappear.

I entered the hall and saw the pool of dried blood. Everything had stopped in one chaotic, provisional moment. Silence reigned, a silence broken by the vague, subterranean noises of the heating system. I stayed in the entrance area for a while, looking at the staircase, and then I climbed the stairs, imagining how your back, your shoulders, your knees, your head must have struck every one of them. When I reached the top step, I looked back down. The shadows of the trees came through the hall window and darted back and forth across the wall like fish. I kept walking toward your room, but I halted in front of the open door without going inside. The bed was unmade. You must have fallen in the morning, maybe a little while before I found you. I went back to the top of the stairs. I wanted to reproduce your steps and elucidate the circumstances of your accident. According to the doctor, it hadn't been caused by a sudden loss of consciousness: the scratches on your arms showed that you'd tried to steady yourself against the walls as you fell.

I retraced my steps over the short distance between bedroom and stairs several times, and then I went back down. Although the staircase showed signs of wear and tear, it was solid. The handrail was firmly attached to the wall and easy to grip. The steps were carefully thought out and well proportioned, with risers seven inches high and treads twelve inches deep, for maximum safety. The most important consideration in their modest design had clearly been practicality. As I looked at the steps, a thought crossed my mind for the first time: maybe your fall hadn't been an accident. You were a strong woman, in complete control of yourself and your body. Your movements succeeded one another elegantly and precisely. On our walks, it was you who set the pace. There were even some times when you went so far as to poke fun at me: "Come on, let's lengthen those little strides, you're walking like an old dandy," you'd say as you passed me. I tried to recall the image of you lying on the floor, the position of your arms, the angle of your legs, your naked pubis, but the vision was too raw and an internal filter, unable to fix it in my consciousness, rejected it. I went out into the yard to feed the dogs. Then I went back inside and threw myself on the floor, in the exact spot where you'd fallen. What were your thoughts, I wondered, as you lay there, in that second before you slipped into unconsciousness?

Some constellations I had never noticed before were portrayed on the ceiling. The figures, thin lines traced on a light blue background, made me think of the ones that watch over travelers from on high in Grand Central Station in New York. I remembered your obsession with the universe and the stars, and their persistent evocation in your writings. That drawing on the ceiling may have been the last thing you saw.

A current of cold air went through my arms, my legs, my backbone. I remembered the wide-open kitchen door, and suddenly what a few minutes ago had been nothing but a vague hunch turned into a certainty: you hadn't made a misstep; something or someone had caused your fall.

I searched the Internet for the number of the PDI, the Investigations Police, and gave them a call. While I was telling a weary-voiced woman what had happened, I felt a strong urge to hang up. I knew what she was thinking, and what everyone I disclosed my suspicions to would think, namely that you were an old woman who stumbled and fell down the stairs. It must happen every day in every corner of the world, hundreds of times, thousands of times, older women and older men suffering fatal accidents, and it never occurs to anyone to think that anything other than the victim's old age might have been the cause. I had no proof. There was nobody now who could testify to your physical strength and the precision of your movements. When I finished my explanation, the woman informed me that the first thing I would have to do would be to procure a medical report corroborating my suspicions, and with that in hand I'd be able to apply to the public prosecutor and request that the PDI begin an investigation.

4.
EMILIA

Bare trees and gray streets.

That was my first impression of Santiago.

I arrived in Chile only a few months before the August morning when Vera Sigall fell down the stairs. My plan was to gather the material I needed to finish the thesis I was writing on her work. I was well aware it would be difficult, but I nevertheless cherished the hope of meeting her.

Although my mother had been born here, my only clear memories of Chile involved the sea and her head, bobbing in and out of sight on the great expanse of water. My grandparents had died in an accident when I was four, and since then my mother had lost contact with the rest of her family, who presumably were still living in La Serena.

Fortunately, my dad had managed to find me a place to live. It was an apartment that belonged to a Chilean who had been a student with him in Grenoble, and who had agreed to rent the place to me at a price my modest budget could afford. My apartment—if it could be called that—was a group of structures on the roof of a nine-story building facing Bustamante Park, a few blocks from General Joffré Street. The place consisted of a main room, a kitchen, and a bath, none of them connected. To go from one room to another, you had to step out into the open air, take a few steps across a broad terrace, and go back inside. The main room was small and papered in a floral pattern faded by the sun. On the bed was a colorful, hand-sewn eiderdown comforter. There was also a rickety armchair covered in blue velvet, some empty shelves where I put the books I'd brought with me, and a desk pushed against the window, over which hung a mirror in a pewter frame. The kitchen was even more cramped, but it boasted the essential utensils and a chiming clock whose ticktock marked the passage of time.

After unpacking my suitcase, I started getting nervous again. I had a mission to accomplish, a job to do, but I knew that the reason why I was there was one I hadn't explicitly discussed with Jérôme. One I myself didn't have the courage to face.

We'd met as children and classmates, and ever since then, with the exception of the period we called "the accident," we'd always been together. We shared our homework, our games, our reading. His father worked for Caterpillar, assembling pieces of gigantic bulldozers in a world that seemed alien to Jérôme and his interests. By contrast, when he was at our house, Jérôme felt at home. When his interest in astronomy became evident, my parents accepted him as a pupil. By the age of twenty-four, he was my father's right-hand man on the Schmidt telescope.

Our childhood bond had lasted until the present time, when we were grown, and it had made us into a couple, although of a strange kind, inasmuch as we had never touched. A few weeks before I left for Chile, Jérôme had proposed that we get married upon my return. We were having dinner in a restaurant in the center of Grenoble.

"Jérôme, we can't—"

"That's not important," he interrupted.

"But it is to me."

I myself didn't know what I meant. Maybe I was referring to my conviction that a normal human being like Jérôme is incapable of living without touching another person, without the embrace that seals his love, or maybe to the unutterable idea that somewhere, somewhere, there was someone who would be able to defrost me. Jérôme wasn't any more interested in physical expressions of love than I was, but his lack of interest wasn't a conscious phobia like mine. Plunged in his observations of heavenly bodies, he had no room for the terrestrial. One thing was certain: Jérôme and I had spent our lives in separate orbits, like two solitary planets.

That first evening I got a chair out of the kitchen, placed it in a corner of the big roof terrace, and sat down to read. The windows in the distance, touched by the winter sun, held its light. Pigeons were strutting defiantly on the rooftops and courting one another. On a nearby roof terrace, a Chilean flag was waving like a flame against the background of gray sky.

As the day started to fade, it was filled with icy reflections. I went into the bedroom and wrote to Jérôme, describing the details of my trip, of my new home, of the view I had over the city. It was only when I put all that into words for him that everything I'd experienced since my departure settled into my consciousness and became real.

I hardly slept that night. The next day I was to visit the Bombal Library, whose collection included manuscripts, papers, and working notes donated by Vera Sigall. Horacio Infante, a distinguished Chilean poet residing in Paris, had put me in touch with the library and helped me obtain permission to work there. I was longing to submerge myself in that material, which no one had yet touched. I was sure it would open a path for me, a road leading to new dimensions of Vera Sigall's work. But not only that.

In this corner of the world, separated from Jérôme, there were many things I didn't know; life appeared before me, vast and hazy at the same time, with neither beginning nor end.

5.
DANIEL

Once the doctor had given me, all unwillingly, a report in which he accepted the possibility that your fall wasn't an accident, I submitted the case to the public prosecutor's office, and a few days later I received a call from the Investigations Police. They arranged to come to your house that afternoon.

While I waited for them, I went out into your yard and looked at your study. Its design had caused our first and only argument. I thought it should have big windows that would let the light and the greenness in, but you wanted little windowlets that would safeguard your privacy, isolate you, provide you with a timeless interior space. I remember the sketches I made for you and your flattering words when you described the proportions of the glassed-in room I'd designed for you. Nevertheless, your decision was categorical, you wanted a black box your characters couldn't escape from. When I showed you the Zumthor chapel, it fascinated you, with its burnt-wood walls and its single opening above and the light falling in.

"That's what I want!" you said. And together we designed a study halfway between your black box and my glass one.

I crossed the yard and went in. There, inside your study, a life had remained suspended. The yellow daffodils in the vase had withered, and the book you'd been reading, Katherine Mansfield's diary with a foreword by Virginia Woolf, lay open, face down, on your chaise longue. Once again I looked at the picture on one of the shelves, the only photo of yourself that you kept in your house, apart from the one of you and your father. I never stopped being surprised that you'd chosen that particular photograph. You're standing up, your knees bent, your arms extended downward, your hands open, in a posture that shows you must have really known how to do the twist. You're looking at the camera with a mysterious smile, as if you're hiding a secret behind it and daring the photographer to discover what it is. Your serious-looking companion is watching you in tense futility, with the fixed gaze of a man confronted by someone who exceeds not only his expectations but also his possibilities. The picture you always kept on your table also held my attention for a while. It was a black-and-white photograph of a man with a dark beard bent over a handwriting exercise, the work of a little girl no older than five. The year was 1923, and that child was you. One day you told me the story: "My father was determined that I should learn to read and write. According to him, knowledge was the only thing that couldn't be snatched away from us."

A few days after the photographer, Alter Kacyzne, took that photograph, the town of Chechelnyk was invaded.

"My father blew out the candles, and we stayed where we were without moving and looked out through the drawn curtains while dozens of men ran about in the street, shouting, banging on doors with clubs and gun butts, breaking windows, dragging our neighbors outside and ransacking their houses."

I remember your telling me about your neighbor Danya. About her open, empty eyes. Four armed men were already ripping her clothes to shreds in front of the door to her house when your mother covered your eyes and held you close. You had never before spoken to me about that horror.

"Write it," I told you. And for the first time, you looked at me with contempt, as if saying, *You have no idea.* That was your silent space, and I never tried to profane it again.

The photograph on your shelf was an exceptionally fine one, and I became interested in finding out about the man who had taken it. I discovered that Kacyzne had been a great photographer. At the end of the First World War, he dedicated himself to chronicling the customs and lives of the Jews, going from town to town and trying to capture their culture. Many years after taking that picture of you and your father, Kacyzne left Poland, running from the Nazis, but when he reached Ternopil in 1941, they had already occupied the city, and he was beaten to death by Ukrainian collaborators. His wife Khana, a very beautiful woman who accompanied him on his photographic wanderings, died in a concentration camp. Their daughter survived by hiding in Poland as a non-Jewish citizen.

I left your study grieving all the harder and determined not to rest until I discovered what had happened to you the morning of your fall. I made myself some coffee and sat down at the kitchen table to wait. I thought about Gracia, about her wide mouth and her lopsided smile, which seemed to arise from a sense of irony, a shrewd apprehension of things and life. I also thought about the anniversary party she'd planned with so much care for that weekend, when we were to celebrate seven years of marriage. And although I knew Gracia was eagerly and even impatiently anticipating this celebration, I was going to be obliged to tell her that we had to cancel it. I wasn't capable of going through the vicissitudes, efforts, and pretensions that a party required.

I was deep in thought when the doorbell rang. The sound made me jump. I opened the door to a man of slight build and short stature. "I'm Detective Segundo Álvarez," he said by way of greeting.

He had an elongated face. His eyes were so black that it was impossible to tell where the irises stopped and the pupils began.

"Do you mind if I take a look around?"

He had on jeans and an impeccable blue parka. You could sense the care he took with his appearance; he wore his thinning hair combed back and had recently shaved. Nevertheless, the large bags under his eyes spoke of a life that wasn't in any way orderly or easy. I showed him the place at the foot of the stairs where you'd fallen, and the pool of blood, which was now dry. I mentioned that I'd found the kitchen door wide open that morning. Then we went up to the second floor. My cell phone rang while we were climbing the stairs; I tried to ignore it, but the detective gave me an expectant look. I took the phone out of my pocket, glanced at the screen, and silenced the call.

"You're not going to answer it?"

"I didn't recognize the number," I lied.

I explained my technical assessments of the stairs and the handrail, but he ran his eyes over things quickly, as if none of them represented a matter of interest to him. I had the impression that he was just going through the motions of his job, knowing in advance that everything he might do would be, when all was said and done, a waste of time. When we returned to the first floor, Detective Álvarez turned his attention to me.

"Mr. Daniel Estévez, right?"

"Exactly right," I said solicitously.

"What is your relationship with the lady?"

"I'm her neighbor."

"And how did you get in here?"

"I have a key. She gave it to me several years ago."

"Why didn't you call us immediately?"

"Because at first I thought it had been an accident."

"And what makes you now think that it wasn't?"

I explained again about the handrails and the stairs, I told him about your agility and about what good physical shape you were in for your age. I showed him into the kitchen, and we sat at the table in front of the window. I didn't want that scene to end in the living room, in front of your books and your most prized possessions. I offered the detective a cup of coffee, but he turned it down. He examined the door. I insisted that my having found it wide open was irrefutable proof something out of the ordinary had happened. He asked me who else was in your life; he wanted the names, addresses, and phone numbers of any relatives, friends, and acquaintances of yours who might have had some business with you. And as I knew little or nothing about any of that, my replies to his questions, which at first had come without hesitation, gradually turned stammering and unsure. He asked me if I'd come across any signs of violence when I found you on the floor, if you kept valuables in the house, and if anything was missing. I told him that some of your pictures had value, especially a portrait of you, a work of considerable size, painted by De Chirico. He asked me to show it to him and took a photo of it with his cell phone. He also photographed your Negret sculpture and some other paintings I pointed out to him. He'd send some technicians, he said, to gather fingerprints. My phone rang again. I knew who it was, and I silenced the phone without looking.

He asked me how we met, you and I, how often I saw you, how I earned my living, who lived with me. I told him that I'd spent the days preceding your fall on a trip to the north, in a place called Los Peumos. He asked me when I'd arrived there and what the reason for my trip was. I told him that I was an architect, and that I'd been asked to take on a hotel-building project. I was lying again. I wasn't about to confess to a stranger the real reason for my northern journey. Although the air was cool, I'd begun to perspire, and Detective Álvarez must have noticed. Lastly, he asked me when was the last time I'd been with you, and I said it was before I left. I was still lying to him. After that, he brought his visit to a close.

"You have to stop coming into Mrs. Sigall's house. We don't know that she would have wanted you to enter the place in her absence. Does anyone else have a house key?"

"María. She comes once a week to do the cleaning."

He asked me if I knew her full name and how to get in touch with her, and I gave him her cell phone number.

"When does she come?"

"She comes on Tuesdays. On the Tuesday after the accident, I called her and told her not to come. But she'll be here next week."

Having finished the interrogation, Detective Álvarez went back into the kitchen and bolted the door. He asked for my key as well and placed it in a plastic bag, which he then sealed. With a hand gesture and a lowered head, he requested that I leave your house.

That evening, however, contravening his instructions, I went in again. I had another key, a backup copy I'd made and kept in a desk drawer. I searched every corner of your house, looking for any sign that an object was missing or out of place. I went through your closet—discreetly—where, amid your shoes, you kept your strongbox. Everything was where it should be, untouched. A stopped life was holding its breath, waiting for you to come back so it could get going again. I knew that chaos of yours very well. I remembered how mischievously you'd quote Einstein by way of defending yourself. Something like, if a cluttered desk was a sign of a cluttered mind, what should we think about an empty desk? Apparently, if someone had entered your house, they hadn't done so in order to rob you. But why, then? Who?

6.
EMILIA

My tutor at the university had obtained a grant for me, but it barely covered my expenses. And so, with some of my savings, I bought a Pashley bicycle and applied to work as a delivery girl for the neighborhood fruit and vegetable market. The owner, Don José, accepted me right away. He was the son of Spanish immigrants who had arrived on the *Winnipeg* in 1939. He'd never lived in Spain, but he still had a Spanish accent, which he must have inherited from his parents. He wore a beret, a mustache, and a pair of suspenders, with his stout belly protruding between them. You entered the shop by going down three steps, on one of which a black cat was usually lying. Every morning after making my deliveries, I'd ride my bicycle to the Bombal Library on Condell Street.

The first day, a small, slender woman opened the door. Although she wasn't extremely old, she walked with a stick and her hair was white. As soon as I came in, she showed me into a room almost entirely occupied by a mahogany desk. Light barely entered the room through some long, heavy, velvet curtains. Everything there seemed to have been in place for a long time, and colors and objects blended into a single, uniform substance.

The library had been founded by a wealthy heiress in the 1950s. Its mission was to collect and recover texts composed by Latin American women who were storytellers and poets, but it also held a collection of poems and letters written by anonymous women of Anglo-Saxon origin in the nineteenth century.

"My name is Rosa Espinoza. Tell me how I can help you," she said after we were both sitting down, she at the desk, which was loaded with books, and I across from her.

I wondered about her name, "Thorny Rose." Either her parents had given it to her on purpose—which would have been cruel—or they hadn't noticed what they were doing.

Without waiting for my reply, Mrs. Espinoza proceeded to ask me a string of questions: address, age, contact information for my professors in France, course of study. Things like that. Using an antiquated computer, she slowly and sternly recorded my responses while scrutinizing me through her eyeglasses as though I were hiding a bomb in my backpack.

"And what do you propose to do here?" she asked in conclusion.

She removed her glasses, closed them, and held them like a pointed weapon as she crossed her arms on the desk. I was finding it difficult to understand what was going on. Horacio Infante had insisted that all I would have to do was to show up at the library and start working.

"You really don't know?"

The woman shook her head. Her pearl earrings shed sparkles on her shoulders. She was dressed in bright colors that played off against her white hair. I sat there in silence. I didn't want to tell her the real reason that had brought me there. I kept that closed up inside me, where it had no limits. To name it, on the other hand, would have been a way of imprisoning it and mutilating it. Therefore, I had come up with a project that would serve as a screen: to catalog the papers and archives Vera Sigall had donated to the library two years ago and which, according to Mr. Roche's inquiries, had remained untouched ever since.

"Perhaps you might like a cup of tea before you explain."

A strange gleam shone in her eyes, which were surrounded by wrinkles.

"I'd love some tea," I said, and she disappeared.

Through the small opening between the heavy curtains, I could make out the bare branches of the trees, standing out like filigree against the gray sky.

"*A world of trees without stars*," I murmured. Those were the last words spoken by Javier, the main character in Vera Sigall's first novel.

Mrs. Espinoza returned, followed by a man carrying a silver tray with a grayish-blue teapot and two cups of the same color. The man placed the tray on the desk, took Mrs. Espinoza's stick, and helped her sit down.

"Thank you, Efraín," she said with a smile. "Efraín is the gardener, my chauffeur, and the guardian of all this," she added after he had disappeared.

The fragrance of tea and spices filled the room. Mrs. Espinoza served us both, frugally.

"It's rather hot, be careful," she said. After a pause, she went on: "And now, perhaps you can tell me the purpose of your visit to this place."

She raised her head, hoping that something unexpected but at the same time familiar would arise from my words, like a pigeon from a magician's hat.

"What I want to do...," I said, and stopped.

"Come now. Speak."

Her voice sounded kind but firm.

She leaned her head against the back of her chair and fixed her uncosmeticized eyes on mine.

"Well, what I want to do is to analyze the different meanings that the stars and the planets have in Vera Sigall's writing. To discover their origin. That's in very broad terms. I've studied this topic for some time without getting very far."

I don't know why I did it, but in front of that woman I articulated, for the first time, the reason that had brought me there. That had given me the strength to cross the pond. My intuition told me that something was hidden in Vera Sigall's stars. Something that went beyond the fiction, beyond the characters and the stories. And the words too. I also sensed that if I could find it, I'd find something of myself. This was a perception so vague and elusive that it often faded away. I lowered my eyes. My hands were perspiring.

"As soon as I saw you, I knew Horacio Infante must have been mistaken, I knew your real purpose couldn't be to catalog Vera Sigall's work. You don't look like a cataloger."

I didn't know how to hug people. But I wished I could.

With her as my guide, I toured the library, a two-story building in the English style. The large reading room on the ground floor was at the scholars' disposal. A stool that had belonged to Alfonsina Storni stood in a display case in one corner. As Mrs. Espinoza explained, Alfonsina used to take that stool with her on her long walks on the high plateau so that she could have something to sit on when she stopped to think. The library itself was on the upper floor. There were three large rooms, in one of them a large card catalog with drawers classified by authoress. I managed to make out some of the names: Clarice Lispector, Elena Garro, Silvina Ocampo, and Alejandra Pizarnik.

A short while later, I was sitting in a room on the first floor, in front of one of the boxes Vera Sigall had donated to the library. A group of photographs bound with black ribbon drew my attention. There aren't many pictures of Vera Sigall. The press and the publishers of her books always printed the same one, in which she seems to be trying to hide her beauty behind a scathing seriousness. I undid the knot carefully. There were five black-and-white photos. Four of them were of people I didn't recognize. The fifth was an oval-matted photograph of Vera with her parents, Arón and Emma Sigall. The thick-faced, coarse-looking mother gazes at the camera with a concerned expression, as if she knows fate has a difficult future in store for her, and she's anticipating it unflinchingly. The father, wearing a humble suit of clothes appropriate for someone accustomed to hard work, gives the camera a strict, determined stare. Vera, a little girl no more than seven years old, has an uneasy, melancholy air about her.

In one of the most important books published on Vera Sigall's work, its author—Benjamin Moser—points out that everything having to do with her biographical details is ambiguous and often contradictory. Nobody knows for certain how old she was when her parents made their escape from the town of Chechelnyk in Ukraine, fleeing the pogroms. According to what Moser was able to verify, they arrived in Moldavia on the Dniester River, traveling by canoe. The exact date when they reached Romania and the journey they made afterward to arrive in Chile are lost in the mist. Throughout her life, Vera surrounded herself with enigmas, and in the few interviews that she agreed to, she generally hid behind a reiterated response: "My great mystery is that I have no mystery."

I remember the first time I read one of her texts. The language changed in her hands. Words reflected and reproduced one another, like images in crossed mirrors, creating a sensation of uncertainty.

I put the photograph on the table and closed my eyes. I needed to assimilate the emotion that being in Vera Sigall's world aroused in me. I thought that maybe I'd finally found my place, within those old walls, within the souls of all those women. Nobody could reach me there. Nobody could demand what I could never give.

I got back on my bike before darkness fell. The rays of the sun were crossing the sky like darts, bouncing off the windows of the tall glass buildings. I was climbing the stairs to my rooftop apartment when I ran into my ninth-floor neighbors. They introduced themselves as Juan and Francisco. Juan was tall and dark-haired; his demeanor was easygoing, his clothes fastidious and elegant. Francisco was short and stocky, with stiff blond hair and lively eyes; his worn-out jeans and his sweater bore traces of paint.

"You're Emilia Husson, right?" Juan asked me. With friendly formality, he held out one big, swarthy hand. I nodded affirmation but didn't take his hand. Maybe he could read in my eyes that my refusal had no disdain in it, for he disregarded the offense and went on: "As you see, we've been interrogating the super. You're Emilia, and you come from Paris."

"Well, not exactly Paris. I live in Grenoble, but I don't suppose that makes much difference right at the moment."

The two men gave me unambiguously friendly smiles.

"It's been more than a year since anyone lived on the roof. We were worried about who might move in. I'm glad it's you, Emilia," said Juan, taking some keys out of his pocket.

"Hope we see you again soon," said Francisco, and they disappeared into their apartment.

In my rooftop home, I washed the plates left over from dinner and then turned on my computer. I had a long email from Jérôme. He was leaving the next day on one of his mountaineering expeditions; this time he'd try to reach the top of Mount Elbrus. After reading his message, I wrote him back and told him about my meeting with Mrs. Espinoza, about the dusty smell, about Efraín, the solemn gardener, about the aromatic tea that changed the order of things like a magic potion. I also told him about the photograph of Vera Sigall I'd found, and about her uneasy eyes, which seemed to be waiting for something.

7.
DANIEL

With both hands, Gracia piled her hair on the top of her head and then shook it loose. Although she was perfectly dressed for her working day, she looked tired.

"You don't understand," I told her for the *n*th time.

"Yes I do. But I'm alive, right here at your side. And she isn't," she declared, banging her coffee cup against her saucer.

We were sitting at the kitchen table and looking out the window. The garden, paralyzed by the cold, was covered with haze. We'd been arguing for much of the night, and we were both tired. The offenses we'd given each other were still floating in the air, wounding us with their sharp points. It had been a bitter contest, with no concessions given.

It was true that Gracia had been planning our anniversary party for weeks, that she'd already hired waiters and a caterer, and that the majority of the guests had confirmed their intention to attend, but even so, it hurt me that she didn't understand my inability to celebrate while you were lying unconscious in that bed. The mere fact of discussing the matter constituted a defeat in advance. I would have wanted Gracia to be the one to propose canceling the party, while she, on the other hand, would have liked me to be so excited by the prospect of our celebration that I'd be able to forget you for a few hours.

"If I had agreed to let you cook, we wouldn't be having this fight," she pointed out.

"I'm shocked by how little you know me, Gracia. After so many years," I said, furious and defeated at the same time. The battle was in its last throes.

When Gracia had started to talk about celebrating our anniversary, I'd toyed with the idea of preparing the feast myself. I figured it would be a good learning opportunity. But Gracia was against it, and I gave in.

"Don't expect me for dinner. I've got to stay at the station later than usual," she informed me, taking the last sip of her coffee.

I'd made breakfast—scrambled eggs and toast—which neither of us had touched.

"I can wait for you."

"Suit yourself," she said. She got up from the table, picked up her briefcase, and left without a good-bye, slamming the door as she went out.

I made myself another cup of black coffee and sat down again. I remembered our conversations in your study, and how you'd made me see the stuff marital relationships are made of. Stuff whose makeup includes all the ingredients they need to self-destruct. I always resisted believing you.

In the end, it's just a matter of will, I used to tell you. The will to love, and to be faithful to the object of your affection. But then you told me about the voraciousness of love, about its longing to swallow the beloved and ensure that he or she breathes only through us. But above all, you talked about love's secret desire to be realized without transactions and without words, moved solely by its own essence, by its supposed unconditionality.

I went out into the yard with the cup of coffee in my hands. The morning frost crackled in the air. Everything was still, constrained. I heard voices. I went over to the fence that separated your house from mine and pricked up my ears. It was Detective Álvarez, talking with María. She had her checked apron on, and she was pointing out the gate that connected our yards.

I heard the detective call out to me. "Mr. Estévez," he said. "Just the man I wanted to talk to."

I went over to them. María gave me a suspicious look. She'd never understood our long hours behind closed doors in your study, which was now hushed and solitary and staring at us, with its little windows, from the end of the yard. Charly and Arthur emerged from the bushes and came up to me, their tails flailing the air. Detective Álvarez greeted me with forced familiarity and kept talking to María. While they conversed, I let my eyes stray to your garden. The branches of the walnut tree were looking pensively at the ground. That was when I noticed your callas. Someone had pulled up a good number of them. As I got closer, I realized that their stems had been cleanly snipped with pruning scissors. I smiled. Maybe you'd fulfilled your secret desire to steal your own flowers. I thought about Gracia again. For her, the world was divided between those who get tangled up in it and fail, and those who use it to achieve their goals and succeed.

The cell phone in my pocket began to vibrate. I didn't need to look at the screen to know who it was. I let it ring, thinking all the while that maybe what I should do was change my number and disappear.

"Mr. Estévez." The detective's voice came from behind me. "Can we talk?"

"Yes, yes," I said, embarrassed. Without knowing it, I'd walked toward the callas.

He demanded that I go over, once again, the details of the morning when I found you. He asked me if I'd seen anything or anyone suspicious. I remembered the tramp, but naming him would have been a way of accusing him, and that seemed unjust to me. I was convinced that he was harmless. The detective wanted to know if you'd received any visits or attended any kind of special event in the past weeks, and I mentioned your lunch with your friend Horacio Infante at his daughter's house. Álvarez also asked how many days I'd been away from Santiago, and whether, during that time, I'd had any contact with you. I told him I'd left Thursday morning and returned Sunday night. Lying again. That same evening, while I was walking home after being with you in the hospital, I got a message from Gracia on my cell phone. "Everything's canceled." I felt immense tenderness for her, for the efforts she was making to reconcile our differences. I stopped at the supermarket and bought the ingredients to make a pot roast.

It didn't matter that she was working later than usual, because that would give me enough time to prepare dinner with the calm I needed.

While I chopped the carrots and the garlic cloves, I thought again about the restaurant by the sea. It was a fantasy I'd been concocting for some time. I'd drawn up the plans and even devised some recipes, keeping everything fresh and simple and using spices typical of this end of the earth but forgotten in our country. I didn't want you to have bad feelings about Gracia, so I never told you this, but she hated the idea. She had married an architect, she used to say, not a cook in a beach bar.

I left the kitchen at midnight. I finished a bottle of pinot noir, and the stew remained untouched in the pot. Gracia hadn't come home. I fell asleep on top of the comforter on our bed, with every light in the house blazing.

Although you never asked me about it, I always knew my relationship with Gracia was hard for you to understand.

I was sixteen and she was twenty when we met. My parents had gone away on a trip, leaving me and my little sister with an aunt and uncle. My cousin Ricardo, six years my senior, was sullen and violent. He spent most of his time shut up in his room, studying or talking on the telephone, and when he came out, he never missed the chance to make fun of me, to shove me around, or to ignore my presence. It was, therefore, totally unexpected when he came into the living room where my sister and I were watching Saturday night television and invited me to a party. "Rats need air too," he said in his sarcastic tone.

"Rat" was what he'd called me ever since we were little. I figured Ricardo—like many of my friends—planned to crash some party and wanted me to smooth the way for him. At the time, I was a student in an all-boys' school, and the struggle to come into contact with persons of the opposite sex occupied the greater part of my schoolmates' time and efforts. But I'd already realized that I didn't feel the need to go out in search of female company. I'd never had a girlfriend, not for lack of opportunities, but because something essential in me had been shattered.

I must have been twelve, or maybe thirteen, when I was sexually assaulted for the first time. We were moving house in a few days, and one of my mother's friends had come to help her pack up. They arranged things, drank tea, went upstairs, came downstairs. Every time the woman passed the door of my room, she opened it and told me I was the cutest boy she'd ever seen. She came in at least five times, and every time she stayed a little longer. On one such occasion, she locked the door and touched me. I broke away from her violently, grabbed my soccer ball, and went out into the yard. She joined me shortly afterward. That night, I woke up with a fever. "A virus," my mother said. But I knew there wasn't any question of a virus. The effect I produced on other people drove me crazy and distanced me from the world. It also made my relationships with my peers difficult. They knew what was going on, and my presence made them feel uncomfortable. Some, however, had discovered that it could have a certain usefulness, for example in attracting the attention of the best-looking girls, or in saving them—the boys—from being thrown out of parties to which they hadn't been invited. All the same, I would slip away quickly, go back out to the street, and set out for home with a sensation of defeat.

After Ricardo abandoned me at the very door of the party, I wandered around the house. In the living room, four girls were sitting on a sofa and talking excitedly. Three of them saw me and started whispering among themselves. The fourth, ignoring my presence and the murmurs of her friends, kept on talking. It was Gracia, holding a glass of beer in one hand, laughing, playing with her hair. She had sparkling eyes and a smile that made her look like someone who knew a lot about life. She spoke with assurance, and without being the prettiest, she emanated a great deal of powerful energy. For the first time, I felt the desire to get closer to a woman. But I didn't know how. After walking around for a bit, I saw Gracia and one of her girlfriends go into the kitchen, and so I followed them. The kitchen was elongated, like a train car, and crammed with people. By the time I managed to get in, Gracia had disappeared. I drank a couple glasses of wine. I needed to get my courage up so that I could approach her when I found her again. A door opened onto a little concrete patio, where a group of people were gathered around a brazier. I joined them and warmed my hands at the fire. A woman wearing a hat that came down to her nose offered me a sip of pisco brandy from a plastic cup. I drained it in one go. A few seconds later, I began to feel queasy. In a corner of the yard, behind the only tree, I saw the girls again. Gracia was a diminutive person; the black skirt she was wearing revealed a pair of strong, shapely legs. She was the one who was doing the talking, while the other girl nodded attentively, as if receiving some lesson. In spite of the darkness, I got the impression that Gracia was gazing at me and smiling. I felt again the excitement I'd felt a little while before. I was resolved to talk to her. I asked the girl in the hat to give me another sip of pisco and once again drained the half-full cup she handed me. Ricardo appeared in the yard and headed for Gracia and her friend. He was taller and more powerfully built than the other guys. He put his arm around Gracia's waist as though she belonged to him and kissed her on the mouth.

"Come here, Rat," he called to me.

At that moment, we heard "Happy Birthday to You" being sung inside the house, and we went back in. A chubby young girl was carrying a cake that resembled something halfway between a sculpture and a pile of scrap. Before the song ended, I slipped through the crowd and went in search of a bathroom. I found one just in time to raise the toilet lid and expel some foul-smelling, brownish matter. I closed the lid and sat on it. Now I felt exhausted, and my nausea hadn't dissipated at all. Somebody knocked on the door.

"Are you okay?" a voice asked.

Before I could say anything, Gracia was already in the bathroom. "What happened to you?" As I didn't open my mouth, she answered her own question. "You're not used to drinking, right?" I nodded.

I felt ashamed. The smell in there must have been appalling. Gracia sat on the side of the bathtub and lit a cigarette, probably an effort to combat the pestilential stench. She took a deep breath and then blew the smoke at the ceiling. She was sitting with her legs crossed at the ankles.

"Feeling better?" she asked me.

I explained that I'd mixed wine and pisco, which had proved to be a fatal combination. I also confessed that I'd done it so that I'd have the guts to talk to her. She remained silent. I thought she'd get up and leave the bathroom, but she disregarded my remark and, with a radiant expression on her face, asked me, "Have you thought about what you're going to study at the university?"

In spite of the stuffiness of her question, she looked genuinely interested.

"Architecture."

She told me she'd thought about architecture too, but in the end she'd opted for engineering because she wasn't talented enough. "If you're not capable of creating something memorable, it's better to forget it," she pointed out gravely.

I was impressed that things were so clear to her, and that she set the bar so high for herself. I had never planned things out like that. I simply relished the idea of building houses. I drew designs for them in all my exercise books and notebooks. I had some good books on architecture, and they made me think there was a language beyond words that I could use to express myself. We discovered that, like all aspirants, we both admired Frank Lloyd Wright, but that our favorites weren't the best known of his houses; they were the ones in a minor key, such as the Robie House. Gracia asked me straightforward, interesting questions. She kept bursting into laughter, often at her own comments, not because she was self-centered—or so it appeared to me at the time—but because they represented an opportunity for celebration. She lit her third cigarette, and then we heard knocks on the door.

"Gracia, are you in there?"

It was Ricardo's voice, coming in through the gap between the doorjamb and the door, ruining everything.

"I'll be out in a minute," she replied.

"But what have you been doing in there all this time? Are you with somebody?"

"I'll be out in a minute," Gracia repeated, without budging an inch.

A few seconds passed. A strange happiness overcame me. The life I'd been waiting for was finally beginning. Gracia opened the door. Ricardo's face was flushed, and the pupils of his eyes were so dilated that the irises had disappeared.

"With the rat!" he shouted. "I can't believe it!" He thrust his torso forward and accompanied his words with energetic hand gestures. He was blocking the bathroom door so we couldn't get out.

"He felt sick. I stayed with him until he felt better," Gracia said firmly. She leaned on the doorjamb, crossed her arms, and made an impatient face. I remained in position a few steps behind her.

"Stayed with him?" Ricardo yelled, and then he clicked his tongue. "Are you taking me for a fool? Do you really think I'm going to buy that?"

"Can you let me pass, please?"

Ricardo grabbed her by the arm and stopped her. "Where do you think you're going? And you," he added in my direction, "you're going to pay for this, you understand me?"

Despite the pressure he was putting on her arm, Gracia looked at him with contempt. "Let me go!" she yelled.

Ricardo staggered. He was drunk. He glanced at me sideways, with cold disgust, as if I weren't worth looking in the face. With a snort he pivoted around, left the bathroom, and lurched out the front door.

That night Gracia gave me a ride to my aunt and uncle's house in her Peugeot 305. She'd saved her money and bought it. She'd been working since she was sixteen, she told me. She drove in silence through the streets of a Santiago still permeated by the late-night party spirit. She seemed a little downcast. She'd broken up with her boyfriend, and I was responsible.

"Will you be all right?" she asked me before I got out of the car. She messed up my hair the way you do with children and gave me a kiss on the cheek. I must still have stunk. She drove off, tires squealing, and disappeared into the darkness of the street.

Once I'd met her, I found it hard to get her out of my head, and in the following months, hers would be the image that accompanied my masturbation sessions. I held out hope that she would get in touch with me, that our meeting had meant something to her too. But she didn't try, and neither did I. When I was in the fourth year of my architectural studies, we met at an art exhibition and ended up making love that same night, in the apartment she shared with two other women.

At her side, I was safe from the effect I produced on others, protected from myself, from my discouragements and my fears. At her side, everything seemed possible, as her certainties and her practical way of looking at life confirmed. When I finished my studies, we got married. In the world of television broadcast news, Gracia already occupied a prominent position. She had been capable of seeing me as I was, or so I believed. Her look gave me the conviction and the strength necessary to transform myself into the person I dreamed of being.

Vera, I've taken the time to tell you the details of this episode in order for you to understand that it was Gracia's determination that attracted me to her. Maybe from the very first moment, I saw that she had the something I was missing, the thing I unknowingly longed to appropriate for myself. It's in your novels. The hidden destiny that unites people, and whose machinery begins to operate without our noticing it.

8.

EMILIA

I'd been going to the library for two months. Nevertheless, the immense volume of information that confronted me only made me conscious of my gigantic ignorance. I wrote to Jérôme daily, sharing with him the tiniest details of my days. Until I put it in words for him, my new life lacked consistency. And order. And sense. I knew that if I had come this far, it was because I didn't want to disappoint him and his expectations for me. I didn't want to fail him. And I wouldn't.

What I didn't tell him was that in spite of my work delivering produce, I was running out of money before the end of the month. For the first time, I'd felt the pangs of hunger in my stomach, in my head. I'd wake up in the middle of the night with the image of a succulent plate of food firmly fixed in my forebrain and a rumbling in my guts. I wasn't capable of admitting the truth to him. Nevertheless, the omission of this essential fact caused a subtle distance between us. It was as if someone with a scalpel were slowly extracting an organ from inside my body.

One Tuesday afternoon, I got an email from Horacio Infante. He was on a visit to Chile, and he invited me to attend a luncheon hosted by his daughter. They would be celebrating the prize he'd received recently, the International Sky Book Prize, awarded by the Swiss Academy. I wasn't ready to go to an event of that kind and had decided to decline the invitation, but then, at the end of the week, Infante wrote me again to tell me that Vera Sigall would be at the luncheon.

Vera didn't receive strangers. She lived a reclusive, solitary life in some Santiago neighborhood. Her isolation was part of her mystery. The beginnings of her career, applauded by the critics, had also marked the beginning of her legend. She never appeared in literary circles. She never signed her books, and very few people had been able to get close to her. Some had even gone so far as to assert that Vera Sigall didn't exist, and that the name was the pseudonym of a well-known writer who hid behind it out of a desire to free himself from the impositions of his fame. The idea of meeting her set my heart on fire, as if a sun had been thrust inside it. I went out onto the roof and looked at the sky, searching celestial landmarks. I could see them even without seeing them. Venus's elegant, curving path, Saturn's rings, Aldebaran, Betelgeuse. The same ones that Vera had named so many times in her writings, and that secretly united us.

They made me feel like doing crazy things, like jumping, like throwing a ball high up into the sky, like dancing.

• • •

On the day of the luncheon, I woke up at dawn.

It was a bright Saturday. During the night, the wind had cleared the air, and from my vantage point I could make out with unusual clarity the roofs of houses and buildings, their terraces and antennas, which in the distance took on the appearance of masts suspended above the sea. The morning sun filled me with optimism. After making a couple of produce deliveries on my bicycle, I took a shower and dressed with great care. I wanted to make a good impression on Vera Sigall. When I went out, I ran into my neighbors, Francisco and Juan.

"Where are you going, all dressed up?" they asked with their usual good humor.

"To meet a great writer," I said proudly.

Infante's daughter lived in one of the more elevated neighborhoods of the city. I was afraid of getting lost, so I set out too early. Before twelve noon I was already in front of her house, on a classy, tree-lined street called Espoz.

To kill time, I rode around the neighborhood on my bicycle, observing the big houses and their luxuriant gardens, protected behind tall railings. At one-thirty I rang the doorbell. Infante opened the door. He was, as always, elegantly dressed.

"What a pleasure it is to see you, Emilia," he said, without touching me. "Everyone very much wants to meet you."

He carried his eighty-three years well. His hair was gray and thick, his features well marked, and his eyes lively, as befitted one to whom life had been generous. His face must have always contrasted with his wide body, which was hidden under a long jacket that emphasized his low stature and short legs. In the foyer, two boys were fighting for a ball until the taller one picked it up in his hands and disappeared through a door.

"Come, come in, come in."

I followed him down a long corridor whose walls were hung with a series of modern paintings. One of them was a portrait of Infante. A realistic painting of his upper half, with a background that recalled Manet. An aura of power emanated from the subject, and his expression denoted assurance and satisfaction.

In the living room, about ten people were talking and sitting around a table on which there were various trays of little sandwiches. The guests were all older than I was. The formal atmosphere in the room intimidated me. I glanced around rapidly, scanning the company in search of Vera Sigall, but I didn't see her. A short woman wearing no makeup stood up to receive me.

"Welcome, Emilia," she said. "I'm Patricia. My father has told me a lot about you." As she spoke, her gaze wandered over the faces of the company.

I, on the other hand, could feel the attentive eyes of the other guests fixed on me. Infante must have told them about my affliction, which always aroused morbid curiosity. I'd just arrived, and already I was sorry I'd come. I sat in an armchair, and Patricia handed me a glass of champagne. Then she toasted her father, her children, all the other relatives who were there, and, finally, God.

"He's so adorable, and He never forgets us."

She spoke about God like someone she'd dined with a few days before. The conversation continued on its way. Everyone looked at Infante with the curiosity of a museum visitor gazing at a work he can't understand, but which he knows has incalculable value. Sitting straight-backed beside his daughter, Infante enlivened his relatives' conversation. Every now and then he asked me how I was doing and smiled at me. But his attention was elsewhere. He pulled down the sleeves of his jacket, ran a finger around the inside of his shirt collar, and kept looking through the glass door at the corridor.

"Daddy, you haven't eaten anything," Patricia scolded him affectionately.

"Forgive me, sweetheart. The thing is, I haven't recovered from the trip yet."

"The poor man's been traveling for seven weeks. The life of a poet," his daughter remarked, unable to conceal the pride she felt.

The doorbell rang. Infante got up with uncommon agility and disappeared through the living room door. In search of something to hold on to, I looked out the window. In the garden, among the bushes, there were purple hydrangeas.

I remembered Jovana, one of Vera's characters, who liked invading the neighbors' yards and stealing flowers. Discovering their forbidden beauty. Looking around on all sides to make sure there was no witness to her thievery. Reaching out her hand, plucking the flower, pricking herself on the thorns, and fleeing with pounding heart as fast as she could go, endowed with a glory she was certain nothing else could bestow on her.

Infante was slow coming back.

Suddenly, I saw her. She wore a dress in the style of the 1950s and a hooded black cape that was likewise reminiscent of another era. It was as if she had kept herself shut in somewhere, indifferent to the time that was passing outside. Even so, her presence possessed an innate grace, a beauty that the years couldn't overcome. Dark tresses like feathers daubed her gray hair. And while she moved toward us, her numerous bracelets sparkled in the light and made a delicate jingling sound. She carried a bouquet of callas wrapped in cellophane paper. Infante, at her side, was watching her nervously. The chatter around the table stopped.

"My friends, let me introduce you to Vera Sigall."

Vera, standing next to him, seemed shy, even upset, as if despite her advanced age she hadn't yet grown accustomed to the effect she produced on other people. She handed the callas to Patricia, and at the same moment the boys burst into the room, heading for the garden. A woman in a blue apron with a white front followed them outside.

Vera's eyes stopped on me.

It wasn't usual for people to notice my presence. I thanked the God whom Patricia had named with so much familiarity for making the body a closed case, inside which one's feelings remain hidden.

We were at the table in the dining room when Vera said to me, "I have a feeling we've met before."

I was seated opposite her. The table was wide, and there was a certain distance between us, but even so, I could distinguish her velar *r*, which appeared to be the recollection of another language. She had the hoarse, husky voice of the confirmed smoker.

"Never," I replied. "I would remember."

Infante, sitting beside her, shot me an intense, intimidating look. I had the feeling he was searching for something inside me.

"But you look familiar to me, Emilia. Are you sure?"

She opened her eyes wide. Her fine eyebrows seemed to climb even higher up her forehead, waiting for something. Her mouth was bright pink, surrounded by wrinkles. Its well-defined corners indicated reserve.

I again assured her that we were meeting for the first time.

"You shouldn't turn over that material to the library, Vera," said Infante with a smile. "This girl will dig up all your secrets."

Then, suddenly serious, he took a gulp of his drink, throwing his head back so that the liquid would get a good start on its way to the place he wanted it to reach quickly.

"I don't want to disappoint you," Vera warned me. "But everything in there is all lightweight stuff." Then, looking at Infante, not without a certain coquettishness, she asked, "Was it you who put this whole crazy idea in her head?"

She ended each sentence on a rising tone, which despite her age made her seem like a little girl investigating worldly matters for the first time. Infante smiled and raised a hand to his shirt collar to adjust it. His restrained, guarded expression seemed intended to hide, not wholly successfully, the disaster of the years.

"Yes," I replied, "it was Don Horacio who spoke to me about you for the first time." Vera's openness had given me the courage to speak to her. "I was in the third year of a literature major when he suggested I should write my thesis on your work. I hadn't even begun to think about my thesis. But as soon as I began to read you, I realized that he was right. I..." And there I stopped.

I couldn't go on. The words thronged together in my head. My feelings too, all in disorder, all eager to emerge into the open for her sake.

A man at the other end of the table asked Infante some question, one of those questions people ask when they don't know much about poetry but wish to pass for connoisseurs. Infante recognized the nature of the query and answered it with well-disguised sarcasm. The years had done nothing to lighten his heavy jaw, which gave him a belligerent look. I imagined that in his youth he must have intimidated his peers and attracted women. Another man joined the discussion, one who really did seem to know what he was talking about. They struck up a conversation whose principal subject was Infante. Everyone listened. I was impressed by his metamorphosis. I'd observed a tactful servility in his attitude toward Vera; now, however, the man of the podiums stepped out from behind the scenes and displayed his acuteness, his innate ability to attract others' attention with his words.

While he was speaking, I couldn't take my eyes off Vera, who was listening to Infante with her head raised and her hands folded in her lap. An alert, aloof silence enveloped her. I remembered one of her stories, "Simultaneous Worlds," in which a character realizes that he has used words without restraint. That he has transformed them into clowns in order to attract the notice of his peers. In revenge, words make him lose the notion of himself and believe that he's someone else.

After a while, when he and the other two men had finally run out of things to say, Infante turned his attention back to Vera. He offered to pour her some wine and filled her glass. Then, resuming our conversation, he said, "Emilia came to one of my readings in Nanterre. That was five years ago, right?" I nodded. "You had a copy of *Affirmations* for me to sign. It was a first edition, in Spanish. I don't remember where you'd managed to find it."

"It was in my mother's library."

Someone tapped on a glass. It was Patricia's husband. A man in his fifties, with smooth, rosy skin like the belly of a fish. His hair was light and sparse. It fell thinly on his forehead and would soon disappear.

"I want to make a toast to my esteemed father-in-law. And to this prize, which places him among humanity's notable poets. It's a genuine source of pride for me to belong to this family," he said, raising his glass.

Horacio placed his hand on Vera's, enfolding it like a wing. Vera remained unmoving, her unfocused eyes on a region above my head. Infante withdrew his hand, picked up the napkin from his lap, and with a weary gesture wiped his mouth. A boy of about fifteen appeared in the dining room, together with the woman who had gone out into the yard after the other boys. This one had a piece of paper in his hand. He looked upset and might even have been crying. He had Down syndrome.

"Horacito wants to read a poem he wrote for his grandfather. Go on, Horacito, read it," Patricia said.

The boy read the poem in a quavering voice. His reading deficiencies were obvious. I served myself a second portion of steak, potatoes, vegetables, whatever a pair of diligent servers could offer me. I hadn't really eaten for a long time. I was still getting all my nourishment from tin cans, and I was always hungry. Vera left her cutlery lying on the table and listened to the boy, gravely and serenely, as if everything going on there was familiar to her, but distantly. Infante was listening to the boy's words, but every now and then he looked at Vera.

After dessert was over, Patricia invited us to return to the living room. Vera stood up before Horacio, and when she was standing in front of him, he looked up at her from his chair, as if paying homage to her greatness. I wondered what feelings they harbored for each other. Infante had attained, through his poetry, a rare degree of fame. He'd won prizes, and with them money. His poems were recited in the streets of the world. He lived in Paris, in an apartment with a view of the Seine, and his innumerable conquests after the demise of his marriage to Patricia's mother were common knowledge. Vera, by contrast, had always been a hidden treasure. Her work was venerated, in the abstract, by all, but known only to a few. In learned circles, however, Infante's work was considered as "facile" poetry, cloying in its sonorities and simple in its contents. That very simplicity, however, made it accessible, without sacrificing depth. Hence its success, the many translations, the readings all over the world. Hundreds of people would assemble to hear those verses, which had accompanied them for a good part of their lives, and which spoke of things they could identify with.

What did all that mean to those two writers? Was a veiled rivalry lurking behind Infante's solicitous attentiveness and Vera's aloofness? Maybe they were united sentimentally, or had been so at one time. But that didn't explain the strange attitudes they both seemed to have.

While we were walking back to the living room, the boy who'd read the poem threw himself on me. "What are you doing in my house?" he said, forcefully squeezing one of my wrists. "I don't like strangers."

He was a big, well-built boy. His thin blond hair, inherited from his father, fell over his slanted eyelids. A woman who'd been walking beside me looked from one side to another, hoping that someone would stop him. Nobody else in the house noticed what was happening. I couldn't bear that sweaty hand on my skin. I needed to shout, I needed to get out of there.

Then I heard Horacio's voice. "Let her go, Horacito," he said firmly. Vera was at his side. "Let her go *now*."

The boy looked at him defiantly and kept hold of my wrist.

I had begun to shake.

"She's as afraid as you are," Vera said.

The boy let me go. Patricia, realizing what was afoot, seized him by the shoulders and took him away, without explanation and without words. As in a play, when an understudy flubs his lines and has to be rapidly hustled offstage. Vera stepped beside me and put a hand on my shoulder. But this time it didn't produce the usual effect. What was going on?

I was so familiar with Vera's work that sometimes I could predict her sentences or the direction her story would take. When I read her, I had the feeling I was seeing the curtains hung in her mind and hearing the voices speaking to her from somewhere inside before they came to be composed into a text. With an effort, I stayed on my feet, suffocating with emotion. Infante was standing a certain distance away, not taking his eyes off us.

"Are you sure we've never met before?" she asked me once again.

She lit a cigarette, dragged on it with half-closed eyes, and then abruptly fanned the smoke away. There was something theatrical in her movements.

"I'm sure."

In the living room, Infante came up to us. He said something in Vera's ear, and the two of them disappeared through a door. Patricia served coffee while her guests made themselves comfortable in the big armchairs.

I had to get out of there.

I waited a few minutes and then slipped out of the room. At the other end of the entrance hall, I saw Infante and Vera. I stayed where I was, spying on them from a distance. On many occasions, during the months following that evening, I've tried to reconstruct their dialogue. Their words reached me in bits, like pieces of a puzzle thrown into the air. Infante, obviously nervous, was gesticulating with his hands. Silently shaking her head the whole time, Vera kept her eyes fixed in front of her, like someone gazing at a familiar landscape from a high terrace. I thought maybe Infante was asking her for something she was refusing to give him. At one point, he raised his voice. His exasperated tone deviated from the image of composure he usually projected. Something in her had produced that reaction.

"You're leaving me in a difficult position, Vera."

"Nothing's changed," Vera replied, also speaking louder than before. "Everything's the same as before. You just have to trust..."

They both lowered their voices, and I could hear no more. I retraced my steps before they noticed that I'd seen them. I went into the bathroom. When I returned to the living room, they were back too. Vera was saying good-bye to Patricia. Infante stood at Vera's side, waiting for her. Vera turned around, smiled at me, and said, "I'm going, Emilia, but I hope we meet again soon." She glanced at Infante, then at me, and added in a suggestive voice, "I'd like it very much if we could meet again. I'll get your email address from Horacio." She looked at me, smiled, and closed her eyes.

I bade the other guests farewell from a distance and went up to Patricia. She was still serving out coffee, and there were red splotches on her cheeks. She was sweating. I imagined her suspended like a spider in her perfect, fragile web. Then Horacio escorted us to the door.

"We don't have much time," he said to Vera. "I'm leaving on Tuesday. Can we meet again and talk in peace?"

"You may call me, if you want to."

We went out to the street.

"Count on it," said Infante.

A dilapidated taxi with a yellow roof was waiting for Vera on the other side of the railings.

"My faithful Ramiro, always so punctual," she said. "Don't you want us to give you a ride home, Emilia?"

"I came on my bicycle."

I longed to be rid of it so that I could spend more precious time with the woman who'd kept me up at night for the past couple of years.

As I pedaled downhill, heading for home, Vera's words echoed inside my head.

I could hear snippets of a Sunday choir rehearsing somewhere in the city, very far away. An automobile accelerated, and the roar of its engine rose above the other sounds. A clock I may have imagined struck five in the afternoon, and its sounds, haughty and sorrowful at once, sank among the trees.

9 · DANIEL

Two weeks had passed since the accident, and in a couple of days they would start to bring you out of your coma. There was a possibility that you wouldn't wake up. The doctors knew that and so did I, but nobody mentioned it.

Sitting in the armchair facing the bed, I talked to you and asked you questions I answered myself, imagining what your reaction would have been to this or that circumstance. I continued to ignore Detective Álvarez's instructions, and I'd taken various things from your house. I put Kacyzne's photograph on your night table. Also some of your books, so that—if your senses could still discern the world—you'd be able to perceive that bookish smell you used to appreciate so much.

But most importantly, I didn't give up my investigations. I'd started making a list of all the persons you'd mentioned as having been in touch with you in the past months. Journalists, professors, students; people you'd ignored for the most part, just as you usually ignored those who tried to penetrate the barrier you'd erected around yourself. You remembered many of them only by the nicknames you gave them: "the Hellenic girl student," "the symphonic journalist," "the talpid professor," names whose origins I mostly failed to understand. I remembered the psychiatrist who lived in Madrid; according to what you told me, this man, after sending you countless emails that you'd answered with monosyllables, decided to board a plane and fly to Chile. You two had met in a café the week before the accident. After that meeting, you were downcast and even taciturn. I tried to inquire about what had happened, but you didn't want to give me any details. One evening, I found you in your study, standing in front of dozens of sheets of paper, which you'd thrown on the floor. I asked you what had happened, and you told me you'd lost something. Then you started to pick up the pages and wouldn't allow me to help you. Nor would you tell me what it was you'd lost. I asked you if it had anything to do with the psychiatrist, and you remained silent.

I was reading you a recent newspaper article about your friend Infante when my cell phone rang. I got up from the chair next to your bed and looked at the screen. It was Gracia. The previous night, after several weeks of not touching each other, we'd made love again. It had been fast, energetic, and vertiginous.

"You must be crazy!" she shouted at me through the telephone.

I went out into the corridor. If you could hear me reading to you, if my words were able to reach you in that place in the distance where you were, then you could also hear me arguing with Gracia. And the last thing I wanted was to disturb you.

"So what is it now?" I asked wearily.

"You must be crazy," she repeated, without lowering her voice. "A detective came to the channel offices today. It was a huge embarrassment, Daniel. Do you really want to destroy us?"

I was happy that Detective Álvarez had taken my suspicions seriously. However, to hear that Gracia had found out about them was neither happy nor convenient, not at all. I'd kept quiet because I knew in advance what her reaction would be, namely the one she was having at that very moment. Soon she'd be accusing me of idleness and paranoia.

"He asked me a thousand questions about Vera, and I didn't have the slightest idea how to answer any of them. He also asked me where you were the week before the accident, when you got there, what you were doing on the coast, what was your relationship with Vera, et cetera, et cetera. All very unpleasant, Daniel. Vera fell. It's obvious. Nobody with any brains could think the opposite. I don't know what ideas you've got in your head."

While listening to Gracia's diatribe, I walked to the waiting room. A pair of women with tired faces were chatting in whispers. A small child was on the floor, playing with a little blue truck. One of the women fixed her eyes on me. I found her gaze unbearable, turned around, and went back down the corridor. I stopped in front of your door.

"So what did you tell him?" I asked cautiously.

"The truth. What else was I going to tell him? I said you'd gone to the beach because you wanted to think, you wanted to be alone, that sort of thing."

"You really told him that?"

"Of course. What did you want me to say? That you were building the best hotel in the Metropolitan Region?"

The woman stepped into the corridor and looked at me while clumsily pretending not to. I leaned my back against the wall and stared at the floor.

"For example," I said.

"I'm not going to lie to the PDI, I'd have to be crazy."

Those last words of Gracia's struck me. I, on the other hand, had lied indeed. Four times. For the moment, the detective had discovered one of those lies. Maybe Gracia was right, and I was starting to lose my mind. I felt depressed. I had an impulse to confess the truth to her, but just then a nurse went into your room.

"I have to go, Gracia."

"Are you at the hospital?"

"Yes," I replied curtly. "We'll talk tonight. Just stay calm."

"I'm not calm, Daniel. Not calm at all," she said, and hung up.

The woman approached, walking rapidly, as if she'd found the key that would allow her to rob me. I went into your room and shut the door. The nurse took your temperature and then left.

There we were again, you and I, alone in our silent world, our static twilight. And in the distance, bells, songs, sorrows, yearnings, which reminded me of the poem you shared with me one day. I talked to you about Gracia.

• • •

She'd found the announcement one Sunday morning when we were lying in bed and reading the newspaper. "Look," she said, passing me the page.

The notice informed the public of an open competition to design a museum that was to be built on the banks of the Mapocho River and to house the most important collection of Latin American art on the continent. The space would also contain at least one auditorium for theatrical and musical performances. The project would be financed by a foreign foundation and sponsored by the Chilean government. This was, without a doubt, one of the country's most important architectural projects of the past decade. In the circles frequented by architects, it had been the subject of discussion for months.

"I know about that," I said, remaining absorbed in the article I was reading.

"You have to enter the competition," she said, with one of those smiles of hers that had always captivated me.

"Not a chance," I groaned.

"It's what you want to do, Daniel. You'd get to design public spaces, take control of the landscape, transform our city into a more pleasant and interesting place."

I was listening to my own voice, the same set phrases, the same pompous words, which as always didn't sound so ridiculous coming out of her mouth.

"Have you considered that the most important architectural studios in the country started gearing up for this a long time ago? Not to mention all the foreign architects, big and small, and all the ones who have built museums in different parts of the world. It's a gigantic project. Do you understand what I'm telling you?"

"Of course I understand. That's why you have to participate."

I looked at the announcement again. Applicants were given sixty days to submit their designs. I laughed.

"Drop everything and concentrate on this project, Daniel. I'll help you. You won't have to worry about anything else. You can just do the work."

"You're incredible, Gracia."

I hugged her. Gently, I placed my hands on her breasts. They were warm, and her nipples hardened before I touched them. We made love. While she caressed me, I had the impression that she was touching my impenetrable world, opening doors and windows, letting the air in; pure, fresh air, full of good omens.

Throughout those two months, Gracia kept her promise. She pampered me incessantly and allowed no one to disturb my work. She transformed herself into my guardian and provider. Those were sweet days, days brimming with optimism. I spent them, one after another, shut up in my studio, imagining the place I'd always wanted to visit. In some way, the museum was already inside me. The way it fell and then picked itself up in the river, its structures that cleft the sky like wings, its simplicity and purity of line. Like Frank Lloyd Wright in his time, I sought to use indigenous materials and to produce a building that instead of dominating nature transformed itself into its complement. After I sent in my design, we awaited the results together. Long weeks passed, during which Gracia never stopped expressing her confidence. Her certainty frightened me. I didn't want to imagine what would become of us if I should fail. When we learned that my project had been selected as the hands-down winner, what I felt above all was relief. Gracia organized a big party, and together with friends, family, and a handful of envious architects, we celebrated the benevolence of life.

However, neither of us could have imagined what was to come. After the honors and the interviews, the project remained on some faceless, nameless functionary's desk. At first the delay seemed fairly routine. An undertaking of that magnitude entailed a series of stages that had to be completed in order.

"Have you heard anything?" Gracia would ask when she came home from work.

I spent the days revising my plans, adjusting them, improving them, lingering over details I hadn't initially managed to resolve in all their complexity.

"Don't worry, love, they're going to call you soon," she'd say, rebutting my negativity.

But time was passing, and I could smell the stench beginning to rise from the carcass of my project, a stench that pervaded even the remotest corners of our lives. All the same, I continued to go over the plans, visiting my museum's empty rooms and corridors and looking out of its big windows, which instead of opening onto the river now opened onto nothing at all.

After a year had gone by, Gracia started pressuring me to take on other projects. She was right. I couldn't keep on waiting for something that was never going to arrive. But the vanity and thirst for magnificence exhibited by the people who approached me to build their houses became unbearable, to the point where I began to doubt my vocation. And Gracia to doubt me. Eventually the offers of work became scarcer and scarcer and nearly disappeared altogether.

From the beginning, I'd made an effort to be the person both of us wished I were. Gracia's interests were mine. She lived at the beck and call of contingency, incessantly looking at her computer, her cell phone, in search of the latest public vicissitude; she had a passionate interest in our politicians' quarrels, their wheeling and dealing, the state of the currency, declines in the stock market, business minutiae, and I stayed at her side, following her; picking up knowledge as I went, trying to make progress without stumbling, without being caught out in ignorance for lack of a comment or a well-informed opinion, always on the crest of the wave, always with that exultant energy, as if the world, tomorrow, in a few hours, were going to blow up, and we, from our promontory, could watch it explode at our feet. For Gracia, there were no compromises. It was all or nothing. That had been her motto ever since she was a little girl, and she had let me understand it clearly for the first time at the party. Above all, mediocrity had no place in our perfect world. Gracia reflected back to me the image of an extraordinary man, and while her light shone on me, I would continue to be that man. Nevertheless, I gradually stopped striving. It wasn't the gaps in the president's last State of the Nation speech on May 21 that kept me awake, but more insubstantial matters. The construction of a chair, the sketch of an improbable library or of my restaurant, suspended from a cliff above the sea. In one way, to have won that important competition with a project I'd designed in the solitude of my studio and nourished with my dreams and fantasies, to have competed against the most prestigious architectural firms and beaten them, reassured me. My winning had freed me from the burden of demonstrating my worth to Gracia, the world, and myself. I'd received a considerable sum of money for the project, and without incurring great expenses, I could pay my way for a long time to come. However, that freedom didn't suit Gracia and the relationship we'd built. When she would get home and we'd eat the dinner I'd prepared in front of the television set, we began to feel contempt for each other. My passive resistance infuriated her. In the face of her remarks, I remained silent, letting her know that I was indifferent to her universe.

It was then that I started to visit you more often, that I opened the little gate connecting our gardens, that your words and your life, with their foundations in the invisible world, began to trace a road that I fervently hoped would bring me back to myself.

But then you went away, Vera, and you left me stranded halfway down the road, an orphan bereft of your words and your calm silences, an orphan of that world we shared, which was yours and mine, but to which, without you, I don't know how to return.

10.
EMILIA

The Monday after the luncheon at Infante's daughter's house, I made my fruit and vegetable deliveries early and then pedaled eagerly to the library. Happiness kept flapping around like a fish deep inside me.

At nine o'clock in the morning, I was sitting in front of Vera Sigall's materials, which had now been endowed with a new light. I was secure in the knowledge that I'd hear from her soon. Maybe even that same day. At intervals of not more than five minutes, I checked my email. Mrs. Espinoza revolved around me, putting papers in order, changing the locations of books, as if my energy had taken hold of her too.

But something didn't fit. At the luncheon, Vera had mentioned that these boxes didn't contain anything of importance. And yet, everything inside them was important. Photographs, annotated pages, fragments of texts, correspondence. Did that mean that her words had been intended to throw Infante off the scent? Had that been her way of creating complicity between us?

My original idea of finding the archaeology of the heavenly bodies hidden inside her writings now seemed insufficient. There was something more. But which road was the one I needed to follow?

I thought about the act of seeking, about its nature.

A few days previously, I'd lost a package of excellent walnut-and-butter cookies that I'd bought on a sudden impulse. An expensive luxury, and theoretically forbidden. I was sure I'd put those cookies in a drawer in the kitchen, inside a plastic bag with the supermarket's logo. I'd looked in every corner of the drawer, but the bag and its contents had disappeared. Then, just when I was taking out a cup that morning, I found the cookies. They'd been there the whole time, in the exact place where I thought I'd put them, but I didn't remember having taken them out of the plastic bag. Blinded by my idea of what they must look like, I'd run my eyes over them dozens of times without seeing them.

And while I was selecting some documents I'd decided to study more closely, it occurred to me that if I began with a preconceived idea, I could wind up overlooking the essential. If I laid out the route ahead of time and envisioned the form my destiny must take, the most likely result was that I'd arrive empty-handed back at my point of departure. It also occurred to me that the unseen is not something you look for. You simply find it.

In one of Vera's boxes, I came upon a sheet of yellowing paper, a page torn out of a notebook. The writing was

Russian, most probably. It wasn't Vera's handwriting. A Spanish translation was clipped to the page:

A month ago we sold Emma's last brooch, today we sold our shoes and wrapped our feet in rags. We left the city together with a group of neighbors, and by night we were already in the forest. I'm weary, but I haven't lost hope. I don't know where it comes from, but there it is. Vera has turned six. Emma's weak from fever. The rash has appeared on her hands and feet. She's barely able to walk. I hold her hand as we go and carry a bag on my back. Abandoned villages. Rotting bodies, people wiped out by typhus. Desolation. Yahweh: where are you, where?

On the bottom half of the page was a drawing of a river.

We've arrived in Soroca. The houses are lit up. A family invited us to share their table, and we ate bread. White bread, genuine bread.

It was the first real inkling I'd got of Vera's history. The text had been written by her father and is not to be found in Benjamin Moser's literary biography. I thought that maybe at some point Vera had considered putting this material in one of her stories and later given up on the idea. Someone must have translated the text for her, because in her rare interviews, she'd always declared that she'd forgotten her parents' language, and that hers was Spanish. I transcribed the text, both the Spanish version and the original, a process that turned out to be long and tedious, because the Cyrillic letters were extremely hard to reproduce. That night I woke up crying. The voice of Arón, Vera's father, was echoing in my ears.

"Where, where, where, where?"

I found out the next day, Tuesday, August 7.

Mrs. Espinoza was waiting for me in the library with a gloomy expression on her face. "Do you want a cup of coffee?" she asked, and I said yes.

She poured coffee for both of us and sat facing me. She was looking at me attentively, as if waiting for me to say something important. But I had nothing of any significance to tell her.

"You haven't heard?"

I shook my head.

That was when she told me about the accident. Vera had fallen down the stairs in her house the previous day, and now she was lying on a hospital bed, lost in a dream from which she might never wake up.

I walked back to my apartment—I didn't have enough strength to pedal my bike. When I got home, I searched the Internet for anything I could find about Vera's accident. There wasn't a lot of information, and what there was wasn't much different from what Mrs. Espinoza had told me. Photographs had been published: one of her, the same as always, one of the neighbor who'd found her, and one showing the front of her house. Infante, the only person who connected us, had traveled on and was now on the other side of the Atlantic Ocean. I wrote him that same day. He replied in an email from Vienna. A brief, sorrowful note.

I didn't go back to the library the next day. Or on any of the following days.

I hardly got out of bed. I wanted to sink into the same dream as Vera. Nothing made sense anymore. Neither Jérôme, nor my thesis, nor myself.

II.
DANIEL

It had been a few days since the doctors started lowering the dosages of the sedatives. According to the results of your last tests, the hemorrhages in your brain had stopped. It was time to discontinue your medications and disconnect you.

They asked me to remain outside. I spent part of the morning and afternoon pacing up and down the corridor while physicians entered and left your room. Their words were vague and terse, their brows furrowed.

In the afternoon, while I was sitting in the waiting room, a boy no more than seven years old asked me if his father, who was apparently visiting someone in one of the isolation rooms, would be much longer. The boy was playing with a little electronic device. I couldn't answer his question, but I started talking to him so he wouldn't notice how slowly time was passing. He was a vivacious, communicative kid, and while we talked I couldn't stop longing for one of my own. Gracia and I had postponed having a child so many times that now even bringing up the subject seemed somehow comical. In the beginning we cited economic instability as our reason, then we had to get settled in our new house, and always, behind those pretexts, which we both accepted, there was Gracia's career. And by the time all the obstacles had been overcome, it was already very late. I don't know. But days and months and years had succeeded one another, and neither of us had ever again brought up the subject in any energetic and definitive way.

I had already learned how to play the little boy's electronic game when his father came back to the waiting room, looking for him. The child ran to his arms and, without looking at me, disappeared through the elevator doors, holding his father's hand.

Night fell and the physicians vanished, leaving behind them an absolute prohibition on entering your room. Lucy explained that patients of a certain age took longer to wake up, and that I could be waiting for several days. She tried to persuade me to go home, but I knew that even if I did, I wouldn't be able to rest; the thought that you might open your eyes when I wasn't there to welcome you would give me no peace.

I called Gracia and told her I would spend the night in the hospital. She didn't take the news well. "Are you alone?" she asked me.

"And who would I be with?" I asked in my turn.

"I don't know. You tell me."

I imagined her, moving around nervously in our room, the cell phone wedged between her head and her shoulder, putting things in order here and there.

For an instant I thought she might be referring to Teresa, but the idea seemed so lurid that I discarded it. Gracia couldn't possibly know about that. I had acted with the utmost caution. After we hung up, I settled into one of the armchairs in the waiting room and opened the book I'd brought with me.

After your accident, I'd begun to reread your novels. I hadn't confessed that to you in my long monologues at your bedside. I couldn't reveal that I was looking for keys in your work, for anything that might shed some light on your life and that might even lead me to discover what had happened the morning of your fall. It had been days since I'd heard from the detective, and I was already starting to get worried. The next time he got in touch with me, I planned to ask him to give me a number where I might reach him. In one of your drawers, I'd found your engagement book. It was almost empty, but you had noted the luncheon at Infante's daughter's house on the Saturday before your fall and your appointment with the psychiatrist who lived in Madrid. His name was Álvaro Calderón. I looked him up on Google and learned that he was forty-six years old and that he was also a professor of neuropsychiatry at the Complutense University of Madrid. He'd published various articles in specialized magazines. What had your conversation with him been like, and why had it left you perplexed and melancholy? Had he gone back to Spain already, or was he still in Chile?

I drifted into sleep. My slumbers were interrupted by the nocturnal comings and goings of formless beings.

Every now and then I woke up, and the pale white lights in the corridors made me feel as though I were inside a refrigerator. Tormented by the cold—which wasn't real but had been generated inside me—I tried to go back to sleep, but soon afterward I woke up again.

When the first rays of sunlight came through the window in the waiting room, I went to the lavatory and washed my face. Then I went down to the hospital cafeteria and had breakfast. A cup of black coffee and a couple of croissants, which must have been left over from the previous day. I went back up to your floor and ran into Lucy in the corridor.

"She's breathing. But she hasn't woken up. The doctor told me that if I saw you, I should tell you to have patience. He also said you could go in and visit her."

"Will she wake up?" My throat tightened, and my voice barely got out.

"That's something we can't know," Lucy said. She looked embarrassed and went away down the corridor.

Now that the tubes and the respirator were gone, your face recovered its beauty. I didn't know whether it was because you'd been immobile and shut off from sunlight, but even the expressive lines and the wrinkles proper to your eighty-four years appeared to have become less pronounced, and your skin looked smoother and more translucent.

I took your hand and stroked your forehead. I knew you were there, behind your closed, twitching eyelids. Yes, you were there, and the place you occupied in life hadn't closed yet.

In the midmorning, my cell phone rang. It was Horacio Infante, calling from Paris, asking for news of you. It was the first time he'd gotten in touch with me. He sounded disturbed; maybe he'd even had a few drinks too many. I told him that they'd disconnected you from the machines, but that you were still asleep. I was tired and discouraged, and Infante must have noticed. We hung up after a gloomy good-bye that hovered in the air for a long time before disappearing under the sound of your breathing.

Part

TWO

12.
HORACIO

It was the summer of 1951, and I was thirty-three years old. For the past thirteen, I'd lived in various cities, but mostly in Geneva, working for the High Commissioner for Refugees, in whose offices I occupied a minor position. My return was a response—according to the official story—to my mother's plaintive letters, wherein she detailed the multiple infirmities that could, any day, snatch her away to the grave. But the truth is, I was returning home chock-full of anticipation and plans, which included renting a cabin facing the ocean and dedicating myself completely to poetry, or meeting an attractive, intelligent compatriot to share the rest of my life with. From a distance, Chile had turned into the place where all the dark corners of my existence would be filled with light. The Promised Land, the Paradise Lost.

I rented an apartment facing Santa Lucía Hill, in the center of Santiago, in an ancient and somewhat run-down building whose winding staircase creaked amicably. I installed the furniture I'd brought over from Europe, and soon the two-room (bed, living) apartment took on the air of a place that had been lived in for a long time.

After several years of uninterrupted work (due to the idea that any distraction whatsoever could cost me the benefits of my efforts and my labors), now I was enjoying useless activities, such as, for example, walking the streets of my neighborhood. I liked the Parque Forestal, its holm oaks and araucaria trees accompanied by the sound of the river, its strollers, the stillness of the National Library. I'd saved enough money to live on for at least a year, and while I wandered the streets of the city center, I laid plans and imagined my future. It was on one of those strolls that I ran into María Soledad, the sister of a former schoolmate. It had been fifteen years since I'd seen her, but the freckles, the reddish hair, and a slight limp when she walked made her unmistakable. María Soledad told me that her brother—Juan Ignacio by name, the class troublemaker—was living on the old family property, and although her words sounded light and carefree, I sensed that his exile wasn't exactly voluntary. María Soledad worked for a law firm on Moneda Street, and I invited her to come to my little apartment for tea the following week. That same evening, I ventured into an antiques shop and bought a tea service that harmonized well with my furniture. In my various long and solitary sojourns, I'd learned to prepare a great variety of tasty dishes and snacks (with which I'd regaled more than one woman), and on the morning of the appointed day, I baked some scones for María Soledad that were in no way inferior to those served in the most refined English teahouses.

María Soledad arrived right on time. In my adolescent years she had more than once caused me the genital discomfort provoked in us by all girls alike, but although it had been months since I'd had an intimate encounter, María Soledad's presence in my apartment did not arouse in me any sort of desire or fantasy of a sexual nature. I must confess that her freckles didn't help too much, to say nothing of her limp. In those days, I had the idea women ought to display skin that was immaculately smooth and without blemishes, and the image of that proliferation of freckles spreading to private areas, such as her forearms or her crotch, repelled me. I don't know what her intentions were. She was thirty years old and had never married, but I suppose that my naturalness and my absolute lack of affectation ended up relaxing her, and soon we were engaged in an animated conversation, like two old friends.

"Do you remember Rodrigo Bulnes?" María Soledad asked me shortly after she arrived.

I hadn't managed to produce either a yes or a no before she was already elaborating on a meticulous description of the said Bulnes's rise and fall. Then she went on to the decline in Fuentes's fortunes and the—according to her—scandalous story of the couple formed by Isabel Yáñez and a certain Videla. It was my first reminder of one of the characteristics of the Chilean society I'd left behind as a teenager: its tendency to illustrate the world through countless anecdotes concerning other people, whom the person you're talking to, if he has any self-respect, must necessarily know. But perhaps the most salient feature of the practice was that the importance of the account didn't seem to be based so much on the facts as on the protagonists' first and last names. Toward the end of our evening, María Soledad remarked that she was going to attend a luncheon at a cousin's house in the Santiago suburbs that weekend; she would be delighted, she said, if I'd accompany her. María Soledad belonged to one of those families whose ancestors are an integral part of Chilean history. A university rector (whose name is now borne by one of the city's important streets), a couple of senators, and a learned aunt, Doña Eloísa Díaz, the first woman to matriculate at the University of Chile for the study of medicine. Her brother used to talk about "Aunt Isa," even as a child, and what amused him most about her story was that she was obliged, by order of the rector, to attend classes in the company of her mother, and that the two of them had to remain behind a folding screen during anatomy lessons.

The prospect of participating in that world—to which my family had belonged but in which, after my grandfather's massive financial collapse, followed later by my father's, I hadn't had the opportunity to live—never failed to arouse my expectations.

On the appointed day, she picked me up in her Renault Caravelle. Her cousin, she informed me, though an uninteresting woman, had intellectual aspirations, and her husband was a prominent attorney, a partner in the firm where she worked as his secretary and assistant.

We got there at noon. A few cars were already stationed in the spacious, graveled parking area. In the distance, the mountains rose and undulated above the surface of the earth like sinuous bodies. We were walking to the house along a path lined with hedges when the lord of the manor came out to meet us. María Soledad introduced me as an old friend who had been living in Europe, a fact that seemed to arouse a certain curiosity in our host, an interest which in any case faded away as soon as we began to move toward the house. The lawyer was dressed in a white shirt and cream-colored trousers, both impeccably tailored from expensive material, and he had a scarf tied around his neck.

We crossed a little circular garden, passed a French-style fountain, and then went around the side of the house. It was a two-story residence, at once imposing and simple, with satiny white window frames and a brick facade. This building was crowned by a stately, impassive tile roof, with two windows that peered into the distance, their view obstructed by tendrils of climbing ivy. Each element occupied the place corresponding to it, like silent bastions of the established order.

From behind the tall hedge that bordered the path, voices and laughter filled with summery joviality reached our ears. The road ended in a park, where the verdure of summer and the cooling altitude of the sky opened up in all their magnificence. Men and women, casually but elegantly attired, were conversing in groups around wicker tables and deck chairs placed here and there on the grass. Circumspect waiters gazed at the horizon while balancing trays on one hand. Two greyhounds were trotting around, moving their long extremities with sarcastic expressions on their snouts. The entire ambience evoked an English colony, which clashed almost brutally with the soulless neighborhoods and the dwellings made of cardboard and construction waste that we'd spotted along the way.

I soon lost sight of María Soledad, which gave me license to wander among the guests at my ease, a glass of champagne in my hand. Every now and then I'd approach one of the groups, whose members, after greeting me with kindly indifference, resumed their conversations, which consisted for the most part in chitchat about persons unknown to me. The other guests appeared quite cosmopolitan, but on the few occasions when I tried to speak up on some subject, offering a point of view that transcended the borders of our country, they looked at me questioningly, and with a certain disdain. The Andes, apparently, with all their majesty and magnificence, acted as a boundary between their lives and the world.

After a while, I was certain I'd made a mistake in accepting María Soledad's invitation. But above all, I was mortified by the thought that I'd harbored a hope of recovering some sense of belonging. While I roamed around aimlessly, groups formed and dispersed on the grass, then reconstituted themselves in other shapes and colors, like ink stains on green paper. An older gentleman, fine-looking and robust, came up to me.

"You look a bit lost," he said. He had white hair, and his red cheeks (perhaps from the sun, or from the effect of a few glasses too many) were crisscrossed by deep lines that gave him an air of seriousness and experience.

"And so I am," I confessed.

He asked me who I was and how I came to be there. In a few words, I told him the state of things in my life and described my recent return and the work I'd been doing in Geneva, which immediately aroused his interest. He introduced himself in his turn as Manuel Pérez, "a simple businessman." Soon we were talking about current events, such as the recent reelection of Juan Domingo Perón, and about Eleanor Roosevelt, whom he'd had the opportunity to meet when she chaired the United Nations Commission on Human Rights.

Little by little we were being surrounded by other guests, attracted by the presence of my companion, who (judging from the way people were bowing to him) proved to be much more powerful and popular than he'd indicated to me. María Soledad herself rose from the depths of wherever she'd disappeared to and joined our animated group.

That was when I saw her. She was sitting under some elms in one of the wicker deck chairs, talking with two young men. But she seemed to be doing more than just chatting; she was stirring their senses. She exerted the same attraction on me as on the two men, who conversed between themselves while focusing their attention on the effect their words were having on her. The woman's eyes were penetrating but at the same time indifferent, almost cruel. She contemplated her two interlocutors and then ran her eyes over the grass, the poplars, the sky, and the birds that were squawking in the distance. She had a prominent, delicate nose, high cheekbones, thick lips, a wide mouth, and almond-shaped, feline eyes. She wore an extremely simple, cream-colored dress that emphasized her long bones, her shoulders, and her slender arms. Her beauty was of the striking variety that in a less mysterious woman would not have aroused my curiosity. At the time, I had a theory, according to which excessive beauty, in men as in women, caused them to build their lives around that fleeting attribute and in time turned them into indolent and mostly uninteresting people.

María Soledad noticed my interest in the woman, and her face took on a grimace of displeasure.

"She's a Jewess."

I was struck by the scorn in her words, which served only to spur my curiosity and my longing to meet the lady.

"Her name is Vera Sigall," María Soledad went on. "They say her mother died of syphilis after an entire battalion of Soviet soldiers raped her in the village where she lived. I don't believe it. It's just too much, isn't it? You know, Jews love to make up terrible stories they can use to pass themselves off as victims all over the world. I don't know why they can't just turn the page and be like everybody else."

I had no desire to keep listening to María Soledad. I wondered how many of the people present thought the way she did. Every now and then, the woman looked over in our direction. Without curiosity, merely reconnoitering the place. Even so, each time her head turned and the muscles in her slender neck tensed, I couldn't help feeling a certain emotion. Her reddened eyelids gave her a tragic air. Soon I realized that it wasn't me she was observing, and not María Soledad either, but the big, friendly fellow who had welcomed me. Despite my efforts to get rid of María Soledad, she remained at my side, and in whispers, while the rest of the group steered the conversation in new directions, she imparted anecdotes and pieces of information that I suppose she thought indispensable for survival in that milieu.

When lunch began, I managed to get a seat far from María Soledad but then suffered anyway, as I was trapped between two women, friends who ignored my presence and exchanged comments and giggles behind my shoulders. In compensation, I had an excellent view of Vera Sigall, who was sitting at a nearby table. On a couple of occasions, our eyes met, but hers, after stopping for a fraction of a second, and without the slightest change in their distant expression, passed over me as they might a plant. At her side, immersed in conversation, was Pérez with a glass of champagne in his hand, just as when I'd met him a couple of hours previously.

By late afternoon, many of the guests had had too much to drink and were peacefully dozing in the chairs under the elms or loudly talking and laughing. Behind their voices, you could hear the twittering of the birds, but then they fell silent. Afternoon capitulated to evening, and the reddish colors of sunset climbed the sky. Pérez and his wife had disappeared. It was at the end of the soiree, when María Soledad and I were going to her car, that I saw them again. She was keeping him upright with some difficulty, holding him by one arm while he staggered down the gravel path. They were about halfway to the Chevrolet Bel Air that was waiting for them with open doors several meters away when a man dressed in an impeccable gray three-piece suit appeared and relieved Vera of her burden. Not many minutes later, we were driving on the poplar-lined avenue behind their car, which raised a slipstream of dust that obscured my vision of the road, of Pérez, and of Vera Sigall.

13.
EMILIA

The days passed, sealed up in black paper that let no light in.

Don José sent one of his daughters to ask why I hadn't shown up for work. The girl's dark, curly hair fell down to her waist. I told her I had the flu. I don't know if she believed me.

The cans that provided my food came to an end.

On one of those mornings, I went out onto the roof. The city lay at my feet, still half asleep. In the park, the treetops were swaying. Far off, the streetlights started to go out. The cloud ceiling was low, as if the sky had come closer during the night. A hole opened briefly, and I could see an airplane plowing through the clouds. The vision was transient, but true. Behind the gray, opaque expanse of clouds, there was another world.

I just had to reach it.

I took a shower, got dressed, and waited for the morning to settle in. I didn't know exactly why, but I surely knew where I wanted to go. When I stepped into the elevator, I found Juan and Francisco. I must have looked fairly bad, because they asked me if I needed anything. I told them that the writer I'd gone to see had suffered an accident.

Before too long, I was standing in front of the hospital, a white building whose stairway access and high ceilings made it look like a hotel. I went in, approached the reception counter, and asked for her.

"She's in room 405. The elevator's over there," one of the receptionists told me. Her nose was turned up so high that I could see the inside of her nostrils and the little hairs that protected them.

The elevator doors opened onto a waiting room. In one corner, a woman was reading, her face hidden behind her magazine. Two corridors led out of the waiting room, one on either side, until they were lost in darkness. I took the corridor on the left, which according to the signs would bring me to room 405.

I passed in front of Vera's room. Her door was ajar. I couldn't resist the impulse to look in. The shoulders of a man who was sitting on a chair against the door prevented me from seeing inside. I kept walking to the end of the corridor, where a window admitted triangles of light that moved around on the floor. Then I retraced my steps, passed 405 without looking, and sat down in the waiting room.

The heat emanating from the walls contrasted with the cold in my bedroom.

Now the woman had the magazine closed on her lap and her eyes fixed on a cheap reproduction of a Constable painting that was hung on the wall. Serenity was the order of the day in there, as if the world had stopped to listen to the heartbeats of the patients lying behind the shut doors. A nurse walked rapidly through the room.

The swift clatter of her heels resounded in the silence, filling it with expectation. There was a vending machine on one side of the room, and I got up to buy something to eat.

"I was waiting for you," I heard the woman say.

She had an affectionate voice that seemed to contain moist, furtive promises.

I raised my head and saw a tall young man whose dangling arms were like two folded wings, ready to open and take flight. He was wearing threadbare jeans and a white shirt with the sleeves rolled up to his elbows, revealing his thick veins.

A doctor, followed by a pair of young interns, hurried through the room, heading in the same direction as the nurse. Their voices sounded urgent.

The woman got up from her seat and went over to the man. She wore a black dress that despite its high neckline displayed her generous curves. Her high heels made her almost as tall as he was. Her movements were timid, in contrast to the exuberance of her body.

"What are you doing here, Teresa?" the man asked. He sounded angry. His face looked familiar to me.

"You don't answer my calls," she said, and she raised one hand to her throat, as if protecting herself.

I stayed where I was, leaning against the wall next to the vending machine. I sensed that they'd find my presence inconvenient.

"It's not right for you to come here."

"You think I care about that?" she asked, with contained ferocity.

For the second time in two weeks, I was eavesdropping on a conversation between two other people, and I didn't much like the way it made me feel. I was able to sneak a peek at the man's annoyed expression.

"I told you I'd call you when I could," the man said. His tone was harsh, categorical.

"You can't do this to me," she said, almost in a whisper.

"Teresa, please...," he replied. The weary expression on his face made him look older.

With a swift gesture that seemed to spring not from her consciousness or her will but from some other source, the woman touched his lips with her fingers. Reacting brusquely, the man rejected her.

The lines in the corners of the man's thin lips seemed to contain a veiled force, a reserve that could just as well have been hiding something benevolent as something malign. His eyes, by contrast, were friendly. The eyes of a man who observes.

Suddenly I remembered. He was the one who had found Vera Sigall after her accident and taken her to the hospital. I'd seen his photograph on the Internet, during my searches.

The abrupt sound of a banged door reached us, but they didn't appear to notice it. The woman blinked a lot. Her most trivial gestures seemed to arise from her very depths.

There was something intolerably open about her, something almost indecent.

She reached out her hand, and he clasped it without looking at her. After a few seconds, she withdrew it and crossed her arms under her breasts. He fixed his eyes on her, looking serious, and ran his hand over her docile, chestnut-colored hair.

"You shouldn't be here," he repeated.

She moved closer to him and kissed him on the mouth with panting urgency. I thought about Jérôme. He and I had never kissed.

I remembered the first time I'd become aware of my affliction. I was eight. Judging by the countless therapies they'd subjected me to, my parents had noticed something peculiar shortly after I was born.

It was my body.

Even when I was a newborn, my musculature was firm and powerful. Instead of snoozing, overcome like all babies by my new life, I raised my head from the pillows and scrutinized the world through barely opened eyes. Considering all the times I reconstructed events for therapists, those that settled into my consciousness are probably just a "story," remote from the events themselves. A mythology.

It happened at recess. When the bell rang, my classmates ran out to the school playground.

Before going out, I usually arranged my notebooks and put my pencils in their case—even though after recess I'd have to take them out again—and so I was always late for the games on the playground. On that day, however, when I stepped outside, nobody had climbed up to the top of the slide yet. It was higher and steeper than the ones in my neighborhood park. Toward the bottom, before you landed, a bump in the slide made you feel a slight vertigo. A foretaste of life.

There was a heavy thump, and the blood started to flow the instant the back of my head touched the sharp rock. The children around me became quiet, they uttered no sound, like choristers who had suddenly lost their voices. I passed my hand over the cut on my head and felt blood, warm and viscous. I ran to the bathroom and locked the door. My being was running out through that wound, and I was never going to get it back.

Alerted by the children, the teachers started to knock on the bathroom door. But I couldn't open it.

They managed to get in. The cut wasn't bleeding anymore, but according to what they later told my parents, my hands, my arms, and my face were covered with blood.

I don't know what happened inside that bathroom.

The tiles were cold. The morning light came in through an opening in the wall, high up, and offered evidence for the existence of the outside world. The rest is lost, a blur in a gray, formless landscape. In the hospital, they put five stitches in my head. On the way home, in my mother's car, I felt as though my skin had turned itself inside out, leaving raw and exposed everything it was supposed to protect: my guts, my heart, my lungs, my liver, my veins.

A metallic screech broke the silence in the corridor. The man and the woman stepped apart.

When we got home, I went to my room, locked the door, and fell asleep. I heard neither my parents' knocking nor the locksmith they'd called to open the door. I woke up with my fists clenched. I'd pressed my fingernails into my palms so tightly I'd cut them. I lost my appetite and I could hardly speak.

During the following weeks, I underwent various medical examinations. The doctors were looking for evidence of a blow to the head that could have caused a trauma. But they found nothing. My parents, frustrated and unable to understand what was happening to me, blamed the school for negligence. I knew, however, that the process had begun much earlier. When I walked on the concrete patio in the schoolyard, my body wasn't my own. I'd look at my hand, and everything about it would seem strange to me, the white skin, the slender fingers. Sometimes a nameless terror would overcome me and I'd remain paralyzed, not recognizing myself, not recognizing the mechanism that could make each finger move. Furthermore, when I looked into a mirror, sometimes I'd see someone else. It was hard for me to believe that those black eyes, staring out at me in surprise from their sockets, that narrow torso, and those dark, tight braids were "me." My dismay and fear were so intense that I'd forget to breathe, and it was only in the subsequent, agitated huffing, in the hasty search for oxygen to nourish my lungs, that I'd meet up with my body again. After my fall, the episodes of estrangement became more frequent, and contact with the rest of my schoolmates rarer.

My parents had me change schools, and I began a new life. A life in which my body remained inside out. A body no one could touch.

From then on, books became a home for me, solid but also changeable. I became adept at reading anywhere: from one room to another, on the way to school, while I was eating. Nothing could distract my attention from those pages. They sheltered me and at the same time gave me an idea of the universe I was so afraid of. When I discovered the Latin American authors, their effect on me was like a hurricane, a life-changing event. Julio Cortázar's *Hopscotch*, for example: I remember reading about the death of little Rocamadour again and again. His feverish body, the sounds of Brahms, the rain, Oliveira's defeated remoteness, the sharp blows of the old man's stick on their heads, the darkness, and then the irrefutable evidence of death.

From one of the rooms came the sound of voices and a high-pitched wail.

"Stay calm, it's not her," I heard the woman say.

Someone had died. Behind one of those doors, someone had left us. And it wasn't Vera.

I went out to the street and got my bicycle. I walked it home, holding on to it with both hands. I was conscious of the air going in and out of my lungs, of my pulse, of guitar chords coming from a half-open window, of the stiff strides of the pedestrians beside me. My empty stomach cried out mutely. But Vera was still alive, and so was I.

I started going to the hospital every day. I didn't know how to explain to Jérôme what was happening to me, because I didn't understand it myself. I stopped visiting the library so that I could spend hour after hour in that waiting room, waiting for something to happen, I didn't know exactly what. I'd just sit down with a book and read. I began to study Horacio Infante's work. I'd never been interested in it before, but now, seen in the light of our meeting in his daughter's house and against the background of his mysterious relationship with Vera, his verses had filled up with question marks. I walked up and down the corridor where Vera's room was, hoping for a chance to see her sleeping face. Which I succeeded in doing, more than once. There she was, behind her closed eyes. The same woman who had instilled hope in me, the woman who'd touched me. I had hoped our contact would last.

But what made me visit the hospital every day was the certainty that if I went away from Vera Sigall, I'd succumb to fear, to anxiety, and before I knew it I'd be flying over the Atlantic on the way to Grenoble, on the way to the known, and everything would go back to being the way it had been until then: mute and still. I'd come this far for her, and it was her presence, on the other side of that door, that sustained me and propelled me toward a place I didn't know; but I knew it was there for me.

14.
DANIEL

When I got to the hospital, Lucy and one of her colleagues were stationed at the door of your room. A few meters away, in the corridor, three older ladies were speaking in low voices and looking at the two nurses. I hurried over to Lucy and asked her what was happening.

"News has spread that Mrs. Sigall has shown some signs of recovery. One of her friends, the tallest one," Lucy said, surreptitiously indicating one of the women, "claims to have seen her move her fingers, so she called the press on the spot. I had stepped out for a moment, and when I came back, I didn't see anything...Oh God, here they come!"

I turned around and saw three men walking down the corridor toward us. One of them carried a camera. The doctor who received you the morning you arrived at the hospital was coming with them. Some distance behind them, I again saw the girl who had been sitting alone in the waiting room for the past couple of weeks. She had a pageboy haircut and wore thick eyeglasses with black frames. She was a slight, short person, and she dressed in a way that was so archaic as to seem unconventional: pleated Scottish skirt, down to her knees; turtleneck sweater covering a flat chest; thick wool socks; and flat-heeled, lace-up ankle boots. She looked like a little girl, with the exception of her black eyes, which displayed a mature wariness under her thick eyebrows. The journalists, fortunately, contented themselves with a few responses from the doctor, as they were in a great hurry. Some semi-celebrity had convened a press conference on the other side of Santiago to announce his divorce from another semi-celebrity. The doctor entered your room and left the door half open. The girl with the lace-up boots stood in front of it, looking inside. She looked completely absorbed, like someone studying an equation written on a blackboard. She had a book in her arms and pressed it against her breast, never taking her eyes off you. My first impulse was to close the door, but her intense concentration stopped me. After a few seconds, she seemed to emerge from the trance that the sight of you had provoked in her and looked around in embarrassment. I was the only one who appeared to notice her presence. She raised her eyes, gave me a sidelong glance, and wiped her nose with the palm of her hand. Before she hurried off down the corridor, I smiled at her, but she didn't smile back. I thought I saw in her eyes a certain contempt, and at the same time an appeal. I thought about a helium balloon drifting off, dangling its cord in the air, wishing that someone would grab it and haul it back down to earth.

The detective kept on not getting in touch with me. I had tried to reach him, but my attempts had perished in the tangle of telephone operators who passed my calls to one another like some endless relay. I hadn't made much progress in my own investigations either, but the idea that your fall hadn't been accidental, instead of fading, grew stronger day by day. I knew that such things happen, people fall, people have accidents, people die, but not you, not you.

15. HORACIO

I saw Vera Sigall again six months later, at a reception in the Argentine embassy. I'd been able to get María Soledad to talk to me about her on our way back from the afternoon in the country. That was how I'd learned that Manuel Pérez, Vera's husband, was her senior by twenty years, that he'd had two previous marriages, and that, in the ten years of their union, Vera had never ceased being unfaithful to him. María Soledad declared her not only a whore, but also a social climber. What bothered her most was the fact that Vera, "a Jewess," had entered into a marriage with Manuel Pérez. According to María Soledad, Pérez was a scion of "the noblest lineage in the country," an assessment that obliged me to repress a laugh, given that those lines of descent she was alluding to were formed by the descendants of some desperately impoverished Spaniards who had come to Chile to seek their fortune.

If I must be strictly accurate, I should disclose that I'd seen Vera Sigall on three occasions prior to our meeting at the embassy. The first was in front of the doors of the

Municipal Theater in Santiago. There, after letting her gaze rest on me for a fraction of a second, as if my features looked somehow familiar but produced no greater interest, she turned her eyes to her companion, a good-looking man who reminded me of María Soledad's accusation and therefore made me feel slightly uneasy. The second time, I spotted her through the windows of Darío Carmona's bookstore. I was tempted to go in, but she, sitting on a stool with a book in her hands, was looking straight ahead with half-closed eyes. Her solitude and her stillness expressed strength, but at the same time they betrayed her fragility. The potential embarrassment of interrupting her when she was so deep in thought and the certainty that she would once again look at me without seeing me made me give up. The third time was outside Café Paula, on the corner of San Antonio and Agustinas. She was with a little boy, and she was squatting down on the pavement, wiping his mouth with a handkerchief. The child clutched his ice cream cone and docilely let himself be worked on. He had the thinness of a convalescent and his mother's high cheekbones and almond eyes. Vera studied him with an expression of immense sweetness. When she finished, she caressed his face. I thought her gesture was a sort of once-over, verifying that the boy was still there, at her side, and that he was hers.

The past six months had been fruitful ones for me. Above all, I'd succeeded, with the help of a friend who worked in a print shop, in publishing a book of poems, and the reviews, though far from numerous, had all been positive. There had been change in other areas as well.

My savings had turned out to be scantier, or my expenses more abundant, than I had foreseen, and I'd had to accept a job with the United Nations, which entailed returning to Geneva for some time. My departure was a few weeks away.

I remember that in the long meetings I had to attend for my new job, I developed a habit of making lists in my notebooks of the women with whom I'd had relationships, cataloging them according to a crude scale which took into account their beauty rating and the degree of their liberalism in sexual matters. Each name was accompanied by a coded letter: S for sublime, P for passable, I for inadequate, and LTI for less than inadequate. Later I scrawled over and scratched out those lists, hiding the identities of the women involved, the majority of whom were married, while others were engaged and on the verge of entering into matrimony. I wasn't proud of my adventures, but I consoled myself with the thought that I hadn't simply had intercourse with those women; I'd given something of myself to each one. María Soledad's talk about Vera Sigall's recurring infidelities hadn't escaped my notice, and in some part of my consciousness I harbored the hope of adding her name to my list. In those days, I was convinced that a man's true path was the one that led to the next woman he would kiss, or better yet, if the conditions were right, take to bed.

In my daydreams, I pictured Vera Sigall's gaze finally coming to rest on me, recognizing our mutual roots in the wasteland of the landless. But that night in the Argentine embassy, things happened in a way I would have been unable to imagine even in my cheekiest fantasies.

The ambassador's residence was one of the most magnificent in the city. From every object, from every corner emanated an aura of luxury and good taste, and through the windows you could see the vast park that surrounded the house. I spotted Vera the moment she came in. She was wearing a violet-colored dress with a flared skirt that accentuated her slender waist. In this setting, her presence projected a looseness, an ease I hadn't noticed the previous time. While conversing with a group of women, Vera laughed, gesticulated, lent an ear to the comments of the others, and agreed with them completely. It was obvious that this display of worldliness (which to my aspiring poet's critical eyes appeared ostentatious and false) came naturally to her. I felt a touch of disappointment, and throughout the rest of the evening, I refrained from making any effort to approach her. Manuel Pérez was utterly absorbed in one of his conversations, his hands clasped behind his back, his body slightly stooped. It was only when we were preparing to move to the dining tables that Pérez and Vera Sigall rejoined each other. I noticed, however, that in the course of those months, the years seemed to have fallen on Manuel Pérez with all their weight. Even his impeccably tailored suit was too large for his body, which was obviously thinner. Vera went to him and whispered something in his ear, and after she took his arm, they walked together to their table. I noticed that the man, even though he kept looking determinedly straight ahead, staggered a little, and that after he sat down it took him a few seconds to catch his breath. Vera and her husband were seated at a table next to mine, but behind me, so I didn't have an opportunity to observe them during the dinner. After so many years, when I try to put together what happened next, I realize that the events as they occurred are distorted by the multiple versions of them that Vera and I re-created over the course of time, endowing them with subjectivity and with a patina of romanticism that they doubtless didn't have. There are moments like that. Moments that in time turn into shared fables. We reconstruct them with the purpose of accommodating them to our story and transforming them into something we can hoard.

I remember that a big teardrop chandelier, projecting its beams onto the women's powdered faces, revealed their imperfections. The music of a string quartet tempered the atmosphere from the far end of the dining room, producing a sound that served as a background to the voices and the laughter and gave the scene a soft texture. It was from the depths of that harmony that the shouts burst out.

"How dare you speak that way about Mussolini?" a woman cried out.

"And you, how dare you falsify history, Madam?" That was Vera's voice I was hearing, clear as the sound of glass shattering in the midst of silence. I turned my head and saw her. There was something in her eyes wild and sad at once.

"What's your moral authority? That you're a Jew? That you're destroying the life of a man like—"

"Don't you dare, Sonia," Manuel Pérez interrupted her.

"Ladies, gentlemen...," another man shouted.

"Is it possible you haven't noticed, Manuel?" said the woman, shouting as before.

"What I've noticed is that I have no patience for this much ignorance and stupidity," Manuel said caustically, rising to his feet so violently that he overturned his chair.

"Leave it, it's not worth the trouble," I heard Vera say. She too rose from her seat and put her bare arm around Manuel's shoulders.

Everyone in the room had fallen silent, and now you could clearly hear the strings playing in the background, like the soundtrack of a tragedy. In the midst of the silence, broken only by the music, the two of them passed through the room, making their way among the tables before the astonished eyes of the other attendees. Vera displayed the confident composure of her youth, her chin held high, her cold eyes staring straight ahead, while Pérez walked slowly beside her, holding on to her arm. I got up from my table and joined the couple. Although Manuel had lost some size in the past few months, he was still a big man. I took him by one elbow, while Vera did the same with the other, and we continued on like that, heading for the doors of the room. The plush carpets that absorbed our footfalls also made it harder to walk, as if a force from the center of the earth were contending against our efforts to maintain our dignity. An embassy official, whose hair seemed to have been parted in the center of his head with a ruler, came up to us and babbled some confused words in a markedly Argentine accent, so that it wasn't clear whether he was trying to dissuade us from our flight or encourage it. In any case, whatever he may have been saying, there was no way back. The same chauffeur as before, on the occasion of the afternoon in the country, was waiting for the Pérez couple at the gates of the embassy. The sound of music reached us from inside the house.

"We can give you a ride," Vera muttered. I could see in her eyes both her fortitude and her desolation. I liked the way she took for granted that I wouldn't be going back inside. I also liked her addressing me with the informal *tu*.

Together we helped settle Manuel in the front seat, and then Vera and I got in the back. The house behind us, with light streaming from every window, evoked the image of a cruise ship from which we'd disembarked and which was now sailing imperturbably on. Its passengers must have resumed their chatter by then, having already forgotten the unpleasant moment Pérez and his wife had made them go through. The chauffeur started the engine, and I opened my window. We drove through the solitary Santiago streets. At regular intervals, we passed barefoot men pushing carts crammed with packages and newspapers. Manuel was breathing heavily. With eyes closed, he began to hurl insults. In the distance, we could make out San Cristóbal Hill. While Vera was looking out at the street, and although I felt a little wretched for what I was doing, I watched her breasts rise and fall with her breathing, and if I arranged myself at a certain angle, I could even see her cleavage narrow and widen. Her body gave off a fresh aroma of soap.

"Where would you like us to drop you?" I heard Vera ask me. "Horacio Infante, right?" I was impressed that she knew my name.

I stated my address, and we drove on without saying a word.

"He needs me," she said, adding a few seconds later, "And I need him."

When we stopped in front of the doors of my building, Manuel was snoring laboriously and breathing with difficulty.

"He'll be fine," Vera declared.

I got out of the car, and while I was taking my keys out of my overcoat, she rolled down her window and said, "Thank you, Horacio."

The morning after that strange soiree at the Argentine embassy, I found myself standing outside my apartment building with one of my neighbors. He'd seen me coming home the previous night, and he'd recognized Manuel Pérez inside the car. I imagined him peering through the curtains on one of the windows of his first-floor apartment and felt disgusted. He was a man of immaculate appearance, with a sparse little gray mustache, who had retired from some position in public service and devoted the greater part of his time to walking his dog in the neighborhood. From him I learned that the Pérez family had made its fortune in mining, and that Pérez himself, as a businessman, had for years been in charge of amassing and increasing that fortune. The same day, I went to the National Library. I was looking for a book by a forgotten poet of the Golden

Age, a friend of Lope de Vega, when it occurred to me that perhaps there was some historical work in which I could find more information about the Pérez family.

What I found corroborated and amplified my neighbor's revelations, but it didn't help me conceive a fuller or more exact idea of Pérez. In any case, I'd already learned that in their zeal for generalities, history books, like museums, swallow up the particularities of the men and women who inform them, exalting the identities of only a few. Or—to put it more succinctly—if I want to understand, I always turn to novels and poetry.

A few days later, I would have a chance to learn more. An old friend from my school days, Miguel Sanfeliú, invited me to lunch at the Club de la Unión.

We were preparing to drink a final liqueur in the club's great room, the one with the checkerboard floor, when a man came over to us and sat at our table. He held a cigar clamped between his teeth. A bald-headed man seated at a grand piano was playing a Debussy piece without much conviction.

"Bernardo Ruiz, pleased to meet you," our new companion introduced himself, and then, without any preamble whatsoever, he asked me, "Have you known them for a long time?" I noted a slight disdain in his tone.

"I don't know who you're talking about," I answered apprehensively.

"I'm talking about Manuel Pérez and his wife," he explained, and then, without taking the cigar out of his mouth, he exhaled a great cloud of smoke, which came apart a few centimeters from his face.

"The truth is, I don't know them at all," I said.

In the mirror in front of me, one of the many that covered the walls of the room, I saw a man whose every gesture was full of an arrogant and almost absurd conviction. His hair was poorly cut and his face beardless. Only a few fractions of a second elapsed before I realized I was looking at myself.

"In that case, I'd say your 'performance' of the other night was even more spectacular than it appeared," replied Ruiz.

"What are you talking about?" asked Sanfeliú.

In a few words, our new companion explained to my friend what had occurred at the embassy, and Sanfeliú laughed heartily. One of the candles burning in front of the mirrors went out, leaving us sitting in a shadowy corner. The pianist stopped playing, adjusted his bow tie, and got up heavily from his piano bench.

"I didn't know you had quixotic inclinations," said my friend, laughing.

"Well, what's certain is that they're both a mystery to me," I ventured.

"I can tell," said Ruiz, smiling with one side of his mouth, and I sensed that he was savoring in advance the revelations he was about to make to me.

All of a sudden, as I was looking at his ruddy face, his double chin, and the carefully arranged yellow curls on his broad skull, I thought about Scarlett O'Hara's gossipy aunt.

"It happened more than fifteen years ago but even so, there are many people who haven't forgiven him, especially members of his family. And as you surely must know, the Pérez Somavía family is related to *le tout Santiago*," he said, pronouncing these last words with a French accent.

"Explain what you mean, please," I asked him.

And thus I learned that Pérez had been, from the shadows, one of the main architects of the migration of twenty thousand Jews to Brazil between 1938 and 1941, together with his friend the Bolivian mining magnate Mauricio Hochschild.

"But what makes this all the more interesting is that Manuel's father, Don Jorge Pérez, was one of the founders of the Nazi Party in Chile."

A group of men entered the room; their shoes resounded on the tiled floor. Two of the men walked ahead, in animated conversation, while the others followed them in silence.

"Don Jorge was the principal investor in the Nazi newspaper *El Trabajo* and also a friend of Keller, you know, the ignoramus with pretensions to divinity. Manuel defied not only his class, teaming up with a Bolivian Jewish tycoon, but also and above all his father. Recall that in those days, the majority of Latin American countries, faced with the Nazi occupation of Europe, had closed their doors to Jewish immigrants. Manuel's actions destroyed his father. It's said that Don Jorge sent part of his fortune to Germany to finance some obscure experiment that involved the bodies of Jews who had died in the gas chambers. But of course, so far no one has been able to corroborate that. Sometime afterward, the father had a brain hemorrhage, and that was the end of him. Everyone accused Manuel of having caused it."

"And how about Vera Sigall?"

"What do you mean?"

"What does Vera have to do with all this? She's a Jew. She even has a slight accent."

"Ah, that's another story, but I can assure you that Pérez married her so he could finish destroying his relationship with his family. Some say it was his way of redeeming the guilt and shame that weighed on him because of his father's actions. But not much is known about her. I've seen her a couple of times, she's extremely beautiful, there's no doubt about that. They say she has a very sharp tongue and an excess of intelligence."

At this point, my friend Sanfeliú was looking rather insistently at his watch, and soon he got up to leave. He had a meeting to go to. He offered to give me a ride in his car, but I preferred to walk. The information I'd just received had shocked me. I must confess that I even felt a little envious of Pérez. From my place amid the Byzantine workings of the UN Refugee Agency, I would never be able to do anything so impressive and important as what he'd done.

After a few days, I received a missive from Vera, delivered to me by my concierge. The envelope bore no postage stamps, which made me think it had been brought by the chauffeur. In it Vera thanked me again. She'd read my book of poems, concerning which she made a few acute and insightful comments. She'd even detected my allusions, which heretofore nobody had discovered or commented on, to Saint-John Perse. She didn't mention the possibility of another meeting, but on the back of the envelope she'd written her address, in clear, neat letters.

At the end of that month I left Santiago for Geneva, and it would be a year before I'd see Vera again.

16.
EMILIA

One afternoon, I passed a store that sold articles for terraces and balconies, went in, and bought a white, four-legged canopy, which I installed against the kitchen wall.

When the cold was less penetrating, I'd station myself under that canopy and watch the sunset. From my observation post, I could see the four corners of the city, the Andes, the Chilean Coastal Range, and the sky, in its fullest extension. And if I peered over the railing, I could even catch a glimpse of the hustle and bustle in the street below—all those human beings, endlessly moving, the cars, the bicycles, the grocery store across the street, illuminated night and day by neon lights, and one side of the bakery, which was always crowded with people looking for the fresh bread that came out of its ovens. I liked to hear the general racket.

The silence of my little world pained me.

The six hours separating me from Jérôme were as unbridgeable as the thousands of kilometers of sea and land I'd flown over.

Shaken by the breeze, my canopy moved, lively and ethereal. It made me think about the sails of a ship. Then I imagined that I was sailing to faraway lands from which I would never return. On other occasions, I'd imagine I was under a tent in the desert, and soon I'd see a comet cross the bright, gigantic sky. I liked that momentary sensation of living adrift, like a jellyfish, in the midst of the colors of sunset.

But on most evenings, when I returned from the hospital, I'd sit at my writing table and concentrate my efforts on what by then constituted the focal point of my studies: the relation between Infante's work and Vera Sigall's. I'd discovered that his verses frequently appeared in her work. Especially the early poems, the most powerful ones, the ones that catapulted Infante to a place among the most respected Spanish-language poets of our time. I began to make a register of all the paragraphs in which Vera alluded to his verses or reproduced extracts from them. I included the context, as well as a description of the characters who made the allusions. In certain cases, such passages formed part of a character's stream of consciousness, providing ideas that concluded long reflections and granting them, in the end, the power they required. In others, the allusions occurred in dialogue, producing a discordant note that evoked the character's particular world. Often, the meaning of a poem was the origin of a scene, of a conflict, of a segment of the story, and those parallels were what most intrigued me. I spent several days in a close study of Vera's third novel, *The Highest Trapeze*. The connection between Infante's verses and the novel's story operated on various levels, in both form and content.

In the novel, the two main characters, Octavio and Sinalefa, have a *clandestine encounter* in a city perpetually covered with snow. Both are married, though not to each other, and they live on different continents. Sinalefa has agreed to meet Octavio in this *unfathomable city*. And there they are, together and solitary at once, *having no expectations, making no requests*, wandering the snow-covered streets, neither asking the other what the essential meaning of this encounter is, fearful of unleashing feelings, of confessing to themselves and to the other that *I was an outlet for your rage and your boredom, in the antechamber of that New York snow*. And as they walk along, little by little they begin to reveal to each other their previous infidelities, *small-scale, virtually forgotten adventures*. Infante's verses were structured like Japanese tanka: five lines containing, respectively, five, seven, five, seven, and seven syllables.

...a few small-scale adventures,
now virtually forgotten,

the kind we never
boast about, and not because
we are so discreet,
but because, to tell the truth,
they weren't so important,

and yet as time passed
they kept on growing until
they got big enough

to be great thorns in our sides,
pricking us and torturing

our minds with onslaughts
of wholly unjustified
jealousy, or at
least that's how I would prefer
to think about it at this

late date, and it is
moreover what you yourself
always said, isn't
it, looking at me with your
earnest inquisitive eyes

Octavio and Sinalefa continue to meet in different places all over the world. But although the settings change, one after the other, the real and most dangerous journey they take together is the one to the underlying springs of jealousy. What started as a game in the streets of the city turns into an obsession. *I can't tell why we / did it, but here it / is, there's no way back.* Octavio discovers the painful pleasure of imagining Sinalefa's naked body being caressed and possessed by another man. *Pain, and a thousand / suspicions, without / redemption, without / escape, are all that's / left. The nights go by / like this, pregnant with / insomnia, while somber, / suffocating cries / shiver our souls.*

I was certain I'd discovered something important. A hidden secret no one had seen before. Vera wove Infante's verses like threads into her prose.

I went out onto the roof.

The sun had gone into hiding some time ago. A thousand questions were spinning around in my head. I could hear Vera's bracelets jingling, and she seemed to be saying to me, "Watch out, watch out."

Besides Benjamin Moser, two academics and an important critic had studied Vera's work in detail. All three of them had a good command of Spanish, as was evident from their observations and the acuity of their analyses. However, none of these studies mentioned what I'd discovered. Probably none of them knew much about Infante's poetry. Obviously, Vera was employing allusions. But the fact that what she'd done was a standard practice didn't in any way lessen the value and mystery of my discovery. Or at least, that was what I wanted to believe. I thought that maybe it was a secret code, a game that both had agreed to. Perhaps in Infante's verses, which I wasn't completely familiar with, there were also excerpts from Vera's work.

I took several turns around the terrace, lost in these reflections. Night had fallen some time since. I went into the kitchen and opened a can of tuna. I sliced a tomato and mixed the slices with the fish, adding a few lettuce leaves and a hard-boiled egg I hadn't eaten the night before. I filled a glass with water and carried my little meal to my bedchamber. I usually ate while sitting at my writing table, reading some text or making notes in my notebook. But that night, even though I'd eaten nothing all day, I had trouble swallowing so much as a single mouthful. The easiest conclusion was to assume that Infante and Vera Sigall had been lovers. I tried to recall the details of the luncheon at his daughter's home. Including the conversation I'd overheard in the entrance hall.

Back then, I didn't know what relationships between adults were like. I was barely familiar with those between kids of my own age. But even with all my limitations and ignorance, at that luncheon I could see that what I was watching was more than just the meeting of two former lovers. They were bound together by a complex weave of feelings. The result, I was sure, of a backstory compounded of powerful sentiments, which included much more than the ghost of love.

17.
DANIEL

It was after twelve noon when I left your room to go to a little restaurant a couple of blocks from the hospital for lunch. The air in the corridor was thick and humid, like the air in a greenhouse.

I hadn't seen her arrive, but there she was again, sitting in the waiting room with a book on her lap. Instead of continuing on my way, I stopped and observed her from the corridor. She'd been showing up every day for nearly a month. Since the incident with the reporters, our eyes had met a few times, and I'd caught a glimpse of the force in her gaze. She looked like someone from another era, untouched by the changes of the modern world. It wasn't just her outfits—pleated skirts, thick wool socks, ankle boots—and her unmade-up, white, round face, but her mind too seemed to be afloat in time. It was hard to say how old she was. She had the appearance of a fifteen-year-old girl, but her isolation, which surrounded her like an iron curtain, suggested she might be a grown woman.

She got up and started to walk toward the elevator, her backpack slung over her shoulder. I decided to follow her. I ran down the stairs and reached the first floor at the same moment the elevator doors opened. I went out on the street. It was a cold September day. For an instant, I lost her in a group of children who suddenly came around the corner. She crossed the street with hunched shoulders, her arms folded across her chest, her eyes on the ground. She walked a few meters on the path that runs along the Mapocho River and sat down on a bench. She reached into her backpack, took out a package of cookies, opened it carefully, and ate one, taking tiny bites. And likewise with the rest, one after another, her gaze concentrated on the automobiles making their way along Santa María Avenue, as if that act were part of a ritual. I had the impression that I was violating her privacy. I thought about turning around and going, but something held me there. Her dark eyes, visible behind her sunglasses, now seemed defenseless. I walked over to the bench and sat down beside her. Without looking at me, she leaped to her feet and clutched her backpack in her arms.

"Don't go away," I said to her.

She was breathing rapidly, and all her senses seemed to be heightened. She put me in mind of a doe in open country, exposed to the untimely appearance of a predator.

"Don't be afraid of me," I said.

"That's two don'ts in less than a minute," she said. Her breath erupted from her mouth in clouds that dispersed in the cold air.

With one hand, she pushed aside her shiny black bangs, which immediately fell back over her eyes. Her voice was thin but firm, and she had a hint of a foreign accent. Bright sunlight suddenly penetrated a gap in the cloud cover, making her furrow her forehead. Her thick dark eyebrows seemed to meet in the center. She kept looking toward the street.

"I wish you'd stay," I said, careful this time not to let any furtive don'ts slip out among my words.

She sat down on the opposite end of the bench, rubbed her nose, and then thrust both hands between her knees. We remained in silence.

"I was on my way to get some lunch. Come with me, if you like," I proposed.

She shook her head. Her feet were pressed very close together, her body tense. She didn't look at me, but I could see her profile, serious and expectant at the same time. Any minute, she'd get up and disappear.

"There's a neighborhood restaurant a block or two from here. They serve a fabulous soup," I insisted.

She got up without saying a word and just stood there, not looking at me but also not making any move to leave.

"I'm going to take that as a yes," I said, with no expectation of a reply.

The girl let her eyes glide over me and then immediately fixed them on the ground. I started walking in the direction of the restaurant and she followed, a few steps behind me.

18.
EMILIA

I was hungry, and the idea of a plate of hot food was stronger than my fears.

He went ahead, turning around at intervals to check on me. He walked at an unhurried, natural pace. In spite of the sunshine, the cold gripped me with both hands. A couple of blocks farther on, he stopped in front of a restaurant. The plant climbing around the door had leaves that shone as if someone had oiled them. As we were going in, I stumbled. That was when he took me by the elbow, which made me jump.

"Are you okay?"

"Yes," I said, hanging my head and looking at my shoes. Then I said, "You may not touch me. You understand?"

"I understand."

I was impressed by his response. Clear and unequivocal.

"I'm Daniel Estévez," he said when we entered.

"I'm Emilia Husson."

The dining room was small, and crocheted curtains hung over its windows. Most of the customers could not have been younger than seventy. Some were laughing and talking familiarly from one table to another. The aromas coming from the kitchen hung suspended in the air and struck my senses. I started sweating, and my stomach felt even more intensely empty. As we passed, the ladies looked at Daniel. A few smiled at him, and he smiled back. One of them stopped him, and he asked her, "Were you able to get your key copied, Mrs. Marta?"

The woman replied with a smile while looking archly out of the corner of her eye at her lady friends, all as ancient as she.

We sat at the only unoccupied table, where the wrinkled eyes and the aromas followed us. A ceiling light shed a weary glow.

"In a novel I read as a teenager, there was a girl called Miss Husson who drove me crazy," said Daniel, laughing.

"What was she like?" I asked.

"Besides super sexy?" he replied, still laughing.

"Besides that," I said, turning red.

"She was diabolically intelligent."

I lowered my eyes and fastened them on the menu.

"Would you like to order? Pick whatever you want," he added, changing the subject when he saw that his words had embarrassed me.

"Really?"

"Yes, of course!" he exclaimed.

I studied the menu. Meanwhile, Daniel ordered a carafe of water and two glasses of wine.

"I'll have the minestrone. And then the steak with fried potatoes, and for dessert the baked apples with cinnamon."

He burst out laughing and then said, "You obviously know what you want."

"So I do."

"You've chosen very well. I'd say those are the best dishes they have. I make a minestrone almost as good as theirs."

"How do you do it?"

"Are you really interested?"

I'd never been curious about kitchen secrets, but now they seemed like the most fascinating subject in the world. Waiters came and went, carrying steaming plates. Daniel pulled down his sweater cuffs, tossed his hair back with one hand, and started talking.

"Well, the first thing you have to do is brown some salt pork in olive oil. Then you put in chopped carrots, celery, and onions. So your pot should be fairly large, right? Next you add beans and crushed tomatoes and sauté everything for a little while, not long. Pour in some stock and simmer for at least forty minutes. Afterward you add pasta, garlic, a little parsley, and chopped basil, and you cook the soup for ten more minutes."

When he smiled, two dimples appeared in his cheeks. His voice made me warm. While I was listening to him, I registered the slow movements of the old folks around me, their sagging faces, their fallen cheeks, their heavy eyelids. I took a sip of wine, and its heat poured into my empty stomach.

"Oh, and in the end you add a few spinach leaves, right before you take the pot off the heat, so that the spinach keeps its fresh green color. Also, very important: you serve the soup with grated Parmesan cheese and a little olive oil."

"It sounds delicious," I remarked enthusiastically. A few specks of dust, touched by the sun, were dancing on the table.

"I could make it for you someday," he said. There was excitement in his voice, as if the words were a taste in his mouth.

I didn't like him saying that. It implied a kind of rushed intimacy. My face must have reflected my feelings. He fell silent. The atmosphere became denser. And under that thick layer was me. I mustn't forget that hunger was my motivation for coming to this place.

His cell phone rang. He reached into his jacket pocket, took out the phone, silenced it, and laid it on the table. The display screen stayed lit for a few seconds, and in the course of the following minutes it lit up again several times. Somebody was desperately trying to communicate with Daniel, who was ignoring whoever it was. We ate without talking, still enchanted by the lost spell of a few moments before.

The last time I'd been in a restaurant, I was with Jérôme. Now he'd let eight days go by without responding to my emails. I wanted to believe that he was on one of his exploratory trips and had forgotten to tell me he wouldn't have a signal. When I was a girl, my father would disappear for weeks. In those days, cell phones were a rarity, and as far as he was concerned, sending a postcard was inconceivable. I missed him. I'd count the days he was gone, not knowing how many there would be. Not knowing when I'd see him come through the door of our house, wearing his explorer pants, with his hair all tangled and his skin ruddy from long hours outdoors. I imagined that a hole opened in the middle of the earth. A hole my father would disappear through. And now, faced with Jérôme's silence, I could feel that anxiety again.

The carafe of water, in all its still simplicity, stood in the center of the table. While we were eating, on one or two occasions I raised my eyes and met Daniel's. There was something inquisitive about the way they were shining. As if he found himself in the presence of an insect he'd been looking for.

"Do you have someone who's a patient in the hospital?" he asked me.

By then, we'd finished the first course.

I nodded. I didn't tell him we both went there to visit Vera Sigall. I figured that if I admitted the truth, the precarious balance I'd reached with my visits would break.

"Your tenacity impresses me. You never miss a day, not one."

"Yours impresses me too."

He laughed. His shoulders shook like treetops. I could tell from the look in his eyes that he was inclined to be cheerful. We fell silent again. The main course and the dessert were still to come.

"My dream is to have a restaurant," he said all of a sudden. There was a pause, and then he added, "Clinging to the face of a cliff, overlooking the sea."

"Why a cliff?"

"I like the idea of being suspended. I've already made the drawings. I'm an architect."

"Do you build houses?"

"Not many," he said, laughing again.

"Why do you always dream about your restaurant?" He looked at me with wide-open eyes and kept on laughing. I went on: "I'm used to succeeding. When I want something very, very much, I lose interest in everything else. And since nothing interests me anymore, everything stops working."

"You're talking about passion."

"Passion?"

I had one hand on the table, and I hid it under the tablecloth.

"About passion and what we're prepared to do for its sake," he said with a certain severity.

"And that's your passion? To build a restaurant on the side of a cliff?"

"Yes, one among others, of course," he declared, laughing. "And you?"

He caught me by surprise.

"Letters and stars."

"I had a friend," he remarked, and stopped. "Have. I have a friend, a woman with the same passions as you. She's the friend I visit every day in the hospital."

I couldn't go on hiding the truth. If I did, there would be no way back. Daniel seemed like a good person, and I didn't have many good persons around me. The equation was easy to solve.

"I want to tell you something."

His entire body straightened up, on the alert.

"I come to the hospital every day for Vera Sigall."

"I guessed as much." He smiled and crossed his arms, as if someone had put a trophy in them.

"Really? Why?"

"Because you're always alone, because you spend your time reading, and most of all, because you have an air about you, a hint of foreign lands, just like her."

"You knew!" I exclaimed, trying to cushion the weight of his last words and the emotion they caused in me.

He could have observed that he'd discovered me sniffing around her door or seen me reading one of her books. Anything. But no. He'd said we had the same air about us. The same air!

His words encouraged me to talk to him. I told him I was writing my thesis on Vera's work, but now, since her accident, I'd lost my way. Only her nearness as she lay prostrate on her hospital bed allowed me to continue. However, I didn't tell him about the progress I'd made in establishing the relationship between Infante's work and hers. I was still submerged in their texts like a treasure seeker, without a map or coordinates, without knowing the nature of the riches I was setting out in search of. I finished talking and felt exhausted.

Daniel hadn't moved.

I believe the two of us were evaluating the dimension of that meeting, of the fact that we were both there, he and I, talking about the woman we both visited daily, each of us for his or her own reasons. He told me about the accident and how he'd found her. He described events and ideas in simple words, without pompous or fancy turns of phrase, and above all without melodramatic twists. I thought about how words sometimes get detached from the events they narrate and start to play other roles. What was important just then wasn't the details Daniel was furnishing but the fact that he was revealing them to me, that we were sharing them, and that they possessed the same significance for both of us.

Vera Sigall's accident had left Daniel in a state as confused and bereft as my own.

His cell phone, still on the table, lit up again, silently but persistently. We went out to the street and walked together to the hospital. It was just a few blocks away, and we both remained silent. The leaves on the trees, shaken by the light wind, spoke in whispers among themselves.

We said good-bye at the doors of the hospital. He asked me if I'd be back the next day, and I said I would.

"Then we'll see each other," he said.

He went inside, and I started walking down the street.

My bicycle was in the hospital's underground parking garage, but I needed to separate from Daniel right away. To restore order. I walked rapidly through the Bellavista neighborhood. Absorbing the external world. The blue-and-white houses, the stray dogs, the smells seeping through the air. After a while, Daniel's voice got left behind.

Only then did I return to the hospital, collect my bicycle, and go back to my rooftop rooms. While I pedaled, I remembered the brief contact of Daniel's hand on my elbow. I also remembered when I was a teenager and I'd fill notebooks and exercise books with questions: Are animals aware of their bodies? If the body changes, does what's inside it change too? Where is my "me"? On the outside or on the inside? If someone had given me the choice, I would have chosen to get rid of my body. I dreamed awake of a world in which, stripped of all corporeal materiality, hearts and consciousnesses could meet in a true and absolute way.

19.
HORACIO

A few months after my arrival in Geneva, I plucked up the courage to send Vera a letter. I wrote it over the course of several days, sitting in front of my window, from which I was able to see the shore of Lake Geneva. I'd moved into an apartment that had been furnished pretentiously but shabbily: glass chandeliers, Persian rugs, French furniture, and porcelain plates and cups, the majority of which were missing their handles. It was a lowly place, but despite everything, I liked it there. In the letter, I told Vera about my work, about my long, sleepless nights, about my poems and my discoveries, about how, while I was writing, emotion would raise my pulse rate and—together with euphoria—overcome my fear. I never managed to explain to her, neither in that letter nor in any of the ones that followed, the nature of that fear, because I was incapable of articulating it, even to myself. What's certain is that I was afraid my creativity would dry up, or that it was nothing but an illusion anyway, the product of my longing to be a writer. However, my deepest fear—alas—was that I lacked talent.

In any case, even though I employed a personal tone in that first letter, I didn't reveal the feelings I'd been harboring for her ever since before I left for Geneva. Her reply came after a couple of weeks. Vera welcomed and adopted the familiar, intimate tone I'd established.

And thus it was that we began an epistolary dialogue notable for the balance we achieved between confiding in each other and maintaining a respectful distance. In her letters, Vera recounted anecdotes that acquired dazzling grace and significance under her pen. Nevertheless, some of them had a lighthearted, festive air that seemed artificial. I had the feeling she was hiding something from me, that in her witty and generally optimistic letters the very center of her life remained hidden and encapsulated. As she would confess to me years later, it was in those letters—many of which she never sent—that she discovered the exaltation of putting one word next to another and verifying that together they acquired a meaning and a sonority which produced something new and unique. This was a territory all her own, and little by little she would begin to transform it into her true homeland. She told me about her reading, about her early discovery of Faulkner, about Borges's labyrinthine stories, about Kafka. Every now and then she would venture to send me a poem. Vera had full awareness of each word's weight, and also of its brilliance or opacity. She treated words with caution, never making a false move, and the example of such prudence, combined with her passion, made my own writing come alive in an unprecedented way.

In one of her letters, she confirmed that the little boy I'd seen in front of the café was her son, a six-year-old named Julián. She talked a lot about him, describing the walks they often took together to the center of the city or to the zoo, where they'd watch the animals, especially the birds, for hours. Julián suffered from some kind of pulmonary deficiency that kept him from going to school, so he spent long periods of time at home, where Vera would instruct him in the subjects she considered important. With his mother beside him, Julián was starting to read *The Lion, the Witch and the Wardrobe*. It was obvious that she adored her son, and his periodic relapses and subsequent confinement probably gave Vera the opportunity to construct a separate world with him, a world of their own.

That was the spring when Editorial Orbe published my second book. There were only about twelve poems in it, but it got a better reception than my first one had, which caused me to begin to entertain, in some part of my consciousness, the idea of dedicating myself to writing full time. Nevertheless, I knew that the moment had not yet come.

Toward the end of that same year, I was invited by an international organization to participate in a conference on migrations that would be held in New York. One night, while I was writing to Vera, I imagined the two of us walking on the streets of the big city, and on a sudden impulse I proposed to her that we should meet there. Timid hints had crept into our recent letters, on both sides, intimations that behind those missives, which regularly crossed the Atlantic, stood two flesh-and-blood persons, a man and a woman, who desired each other. I was aware that I risked being rejected, aware of how insane a project it was to invite to a place so remote from both of us a married woman with whom I had spoken on a mere two occasions and whom, above all, I had never touched.

Vera's letter of reply took longer than usual to arrive. There were days when I thought she would never respond to me at all. It had been a mistake, I thought, to cross that ineffable line, which paradoxically had enabled us to grow close. During the vicissitudes of daily life, when I'd remember that I still hadn't received a reply from her, and that maybe I never would, I'd promise myself that if she'd only write to me, I would never try anything like that again. Our friendship had been forged in letters, and to try to give it another form was to destroy it. I decided to write and beg her pardon for my outburst, but on the very day when I resolved to do that, I received her reply.

She wrote about a birthday party she'd gone to with Pérez, lingering over those details that only she saw, and that revealed her ability to understand human nature. I was relieved. Vera had serenely ignored my foolish proposal. However, under her signature, there was a note. Very brief, but it transformed everything: "My senses are shutting down. When?"

20.

DANIEL

After leaving Emilia outside the hospital, I got myself some coffee on the ground floor before going up to your room. Along the way, I never stopped thinking about her. But not the same way I thought about other women. Fragility and force emanated from her being simultaneously and aroused contradictory impulses in me. On the one hand, I wanted to protect her from whatever was tormenting her, as I believed; and on the other, her presence made me afraid I could be approaching something that might do me harm.

Detective Álvarez was in the waiting room. I was happy to see him, a feeling I'd never expected to come over me in anticipation of a policeman's company.

"I need to talk to you. Is here all right, or would you prefer somewhere else?" he asked.

"Have you discovered something?" I inquired excitedly, adding, "There's a cafeteria on the ground floor, we can talk there."

When we were seated at a table, I gave him the list I'd put together and talked about Calderón, the psychiatrist and Complutense University professor you'd met with the week before the accident. I told him about your anxiety after your meeting with the professor and suggested that he should verify whether Calderón was still in Chile.

The detective listened to me with courteous reserve and then said, "I'll get right to the point, Mr. Estévez, all right?" I nodded and he went on, "There are a few things that don't fit, and I'd like you to clear them up for me."

Instinctively, I sat up in my chair.

"I've made some inquiries. It appears that you settled your account at Los Peumos, the hotel you stayed in the week before the accident, on the morning of Saturday, August 4. Both you and your wife maintain that you arrived back home on Sunday night. Where were you from Saturday morning to Sunday night?"

"This is all completely ridiculous," I blurted out, almost shouting.

"Please don't get angry," he said, looking worried. "The thing is, I can't leave any loose ends. That's my job. If something doesn't fit, I have to make it fit."

"This is a personal matter that I don't have to share with you," I said, speaking firmly. "My sole intention is to clear up what happened to Vera, and my private life has nothing to do with that."

"You surely understand that I've been talking with other people. With your neighbors, with the doctor who attended her, with your wife, Mrs. Gracia Silva."

"Yes, I've already been told about that," I said, irritated at the memory of my argument with Gracia. Thanks to her, this detective was perfectly aware that I'd lied to him. "Do you really want to know?" I asked curtly.

"If it's not too much of a bother."

"I went to look at a site near Los Peumos. And that night, Saturday night, I camped out there."

"Camped out?"

"That's right. I think I still have the tent in the trunk of my car, if you'd like to take a look."

"That won't be necessary."

I had in fact camped at the site. I wanted to identify the exact path of the sun over the place where I imagined my restaurant would have to be built. A wasted effort, since the site wasn't mine and—given its value—would be impossible for me to acquire. The version I gave the detective, however, wasn't completely accurate. I hadn't camped there on the Saturday, but during the week. I'd spent Saturday night and the following Sunday with Teresa.

I'm not proud of what I'm about to tell you, although in any case you probably know it already. Teresa, the woman who was with me when I visited you that Sunday, the one I introduced as a childhood friend, was my lover. I speak in the past tense, because she isn't anymore. We met as children. She lived a few doors down from us and was my sister's good friend. A shy girl, not very attractive, who would hide in corners and follow me with her eyes. I ran into her again a little more than a year ago. It was a perfectly ordinary encounter, hardly worthy of being described. A line at the supermarket, a woman looking at me, then her name, the memory of the chubby little girl, laughter, the exchange of telephone numbers, the messages, the first date, the trysting hotel, the successive meetings. Why? Because Teresa knew the little boy I once was, knew my former innocence; because of all the possible occupations, she'd chosen to be a veterinarian, a profession for which, like dentistry, Gracia had contempt; because Teresa was weak and insecure, and with her I recovered, at least for as long as we were together, my lost mettle, my sense of myself; and because for some time, Gracia had begun to avoid me sexually. Since I no longer had the energy to follow her in her dizzying race to success, refusing to have sex was her way of exercising power over me. A power I never imagined could be so brutal. If there was one thing I was clear about when I married Gracia, it was that I wouldn't be unfaithful to her. Adultery seemed vulgar, a facile and immediate way for weak, crude men to brighten their gray lives. I was convinced that fidelity gave substance to my own life, a life that otherwise would have degenerated into a sequence of transient and insubstantial sensations and been emptied of content. Fidelity wasn't a moral value, it was an existential one.

Yet in spite of all that, there I was, devising crafty assignations with Teresa. I'm not trying to justify myself, but those meetings served to dissipate the cloud of failure that hung over me.

So there, I've said it. I know you won't judge me, but even so, I don't feel better for having confessed to you. That Sunday, when I brought Teresa to your house, I knew you knew, and I also knew I was making you an accomplice of my cheating without your consent. I was violating your trust.

Although the notion may sound ridiculous, it suddenly occurred to me that our clandestine visit to your house and your fall a few hours later might be connected in some hidden and unthinkable way.

21.
EMILIA

For the second day in a row, after my morning produce deliveries, I went back to my rooftop quarters. My investigations were following their course. After analyzing *The Highest Trapeze*, I'd addressed myself to the study of Vera Sigall's second novel, *Dried Flowers and Such*.

That was the work in which she'd begun to develop the abstract, almost allegorical language that would later become part of her imaginary world. Infante's verses were woven into *Dried Flowers* in a subtler and at the same time more defining way. The tone of the prose seemed to have its origin in the poetry. I spent hours sitting at my writing table, going from Vera's texts to Infante's verses, relentlessly, my fists clenched from the frustration of not seeing the connections. Until suddenly I saw them.

Three or four words. Hidden in the folds of the plot. At first I was greatly surprised, and then I got excited.

I remembered the way my father had searched for his dead stars. Barely visible stars, rapid in movement and weak in luminosity. The only way to spot them is to search near the sun. The sun's light reveals their movements. I remember how excited my father would be when he came home in the morning after having discovered a new dead star amid the dark matter of the firmament. He would follow that star night after night. Until he was certain that it was there. And that it was his.

In the same way, I discovered, hidden in the complex fabric of Vera's words and stories, a verse of Infante's I could see only when it was illuminated by the light of a sun that made it visible to my eyes.

Vera's and Infante's works were connected—there could be no doubt about that. Now it was a question of finding out why.

I remembered my first encounter with Infante. It was in Nanterre, after one of his talks. With dozens of other students, I was waiting my turn to ask him to sign one of his books for me. Infante had read some of his poems to a numerous audience. He'd done so without affectation, but with a distance and a terseness that might perhaps have been hiding a certain timidity. He was dressed rather formally: dark blue double-breasted jacket, light pants. I was struck by his thick eyebrows, under which his eyes were solidly ensconced. His gestures were slow and reserved.

"Where did you dig this up?" he asked me, when he saw the book I'd brought.

It was an edition of his first collection of poems, *Admonitions*. My mother must have bought it in a used bookshop, because its first page was torn out.

He asked my name so he could write a dedication.

"Emilia Husson Vásquez."

He looked up from the book and wanted to know if my mother was Chilean.

Back in those days, I used to give my whole name, including both parents' surnames, Spanish style. I liked the way they sounded together. Husson was soft, with its mute *H* and its two *s*'s, and it rhymed with the winds of the monsoon. Vásquez made me think of a warrior. The *V* and the *z* were the shields protecting him from its enemies, while the *q* was planted in the center, like a lance. I remember Infante's eyes, staring at me. I remember the great sympathy I saw in them, and the calm with which he ignored the long line of people waiting their turn and asked me how old I was, what I was studying, where I'd grown up. Questions that I, unable to concentrate, answered in monosyllables. He wrote his telephone number on the first page of the book and told me to call him whenever I felt like it. I left the venue under the curious eyes of the other students, who had witnessed the scene.

I waited a few days so as not to appear anxious and then called him up. He picked up the phone at once and proposed that we meet in the Père-Lachaise Cemetery.

While we were walking among the tombs, Horacio Infante gave me a gift: a novel by Vera Sigall. I'd heard talk of her in the university, but I'd never read her. Everything that came out of my mouth sounded banal and insignificant to me in the presence of that older, learned man, who represented the world I aspired to belong to. Over the following days, I never stopped wondering why Horacio Infante had taken the time to get together with me. I couldn't have been the first student of literature with a Chilean mother that he'd met as he traveled all over the world. We were standing in front of Pierre Abelard's grave when he asked me about my parents.

"Your parents worked in the Nice Observatory, didn't they?"

"Yes, before I was born. Do you know them?" I asked, surprised at his question.

"Not personally," he said. "Your mother's name is Pilar. Pilar Vásquez, right?" I nodded. "We Chileans generally know our countrymen's itineraries, especially in your mother's case. To be a woman astronomer and work in one of the most important observatories in the world—that's pretty extraordinary. Although I'm no expert, the stars have always fascinated me. It must be Huidobro's influence, maybe."

"One of my father's most important essays begins with a quotation from *Altazor*: *I feel a telescope, aimed at me like a revolver,*" I recited. I don't know where I got the nerve to do that.

"*A comet's tail, stuffed with eternity, lashes my face and proceeds on its way,*" he continued. Then he smiled, and a pallid glow hung suspended in his eyes.

Without words, and without doing anything other than slowing his pace, he was, I felt, urging me to talk. I didn't know why he was doing that. I told him that my father wasn't my father. I also told him it made no difference to me. Because even though we had no ties of blood, we were both made out of the same stuff.

He stopped. His eyes sparkled when he looked at me. He asked me to talk about my father. About his work, about the stars he'd discovered. I told him that when I was a little girl, after my mother had given up her telescopic activities to concentrate on mathematics, we used to meet him on weekends in the Calern Observatory, where he worked. Infante's attention, which was like a soft light focused on me, exhorted me to go on. I told him he usually spent his nights examining the sky and went to bed at sunrise. The observation room was at the end of a corridor where there were always beer bottles and plates with the remnants of meals. The room had a single high window. Standing in the middle of the room and occupying almost the entire space was a gigantic machine. It was used to take photographs and to measure the positions of the heavenly bodies. When I visited him, my father would let me put the photographic plates in numerical order and transcribe the information they contained onto a board. The approximate temperature of the star, its position, its latitude and longitude, and the general location of the image in the sky. This allowed him to compare the information with that on other, previously recorded plates and thus to know whether the star had been there before or not. The challenge was to find dead stars, and also to see them being born or dying. I remember one year when my father discovered sixty-four stars, thirty-two of which were dead.

I spoke as though I were putting together a collage whose images I'd gathered together some time before. I looked at Infante. There was a watery gleam in his eyes, reflecting everything around us in its naked form.

I couldn't have known, at that moment, the full significance of his questions, or the emotions my words triggered in him.

A few weeks after our walk through Père-Lachaise, I found in my university mailbox a package with Vera Sigall's complete works and three scholarly studies that had been published about her fiction. After our meeting in the cemetery, and despite the fact that he spent long periods of time outside of France, Infante never lost contact with me. A year later, after I announced my intention to write my thesis on her, the departmental office received another package for me, Walt Whitman's *Leaves of Grass*, in a lovely Alba edition. In its pages I came across a sheet of paper with some of the poet's lines, transcribed for me by Infante in his own hand:

Not I, nor anyone else can travel that road for you.
You must travel it by yourself.
It is not far, it is within reach.
Perhaps you have been on it since you were born, and did not know.
Perhaps it is everywhere—on water and land.

I thought it suitable for the journey I was embarking on. Infante had shown me Vera Sigall's work, but now choosing the route was up to me.

Had Horacio Infante counted on my coming this far? Was it by any chance a scheme he'd been concocting in meticulous detail ever since that first meeting of ours at the university? For what? Why?

I was sitting at my writing table, with the tray and my empty dinner plate pushed to one side, when all at once the response came to me. It shook me so hard that I had to go outside and take some deep breaths to calm myself.

Infante had used me. The thesis I was going to write, which he himself would take care of disseminating through his contacts in the literary world, would emphasize the enormous influence he'd had on the work of a cult writer like Vera Sigall. At first I thought he'd done it out of simple vanity. But I soon realized it was much more than that. It would be a blow to his detractors, to the group of critics and academics who had looked down on him from their high places. I didn't care about being the bearer of the good news. On the contrary, some part of me felt pleased that I was the one he'd chosen. What I couldn't forgive Infante for was his having manipulated me like one of the many marionettes who I imagined had helped him forge his career and his fame. I also realized that if he'd fed me the story directly, I wouldn't have believed I'd made a discovery. And probably, even knowing the benefits it could have brought me, I would have abandoned the project out of pride.

But why me? Why a simple student of literature? Why not one of the many critics who had been praising him for lo these many years?

I needed an answer. I needed to know more.

I went back into my room and wrote him an email describing my finds. It was an enthusiastic message, in which I expressed my excitement at the magnitude of my discovery. After having gone round and round with my thesis, I'd finally found the path he'd pointed out to me through Whitman's poem. I'd been looking for it in the stars, and nevertheless I'd found it in a very different place, at the very starting point of the whole journey: *Him*. I thought my words sufficiently flattering to keep my true feelings from showing through, and at the same time to open the door that would allow me to go on with my investigation.

After sending him the email, I put both hands on the table and looked at my gigantic shadow on the wall. I had a feeling of triumph. As if I'd been observing the world from its fringes, and now someone had pushed me to the center.

A yellow cat appeared in my window.

His jasper eyes met mine. Then he checked out my room, arched his back, jumped, and disappeared. I had to tell Jérôme about what I'd discovered. Although he hadn't answered my emails for ten days, I'd kept on writing to him. This time, however, after a couple of sentences, I got a feeling I'd never had before: among the countless masks I kept hidden in the corners of my room, one of them, the shiniest, had jumped on me. One I didn't want to write to Jérôme about.

Over the years, each of us had played a part. Nobody had assigned us these roles, but both of us had settled into them as into a soft armchair. When we were together, isolated in our own particular world, it was as if we constituted a single being. It frightened me to be bound to someone so categorically and at the same time to feel so alone.

The cat appeared on the windowsill again and proceeded to clean one of his shoulder blades with his pink tongue. The rising moon was shining, close and bright. As if someone had cut it out, painted it, and pasted it to my window.

The following morning, like every other day, began with produce deliveries. I'd come to know my customers, most of them older people who'd appear at their doors wearing slippers and strike up a brief conversation with me. That was how I learned that the delivery boy who was my predecessor had been run over and killed a few blocks from the fruit and vegetable store, that Don José had Gypsy ancestors, and that if you found him in a good mood, you could get him to take out his guitar and play you a little Paco de Lucía. But that day I was in a hurry. I wanted to get to the library and search for more clues to help me understand the relationship between Infante and Vera Sigall. My neighbor Juan and I met in the elevator. He asked me about my friend who'd had the accident, and without realizing it, I started telling him about Vera Sigall, about the state she was in, about the hours I was spending in the waiting room. I don't know why I did that. Maybe because I had to tell somebody.

As soon as I arrived at the library, I dived into Vera Sigall's boxes again. I had the feeling I was seeing them for the first time, because my view of the material before me was so different now. My investigation had taken on the guise of a sleuthing expedition, and I already knew that what I was looking for could be hidden under the most diverse forms. I'd brought along a bag of fried potatoes, and when lunchtime came around, I ate them in the garden. By the end of the afternoon, I'd reviewed a significant amount of the material. Among other things, I'd set aside a 1952 letter addressed to an unnamed correspondent in which Vera Sigall talks about her son Julián. The boy has been ill, and she fears for his health. "He's very fragile," she writes. "He wasn't born to take the hard knocks of life, or the blows of cruelty." "Everything upsets him." "His cheeks have a demoralized color." She also talks about her reading, namely Flannery O'Connor's short stories, especially one called "A View of the Woods." Then she returns, in virtually obsessive detail, to the subject of her son. "His black eyes are impertinent, like fire." I recalled my own eyes, also black, and thought I would have liked it if someone had described them that way. The letter ends abruptly: "I can't put into words what matters most. It escapes me, like the color of invisible things." When I saw that sentence, I thought it contained the seed from which her quest, the one both she and her characters were on, sprang. The search for the "thing" that mediated between the individual and the object, and which disappeared when she tried to capture it.

I also set aside some notes, written on paper napkins, that were roughly contemporary with the letter: "Green is man, white is woman." And another: "Red can be son or daughter." I remembered a poem by Infante in which he recalls images from his childhood and assigns each of them a color.

"Green," "white," "son," "daughter," I muttered. I felt as though I'd been condemned to spend my life turning words over to see what they were hiding, just as when I was a little girl and I'd lift up rocks to see the earthworms that lived in the darkness underneath.

22.
HORACIO

I arrived in a snow-covered New York City one December morning in 1953. I'd attempted, without success, to reserve a room in the Chelsea Hotel, which was in the midst of one of its many moments of splendor, and its rooms were occupied by musicians, playwrights, actors, and—most important to me—poets, who lived there for long periods of time. Undaunted, I'd managed to book a room in a nearby hotel that would allow me, at least when I passed the Chelsea's doors, to breathe the "creative" air that was supposed to emanate from it.

Vera was arriving from Chile on a long flight with planned stops in Lima, Guayaquil, Panama City, and Miami. I waited for her, first pacing around my room, then walking back and forth in the hotel lobby, and eventually tramping through the neighboring streets. I was used to experiencing a certain nervousness at the prospect of an encounter with a woman. My list had grown during the recent months in Geneva, but not considerably. Conquest seemed to come pretty naturally to me.

Such assignations featured a proper balance of romanticism, expectation, and adventure. I must confess that on some occasions, after reaching the point where the impending conquest was a sure thing, I would just as soon have declared myself satisfied and skipped consummating the act itself, like a fisherman who savors the desperate tugging on his line for a while and then sets his prey free. But I suppose good manners and pride prevented me from doing that.

When Vera's cab stopped in front of the hotel, I was waiting for her at the entrance, under the marquee. The double doors were opening and closing without letup. So much time had passed since I'd been in her company, and our moments together had been so scanty, that her image had grown distorted in my memory. At the age of thirty-five, a year older than me, she radiated youthfulness, but even so, time had clearly not passed over her in vain. I was afraid of what she might think of me. I should add that those unequivocal signs of her maturity, instead of disappointing me, heightened my desire. She wore a long coat of silver fox fur that gave her a majestic air. She set her suitcase on the ground, and we exchanged cautious cheek kisses. Once again I smelled that soapy fragrance I'd noticed almost a year previously, and it made the hair on the back of my neck stand up.

"I'm hungry," she said, smiling and brushing the hair from her forehead with one smooth gesture.

"We can put your bags in the room and then go out," I proposed.

I hadn't been able to reserve a room with a street view, and so our window faced the back and overlooked an ice-skating rink surrounded by buildings on all sides. We stood at the window, with our coats on and our hands thrust into our pockets, and watched together as two young people on skates, holding hands, emerged from a little wooden house in Hansel and Gretel style and began to pirouette on the ice.

"Shall we go?" I suggested, a little nervously. And we went out to the street.

I took her to breakfast at a diner on Twenty-fourth Street. It was diabolically cold. The sounds of the pedestrians' footsteps and the passing automobiles were absorbed by a layer of snow.

Once inside the diner, we took a seat next to a window that offered a good view of the street. Vera took off her coat. She was wearing a vermilion silk sweater that highlighted her pale skin. She pushed her sleeves up past her delicate wrists and, after studying the menu attentively, ordered coffee with milk, toast with marmalade, and a slice of strawberry pie. We spoke about her trip and mine, about the disagreeable sensation of landing on an all-white surface. The pleasure Vera took in eating produced a feeling of tranquillity in me. When we fell silent for a second, I spoke to her about something I'd been turning over in my mind for weeks.

"After you decided to meet me here, you wrote, 'My senses are shutting down.' What did you mean by that?"

Vera turned toward the window. Droplets of water sparkled on the glass. "I don't remember. I really don't. I can imagine the feeling, but I don't remember it. Maybe I was referring to the way one gradually loses the ability to perceive the world. Or maybe not even that, maybe..." She stopped in the middle of her sentence.

With one index finger, she drew a line on the foggy window. I noticed that she wore a ring composed of three interlaced circlets on her right hand.

"Maybe what?"

"Maybe I just said it like that, the way I made this line. Can you see it from there?"

The dim exterior light slipped in through the line Vera had drawn.

Instead of going back to the hotel, we walked through the snowy streets, and with each step we seemed to conquer a new stretch of territory. Or rather, to adjust reality to match the path we'd covered in our correspondence. Even so, when I saw her walking on the icy sidewalk, stepping along merrily and a little unsurely, her shoulders straight and her fur coat hanging down to the ground, I couldn't help feeling alienation again. The wind blew, slipping under my shirt collar. We went into a couple of art galleries to take shelter from the cold, and in one of them we found, along with works by other Latin American painters of lesser note, a canvas by Jesús Rafael Soto. One of his first geometrical and abstract paintings, with flat, brilliant colors. Soto was living in Paris at the time he produced this piece, and he hadn't yet reached the level of fame he would later achieve. Vera impressed me by recognizing his work. I had so many questions to ask her; behind that face—the high cheekbones, the green eyes that looked on everything with enthusiasm and delight—there were so many mysteries.

"Do you do this often?" she asked me as we were walking toward Grand Central Station.

Her question took me by surprise. "How about you?" I asked.

She laughed heartily. "That's cheating. I asked you first," she said, sounding like both a child and an experienced woman.

"Aside from a partner I had a long relationship with, I've never spent the night with a woman."

I had spoken honestly. In my previous romantic encounters, I'd always made sure that my companions in adventure had their own rooms in the hotels where we met. And when assignations took place in my apartment, I'd take my date home before sleep could overcome us.

"How about you?" I asked, returning to the charge.

"Manuel's not the only man I've been with," she replied.

I remembered what María Soledad had told me and was pierced by an instantaneous stab of jealousy. I imagined all the times when Vera, behind her husband's back, had delivered herself into other men's arms. We kept walking at a good pace and didn't speak again. A driver hit his brakes and skidded on the icy asphalt. We both shuddered. Vera grabbed my arm, and we continued our march.

When we got to Grand Central, the cold was nearly unbearable. We went upstairs to the second floor, sat at a table on the west balcony, and spent several minutes warming our hands with our breath. High above us, the aqua-green ceiling and its constellations made us forget the harshness of the winter. Down on the concourse, men in dark suits and women dressed with careful elegance were hurrying around.

After a glass of wine, Vera displayed the worldliness and self-confidence I'd glimpsed at the Argentine embassy. She spoke at ease, sliding from one subject to another, laughed blithely, moved her hands about, and lit her cigarettes with a gold lighter. But I also caught sight again of the distant look she'd had that day in the country, or the melancholy I'd observed one evening through the window of a bookstore. Especially when she fell silent, took a deep drag on her cigarette, and stretched her neck out toward the vaulted heights of the station. All of a sudden, as though impelled to emerge from her world and obliged to adopt an attitude both courageous and merry, she rose from her seat, drew herself up to her full height in front of me, and said, "Horacio Infante, I want you to know I'm never going to hang on your neck."

She exhaled smoke toward the ceiling and fixed her eyes for a second on one of the delicate drawings, perhaps the centaur or the winged horse, as if she needed a witness to her words. Having said them, she sat back down. I stared at the pallor of her cheeks. An unseen weight seemed to be holding her in some dark place. But at the same time, her expression was defiant, not unmarked by irony, and above all, shot through with eroticism.

Much later, I would figure out that those words, spoken in a place unfamiliar to me at the time, had triggered my fervent resolution to conquer Vera Sigall's heart.

We finished lunch and went out to the street. Snow was falling again. It couldn't have been later than four o'clock, but it was already getting dark. Tiny crystals of snow hung suspended on Vera's long eyelashes. We buttoned up our overcoats and hid our gloved hands in our pockets. We walked a few blocks in the snow and then took a taxi to the hotel. We'd passed the day wandering around the city, and now the moment when we would find ourselves alone together was at hand. I felt immensely anxious. Judging by my lists, and according to my self-image, I was an experienced man. So what was happening to me? Could it be, by any chance, that I was afraid of hurting her? Or was it, maybe, a premonition that she might destroy something in me?

Sitting in the taxi, wrapped up in our overcoats, we gazed in silence at the illuminated store windows. In the glow of the streetlights, the snowflakes turned golden.

We climbed up the hotel stairs without haste. In the darkened windows of our room, we could see only the outlines of our standing figures. We kissed. I remember the warmth of her body against mine. On the sheets, her white nakedness caused me a certain sadness. Not because there was anything pathetic about it; on the contrary, Vera was even more desirable than I had imagined. Every female body has its own special characteristics, but on the other hand, they're all the same. And Vera's was, in the final analysis, just one more of the many I had known, and that fact, so banal and so vulgar, was what made me sad. At that moment, I wanted everything that happened between us to be unprecedented, for her, for me; while the snow kept falling peacefully on the other side of our window, I wanted us to discover together, for the first time, the pleasures of merging with another's body. It was this longing that gave every gesture, every advance, a fresh imprint, at once breathtaking and melancholy.

We fell asleep under the bedcovers, my hand on her hip, our breaths colliding.

When I woke up the next morning, Vera was sitting on the edge of the bed and looking at me, an unlit cigarette in her fingers. It had stopped snowing outside, and the room was drowned in a cold white light. Soon we were making love again, with even more assurance, as if her body and mine recognized each other over and above the brief experience they'd shared during the past few hours.

That evening we went to a performance of *The Cherry Orchard*. Dark though it was in the theater, I was able to see that Vera was crying. I wondered what it was in those lives, created by Chekhov to express the dreariness of human existence, that could move her so, and later I was sorely tempted to ask her. But the level of physical intimacy we'd reached didn't translate into total confidence and trust. We could show each other our naked bodies, touch each other, make love, but what lay hidden under our skin still constituted a territory to be explored with caution.

Back out on the street after the play, we found the cold even more penetrating than it had been the previous day. We walked to an Italian restaurant about half a block away. The thick white layer of snow continued to absorb sounds, and the air was filled with a calming, almost mystical silence. Vera had asked me to bring along my latest poems, so I was carrying some of them in a folder under my arm. While we were walking, I tried to help Vera step across a frozen puddle and dropped the folder. Papers flew out and lay scattered on the frosty sidewalk. With incredible good humor, we gathered up each page, many of them already useless, and put them back in the folder. Vera, however, took one page, stopped under a streetlight, and read the poem in silence; then she raised her eyes and looked at me. "You've got talent, Horacio Infante," she said with a serious expression in her eyes, behind which I detected a mischievous glint. "You'll go far. But I wouldn't use the word *dayspring*. At least not in this sentence."

I knew where that word was, between two longer words, together forming a prayer whose purity had enthralled me. Which was precisely what Vera meant to point out, namely that the word thus placed was too conscious of itself and of how it would affect the others, and that this made it stand out in a way that destroyed the poem. Her astuteness and her conviction impressed me. Not only was she right, but her commentary evoked a new criterion for putting words together. Pride wouldn't allow me to concede that her point was well taken, but I did agree, feigning lightheartedness, to give the matter some thought.

We went into the restaurant and ordered a bottle of wine. Vera looked jolly. Her pale face glowed in contrast with her black turtleneck sweater and the pearl necklace she'd put on. Seated facing her in that little oasis, I wondered if Vera had told anyone about her trip to meet me, and the idea that she must necessarily have lied—to Pérez, certainly—didn't please me at all. At that moment, I couldn't know how concealment and deception, in their most disturbing and intricate forms, would become a central theme and, at the same time, an engine that would define her life and mine.

I asked her to talk to me about her son Julián.

"He's obsessed with the stars," she said, her eyes shining. She paused to think for a few seconds and then went on: "He would have marveled at the constellations we saw yesterday on the ceiling in Grand Central Station."

She took a cigarette out of her evening bag and flicked the lighter with a firm hand, without turning her eyes on me, as if this was her way of closing a book that had to stay closed for now.

Toward the end of the evening, when we were splitting a red currant tart, she asked me, "How many?"

"How many what?" I asked, smiling.

"Women," she answered.

There was no trace of resentment in her expression, but rather a genuine and somehow morbid curiosity.

"Thirty-three."

"You keep count?" She laughed flightily, but without affectation.

"On occasion..." was my cautious reply.

In spite of her evident good mood, I didn't know how far this particular subject could take us. Above the building across the street, among the clouds, an astonishing half-moon appeared, lighting them up.

"And you?"

The idea that Vera was an experienced woman, an inhabitant of territory in those days reserved for men, increased both my excitement and my confusion. Outside the moon had hidden itself behind the clouds again, leaving a white background of nocturnal light.

"And you?" I asked, once again.

"Do you really want to know?" She drew deeply on her cigarette. Her gaze grew intense.

My desire for her escalated.

"I was twenty-two when I married. Since then I've had two. I didn't spend more than two nights with either of them, and neither ever heard me say a single affectionate word."

"So counting our nights, that makes three," I replied.

"But don't expect affection from me," she said, suddenly serious, though still absolutely dramatic.

I had never been much for sweet-talking my lovers either. Although admittedly, the use of such language by some of the women I'd been involved with had in certain instances made me yield more than was advisable. I remembered Francisca, an oversized accountant, married to a more or less mediocre colleague who mistreated her. She used to call me "sweetheart" or "honey," epithets that undermined my plans to keep her at a distance. Maybe it was the absence of that amorous lexicon throughout my life that produced the malfunction. My having been surrounded by people not given to displays of affection beyond the limits of what was acceptable for an emotionally austere upbringing. At some point I was even tempted to ask her to leave her husband and make a new life with me. But I didn't do it. As it happened, she left him anyway. I realized then that I didn't love her at all, that the woman hiding behind her sugary words and her unconditional surrender had in reality but one desire, to escape the life she was living, and when all was said and done, all I represented for her was a vehicle that would carry her to her goal. My suspicions weren't unfounded. Not long after breaking up with me, she was impregnated by another man, and when he washed his hands of the entire affair, she got desperate and asked me to marry her. I told Vera about Francisca in vague terms and never named her. I also talked about María Angélica, a Colombian with whom I'd had a recent fling. A slight, ambitious woman who'd committed the sin of loving me more than I was disposed to bear. The situation had brought to light a depth of cruelty that simultaneously disconcerted and demoralized me. I was impressed by the good-humored way Vera listened to these excerpts from my romantic life. As if, instead of distressing her, they not only lightened her heart but also made me more attractive in her eyes. This was paradoxical, because there was nothing even vaguely heroic about either of those affairs; on the contrary, they made evident a certain lack of integrity and a lot of cynicism and coldness.

When I pointed that out to her, she replied, "I like that you speak to me honestly," tossing her hair to one side and holding it there with one hand on her shoulder.

I was trying to give her an adequate response when she pointed at the window and exclaimed, "Look!"

The past always returns in the form of small things. And what comes back to my memory now is the transparent and gleaming veil of snow, carried along by a breath of wind, that moved past our window. Vera extended an arm over the table and touched my hand.

It was almost midnight when we left the restaurant. The temperature had gone up a few degrees, and thin streams of dirty, icy water were running in the gutters. We'd had quite a lot to drink. Vera stumbled and then laughed, as if the fact of being intoxicated amused her in a particular way. We must have hailed the last taxi that was still cruising the streets that night. Back in the hotel, we embraced anxiously at the door of our room. One of our neighbors had held a little banquet, and its remains were piled up in the corridor.

On the day we left, a timid sun was falling on the half-thawed snow. Vera and I said our farewells in the airport. I watched her moving away from me, past the partition, and I thought that our confessions, instead of inflaming the passion each of us felt for the other, had established its limits. We both feared to venture to the place where our meeting could have taken us. During the days we spent together, we never spoke, not even once, about the future, or about the possibility of seeing each other again.

23.
DANIEL

I hadn't thought seeing her would make me so happy. There she was again, sitting in the little room, the same as always, with her ankle boots and her pleated skirt and that look of having come from another time. Her short hair was held in place by two red barrettes. During the four days when she hadn't appeared in the hospital, I'd been waiting for her without admitting it to myself.

"Hello," she said with a shy smile and turned her eyes back to the book she had in her lap.

She didn't seem the least bit happy, which made me think that perhaps our lunch together hadn't meant much to her.

"Would you like to go in and see her?" I asked.

"You mean I can?" she asked in turn, gazing up hopefully.

"Of course, come on," I said, starting to walk to your room.

The curtains were drawn, and a timid beam of light fell on your sleeping face. You'd grown thinner, and your delicate, fragile skin appeared to be glued onto your cheekbones. Emilia approached your bed and observed you for a long time without saying a word. She clasped her forearms in her hands, as though she felt cold.

"She's smiling," Emilia remarked.

I looked at you, as I'd looked at you so often in the course of those months, and for the first time I saw a smile hidden under the uniform veil of your sleep.

"It's true."

"*Far away, Arcturus floats, looking sidelong at Unukalhai,*" she murmured.

"What did you say?" I asked, puzzled.

"She understands," she replied, a big smile lighting up her face.

"You think she can hear you?"

"Obviously."

"I talk to her too."

"I know."

"How do you know?"

"Because I've heard you."

I smiled. From the corridor, we could hear the voices of children, who must have been visiting another patient.

"But you didn't answer my question. What were you saying?"

"It's a line of poetry," she conceded. "Arcturus is one of the brightest stars in the northern hemisphere, but it's dying. When it finishes dying, it'll have a hard crust, and it will stop burning."

When it came to stars, I knew nothing, and I had no idea how to answer her. I figured you were laughing in your sleep. A girl wearing wool socks and ankle boots had left me speechless.

"Sit down," I said, offering her one of the two little chairs in your room.

She looked at me with her black, wide-open eyes, as if I were offering her one of her stars. I noticed she never closed her lips completely, producing a little black orifice the size of a small pea in the center of her mouth. Soon we were both conversing with you, as naturally as I'd been doing for the past several months, but now the conversation was more animated. Until then, I'd pretended to avoid a fact that struck me every morning, every night, when with my head turned toward the wall I'd hear Gracia breathing on the other side of the bed. Only at that moment, listening to Emilia talk to you helter-skelter about Infante, about the allusions you made to his work, about Sinalefa and Octavio and all the characters that seemed to come alive in his voice, did the entire notion of my solitude make its presence known. I felt like hugging her. I got up from the chair and walked over to the window. She remained silent, watching me with those odd eyes of hers, which made me think I was the one looking at myself, and what I saw was reflected in her eyes.

"Is something wrong?" she asked.

"No, no, it's just that I've spent more than two months talking alone in this room, you see, and then you come along, and...well..."

"And I talk too," she said, and burst out laughing.

My cell phone rang again. It was Teresa. On the morning when she appeared in the hospital, I'd made myself clear: I didn't want to see her again. After your fall, things had changed, I had changed, and in this new order she had no place. I silenced the phone, just as I did every time her number appeared on my screen, and in the next hour it lit up several more times. I thought the best thing to do would be to call her after I left the hospital, talk to her one more time, and make her understand that our affair was over, and why. Unfortunately, I forgot to call.

From that day on, Emilia started to wait for me in the little room and not until I invited her to come along did she get up from her seat and walk with me down the corridor to your room. When I left Emilia and returned to Gracia's cold, distant, but cordial company, I felt restless. Everything about that young woman struck me as at once familiar and strange. She inhabited a world that reminded me of yours. Sometimes she was still and silent, as if she'd forgotten herself and us, and at such times an ancient air enveloped her, an air that made her look older than her actual twenty-four years. She liked it when I told her stories that had to do with you. She was interested in the most insignificant details, and she asked me questions that revealed her thorough knowledge of your work. I liked recalling our days for her. We both knew that you, from the depths of your silence, were listening to us. Like you, she didn't talk about herself very much. And when she did, she used succinct, evasive sentences that made me remember the day in the restaurant when I took hold of her elbow and she immediately made me let go. I'd never tried to touch her again since that day, nor had I managed to get up the nerve to ask her the reason for her reaction.

At a certain hour, the habitual rhythm would stop, and the hospital would become a silent place again. Then we'd have the impression that we were on an island, where you and the two of us were the only inhabitants.

On one of those afternoons, while I was telling Emilia about our walks on San Cristóbal Hill, Detective Álvarez turned up again. Lucy announced his arrival. I met him in the waiting room.

"How are you, Mr. Estévez?" he greeted me. "If you don't mind, I'd like to have a few brief words with you. I've made some more progress."

"I'm with a friend," I said. "Wait for me a second while I go and let her know."

I went back to your room, and from the doorway I saw that Emilia was speaking to you in whispers. She'd moved her little chair closer to your bed and was clasping one of your hands in hers. She said my name.

"Are you talking to her about me?" I asked, and she jumped. She let go of your hand and hid hers in her armpits.

"I just wanted to know how your name sounded when she heard it," she replied, blushing. I could see myself in her black eyes, behind which she seemed to be living through something indomitable and sad.

I remembered what you used to say. That when we utter a name, invisible threads attach us to the person we're naming.

"Well, coming from your mouth, it sounded different to me. Like the name of a good person."

"And you're not one, by any chance?" she asked, rubbing her nose with the palm of her hand.

"I don't know, sometimes I think everything I touch turns out bad."

"Everything, everything, everything, that's not possible. Maybe some things." We both laughed. And she opened her hands and said, "You see?"

I told her about my suspicions related to your fall and to the detective's presence in the hospital. The smile disappeared from her face. Through the window came the light of the setting sun, deploying its shy springtime strength. She wanted more details, and I promised to fill her in when I was finished with him.

"You don't mind if I stay alone with Vera?"

"It's fantastic that you're here, Emilia," I said, and left the room.

Detective Álvarez was waiting for me in front of the elevator doors. We went down to the cafeteria and sat at a table by the window. We ordered two coffees. The air was hot and humid. Behind the counter, a waiter sitting on a high stool was watching a soccer match on a television screen mounted on the wall.

"I went to see Teresa Peña," Detective Álvarez said, and cleared his throat.

"What does she have to do with anything?" I asked curtly, unable to hide my surprise and displeasure.

"You tell me," the detective said, barely opening his mouth, as if he were hiding the key to the mystery under his tongue.

I had the impression I was in one of those bad television series where both accusers and accused make the same gestures and seem to come from the same mold. Succinct questions and answers, expected movements and silences, impersonal setting, no-man's-land. On the television screen, a goalkeeper lunged to his left as the ball was kicked to his right. The goalie contorted himself incredibly, and the ball, which seemed to have already crossed the goal, caromed off his right ankle and sailed far in the opposite direction. The waiter leaped to his feet, raised both fists, and stifled a shout of jubilation.

I felt an urge to speed up the process, to tell Álvarez everything in one long outburst; even though what would happen immediately afterward was all too foreseeable, a part of me wanted to experience it in all its nuances. This sensation was similar, I imagine, to what people feel who get pleasure from inflicting pain on themselves.

I didn't want to ask Álvarez how he'd landed on Teresa. I wasn't ready for us to become friends and confidants. In any case, I didn't have long to wait for an answer to my unasked question. It was Teresa who had approached the PDI. At some point during our conversation in the hospital, I'd mentioned my suspicions and told her I'd contacted the police. Teresa had furnished the detective with an abundance of details concerning our visit to your house. She had, in fact, told him everything.

After the detective had gone, leaving me sitting at the table with two cold, untouched cups of coffee, I experienced a strange feeling of freedom. The game of concealment was over for me. There was even a possibility that Álvarez might speak to Gracia again, and everything would come to light.

24.
EMILIA

It wasn't a good sign.

While I was waiting for him, I could hardly concentrate on anything other than waiting for him.

When I heard his footsteps on the little stairway that led to the roof terrace, I left my bedroom and stationed myself in front of the door to the kitchen.

"Hello," he greeted me. He put his grocery bags down and looked around. The retreating sun had colored the clouds. To the west, the shades of orange were dense and vivid. To the east, the mountain range and the buildings were tinted a uniform pink, as if someone had taken the rest of the colors out of them.

"This place is fantastic!" Daniel exclaimed, turning in a circle.

We went into the kitchen, and before long he was cooking things, using a big frying pan he'd brought along with him. Bacon, giant mushrooms, peppers, olive oil. We took the kitchen table and chairs outside and put them under the white canopy, which was rippling in the breeze. As we enjoyed our meal in view of that November sunset, the buildings distanced themselves. One block after another, until they disappeared. And then the lights started to come on. Here and there, like fireflies. The dull roar of motors faded far away.

The solitude I'd felt so often at that same hour, in that same spot, was growing softer.

"You know what? This could be the place I've been looking for," he said.

He was looking straight ahead, holding his glass at eye level and peering through it.

"What do you mean?"

"This place is like a cliff."

I burst out laughing. All around us, the vast expanse of the city sparkled. "You're completely right," I declared enthusiastically, clapping my hands. "It's perfect, Daniel."

By the time we'd finished dessert—mulberry ice cream garnished with blueberries—we'd already outlined a strategy. Daniel would prepare a big dinner, and we'd invite some of his friends, my neighbors, and other guests who might occur to us along the way. Maybe even one or two food critics. It wouldn't be an open restaurant, but rather a place for people who wanted to share a special dinner with their friends.

"The Transatlantic. Do you like that name?" he asked me.

"It's like what I imagine whenever I'm out here. I picture myself living in a gigantic ship that's getting ready to cross the ocean."

High in the sky, the crescent moon was a sliver with two pointy ends. Like stalactites. Happiness takes the oddest roads on its way to you, I thought. And moves to its own rhythm. There's no way of summoning it, nowhere to wait for it. It appears, or it never appears at all.

We spent a good while strolling around the terrace, imagining the locations of the tables, the color of the tablecloths, the style of the chairs, the kinds of trees and flowers we'd fill the space with. We even went so far as to plan an expansion of the kitchen.

When we sat back down for the second round of ice cream, Daniel told me about the policeman. The day before, after the cop left, Daniel had been too depressed to talk to me about him. The Sunday before the accident, Daniel and the woman I'd seen him with in the hospital had been in Vera's house. Her name was Teresa, and they'd been lovers.

Lovers. A long, hissing *s* penetrated into the remotest channels of my ears when he pronounced that word. Lovers sleep satiated, snuggling between the sheets. They exchange fluids. Saliva for saliva. Their bodies embrace. Their mouths scour each other's sweaty skin. I felt nauseous.

"I apologize for telling you all this. In the final analysis, it's not important at all," he said, perhaps noticing my discomfort.

"No, no, of course it is," I said, sitting up straight in my chair. "You know what? I'm like you, I don't think Vera's fall was an accident. When I was with her, I was impressed by the strength she projected, by how lively she was. She wasn't an old lady who slips and falls down the stairs. She just wasn't. But what, then?"

"That's a question that gnaws at my brain, Emilia. What made her take such a violent fall? What really happened?"

"I'm going to say something foolish. But since we've reached this point..."

I stopped talking.

"Tell me."

"Do you know Horacio Infante?"

"Not personally. Vera mentioned him from time to time."

I tried to explain what I'd observed during the luncheon. Their complicity, the respect he'd shown her, the complex choreography of gestures in which I thought I perceived sentiments that in a strange way united them. In their tête-à-tête, Infante had not only looked exasperated, he'd even been rude to her.

I also told him about my discoveries, about how Infante's poems showed up in Vera's texts. I emphasized the fact that she'd never mentioned the relationship between her work and his, and that for his part, Infante had guided me, without my knowing it, to the discovery of his secret.

"Everything you're telling me is incredible and relevant," Daniel declared.

He told me that on the day of the accident, knowing that Vera had been to lunch with Infante that same weekend, he'd used his wife's television contacts to obtain the poet's telephone number and called him up. When Daniel told him what had happened to Vera, Infante had sounded dismayed, but he'd never appeared at the hospital and wasn't heard from until two weeks later, when he called Daniel from Paris to ask about Vera.

Then I told Daniel about writing to Infante and informing him of my discoveries. Not once, but several times, I said, and to this day he hasn't answered me. Neither Daniel nor I knew what we were talking about. Or where our words were headed. Nor did we know if there was any link between what we were telling each other, and if so, whether it had anything to do with Vera's fall. The possibility that it did was too remote for us to be able merely to imagine it. But even so, some connection had been made in our minds, and for a long time we tried to add information to what we'd already put on the table, with the aim of prying open some little chink through which a hypothesis might enter. It was then that he told me about the Spanish psychiatrist, Dr. Calderón, and about Vera's strange sadness after her meeting with him a few days before her fall.

"In spite of her general moodiness, I'd never seen her like that, Emilia. The afternoon when I surprised her in her study, I was convinced that she was looking for something that had to do with him. There was desperation in her eyes, a sort of vulnerability...I don't know how to explain it."

"It didn't occur to you to look through her papers?" I asked cautiously. "The ones she keeps in her study?"

"No," he answered sharply.

"I understand," I said. "I would never have been able to snoop around in her writings and her documents in the library if I weren't certain she'd donated them herself."

It was almost midnight when we stopped talking. Against the background of darkness, the city lights looked like phosphorescent fish twinkling in a great sea. We remained seated at the table.

"Transatlantic," I murmured. "Pretty name."

"I haven't felt this good in a long time," Daniel said.

"Likewise."

As soon as I said that word, I regretted it. I stood up suddenly, confused.

"What's wrong?"

"Nothing."

"You're afraid, right?"

"Yes."

"Me too."

"But your fear isn't the same as mine."

"How do you know?"

"I know."

"Sit down," he said. I obeyed.

We stayed that way for a few moments, the two of us: me, breathing irregularly, and him, looking at me. I had both hands on the table, like a defendant awaiting a verdict. He moved his hand closer to my hands, without touching them. He moved it again, close enough to put his fingertips on mine. I opened my hand slightly, and our fingers intertwined, forming a kind of weave that disappeared when he placed his other hand on the back of mine and covered it.

For the first time, I understood one of Vera's characters, who discovers one day that what complicates talking is having to use words. That contact was a way of communicating with each other. And when I saw it that way, I had no urge to flee.

But even so, I was still afraid.

Afraid that Daniel would try to go farther. At the end of a minute, he picked up his wineglass again and drank from it in silence. He hadn't crossed the threshold, and while I felt relieved, at the same time a part of me resented him for not having made more of an effort.

He must necessarily have noticed how uneasy I was. However, he hadn't tried to ask me any questions. And I was grateful to him for that. All my explanations, the sequence of events I'd constructed in my eagerness to enclose my "condition" inside a coherent story, had long since been voided of their contents. The past is like that, I suppose. We need to freeze it in a single dimension so that we can handle it, while nevertheless knowing that by doing so we're avoiding its complex truth.

Over the course of the following days, I tried to reconstruct in my memory the feel of his skin, its texture, in contact with mine, to recall how much pressure he'd exerted and the warmth that had filtered into me, as light through a closed door faintly illuminates a darkened room.

25.
HORACIO

After our meeting in New York, we started to write each other every day. The level of physical intimacy we'd reached in those three days was now translated into a mounting epistolary passion. Nevertheless, when I told her I loved her for the first time, as simply as that—"I love you very much"—Vera wrote to say that she would never leave Pérez, that she'd managed to build a family by dint of great effort, and that although she loved me too, that feeling would never be able to overshadow what she felt for her husband. Her response, disproportionate in relation to the simple and hardly compromising letters I'd been sending her, made me understand not only that the bond uniting her to Pérez was made of some apparently indestructible material that I didn't recognize, but also that Vera took words seriously. From that time forward, I began to use them with extreme caution, and when the word *love* appeared in our correspondence, it did so after hundreds of other, weaker words that had nonetheless prepared the way for that one. What I felt for Vera was genuine, of that I had no doubt. But I wasn't about to forget what she'd said in Grand Central Station; the limits she'd imposed by warning me that I could never be more for her than what I was at that moment had resonated with me as a challenge. Her resistance was the stimulus that incited me to overcome it. And there was nothing new about that, after all. Millennia ago, Ovid advised married women to close their bedroom doors and make access difficult for their husbands in order to arouse their desires.

It was only after nine months had passed that we finally saw each other again. A few days after my thirty-sixth birthday.

During that time, her life and mine had gone through ups and downs. Pérez had taken Julián to view the stars through a big telescope for the first time; Vera had spent nearly three weeks in bed with a bronchial infection, and her letters had turned gloomy; I'd moved to a bigger, brighter apartment and published *Corolla*, my third book of poems.

We saw each other again in Rio de Janeiro one Saturday in August 1954, on the occasion of a United Nations conference that was taking place in that city. My flight arrived a few hours before hers, and I waited for her in the airport. A man standing a few meters away from me was ringing two iron bells suspended from a cambered arch. They made piercing sounds in samba rhythm. I took up a position against the wall, and I can clearly remember the moment when, as I was reading *Paradise Lost*, I heard her voice.

"Horacio," she said, calling to me from some distance away. It was the first time she'd ever said my first name without adding my last.

In the few seconds that it took her to reach me, I had the feeling that the man whose name she'd said wasn't me, that in her mouth I lost my identity. This sentiment would grow stronger as time passed.

We embraced shyly. She gave off the same fresh, penetrating scent I'd noticed the very first time I ever got close to her. After we let go, we exchanged gazes, smiling nervously, and then we started walking toward the terminal doors, peering at each other sidelong, recognizing each other. Vera was wearing a pink dress, and in spite of her thirty-seven years, her smooth white skin had an almost adolescent glow. Once again, I had the sense of alienation I'd felt when I saw her in New York. On each occasion, Vera was the same woman and another, both at once. She'd lost a bit of weight, and all her features appeared accentuated: her cheekbones higher, her nose pointier, her mouth bigger. An automobile from the United Nations was waiting for us outside the entrance to the airport. For a moment I thought uneasily that travel, airports, and official automobiles were old hat to Vera, and that this trip was in some way a pallid duplication of what she was used to as Pérez's wife. I had to make an effort to keep this reflection from tarnishing the joy that my anticipation of her body produced in me. We drove into Rio in silence, holding hands, gazing at each other and smiling. Vera pressed her thigh against mine.

The city that received us had the bright, festive atmosphere of those years, when you could peer far out into the darkness of the sea from the side of the road. The wind was shaking the palm trees, and we could see the sand swirling around in the few illuminated areas of the beach. A car passed us. Its radio was playing, at full blast, Johnnie Ray's song "Cry," which had been all the rage for some time.

From the following day on, after the morning meetings I had to attend were over, we closed ourselves in our room and almost never went out. The sea, spread out before our eyes in all its enormous vastness, produced an impression of spaciousness and freedom, despite our rather close quarters. But the real freedom was, of course, inside, between those four walls, in our amorous encounters, which attained a degree of erotic intensity I had never reached before. At night, the distant sounds of the sambas and the wind, gently beating against our window, accompanied the urgency with which each of us sought the other's touch.

The morning of our second day in Rio, Vera said she wanted to read aloud the poems in my new book. Wearing high-heeled shoes with black tips and a long nightdress, she stationed herself against the window. Behind her the sea was visible, smooth and whitish, as if covered by an immense, freshly ironed cloth.

"Why are you wearing shoes?" I asked her, laughing.

"For decorum." With her thick hair loose on her shoulders, she performed a ballerina's pirouette.

Before the book of poems was published, I'd sent them to her one by one, and her acute, substantive comments had become indispensable. After I read her observations, I'd even left some poems out, and I'd changed others in essence or form, with the result that, taken as a whole, they'd turned out far superior to what they'd been originally. She read them standing up, her profile serious and angular, her shapely figure outlined against the window, while the cries of a group of kids playing ball reached us from Copacabana Beach. Vera read my poems calmly, without heavy emphases or theatricality, but with a depth that gave the words, as she spoke them, a new dimension. All this made me feel ineffably happy, as if it were the antechamber to the future that was awaiting me.

On the first afternoon, while we were both dozing on the damp sheets with the five-bladed ceiling fan whirling overhead, Vera said, "Horacio Infante." Her voice, breaking the drowsy silence, sounded as though a bubble had burst inside her throat.

"What?" I asked, rubbing my eyes.

She rolled to her knees on the bed, her torso erect, her breasts pointing toward the window, her eyes shining hopefully. We hadn't turned on the lights, and the last rays of the setting sun, entering horizontally through our window, made the room look like a phosphorescent box.

"I brought something for you," she said, stretching her arms above her head and clasping her hands. The pale skin of her armpits gleamed in the yellowish light.

Then she bounded off the bed and took a notebook with red covers out of her suitcase. "I've been writing," she said, her cheeks flushing slightly.

"Poems?"

"No, no, no," she replied vehemently. "I couldn't," she added, pursing her mouth and looking at the floor. "They're short stories."

She cradled the notebook in both arms against her naked breasts. She looked like a teenager. That was something that happened frequently, especially after we'd made love and she was lying relaxed on the pillows, looking me in the eyes with a placid, satisfied smile.

"Promise to be indulgent. Not like me with you."

"You're ruthless."

"I know."

"I promise," I said. "I'm dying to hear you read them."

"I'd prefer that you read them yourself. There are only two." She thrust the notebook under her pillows, walked over to the closet, and took out a very simple white dress.

"What are you doing?"

"I'm going to take a walk while you read. I can't stay here. I'd die of nervousness."

"But I can't let you go."

"Of course you can."

She hadn't put on a bra, and her nipples showed through the thin fabric of her dress. I felt desire for her and also a twinge of jealousy at the thought that other men would see her and feel the same way I did.

"Stay close to the hotel. Don't go very far. It's dangerous," I declared.

She gave me a kiss, told me not to worry, put on some low-heeled white shoes, picked up her purse, and left. I took her notebook out from under the pillows where she'd left it and started reading. Down in the street, a horn sounded for a while and then sank into the background hum. From the first sentence, I knew that the text before my eyes was both very accomplished and very unusual.

The first piece was about a girl who tells her bedridden mother stories while the older woman is in an advanced stage of dementia and dying of syphilis. I remembered María Soledad's words, and I was moved at the thought that the text I was holding in my hands might be based on Vera's life, on that life I'd barely gotten a glimpse of. The stories the girl tells her mother transport them to a world filled with details, characters, smells, and places. It's as if her mother's illness belongs to the world of horror, of the implausible, and needs to touch reality through fiction. Day by day, the girl's efforts grow increasingly desperate, while her mother ineluctably continues to die. It's at this point that the narrative, without resorting to dramatics, becomes almost unbearable, and I had to stop reading it. I opened the window and tried in vain to spot Vera among the people walking along the seashore. A little airplane crossed the sky. The beach umbrellas vibrated in the wind. The bathers had disappeared, and a peaceful solitude reigned over the sand. After a few minutes, deeply affected, I went back to my reading. Vera's innate talent aroused feelings in me that were at once troubled and exultant. Ambiguous. I read the second story. It was less touching than the first, but equally well told. The rest of the red notebook was blank. Most probably, she'd transcribed the two stories from her original drafts, because neither of the two contained so much as a blot. They possessed the same precision that she'd brought to bear on my poems. I looked out the window again. Very far away, I could make out a group of young people playing volleyball in the fading twilight. I needed to express to Vera what she doubtless already knew. I needed to tell her, furthermore, that I would support her, I would guide her, I would be at her side on the road that she must inevitably travel. She had to keep on writing; she had to show the world that she was already a great writer.

I waited for her—impatient, excited, inflamed. When she knocked on the door of our room, I rushed to open it and embraced her.

"Did you like them?" she asked, as best she could, between my hindering kisses.

I kissed and hugged her again.

"Yes, yes, yes. You're a great writer, Vera Sigall."

That night we put on fancy clothes and went out to celebrate.

After our days together, we traveled the road to the airport without talking. But it wasn't the same silence as after our arrival. It was a sad, downcast silence. We were separating again, and once again, we hadn't discussed when or where our next meeting would be. A deliberate omission, which we executed with feigned naturalness, masking our feelings.

26.
DANIEL

I was coming back home after my daily jog when I heard my cell phone ringing in the kitchen. Teresa hadn't called me since the revelation she'd made to the police about us, but even so, every time I heard my phone's ringtone, I thought it might be her. Her revenge for being "dumped," which was how she referred to the fact that I'd broken off our relationship, had been savage enough to make me start to feel afraid of her. I looked at the screen. The number wasn't familiar.

"Excuse me for bothering you, Mr. Estévez." I recognized Detective Álvarez's voice. "There were just a couple of things I wanted to discuss with you."

He'd never called me before. All our conversations had taken place either in your house or at the hospital.

"It seems..." He paused.

"Tell me," I said firmly.

"Well, I just wanted to inform you that your wife knows about your affair," he said. The embarrassment in his voice was unmistakable.

"I see," I said.

I remembered that night when I was waiting for you to come out of your coma and Gracia asked me if I was alone.

"I want you to know that she didn't find out from me. She was the one who told me about it. She said she'd seen the two of you go into Mrs. Sigall's house the Sunday before the accident."

"I see," I repeated, stunned.

I looked around. On the chest of drawers, an amber-colored ceramic vase held a bouquet of gardenias on the verge of withering.

"And the second thing, Mr. Estévez. It seems that several of your neighbors have talked to us about a vagrant who's been loitering around the neighborhood for the past year. Have you seen him?"

"Yes, of course."

The detective told me he was looking for the bum so he could question him. I didn't mention having run into him on the very day of the accident. If I saw him, Álvarez said, I should please call him immediately. I asked him if he considered the man a suspect. Nobody and nothing could be excluded at this stage, he replied, but his main interest in talking to the vagrant was to determine whether he'd seen anything out of the ordinary that morning.

Before ending the call, I stood in front of the window for a little while with my cell phone in my hand. The plum tree I'd planted the year before was blooming for the first time. The clear, serenely azure sky looked unusually pellucid. I closed my eyes to shut out the image of that anachronistic spring, which was painful to behold. Then I sat on the bed, and there I remained a long time, still perspiring from my jog. My feelings were so confused I couldn't think straight. How long had Gracia known about Teresa? I thought about how she must have suffered and felt immense tenderness for her and an urgent need to soothe her, talk to her, explain to her. I saw my refusal to celebrate our anniversary in a new light, I saw what it must have signified to her, I saw her misty eyes and her disappointment. I felt an impulse to call her on her cell phone and beg her forgiveness. I punched myself in the head a few times. After all the efforts Gracia had made to help me, how could I have made her suffer this way? I recalled her behavior of the past weeks, searching my recollection for some signs of the hatred and rage she must have felt, but I couldn't come up with anything. Maybe Gracia had stopped loving me. But then, why hadn't she confronted me instead of repeating that farce day after day? Could she by any chance have feared that I might acknowledge my fault and leave her? The idea of Gracia fearful at the prospect of losing what we'd built together was painful to me, but at the same time not completely convincing. A thought that overshadowed all the others made me leap to my feet: Gracia must have a lover, and the discovery of my infidelity had salved her conscience enough to let her persist in her own. I opened the window. The calm that reigned in the garden seemed artificial. Everything had acquired a patina of falsity. By not confronting me, Gracia had merely been playing for time. The time she needed to figure out where the feelings she had for this other man might lead her. We were even. She had hers, I had mine. Meanwhile, we could go on with our lives. At its worst, our living together had never been hellish, and—for different reasons—it suited both of us. My sweaty T-shirt was stuck to my body, and the morning breeze chilled my arms. I was impressed by the lack of emotion with which these thoughts crossed my mind. There was, nevertheless, something that didn't fit. If Gracia wanted to preserve the status quo, why had she talked to the detective? What did she gain by doing that? Revenge, like Teresa? She must have considered the possibility that shame was the reason why I'd kept our visit to your house that Sunday hidden from her. Talking to the detective was her way of making sure he knew, no matter what consequences that knowledge might have for my life or ours.

I'd already contemplated, in more than one form, a scenario in which Gracia had a lover. Given her physical charms, her professional prominence, and her discontent with our marriage, it was quite probable that a man who could make her feel better would emerge. But it was hard for me to swallow the idea that things between us had reached such a climactic point that she'd actually try to do me harm.

I went into the bathroom and turned on the water in the shower. I stayed in there a good while, with the water buffeting me and steam filling the cubicle, until all trace of reality disappeared. Leaning against the wall, I was overcome by a feeling of sorrow heavier than anything I'd felt since my childhood.

I didn't visit you in the hospital that day. I sat in front of my computer and added the finishing touches to the dinner menu at the Transatlantic, which I'd been thinking about. Then I completed the details on an expansion project and emailed the final design.

Around midmorning, still unable to shake my disquiet, I took Arthur and Charly out for a walk. We went the same way you and I used to go. Before we reached Los Conquistadores, in front of the liquor store, I thought I saw the bum. I quickened my pace, but when the dogs and I reached the corner, he'd disappeared. We wandered around for a while and then went back to the place where I thought I'd seen him. Under an old cherry tree, I found the string of tin cans he usually carried slung over one shoulder. Charly and Arthur whined and fidgeted with excitement as they sniffed the bundle. I had a thought about calling Álvarez but dismissed it. For some reason I hadn't yet been able to understand, I wanted to be the first to talk to the vagrant. I waited a few minutes for him, figuring that he'd come back to collect his belongings, but he didn't show.

I went back, let the dogs loose in the yard, and entered your study. I spent a long time in there, looking through one of your tiny windows at the green garden. While sitting at your desk, I fell asleep and woke up in a sweat. Then I went home and made myself some mango-scented tea. That's how I spent the day, knowing that what I was doing with this aimless coming and going was waiting for Gracia.

She came home after completing the nightly newscast. I'd made a meat casserole, and as usual we ate in the kitchen, in front of the television. I observed her out of the corner of my eye, and every now and then our eyes met. Gracia held her gaze on me for a second, as though she were about to say something, but then she turned her attention back to the screen, where a couple of teenagers were arguing in a Chevrolet Impala parked by the shore of a deserted lake. I gathered up the dishes and prepared to wash them. Gracia settled into her chair without ungluing her eyes from the TV screen. Now the kids were lying in the grass next to their Impala and stroking each other. I stood watching my wife, and I had the impression that I was looking at a stranger. The terrible truth I'd learned that day gave me no peace. Gracia had not only discovered my involvement with Teresa, she'd also reported me to the police. I had no idea what could be going through her head. I thought again about that place where the other is, the place no one else can reach. About how mistaken I was to believe that what could be seen and touched constituted reality. Real life happened in that other space, hidden under the material appearance of things.

I finished cleaning up and sat down beside her. Our eyes met. I saw in hers the implicit invitation to intimacy I'd always ardently accepted. I was taken by surprise, and given the situation, her look should have repelled me; but instead I got excited. The proposition was coming from a stranger, and everything that happened in those circumstances would be a novelty. I got up to put away the last few things in the kitchen. As I was doing so, Gracia climbed the stairs. Her movements on the upper floor increased my desire. I imagined her curves, her pubis, and I saw, as I hadn't seen in a long time, Gracia's sensual, enticing beauty. I'd caught her more than once in front of the bathroom mirror, gazing at her body, slowly moving her hips from side to side, or cupping her breasts in her hands, and upon my untimely invasion of her privacy, she'd raised her arms and put her hands together over her head, laughing at the sight of her captivating, elegant body and the lustful look on my face. But now the image I'd called to mind so many times during my solitary morning masturbation sessions acquired a new, more exciting overtone, because that body, which I had considered part of myself, no longer belonged to me.

I went into our bedroom. Gracia was in the bathroom, running water into the tub.

Less than half an hour later, we made love, without even once looking into each other's eyes, without an affectionate gesture, without a caress meant to increase our partner's pleasure instead of our own. Both of us knew what the other knew. That mutual knowledge felt like a third person in the room, robbing us of all familiarity while stimulating our senses. Every energetic and desperate movement that Gracia made to feel me more intensely was a way of scorning me, of making me see her power, of showing me the utter uselessness of the carcass attached to the erect member that was giving her pleasure. Stripped of all sentimentality, sex appeared before us with its true face, violent and secret: an act in which the need to satisfy one's own pressing urgency is the only need that counts. At the moment when Gracia reached a climax, I held myself back, counting imaginary sheep, and then, when she had finished and was making a move to detach herself from me, I penetrated her again, deep and hard.

27.
EMILIA

I found Jérôme's letter in my mailbox when I came back from the hospital. It was strange to receive a letter from him. Until then, we'd communicated only through email.

After picking up the letter, I took the elevator to the top floor and then ran up the stairs to my roof terrace. I'd stopped counting the days since Jérôme's last response weeks ago. I was continuing to write him every day, but I had never mentioned my friendship with Daniel. I didn't mean to hide it from him; I was just afraid that putting it into words would make it disappear. That was what Vera said about the soul: you can't write about it directly, because when it's regarded head-on, it vanishes.

I caught my breath and opened the envelope right outside the door of my room:

My Dear Emi,

First things first: I beg your pardon for not having replied to your emails. I could say that I was busy, or that the ascent of the Matterhorn took much longer than I thought it would, or some other thing, but I'd be lying to you, and we've never lied to each other.

After reading that first paragraph, I went into my room. I hung my backpack on the chair and sat down on the bed. The sounds of gurgling pigeons reached me through the window. I looked out in an attempt to calm down. Dusk was falling. The sun was already out of sight. I imagined it moored to the hill before being dragged down the universe. I closed my eyes, longing to find in the darkness inside me the strength to read on. I knew the three pages I was holding in my hands contained the answers to the questions I'd been pondering recently.

I've written this letter dozens of times, but I never manage to say to you what I want to say to you. You know how clumsy I am with words. But today I decided to finish it and mail it to you. So if you've got this letter, that's because I was able to write it, however imperfectly.

So here goes, Emi. Please listen to me patiently, and don't stop reading before you get to the end. I beg you not to hate me, not for my silence and not for my words.

When the idea of your going to Chile came up, I felt really happy, for all the reasons we both know. You'd be able to finish your thesis, get to know as an adult the country where you were born, and all the other things we talked about so many times. But there were many other things we didn't mention. Things you know as well as I do.

I knew that after you left, nothing would ever be the way it was before. Don't think I wasn't afraid. I was deathly afraid that your journey would change you, and that you'd look back and see my smallness. But besides, and this is what I had the most trouble understanding, I knew it would change me too. I was such a child when I arrived at your house. We were both children. And you were so pretty. I needed you. I wanted to live in the world you kept hidden behind your eyelids. (I know, you made up that bit about the world behind your eyelids.) From the moment I entered your house, I never left it again.

I'm rambling. Please forgive me, Emi, the thing is, I realize I've never talked to you about any of this before. The point I'm trying to make is that we each needed the other, and so we created what's called a "symbiotic relationship." And that may be a fine thing for trees, insects, and animals, but it's no good for humans. Because it's impossible always to be there for someone else. A harsh thing to say, right? "Impossible." And that's what I've come to understand, Emi. That your leaving opened up not only all those opportunities we'd talked about already, but also others the two of us may have intuited but never dared to name. I'm trying to be like you and say things in a nice way, but all I do is make them more complicated.

You knew and I knew what could happen. I've already said that, haven't I?

Emi, I'm dating someone. Her name doesn't matter, and besides, it would make you laugh. What's important is that I can't hide the fact from you, nor do I want to. So now you know. I'm trying to picture you, and I know I'm not mistaken when I say you haven't laid this letter aside, you're still stubbornly reading it, though you probably raised your head and looked up for a second. Right? But now you're going on, all the way to the end.

I laid the pages aside, just to contradict his predictions. I had, in fact, looked up at the ceiling. I left the letter on the bed and started to fix dinner. I'd bought some sausages and a box of instant mashed potatoes. I put the food on a tray, and as I'd been doing daily ever since the evenings turned warmer, I carried my meal out to the terrace and ate while looking at the street and the final hustling and bustling of the day.

In the sky, a white line marked the passage of a jet. I looked at its trail for a while and imagined the men and women inside the airplane. Where were they going? How many of them were expecting someone to be waiting for them at the end of their journey, and that someone wouldn't be there?

Night had already fallen on the roofs of the city. I sat on the terrace and resumed my reading.

Forgive me, Emi, for the pain my words have surely caused you. You know the last thing in the world I want to do is to hurt you. You know that. But I want you to think about what I'm going to say now.

Letting you go makes me sorrier than I can express. It's like an enormous bereavement. And I'm not telling you that so you'll pity me, but so you'll know how I feel. Not telling you would be another way of betraying you, of betraying us. But also, and here's the essential point of this letter, I know that you and I need this. We each need to let go of the other. Emi, we both know that our union is based on a precise event that we've never called by its name. I didn't know what I was doing. And now that you've had the courage to leave, I can tell you you weren't responsible for what happened to me. That would have gone on even if you had never existed, because it was something that was inside me, something I had to go through before I could see it. I'm so sorry, Emi, I'm really sorry for having kept you captive in an idea that bound you to me in such an unhealthy way.

What we both need now is to be able to look out on the world from our own center, not from that fictitious center we built for ourselves, which was neither yours nor mine, but which was in a place neither of us knew how to get to. I'm giving you back your life, Emi, so that you can take it in your hands and shape it yourself. That sounds really corny, I know, but the problem is I don't know how to put it any other way.

Love always,

Jérôme

I stayed out on the terrace, sitting with the letter in my hands while my body was enveloped in sounds: the distant barking of dogs, the din of traffic.

I got the shivers and went to my bedroom. I got in bed without undressing and lay there watching the lights the night threw against my window.

Hours passed.

In the distance, trucks were crying out like nocturnal animals. My body had turned into a rigid mass. I lay immobile, trembling. Finally I reached a state of precarious warmth. An ecstatic drowsiness came over me.

I woke up when light dawned through my window. The bed was wet and my feet were frozen, as if I'd set them in a big ice mold. I was sweating. I pulled off the sheets, threw them on the floor, and put on some new ones. The effort left me exhausted. I got back in bed and wrapped myself in the covers. I dozed for a while, awakened with a start, dozed again. Now and then anger took hold of me. I hated Jérôme for having loved me, for having entered into my heart until we were one. For having given my days a meaning and then yanking it away from me. For having gone ahead of me, for having been stronger than me.

In my waking sleep, I remembered a time when I was a girl, walking with my parents and Jérôme on a beach, and we found a blue starfish and put it inside a glass bottle. The starfish had five arms, or rays, and couldn't have measured more than three inches in any direction. We took it home, and although it didn't move at all, it fascinated us; we watched it for the rest of the day. Its suckers were attached to the inside of the bottle, and its surface texture looked like it belonged to a prehistoric animal. In its stillness, it seemed to contain a peculiar wisdom. All of a sudden, to our great surprise, one of the starfish's rays began slowly and laboriously to separate from its body. Then, very slowly, the detached arm started walking perpendicularly up the inside of the bottle, until finally it bumped into the top, which Jérôme was holding firmly closed. The starfish was dismembering itself, shedding body parts to save its life. I sensed a thousand meanings in that breakup. A thousand significations that my child's mind was incapable of taking in. "Let go, let go!" I screamed. "Let it out! It has to get out!" With a violent lunge, I snatched the bottle out of his hands, and it fell to the floor. The single ray and the rest of the starfish's body lay still on the tiles of the kitchen floor, surrounded by shards of broken glass. The creature couldn't move anywhere anymore.

I was that body, I was that ray.

28.
HORACIO

The letters kept crossing the Atlantic. We dwelt obsessively on the few moments we'd spent together, as if each of them were a brick in our ongoing construction of a common past we barely had. We needed to create a world that belonged to us. A vain effort, similar to the one made by the girl who invented stories for her mother in order to stave off her death.

Our correspondence was irregular. I might not receive anything from her for days, and then the postman would bring me three or four letters that had got stalled somewhere in the post office. Words out of step with one another made up our universe. It lacked a present, and a future too.

In the course of those months, Vera wrote more stories. She sent me only excerpts from them, fragments related to our epistolary conversations. For my part, I continued to send her my poems, which she corrected and commented on with great dedication. My work at the United Nations became more demanding, and there didn't seem to be any chance of our seeing each other again anytime soon. Although we didn't talk about it, the lack of prospects began to weigh on us. Her letters and mine exuded desperation. It was in March of the following year, 1955, when what we would eventually come to call the Paris Earthquake took place.

Pérez had to attend a meeting in Paris, and he invited Vera and Julián to join him on a trip through Europe. After his professional obligations were fulfilled, the three of them went to Athens, Istanbul, Barcelona, and other places I can no longer remember. Our correspondence became even more difficult. I couldn't write to her. She sent me postcards, hastily scribbled notes that left me hungry for her letters and deprived of her presence, which was far away in geographical distance but close in what was essential. Her notes were full of loving words, but they never acknowledged the fact that she was traveling with her husband, that they were sleeping together, that they were making love, that Pérez was trying somehow—and today I understand this—to get his wife back, because he was losing her day by day, and he knew it. All this started to weigh on me in an unspeakable way, to the point where one day I woke up with the feeling that it was all senseless, that I couldn't go on letting my life revolve around a woman who would never be mine. I hadn't received anything from her in over a week. Motivated by anxiety and a hidden desire for revenge, I did something I had never done before: I added Vera's name to my list of conquests. There she was, pinned like an insect in a collection—a rare, even unique specimen—along with the others.

After my work was done that day, I wrote her a letter in which I told her that the time for us to break it off had come. I explained that until then we'd lived on the other side of the looking glass, where nothing and no one could touch us. An unreal world that protected us from the dirty truths of this one. Everything that might happen henceforward would only tarnish the beautiful love story we'd lived together. First would come unbearable longing, followed by jealousy, recriminations, and, eventually, the end of love.

But before I could mail the letter, I went home to my apartment and found one of hers. I've kept it all these years:

> *Horacio, my love,*
>
> *Things have happened, and I've spent the whole day deciding whether to tell you about them or keep them quiet. One thing's for certain, I can't bear them alone. I need your wise words. I need you to guide me, my love. I'm crying as I write.*
>
> *Manuel found out about us today. I'd never been there before, in that desperate place, besieged by falsehoods. And it was horrible. Lying. Betraying our love story, denying its existence. Betraying him. I'm hurting everywhere, Horacio, I'm hurting a lot. My emotions are so intense they're suffocating me. And yes, I admit it, for a moment I thought about giving you up, but then the pain was even greater, so great that I felt more afraid than I ever had before. I can't, I can't.*
>
> *Do you remember when you used the word adulterers and I asked you if that was what the world would call us? You said it was, and I cried. You must also remember the time when I rejected*

the word affair. Those two words, adultery and affair, had no connection to what was going on with us. Our union transcends that lexicon of betrayal.

It's not anything we ever talked about, I know.

How does one live this way? How does one live a double life?

I know you weren't expecting this, my darling, and you must be upset. But there's something I want you to know: though you say, at the end of your letters, that you're leaving me with the certainty of your love, I'll go even further: I don't want anyone or anything to stand between us, not distance, not time, nothing, nobody. I don't know how to achieve that state, but it's what I want. I've thought it over and over, here's where I wind up: by your side. As the hours have passed, yesterday's anxiety has gone away. I tell myself that nothing has to change, except that we'll have to be more careful. Manuel's trust in me, which I used to count on, has cracked.

Please tell me something, tell me what you feel, what you think, I've never asked that of you before, but now I need it.

Your Vera, your Vera, your Vera

I kept her words in my hands for a long time. Then I picked up the letter I'd been preparing to send her and tore it up. I got to my feet and went to the window. I looked at the street that ran toward the lake, which was dissolving in the twilight. Her letter had shaken me. I had difficulty staying focused; it was hard to put my feelings and ideas in order. I waited unmoving, observing the movements in the street without seeing them, and nothing happened inside me. No great revelation appeared before my eyes.

Without thinking, I picked up the telephone and called the operator. After a long wait, I succeeded in getting connected. The voice of a hotel receptionist was on the other end of the line, and in a French that bore traces of another language, he asked how he could help me. I requested him to put me through to Mr. Pérez's room. I'd decided that if he answered, I'd hang up at once, and if it was Vera, I'd tell her to pretend to be talking to one of her girlfriends.

"Yes?" I heard her ask.

"Vera?" I could barely make my voice audible.

"Who is it?" This was the first time we'd ever spoken by telephone.

"It's me, Horacio," I whispered. The whole speech I had prepared on the subject of necessary precautions got stuck in my throat.

"Hello," she said breathlessly.

A silence ensued.

"Are you alone?"

"He's in the bathroom," she murmured.

I could hear Pérez's voice some distance away, but I wasn't able to understand his words.

"It's Rebecca," Vera said in a louder voice. "It's about some things she wants me to bring back for her."

I was touched by this evidence that our brains worked the same way. But it also scared me. I felt no pride in the speed and facility with which we concocted and assembled lies. Cold sweat dampened my hands.

"Vera," I mumbled. "I'm just calling to tell you I'm here, I'm not letting you go, I'm not letting go of your hand."

"All right," she said. And in those two words there was a sadness that made me shudder.

"Vera..."

"Yes?"

My thoughts were racing. The line went dead for a few seconds. I imagined how I'd feel once I could no longer hear her voice. I knew then that it would be horrible, and afterward it would become much worse.

"I think about how much you've suffered these past days...Even though it's something that's happening to you, now it's part of our story, it's our seismic event. I'm at your side to do whatever there is to be done."

Through the window, I could see the sodium lights of the street.

"Thanks," she mumbled.

In spite of the word's plainness and how vulnerable it sounded, it was full of messages: need, conviction, fear.

"I love you, Vera."

I heard whistling coming from some nearby apartment. It was a simple melody with martial vestiges that instead of taking shape became vaguer, as if someone were searching his memory for a forgotten harmony.

"Have you seen my tie with the green stripes?" I clearly heard Manuel say.

"Give my love to the children and José," said Vera, and hung up.

I sat there on my bed with the receiver in my hand, elbows on knees, unmoving. My degree of responsibility for what was going on appeared to me in a sudden flash. I saw Vera in all her defenselessness. I didn't know her past, I was ignorant of the nature and strength of the bonds that united her to her husband, a man twenty years her senior. I again recalled her short story about the girl at her mother's deathbed.

I felt immense love for her, a love I wasn't sure I was capable of professing. But at the same time, I had the sensation that I'd fallen into a trap. I didn't feel capable of taking on Vera's life. The words I'd spoken obligated me to assume the consequences they entailed. I went outside and walked the streets aimlessly for at least two hours. On the way back, I stopped at a bar and downed glass after glass until I was good and drunk.

I woke up with a headache. Nothing extraordinary, given the quantity of alcohol I'd imbibed. But it was in that semiconscious state, which rendered me unable to carry out the day's tasks, that I understood what was happening to me. I was falling in love with Vera. Or I'd already fallen in love with her. And that discovery led me to make a decision: I would return to Chile, and I'd be there for her when she needed me. It was an extremely romantic idea that made me remember Vera's words in one of her letters, when after hearing some distinguished professor on the radio, she concluded that those who hide behind the walls of knowledge and reason lose their ability to see the phosphorescence of things. In all probability, my decision to leave everything for her wasn't at all reasonable, but never, before or since, have I felt more alive and closer to reality.

• • •

I arrived in Santiago on June 19, 1955, three months after the Paris Earthquake. I settled into a two-room apartment at 456 Mosqueto Street, opposite a nightclub, and I got a third-rate job in the Foreign Ministry.

Two evenings a week, Vera visited me in my apartment. Little by little, the time we spent together had become essential for both of us. During those hours, apart from making love, reading, and launching into lengthy conversations, we would look out the window at the hustle and bustle on the street below. At a life to which we didn't belong together.

On certain evenings, we'd deconstruct and reconstruct a line or two from one of my poems until we emptied it of its contents, until we grew weary, crumpled up the paper, and with the coldheartedness of someone getting rid of a damaged creature, threw it into the trash basket. Vera was pensive, with an expression on her face that made her look like a little girl. Keeping her eyes fastened on the basket, she said, "There must be a way, Horacio. We just have to look for it."

I loved her then, I loved her with all my overflowing heart.

She almost always brought me food. Dinners prepared at her house by her maid and then reheated in my kitchen. Vera loved eating in bed, whereas I preferred to dine while seated at a table. To tempt her, I'd take out my grandmother's cutlery, which had accompanied me in my travels, I'd light candles, and with a white napkin dangling from my neck, I'd invite her to sit with me. Sometimes we'd burst out laughing, push the plates aside without saying a word, go into the bedroom, and make love.

But sometimes I felt discouraged. Even in those years, our separations were already anything but infrequent. Nevertheless, Vera seemed to be trapped in a Victorian marriage, whose main features were guilt, remorse, and attachment to a union long since dead. Why? I asked myself that, I asked her that, time and time again.

Her answers were always elusive and sometimes even contradictory. She'd allude to Pérez's bad health, to her own weakness, to her fear of his possible reaction. Evasions and contradictions with regard to her personal history and her origins would later become Vera's preferred way of surrounding herself with the aura of mystery that would accompany her for the rest of her life. "Facts bore me," she would say in interviews, after she'd turned into a cult author. Her most frequent responses were "I don't know," "I'm not familiar with that," "I can't say," "It's hard to explain," "I've never heard of that," "There isn't," "It's not," "I don't think so."

Vera often fantasized. I remember an occasion when she arrived at my apartment in distress, locked the door, and said with terror in her eyes, "A man followed me here." Her whole body was shaking. "He's there, outside," she declared, and pressing her purse against her chest, she turned to the wall. "Do you see him?" she asked from her corner.

I looked out at Mosqueto Street and saw nothing under the branches of the jacarandas but the usual bustle.

"I don't see anything."

"He's one of Manuel's friends. I don't know whether he assigned him to follow me or he's doing it on his own initiative. He's always been in love with me."

I looked her in the eyes, and she shied away from my gaze. Before many minutes passed, she'd forgotten about the whole thing, and she was laughing and telling me one of her domestic anecdotes, which always ended in a disaster caused by her general ineptitude. For some reason, Vera had made up the story about the man on her tail. I would later discover that creating stories and acting according to them were normal behavior for her. Vera lived in an intermediate dimension, in which the boundaries between the real and the invented aren't as clear as they are where the rest of us mortals live. I sensed that this was the way she dealt with the distress of leading a double life. Maybe in her secret heart, the life we shared occupied a separate compartment, one of the many where she kept all the things that for one reason or another she preferred not to see, or not to come to terms with.

When the streets were intensely cold and the sky weighed on Santiago like a gray vault, she'd come to my apartment in the late afternoon, sit on the olive-green couch in the living room, and ask me to hold her.

"Thank you, my love," she'd whisper in my arms. "Thank you, thank you, thank you," she'd repeat, with feeling.

And it was at such times that I most needed to get inside her head, to learn her secrets, to understand what there was behind that woman whose paradoxes sometimes inflamed my desire and sometimes aggravated my soul.

As soon as the streetlights started to glow, Vera would pick up her coat, her fur stole, and her purse and leave without saying good-bye (because, she maintained, our farewells made her too sad). She often effected her getaway after we'd made love and I was asleep, and when I woke up, her absence would make my body hurt all over.

29.
DANIEL

When I got to the hospital, the first thing I did was to look for Emilia in the little room where she usually waited for me, but she wasn't there. I waited a few minutes, thinking she might be in the restroom. Then I went into your room and sat on the chair facing you. Lucy had washed your hair and combed it back. Your uncovered forehead showed its furrows and creases. Your lips had a slightly pinkish tint. I'd brought some newspapers so that we could read them together, but I was unable to concentrate. I raised my eyes to look at the door about once a second, imagining it would open and Emilia's dark head would appear. But Emilia didn't come.

After I left to go home that evening, I was walking around the hospital's underground parking garage, looking for my car, when I thought I spotted Dr. Calderón, the psychiatrist. I'd looked at photographs of him on the Internet, and I had a clear memory of his aquiline nose, his tiny eyes, and his long, thin face, features that made him look like an anteater. I tried to catch up with him, but the elevator doors opened and the man disappeared when they closed. I waited for the next elevator, went back up to your floor, entered your room, and there you were. I went out to the waiting room and then walked around the corridors. I called Álvarez, and he answered with his customary throat-clearing. I told him what I'd seen and asked him if he'd been able to verify Calderón's departure date. The man was still in Chile, and the detective had already questioned him. Álvarez had nothing important to say about him but would get in touch with me when he did. Dazed, I sat in the waiting room. My amateurish investigations made me feel useless.

Instead of returning home directly, I drove to the nearest movie theater, which was in a shopping mall. My encounter with Calderón—if it had indeed been him—had left me uneasy, but above all, I didn't much feel like seeing Gracia. Automobiles were zooming through the streets, some drivers sounding their horns, some thrusting a hand through their window and saluting a nonexistent multitude. The Chilean national team must have won a soccer match.

I ate in a joint on Luis Thayer Avenue. At the table next to mine, a couple of office workers were trying to seduce two girls who could have been their daughters.

Back in our neighborhood, I parked my car and took the dogs out for a walk. It was an unusually cold spring night. I got home past midnight and Gracia was asleep, or pretending to be asleep, which came to the same thing. We didn't have to speak or explain ourselves.

• • •

I was hoping to see Emilia the following morning, sitting in the waiting room with her feet together and that smile on her face, waiting for me, but she wasn't there. I went into your room. I couldn't keep still. The hardest thing was the thought that Emilia lived in another world, a place unfamiliar even to her. I grabbed my jacket and went out. It had been two days since she'd shown up at the hospital.

There was little traffic at that time of day, and it didn't take me long to reach Emilia's building. I rang the doorbell, but no one answered. Nor was there a doorkeeper. I therefore decided to wait for someone to go in or out and give me a chance to slip inside. After a while, a woman wearing a kerchief on her head and wheeling a little shopping cart opened the door. Very fine blue veins, reminiscent of the venation of a leaf, hatched her face. I explained to her that I was there to visit the girl who lived on the roof, and the woman let me pass inside. I took the elevator to the ninth floor and then climbed the narrow steps that led to the terrace. Viewed from there at that hour, the city didn't appear very attractive. The car horns, the exhaust fumes, and the leaden substance the sky was shedding transformed Santiago into a threatening place. Only the white canopy, rocking in the breeze, belonged to the world we'd shared a few days before.

The doors of the kitchen, the bathroom, and Emilia's bedroom were locked. I knocked on her door a few times, but there was no response, nor could I detect any movement that might betray her presence inside the room. All of a sudden, however, I heard her voice: "Who is it?"

"It's me, Daniel."

I listened to her coughing and said, "May I come in?"

"I'll open the door," she said, the words barely audible.

Her face was pale and her hair disheveled. She was wearing a blue nightshirt and a scarf. Although it was already November, the last few days had been cold. She was barefoot. The room, dark except for a halo of dim light seeping in between the closed curtains, looked like a box filled with dust. Her bed was unmade, and some crumpled sheets lay in one corner. Emilia seemed not to recognize me at first.

"What are you doing here?" she asked. I noticed that she was trembling.

"Are you all right, Emilia?" I asked her in turn.

"I don't know," she said. She appeared confused.

I stepped into the room, even though she hadn't invited me to come in. The room was cold, as though the winter had taken up residence in there to wait for its next opportunity. The place smelled like Emilia, a flowery scent without the sharp edge perfumes have. Books were piled on the nightstand and the table. On one wall was a row of postcards. Among them, the classic photograph of Virginia Woolf and another of the English poet Rupert Brooke. I pulled a blanket off the bed and handed it to her so she could cover herself. She took it and threw it over her shoulders. She pressed her lips together, rubbed her eyes with one sleeve of her nightshirt, and sat on the bed.

In another corner, I saw a small, smoke-blackened gas heater and a box of matches. I lit the wick, and a thin blue flame glowed in the semidarkness.

"I'm going to fix you a cup of tea. Have you eaten anything?" She shook her head and tried to smile, without complete success. "We'll start with the tea," I said, and I went out onto the roof.

There were some sheets of paper lying on the terrace in front of the kitchen door, apparently carried there by the breeze. The pages were handwritten, in French. I folded them in half and put them in my jacket pocket to give to Emilia. After putting the teakettle on to boil, I opened the refrigerator to see if there was something I could prepare for her, but it was empty. I remembered the impression she'd made on me when I hardly knew her, the feeling that she could vanish at any time. I also remembered what you often told me: it's through details that we can see the essence of things. Now, looking into her empty refrigerator, I understood. Emilia was in transit, not through this country, nor through this time, nor through this geography, but through a much vaster one.

She drank the tea in little sips, sitting up on the bed with her feet tucked under her and the blanket on her shoulders. Her dark straight hair fell over her eyes, which seemed to be contemplating incommunicable subjects. She'd changed in the days since I'd seen her. From underneath her defenselessness, a cutting edge had emerged, like a ridge.

"You've stopped shivering. Do you think you have a fever?" I asked, knowing I couldn't touch her forehead and find out for myself.

She shook her head, and then, looking at me for the first time, she asked, "What day is today?"

Hearing her speak and seeing her pupils fixed on me once more calmed me down. I said, "Friday."

"I must have acquired a cold," she said, using language like what you heard in dubbed films. This, along with her slight accent, made me recall that she had never lived in Chile.

"You have to eat something, Emilia. I'm going to go out and see what's available."

I returned with a couple of chicken-and-avocado sandwiches, a carton of orange juice, and some yogurt. Emilia had put on a pair of jeans I'd never seen before and a checked shirt, and she'd put her hair in a tiny braid that was visible on one side of her neck. She had also opened the curtain. The light drew shapes on the floor. Despite her efforts, she still looked dreadful.

I fetched some plates and put them on her desk. She sat on the edge of the bed, and I took the only available chair. She moved slowly. It was hard for her to bear the weight of her own body. Although I wasn't hungry, I ate to keep her company. I watched her and made useless comments, pointing out how salty the avocado tasted or how delicious the orange juice was. A cold breeze streamed through the half-open window, which I closed. I couldn't get closer to her. Her self-absorption was so deep, her effort to remain seated there so great, that she seemed about to succumb at any moment.

"Would you mind if I lie down again?" she asked, still eating her sandwich.

A fire truck sped down a nearby avenue, its siren vibrating the windowpanes. Emilia stretched out on the bed and stared at the window facing her desk. The pale down on her arms sparkled in the sunlight.

I stayed in my chair, knowing that the only thing I could do was to wait and to take care of her insofar as she allowed me to do so. She turned and gave me a sad smile.

"Thank you," she said.

"I found this." I reached into my jacket pocket, took out the sheets of paper I'd picked up from in front of the kitchen door, and handed them to her. Emilia took the pages without looking at them and laid them on the night table.

"Did you read them?" she asked, leaning forward.

"No!" I exclaimed. "I'd never do anything like that. Besides, my French wouldn't be up to it."

Emilia smiled and pulled on her braid. "It's a letter from my fiancé, Jérôme," she said, smiling again, without conviction. "Or from my ex-fiancé, to be precise."

"I see," I said.

"You're probably wondering how it is that I have a fiancé," she said, rubbing her nose with the palm of her hand, up and down, several times.

"Yes, I *was* wondering about that."

"It's a complicated story. I'm not sure you want to hear it."

"I'd be delighted."

Emilia settled herself on the bed, bent her legs, clasped them in her thin arms, and rested her chin on her knees.

She stayed like that for several minutes. Without speaking, without making the smallest movement. Her shoulders rose and fell with her breathing. The fluctuation was very slight. I felt an urge to put my arms around her.

"His name is Jérôme," she said, breaking the silence. "I already told you that, didn't I?"

I nodded.

"The problem is, I don't know how to begin. Supposedly, you begin at the beginning, but where do things really start? Jérôme, Jérôme," she repeated, bringing her hand to her chin in a pensive gesture. "I well remember the day he arrived in our class. We were all eleven, and the school year had begun four months before. He was small for his age. The expression on his face was both serious and indifferent, like someone who already knows how hard life can be and has decided to ignore it. The teacher had him sit in the back row, and while he walked to his desk, everybody looked at him. He was wearing corduroy trousers and a jacket several sizes too big for him. Ours was a private school, the most expensive one in the city. We didn't know it that first day, but we soon learned that Jérôme had a scholarship. I'd started going to school there the previous year.

"In the second week, disobeying the teacher's instructions, Jérôme sat at the desk next to mine. Nobody had ever shown any interest in sitting there before. I don't know how he knew, but he saw immediately that we had both run aground in the same harbor. Neither of us belonged to the world where we had wound up. But the truth is, he chose me. He made up for everything he lacked in inches and social status with his determination and his demonic intelligence. Every time we took up some new subject, he'd quickly learn it better than all of us, and in class he'd ask questions that stumped the teachers. Most of the time he was bored, and while we were all following the lesson attentively, he'd be writing songs. His idols were Mick Jagger and Bob Dylan. The lyrics of Jérôme's songs seemed to come from the mind of an adult. They spoke of lost loves, of betrayals, of alcohol and drugs. But I'm running on too much..."

She stopped and rubbed her eyes with the tips of her index fingers.

"No, no," I said. "Please go on. If you want, I'll make you some more tea."

"That would be nice," she said, and smiled at me.

Back in her room, I noticed that the light had changed, and instead of the shapes on the floor, the reflected rays of the timid springtime sun glimmered on the wall. The color had returned to Emilia's face, and her movements were no longer as languid as they'd been a little while ago.

"So we started to spend more and more time together. I'm repeating myself—I already told you that."

"No, you didn't."

"My father recognized his intelligence immediately. He enjoyed talking to him. Jérôme made him laugh, which was something my father didn't do much. Jérôme practically began to live with us. When the school day was over, we'd walk to my house together. He lived at the other end of Grenoble, and just when it was starting to get dark, he'd set off for home. On many occasions my father offered to give him a ride in his car, but Jérôme always refused. His life was split in half, and he'd decided that the two parts would never meet.

"I remember the first time I caught him looking at me. We must have been around fourteen, doing our homework on the dining room table. I always took longer than he did, and while he was waiting for me to finish, he'd entertain himself with solving the complicated mathematical equations my father would leave for him. But that time, when I looked up from my notebook, Jérôme's eyes were fixed on me. His grown-up's eyes. He didn't blink when I caught him, and the way he was staring at me made me think of his songs, the ones about broken loves and betrayals, and I looked back down at my notebook.

"That fixed stare was repeated more and more often, and the only way I could think of to ward it off was to ignore it and distance myself from him. I knew I was hurting him, but I wasn't able to deal with the feelings his eyes aroused in me. This is where things get complicated, Daniel. That's why I said it's hard to define where stories really begin. Because mine had started long before."

Emilia sighed and undid her little braid. Her hair, always smooth and lustrous, now looked slightly wavy, which gave her face a more mature appearance. The heater gave a click and went out. I lit it again, a task that required several minutes; when I'd finished, Emilia looked ready to go on. It was then that she told me about her "affliction." It was a confused account, which included a playground slide, blood springing from a head wound she'd suffered, and the concussion this had caused.

"That year and those that followed, I went through a series of therapies, one after another. According to the accepted, official version of my case, my head injury had provoked a rare kind of phobia in me. But there was something more. Something I never mentioned in any of my therapies. At first I kept it hidden in the back of my consciousness so I wouldn't have to see it or face up to it again. And later, I guess, I didn't mention it because I knew if I did it would only cause more pain and complicate things between my parents even more."

Emilia stopped talking for a moment, took a sip of her tea—which must have been cold by then—and went on: "I can still see my mother's tight dress, her voluptuous body, and *him*, with his arms around her bottom. My father was on one of his trips to an observatory in another city and wouldn't return until the weekend. I froze on the stairs and watched the man free her breasts from her dress, bend down, and suck them. It's an image I can still see clearly, my mother's white breasts, the man's brown hands fondling them, his avid eyes, his lips. But it's like an old photograph, without a background, without light. A dead image. This happened a week before the accident on the slide. But in the end, if you ask me what happened, I don't know. In therapy, they tried to make me believe that the mind is like a ball of yarn you can untangle by pulling on one end of the thread. But that's not how it is, Daniel. There's not a single thread, but hundreds, thousands; every day, every endeavor has its own. I figure the reasons why you do one thing or another, or why something inside you breaks, are never definitive. I believe that experiences add up, they accumulate, they interweave. One gets carried over to the other, a wound starts to close or becomes bigger. But ultimately, I don't know. I don't know what it was that triggered my affliction, or exactly when it happened.

"The point is that when Jérôme looked at me that way, my whole body tensed up, and his presence alone started to change me in a way that eventually became unbearable. He continued to come home with me after school, but as soon as my father arrived, I would slip away to my room. And I'd often excuse myself at dinnertime, saying I was tired or I didn't feel very well.

"At the end of that year, I went to Paris with my parents for the holidays. We stayed with some friends of theirs. And when I came back, nothing was the same anymore. Jérôme kept on sitting in the desk next to mine, but he stopped coming home with me.

"I found it shocking that my parents never mentioned his absence, as if it was perfectly natural for him to disappear overnight after being part of our family for three years. Although I never asked them, as time passed I began to suspect that my father, maybe because he was aware of what was going on with me, had spoken to Jérôme. He started to skip school, and eventually we learned that he'd flunked the year.

"Soon summer vacation came, and for two long months I heard no more from or about Jérôme. I never stopped thinking about him. He stayed in the center of my memory. It was something that happened naturally. While I was reading, while I was listening to my parents' conversations or going out with them, my mind would play back the moments I'd spent with him. There were hundreds of memories, and every one of them had left a warm imprint on me, a sense of myself, of my existence and my worth. I started invoking them more and more frequently, and for the rest of the summer, my only wish was to see him again. I'd also thought about the effect that his gaze had produced in me, and I wanted to regain his affection so much that I was even ready to let him touch me. But then the school year began, and Jérôme didn't show up for a single class. According to a rumor that was going around, not only had he failed the year, he'd also lost his scholarship. The phone call came in the middle of the third week. It was a Wednesday."

Emilia swept a lock of her hair behind one ear and fell silent. In the window, two jet trails left behind by an airplane rose high in the sky, in parallel lines, like the two uprights of a ladder.

"Yes, it was a Wednesday. The person talking to me on the telephone was his big brother. He was six years older than Jérôme, and he worked as a mechanic in a car repair shop. He and his girlfriend were going to get married. That was all Jérôme had told us about him. He shouted at me and insulted me, using hard, ugly words. He said I was to blame for what had happened, but I just couldn't understand what he was talking about. When Mama got home that evening, I was sick. Like I am now. But much worse.

"My father managed to find out that Jérôme was in the Grenoble University Hospital. He had tried to commit suicide. But my father didn't tell me that until a few days later, after my fever had gone down and I'd started eating again.

"Jérôme was in a life-or-death struggle for a week. His brother had found him in the garage, inside their father's car with the engine running. His family blamed us and wouldn't allow us to get near him. But every day after class, I'd go and sit in the hospital gardens and look up at the hundreds of windows and imagine that one of them had to be the window in his room. He was released after three weeks. He'd lost weight. I saw him leave the hospital with his brother and their parents. A gray couple, both of them pretty elderly-looking to me, maybe because they'd been aged by what had happened. The brother looked like one of those boys who are always on the point of starting a fight. I went home with conflicting feelings. I felt relieved that Jérôme was out of danger. But at the same time, a heavy, new sorrow had settled over me. A feeling I couldn't give a name to, because it was too painful. In the following days and weeks, my insomnia returned and my appetite went away. I was incapable of concentrating on anything but the idea of seeing Jérôme again. I had no way of reaching him. Jérôme had succeeded in keeping each of his two worlds incommunicado with the other. I took up wandering around the streets of Grenoble after classes and on the weekends. I visited the center of the city, the parks, the record shop—the places we'd gone together. On one of my rambles, it occurred to me that I could leave a trail, so that if Jérôme ever went back to those places, he'd know I'd been there too. I talked to the clerk in the record shop, to the cashier in the supermarket, to the alcoholic beggar Jérôme used to have conversations with whenever we'd happen to run across him, and to the young waitress who'd served us in the café. I asked the people I didn't know so well whether they remembered us, the little short guy and me, and most of the time they said yes, they remembered us, and they inquired about Jérôme. Then I'd ask them to tell him I was looking for him if he should ever turn up there. Also, sometime later, I began to leave notes in the places we'd frequented, our bench in the plaza, our table in the café, some tree we used to stand and talk under. I'd hide the notes in some barely visible nook. As was to be expected, when I went back a few days later to see if they were still there, many of them had disappeared, but many others were untouched and waiting for Jérôme.

"A few days later, as I was leaving school with my backpack on my shoulder, I saw him on the other side of the street. He'd gained back a little weight. He was wearing dark jeans and a blue jacket that weren't two sizes too big for him and made him look handsome. I crossed the street, and he greeted me as if nothing had happened. Like so: 'Hi.' And that was it. He walked home with me, we drank tea in the kitchen, we talked about some of the latest music albums and about the movies that had come out that season, and after my father came home, the four of us sat at the table and had dinner. I never asked him whether he'd found his way back by following the trail I'd left. He'd come back, and that was enough for me.

"After high school, he enrolled in the university to study astronomy, like my parents, and I opted for literature. I never again felt his eyes on me, never again felt that gaze of his that had caused us so much misfortune."

Emilia's face tightened. I felt a heavy weight on my chest. I thought, for the first time, that your own sorrow never seems as intense as what you feel with and for someone else.

She picked up the letter she'd left on the night table and handed me the handwritten pages. I took them without knowing what to do with them.

"Can you read French a little?" she asked me.

"A little."

"Jérôme has very clear penmanship, like a diligent schoolboy," she said with a smile.

I read the letter, and although many words escaped me, I managed to understand its gist. When I raised my eyes, Emilia was looking at me.

"The heavy sorrow you felt after Jérôme left the hospital was guilt, right?" I asked her. She answered by nodding her head. We remained silent for a while...and then: "I'm not certain of what I'm going to tell you, Emilia, nor do I know whether it will seem very important in the end, but I don't think Jérôme has another girlfriend. What tells me so is a kind of male intuition, if I can put it like that. I believe his intention in writing you this letter was to set you free from that guilt."

"Do you really think so?"

The indifferent tone she used to ask this question made me realize that the reasons for the letter, whatever they might have been, weren't what had affected her so much; it was the fact that now she was alone before her life, that she would have to start looking at it from a different viewpoint, and that she had no idea where to start. She looked tired but peaceful, like someone who's gone through a quagmire and come out pretty muddy but has the relief of knowing that now, at least, she's on the other side.

She laid her head on the pillow and pulled up the bed-covers. "You know what?" she said, without looking at me. "I don't think I've ever talked so much all at once."

Her smile was different from all her other smiles. Her sorrow, shut up inside her for so long, had found a way out through words, and now that it was outside, it had changed its form. I took the blanket she'd left hanging on the back of the chair and put it over her, on top of the others. Neither of us said anything for a long time.

"Daniel...," she murmured.

"Yes?"

"Would you sit here, next to me?"

"Of course," I declared, and I moved the chair closer to the bed.

"No. Here, with me."

I sat on the edge of the bed and clasped my knees. She placed her hand on mine. She ran her fingers over the back of my hand, a light touch, but at the same time much more intense than a squeeze. I wished, in that moment, for your clarity; I wanted to be able to speak the right words—the mot juste, as you used to say—or to make precisely the right gesture to turn that moment in the proper direction, whatever that might have been. But I remained as I was, without moving, absorbing her body heat, yielding to the emotion produced in me by the thought that her hand had barely ever felt the warmth of another's touch. She settled in under the covers and closed her eyes.

The knowledge that she'd decided to touch me made me feel unexpectedly free, as though I'd been pardoned for everything I'd said and done up to that point. Her virginity made me long to be a part of her awakening. Before long, her breathing became regular. She'd fallen asleep, her head resting on the pillow, her delicate features tranquil in repose. I slipped out of the room and went out on the terrace. A slight breeze had come up, and the first streetlights were afloat in the dusk.

30.
EMILIA

I woke up at daybreak.

The white moonlight was backing away. I remembered Jérôme and a pain started to spread like a stain in the middle of my chest.

I also remembered that I had fallen asleep holding Daniel's hand.

I looked at my right hand, the one that had touched his. I grazed my cheek with it. Then the base of my neck. It tickled, an electrical discharge that passed through all the rest of my body. I brushed my lips. The wings of my nose. My closed eyelids. I opened my eyes, and my face was reflected in the window glass. The vision of myself, touching my face, shook me. I didn't know how to cope with that feeling.

I took the letter and went out onto the roof. It was a Saturday morning, and the city was sleeping. I sat on the terrace railing and read the letter one more time. My body felt heavy and damp, as if someone had put a wet overcoat on my shoulders. I tried to get my thoughts in order. A soft breeze stirred the white canopy. Again I had the impression that I was sailing on a ship.

I don't know how much time passed. The sun began to beat on my head. I had the feeling that everything I did in those moments had a symbolic significance. I thought about the wartime scenes where, after a night of bombing, the survivors rise up from their hiding places and walk through the now-destroyed streets, looking at one another. Entranced by the simple and miraculous fact of being alive.

I tore up the letter, leaned over the edge of my roof, and threw away the pieces. Some of them were caught by the breeze and flew far away, others headed downward, doing somersaults until I lost sight of them.

I was hungry. I went into the kitchen. On the table I found a cell phone and a note from Daniel.

> *My number's on this cell phone. When you can and you want to, give me a call. I left you some things in the refrigerator.*
> *Daniel*

It had been some time since I'd seen such a well-stocked refrigerator. Various fruits, fresh vegetables, bread, juices, cheeses, butter, and two trays of prepared food.

I thought about Jérôme. About the little boy he was before we came to the threshold of adolescence and his body began to desire mine. I remembered Daniel's hand, delicate and finely shaped. Like a pianist's hand. Its gentle touch. Its branching veins. The slight trembling of both our hands when they touched. I was afraid of my thoughts.

I'd reached a state of equilibrium that allowed me to live. Jérôme had been a part of that equilibrium. And now that he wasn't there, I must maintain it for myself. I couldn't get sidetracked. That had to be my sole resolve. I made coffee and a couple of avocado toasts. Then I took a shower. Under the beating water, eyes closed, I tried to calm down.

When Jérôme started coming to our house again, I decided I wouldn't ever leave him. I was sure he needed me. And it was his need of me that made me get up every morning, start the day, and think, "Yes, I'm alive, and my life doesn't belong to me alone." Sometimes I'd ask him, "How much do you need me, Jérôme?" And he'd reply, "A billion times the distance between Arcturus and Camelopardalis," or, "Not so much, just the distance between Cassiopeia and Alpha Serpentis."

So why was I giving up so easily?

Maybe I could turn things around, explain myself. Remind him that the bond between us was indestructible, that I didn't need the freedom he was going on about. I'd write him an email. That's what I would do. It was strange, but the idea that Jérôme had found a woman didn't make me jealous, it made me afraid. I was struggling against a lugubrious, impalpable enemy.

I stepped out of the shower and got dressed. "Jérôme," I wrote, and then I stopped. I stayed in front of the blank screen for a good while, waiting for the faucet of words to turn on. Suddenly a few appeared, but when I typed them they seemed false, and so I deleted them.

The truth is, I didn't know what to write to him. Words of love had never been a part of our language. Our life in common was woven together out of gestures, expressions we'd never given names to. The time had come.

"I love you, Jérôme," I wrote. One second later, I deleted it. Then I typed my name and sent the blank email.

I closed the computer and pulled my dirty laundry out of the closet. I washed my things and the sheets and hung them out on the roof to dry. The wind lifting my clothes made me think about the paper disks I used to cut out when I was a little girl. At some point I heated up the rice and zucchini Daniel had left me. I ate at my desk. The sun was languishing behind the Coastal Range. I used my shirt-sleeve to keep my tears under control.

After I finished eating, I undressed and tried to sleep. A day had passed. Now I had to gather enough strength to face the next one.

And the one after that.

When I woke up, the sun was striking my window. I must have slept more than fifteen hours. The black stain was still there. But it didn't feel quite so heavy. I got up and called Daniel. A couple of seconds later, I heard his voice,

"Emilia. Are you all right?"

"Yes."

My captivated heart started beating faster.

"I can't tell you how happy I am to hear your voice."

I remained silent.

"Can you hear me?" he asked.

"Yes, yes."

"What are you doing today?"

"I did my laundry yesterday. So today I'm free."

Daniel laughed. "Would you like me to make you a shrimp stew for dinner?"

"I have no idea what that might taste like."

"I could be there around seven, would that be all right?"

"Daniel..."

"Yes?"

"I'm sure I'm going to love it."

"It will be a pleasure to cook for you, my dear Miss Husson."

"Don't call me that," I protested.

"Remember I was crazy about her."

"For that very reason, Mr. Estévez. For that very reason."

Were we flirting? I preferred not to think about it.

At seven on the dot, I heard him coming up the stairs. He was carrying various bags from the supermarket. We went into the kitchen, and while he was fixing the dinner, we drank a glass of white wine. Calmly and meticulously, Daniel cleaned the shrimp and chopped up garlic, peppers, thyme, and bay leaves. There was a hidden pleasure in his movements, and he never stopped smiling.

The evening was warm, so we carried my desk out onto the terrace to serve as a table. We ate the shrimp stew while looking at the city and the gradually waning light in the sky. When we were finished, Daniel took two cigars out of his jacket pocket and offered me one. I hadn't ever smoked before, but nevertheless, I let him light my cigar.

"Don't inhale it," he said, raising his voice above the flame of the lighter, which was cupped in his hands.

High above us, the waxing half-moon crossed the sky, watching over the tides that were spreading under my ship.

"This roof terrace is really incredible," he said.

"We have to set a date for the Transatlantic dinner."

"Do you really want to do that, Emilia?"

"Of course," I declared with conviction.

"I made some drawings a few days ago," he confessed. His eyes were shining.

We talked about remodeling the kitchen and the bathroom. About closing off an area to make a pantry, covering the floor with black and white tiles, bringing up some trees, raising some sails. We kept throwing out ideas for a long time. Laughing at some of them, developing others. Then he explained the style of cuisine he had in mind, simple but also individual. Like what we'd just had for dinner. Daniel's passion was strong enough to wrap both of us in an atmosphere of exquisite promise.

"You know what? I think we ought to get started on it right away," I said. "Don't think about it too much. A dinner party to celebrate the arrival of spring. People are fascinated by that sort of thing. Afterward, later on, we can address the remodeling project."

"You're right," he said enthusiastically.

The evening went on, and we could hear laughter from the street. We remained silent for a long time, looking into the depths of the night. Despite Jérôme, something good—like the curiosity of childhood—seemed to be taking shape out there. I wanted to hold Daniel's hand again. All I had to do was reach out my arm and grasp it. And that's what I did.

His skin was warm.

Keeping hold of his hand, I turned my face to the side opposite the one Daniel was on. My hand and I weren't parts of the same person. I remembered the starfish and how one of its arms detached itself from the rest, so that the creature left part of itself behind. When the bottle fell and broke into a thousand pieces on the floor, my father picked up the detached arm, put it into a cardboard box, and told us to come with him. It was almost dark when we got back to the shore where we'd found the starfish, and we placed the little arm on a wet rock. In the pools, strands of algae and shards of seashells were being ferried back and forth by the moving water. We stayed there for a long time, watching over the starfish, making sure that no wave carried it off. Gradually it started moving again, uncertain and apparently aimless. But little by little it got closer to the edge of the rock and disappeared into a crack. After we got back home, my father told us that when the living conditions of starfish change, they dismember and leave behind a part of themselves in order to survive. "Can you imagine if we humans were capable of doing something like that?" he asked us. At that moment, Jérôme and I imagined ourselves shaking off our hands and our feet, and we didn't think it sounded like a good idea. Nevertheless, after all those years, while I was touching Daniel, I knew I was going to have to get rid of a lot of what I was carrying around. The difficult part was that, like the starfish, I had to be ready to start walking again at once, in a world I didn't know.

"Turn around and look at me," Daniel said.

I looked at him. I had the sense of being in a place with no history and no weight. A diaphanous place, created that very instant.

"Do you remember what Octavio says to Sinalefa?" He was referring to characters in *The Highest Trapeze*.

I laughed. "He says lots of things to her!"

"He says something about how when he looks at her, he can see inside her, he can see a mighty, luminous sphere, wrapped in gauze."

"Oh, yes. When they're sitting in the middle of a little square surrounded by buildings."

"Exactly. That's what I see in you. Something round, luminous, and strong."

"And the gauze?"

"You know the gauze. It's the sphere you don't know."

He laughed.

I would have liked him to tell me I was gorgeous. Or that my eyes were pretty. Or my eyelashes. Or something. But not that comment, which had seemed quite expressive to me when I read it in Vera's novel, but which now, having been subjected to it, I thought sounded abstract. I wanted Daniel to see me in a concrete, tangible way.

I let go of his hand first. I put mine between my knees, and the warmth of his persisted there for a long time.

We washed the dishes and said good night at the kitchen door.

"I'll see you tomorrow in the hospital, right?" he asked.

"Yes. Tomorrow."

"Thanks, Emilia," he said, and went running down the stairs.

I wondered why he'd said that. The person who ought to be thankful was me. Maybe, without realizing it, I'd handed him something I couldn't see and he could. I spent a good while turning round and round in my minuscule room, afraid to get into bed and find sorrow there. I felt a strange lightness. I'd been bound to Jérôme by a strong, thin thread like kite string, and now that the thread had been cut, I could rise above people and things.

At some point, I flopped on the bed, exhausted, without undressing, and that's how I fell asleep.

31.
HORACIO

For Christmas of that year, Vera arrived at my apartment with a pine tree. To decorate it, she also brought cardboard and newspapers, which she used to make ornaments like little hanging monsters. It was touching to see her sitting at the table, concentrating on her task, her face as glowing and unblemished as a young girl's.

"I don't know why I'm decorating this tree," she said as she sat in a chair barefoot and hung her ornaments. "Maybe because of my dad. He didn't celebrate the Christian holy day, but at Christmas he'd give each of us a slice of white bread. According to him, that was the best gift he'd ever been given, and he didn't want to forget it."

It was the first time she'd spoken to me about her father and about that past I'd so often tried to get a glimpse of, without success. She sat on the edge of the couch with her knees together and lit a cigarette. I kept quiet, hoping she'd go on.

"It was when we reached Moldavia. He'd always talk about the sight of those bright lights, of the warm yellow gleam pouring out of the houses, after days spent fleeing into the cold dark. One of the families invited us to come in and eat a slice of bread." She was consuming her cigarette in deep drags and looking straight ahead, almost without blinking. "Sometimes my father would wonder aloud, 'Why, why, why?' He was a simple man, and he never understood why he'd had to suffer like that. It wasn't because he'd done any harm to another or attacked the established order, nor was it because he'd said something that offended anyone or because he'd wished someone ill. No. What had happened had happened because of what they 'were.' And what exactly were they? he wondered. Didn't they have ears, hands, eyes like all the rest? Weren't they made of the selfsame matter? It was something that surpassed the limits of his comprehension. When I was a teenager, I would catch him staring at himself in the mirror, without a trace of vanity, trying to find the invisible mark. By then my mother was already dead."

"And do you remember any of that? The slice of bread, the journey, Moldavia?"

"No. I don't remember anything."

The evening light fell on her features and softened them. She crushed out the stub of her cigarette in the ashtray and slowly, as if overcoming heavy resistance, she got to her feet and went into the kitchen.

"I'm hungry, how about you?" she asked me from there. It was her way of announcing that the conversation was now over.

• • •

We'd agreed to meet again during the week following the Christmas festivities, which meant we couldn't see each other for three long days. However, during the evening on December 25, while I was debating whether to smoke a Havana cigar in the tranquillity of my four walls or to go for a walk downtown, someone rang the doorbell of my apartment. When I opened the door, I found Vera and Julián. They had with them a suitcase and a new bicycle, which must have been a gift the child had received the previous night. It was the second time I'd seen him, and once again I was moved by his resemblance to his mother.

Confused yet also delighted, I invited them inside.

"This is Horacio," Vera said. The obedient Julián reached out his hand to greet me with a deliberate calm that was amusing in a nine-year-old boy.

I picked up the suitcase—an exceedingly heavy object—and we entered my diminutive apartment. When he saw the Christmas tree, Julián exclaimed, "It's very pretty, very pretty. Can we make more decorations?"

"Of course, sweetheart," Vera replied.

With Julián present, I couldn't ask Vera what had happened. Even so, the naturalness with which the two of them entered and then settled into my apartment filled me with happiness. After drinking a glass of water, Vera opened a drawer, took out the scissors and the scraps of cardboard and newspaper she'd made her little figures with, and put her materials on the table.

"There you are, sweetie. We're going to cover our tree with ornaments. Nobody will know there's a Christmas tree underneath. Go over and get me my purse," she said, pointing to the chair she'd left it on. "I've got a surprise for you."

Inside the purse was a silver comet.

"You brought it," said Julián with a grave expression on his face that gave his childish features an unusual and alarming maturity.

It was a big, lightweight comet made of aluminum paper, with four points and a tail that ended in an inverted V. Vera put a chair next to the tree, climbed up on the chair, and set the comet on one of the topmost branches. But despite its lightness, the comet wouldn't stay upright, and instead of flying around the firmament, it seemed to be falling to the ground.

"It looks perfect," Vera observed. "Now I'm going to make some tea, and then I'll help you with the ornaments." She got down off the chair and went into the kitchen, and I followed her.

"What's happened?" I asked anxiously.

"Forgive me."

"Forgive you for what?" We were speaking in whispers.

"For turning up here like this."

"I'm happy you're here, both of you. I'm glad to meet Julián...But that's not the point, you haven't answered my question. What has happened, Vera?"

"Everything's over. But don't worry, I'll stay here only a few days. I'm going to find an apartment to move into as soon as possible."

"Have you left Pérez?" I asked.

Vera, head down, answered with a nod. Her shoulders were level with her ears, and tears were falling from her eyes.

"It's forever," she said, and as she spoke, a cup slipped from her hands and fell to the floor. The pieces lay scattered over the checkerboard tiles.

"Mama, you broke another cup," I heard Julián say from the table where he was working. Vera and I looked at each other and smiled.

"What does Julián know about me?"

"He knows you're a good man."

Once again, Vera was dodging, and this time she used Julián as a barricade.

Before too long, we had her things organized. They would sleep in the bedroom, and I'd take the big Chesterfield chair in the living room.

After breakfast the next day, we went out for a walk. Julián knew the name of every street. He explained that his father often took him to his office and then they'd have tea in Café Paula, across from the Municipal Theater, where I'd seen them with Vera. As we walked, Julián offered comments about historical details of the neighborhood that I'd never heard before. I quickly realized that, despite being a "mama's boy," Julián was a good-natured little guy with an exceptional mind.

That night, while I was shifting around on my couch, searching for sleep, I heard him burst into tears. I listened to Vera whispering to him, trying to calm his sobbing. "It's all right, it's all right," she said. "It's just another nightmare."

Julián's harrowing dreams revealed to me that he—like Vera—lived in two worlds. One was filled with optimism and recognition, and the other, a dark one, appeared while he slept.

We began to live a new life. Julián's summer vacation had already started, and so he spent most of his time with us, except for two afternoons every week and alternate weekends, when Sergio, the same chauffeur who had dropped me off at my apartment three years before, would pick him up outside the door of our building. During the hours when we were alone, Vera and I came together with renewed passion. There were also shared readings, including poems by Rimbaud, T. S. Eliot, and César Vallejo, along with stories by Chekhov and by a Brazilian writer, a woman named Clarice Lispector, who like Vera had a Ukrainian background; her first book, which had reached Vera's hands by way of a Brazilian diplomat, had dazzled her.

In mid-January of that year we began to choose together the poems that I would send to *SUR*, the literary magazine published by Victoria Ocampo. To be published in that magazine was the greatest success that a Latin American poet could have. I'd tried to get in before, but I had never received a response. This time, however, with Vera at my side, I was harboring great expectations.

She maintained that poems should be constructed in such a way that the words exploded, convulsing the meaning they'd had until then. On some occasions, using the same words I'd set down on the paper, Vera would create syntactically odd images that didn't fit with the rest of the poems, and which we would reject forthwith. In years to come, that particular way of using words would be what transformed her into a cult writer. Sometimes she'd suddenly grow pensive, her almond-shaped eyes shifting from one expression to another, and I'd guess at the images passing in front of her pupils, images that she, with all her senses on alert, would try to capture. Then something of each of us would skip over to the other's body, making me think that this must be genuine communication.

In Julián's absence, I asked her again and again to explain to me what had happened with Pérez, but she'd reply that she couldn't tell me, that what had happened didn't belong to her alone, that it was also part of Pérez's private life, and that she owed him that much respect. When she said this, she'd look away and her voice would become almost inaudible.

In the morning I'd leave for work before they woke up. I'd open the bedroom door a crack and look in and see them lying there in an embrace, mother and son, their feline features so pronounced that they looked alert even in sleep. During the day, Vera arranged to be always busy with unending domestic tasks. More than once, I came home to find all the dishes piled up in the kitchen, because she'd planned to wash them but then had forgotten; or there would be a platter with a hard mass on it that had been supposed to end up as a cake but had dried out long since; or my shirts would be spread over the bed because she'd thought she could iron them but after a few passes had realized that her labor was producing catastrophic results. Vera was trying to be the way one "should" be, to do the things one "ought" to do. Her efforts touched me. Nonetheless, under the patina of her will, beneath her efforts to cover up reality with the veil of her own peculiar idea of order, chaos was threatening to burst at any moment into our lives.

Mother and son spent long hours walking the downtown streets of the city. They would bring along Julián's bicycle, and when I got home in the evening, he'd recount all the details of their outings, while Vera would eye him from the olive-green couch.

I was impressed by how simply Julián had left behind his home, his nanny, his comfortable life, and his father to go and live in a stranger's apartment. To him, everything that was happening was a game, for such was the notion that Vera had cultivated in him. A game that involved life. From the very first days, Vera and Julián had started giving names to things. The kitchen knife was Mr. Cutty; the ladle was Mme Roundish; Sir Plushalot was the couch; Miss Stupendous was the only unbroken chair. I had the impression that I was living life surrounded by people.

After dinner, Vera would get up from the table, go into the bedroom, and lie down on the bed. We could hear her voice saying, "You two will excuse me, won't you? It's just that I'm so tired."

Those were my opportunities to talk tête-à-tête with Julián. Although we both knew that Vera was lying awake in the dark bedroom and listening to us, a different sort of intimacy was established between us. Julián got a serious expression on his face and asked me to name the capitals of distant countries, such as Chad or Mali. He also used to speak to me about the stars. He shared the rare ability some people have to make you think you're the one leading the conversation when in fact they're way ahead of you. He would sit up very straight, wielding his cutlery with the manners of a little gentleman, but soon he'd burst out laughing or throw himself under the table in search of an escaped marble, thus reminding me that he was, after all, just a child. I could spend a long time looking at him or listening to him. His being produced a strange fascination in me.

Nevertheless, it was true that at night, while I shifted back and forth from one side of the sofa to the other, what really kept me awake was the thought that our situation couldn't last. I missed the intimacy I used to have with Vera. Even though Julián was a charming little boy, his presence sometimes exasperated me. More than once, I wished he'd return to his father's house. I couldn't continue sleeping on that couch. My means were scanty and barely sufficed to cover our essential expenses. The dinner menu often featured soup of some kind, noodles, and some dubious sausages that Vera would get from a downtown delicatessen. I'd asked for an advance, but that was about to run out too. I didn't know what terms Pérez and Vera had come to, but evidently he wasn't helping her.

Meanwhile, Vera had started writing. On one occasion, there was a sheet of paper on the dining room table with the following words: *To see means to capture the representation of things within the things in themselves.*

She was in the kitchen, bedecked with her cook's apron, and as always when she tried to perform the duties of the lady of the house, chaos reigned. "The chicken's in the oven," she said with a smile. "And yes, I know, it looks as though I hunted it down inside this room."

We both laughed.

"What about this?" I asked, showing her the sheet of paper.

She dried her hands on her apron and got a pack of cigarettes out of her vest pocket. She lit one with her gold lighter and exhaled the smoke hard. Her hands were shaking.

"It's...it's what it's all about, Horacio," she said, focused and urgent. "That's it."

"That's what?" I asked her. "Explain it to me."

"When the word gets put on paper, it's not to describe something that existed before it did, but to create what it's describing. Do you understand?" She raised her hand to her mouth as if she'd said something reckless.

We remained silent. Vera brought me light and darkness at the same time, because she was inciting me to a labor I would find impossible to perform, unless I were to abandon the only territory I didn't distrust: rational thought.

On one of those still, hot summer nights, while we were smoking my last two cigars, Vera said, "Horacio, have you ever thought about how lucky you are to know where you want to go?"

I didn't speak, thinking about what she'd said to me. I saw that her cigar was going out, and then she tried to relight it.

"And you?"

She puffed on her cigar several times and then stretched out her feet, throwing herself back a little in her chair. With her eyes on the cloud of smoke as it broke up in front of her, she said, "I know too. I know where to go."

"And where do you want to go, my love?"

She looked at me attentively, like a bird that had risen to a certain height and was preparing to attack. It was the first time I'd ever seen that expression on her face, and I found it quite unpleasant. It even produced in me a certain resentment.

"I have it all in my head, but I can't take it out now, because it would decompose. Like raw flesh," she said, and she bit her lips, as if she'd surprised herself with the harshness of her words.

"What is it, Vera, please tell me, what is it you have inside that little head that always seems to be somewhere else?"

"Everything," she said firmly.

"But what is it?"

"Listen!" she exclaimed happily, pointing to the radio that had been playing the whole time.

It was the opening notes of the song by César Portillo de la Luz, "In the Distance with You."

"*The world seems different*," Vera sang, rising to turn up the sound.

She caught my hand and asked me to dance. It was a hot night, and our bodies, pressed together, were sweating. I could feel the firmness of her skin, of her buttocks, of her arms around me.

"I love you, Horacio Infante," she whispered in my ear.

Julián had fallen asleep on the sofa.

"We can carry him to the bedroom," she proposed.

We put him to bed, closed the bedroom door, and went back into the living room. For the first time, Vera and I made love while the child was in the apartment with us.

"You'll see. Soon your poems will be in the place they deserve." Her hair was gathered at the neck, and her smooth white face showed the fierce conviction characteristic of idealists.

So there we were, Julián asleep in what until a few weeks ago had been my bed, and she and I silently making love, and the joy I felt was shot through with anxiety and with the sadness of knowing how ephemeral everything was, how transient and fragile.

32.
DANIEL

I got home early in the evening. Emilia and I had worked outside on her roof terrace all day long, organizing our Transatlantic dinner party. I made myself some tea and went into my studio. I'd been sleeping there, in the bed we'd set up for eventual guests, ever since the night when Gracia and I made love like two strangers. That had been almost two weeks ago. There was still no peace between us. What remained was a dry crust, as on one of those dead stars Emilia had described, ready to break off and expose the death of our relationship. Gracia must have felt the same, because she didn't ask me to return to her bed and went on with her days as if, given the circumstances we found ourselves in, that was the best option. Would I have wanted Gracia to put up a fight for us? I don't know. It was hard for me to look at her without thinking about her talking to the detective. It was hard for me to see her anymore as the Gracia I knew and had confided in.

Until then, nothing had happened in our romance terrible enough to justify the place where we now found ourselves, nothing more than an accretion of silences, of oversights, of indifference, of exigencies, of little annoyances, which was settling on our lives from day to day, like an invisible, inoffensive dust. Maybe our big mistake had been to let that dust gradually cover everything, to the point where we couldn't make each other out with any clarity. It was painful to think that my betrayal and hers were the result of an accumulation of little wrong moves.

I was sitting at my desk, pondering these matters while simultaneously answering a few emails, when I recognized, among the sounds coming in through the window, the barking of Charly and Arthur, who were giving tongue with much greater intensity than usual. I went out into the garden and entered yours through the little gate.

"Charly, Arthur!" I shouted, but they kept on barking.

I circled your house, and in the front yard I could hear the sound of the tin cans the bum usually carried, clattering against the sidewalk as he went off. I pushed the grilled gate open and went out onto the street. The tall, thin figure of the vagrant, walking away fast, disappeared around the corner. I remembered that Detective Álvarez had asked me to get in touch with him if I happened to see the bum, but three weeks had passed since then, and they'd probably questioned him already. Charly and Arthur were moving in circles around me, restless, baring their teeth. It was a good opportunity to take them out for a walk. I put on their leashes and we started up the street, toward the hill. A little before we reached the barrier that gives access to vehicles going up the hill, I saw the bum again. He was sitting under a tree and smoking a cigarette. The Borsalino hat on his head had a broken brim. A tabby cat with a blotched ochre coat was prowling around him, but when the cat spotted Charly and Arthur, it sprang behind some bushes.

"Good evening," I said, greeting him as I got close.

"Good evening," he replied, without looking at me. His voice was hoarse, and something arrogant in his tone revealed his bourgeois origins.

Ever since I'd first seen him prowling around our neighborhood, I'd tried to imagine how a man who must have known better days had wound up living on the street. Alcohol, drugs, some kind of psychotic break, abandonment. Despite his destitution, he maintained a haughty attitude, as if he was proud of having detached himself from worldly cares in order to live his life as he saw fit. I stood still in front of him. Charly and Arthur, quiet and expectant, sat down beside me. I longed to broach the subject that was bothering me, but I didn't know how to go about it. In the end, he was the one who broke the silence.

"How's the lady?" he asked, still without looking at me.

"Are you referring to Vera Sigall?" I asked. He assented with a nod, simultaneously extracting a pouch of tobacco and some rolling papers from one of the pockets of his threadbare overcoat. The sour odor he gave off reached me in waves.

"Who else?" he replied.

There was a power relationship in this whole scene that made me uncomfortable. There he was, sprawled against a tree on the sidewalk, and there was I, standing with the two dogs at my side, securely leashed and looking down on him. I could have sat down beside him, but I immediately saw how false that particular gesture would seem, and so I opted to remain where I was. The disparity of perspectives didn't seem to bother him any. In fact, despite his position, which was inferior in every way, it was the vagrant who directed the course of our conversation. He wielded a power over me, the power of one who has nothing to lose. Without looking at me, he calmly started to roll himself a cigarette.

"She's in a state that the doctors call 'locked-in syndrome.' It's as if she were in a coma, but she's not," I explained. It was hard for me to talk about you in those terms, all the more so to a stranger.

"It's been three months," he said, after lighting the cigarette he'd just rolled with the stub of the one that had been in his mouth. He raised his head, and I saw his dun-colored eyes, which seemed immobile, his chapped lips, his awful teeth.

"Three months," I repeated. I had the impression that much more time had passed since that August morning. While we'd been awaiting your return, things had changed. My marriage had fallen apart; I was ready to launch the project we'd talked about so often; and Emilia had appeared.

"She was a great lady," said the vagrant, shaking his head from side to side. "She used to give me books. I've got one with me. I lost the rest," he added, reaching into a decrepit bag and taking out a copy of *Un año* by Juan Emar.

He gazed at the cover of the book for a while, puffing on his cigarette with a sardonic smile on his face, and then put the volume back in the bag. He did everything slowly, as if time had another dimension in his impoverished universe.

"I don't know if you've had an opportunity to talk with the police," I said, and my words sounded absurd to me. A man like him didn't have the "opportunity" to do anything at all; life happened to him, and he had no alternative but to face up to it.

"With the bald detective?"

"The very same," I said with a smile.

After a long silence, he replied, "He wanted to know if I saw anything."

"And?"

"My memory's not too good," he observed, taking another drag on his cigarette.

"That morning you and I ran into each other in the Costanera. You remember?" I asked cautiously.

"We did? I don't remember," he answered indifferently.

I had a feeling he was lying. My muscles tightened. Charly and Arthur sensed my tension and got up from their places, groaning and shaking themselves.

"Stay calm," I said, pulling hard on their leashes.

The bum didn't bat an eye, as if he was certain that, in the final analysis, nothing and no one could do him harm. Or that the harm already done was so great, it didn't matter what happened next. He took off his hat and with one hand threw back some long, thin locks of his gray hair.

I needed to keep the conversation going. "So what did you tell him, then?"

"Nothing much. We talked about what I do every day, my routine, so to speak."

"I see. I'm glad the police haven't been picking on you."

"What do you mean?"

"I don't know, they always have a tendency to imagine things," I pointed out, and my voice, despite my efforts to sound casual, had an inquisitive tone.

"Now that I think about it...," he muttered between his teeth, and stopped. He threw his cigarette butt on the ground and crushed it out with his shoe. He was wearing fingerless gloves, but even so, he was good with his hands.

"Did you say something?" I asked, with badly dissembled curiosity.

"Nothing important."

Then the man shut up and spoke no more.

"But you said something," I insisted.

"Your wife. The lady that's on TV."

"What about her?" I demanded impatiently.

"She went into Mrs. Sigall's house that morning."

My whole body tensed up.

"Are you sure?" My words came out like shotgun pellets.

"I slept on the sidewalk across the street, but then I went away. A friend had tipped me off to a place where they were giving out soup."

"So your memory's not so bad, after all."

"Not when it comes to food and the temperature. Those are things I remember."

"And my wife?" I asked, returning to the charge.

"Nothing else. What I told you. Your wife went into the lady's house."

"Are you sure it was her?"

He looked at me with an expression of mingled irony and rebuke, as if he thought I was making fun of him.

"Well, how long was she there? Did you hear anything?" In spite of my efforts to appear calm, my voice must have sounded desperate. I was dying to ask him if he'd told the detective about Gracia, but that was a way of giving the matter even greater importance. I thought about giving him money, but when I put my hand in my pocket to do so, I realized that it could look like a kind of blackmail to ensure his silence. He must have been aware that what he'd told me about Gracia entering your house that morning was serious enough to get me agitated. There was no point in my trying to hide it.

"I don't know. Like I said, I went off."

Charly and Arthur had started to get restless again. The man remained impassive.

"Did you talk to the detective about this?" I asked, unable to restrain myself.

"It's none of his business."

"But what about you? What do you think?" I felt like a child looking for an adult who could assure him that the earth was round and he wasn't going to fall off of it.

The man gave me a sidelong glance and smiled ironically, displaying his mistreated teeth. "What I think isn't important. What's important is what you think." He wiped his mouth on his overcoat sleeve and looked across the street. He considered our conversation over.

I was left with no alternative but to take my leave of him and continue on my walk. I looked back and saw him digging in his bag with the same calm indifference he'd brought to our little chat. He was back in his world.

I made a little tour of the neighborhood with Charly and Arthur. The vagrant's information had left me perplexed and confounded. I wondered if all investigations suffered the same fate as my own, if at some point in the search the investigator always realizes that he's been conducting an inquiry into himself and his story and his place in the world. Like Oedipus, who after seeking his father Laius's murderer in every corner of his kingdom returns to the initial site, to the starting point, to himself. What appeared before my eyes wasn't you, but the receptacle Gracia and I had thrown our trash into, day after day.

I quickened my pace. It was the hour when the depths of the sky turn dark again and the low-lying evening sun lights up walls and facades. I gave Charly and Arthur some water and went back home. As soon as I entered, I knew that Gracia was there. I remembered that she was going to Lima that evening to do a news story. She was surely upstairs, packing her suitcase. I went up close to the landing and told her I'd fix us a light supper.

"That won't be necessary. I'll eat on the plane," she said.

I went into the kitchen and made myself some tea. I didn't want to go upstairs and have to look her in the eye.

I was afraid of what I might find. Then I went back to my desk and, out of pure inertia, turned on the computer.

After a while, Gracia appeared in my doorway. She wore a sand-colored dress, simply and elegantly tailored, high heels, and a gray overcoat. She was looking at me with the restrained, distant expression I knew well, the same one she showed the TV cameras, the one she'd been displaying, more and more often, to me. A kind of disguise that hid her true nature.

"After I do the story, I'm going to stay with some friends in Lima. I'll be at their house until Tuesday. I asked for a few days off—I'm really tired." She sighed, transferring her weight from one foot to the other.

"Will you sit down for a minute?"

It was imperative that I ask her about her visit to you. If she'd seen or sensed any particular detail that might have foreshadowed what was to happen later, I needed to know what it was, and I needed to hear her repeat to me the words you and she exchanged. The urgency I felt to know those things was almost painful. Maybe Gracia held the keys to clarifying the mystery. She looked at her wristwatch, and her hair fell over her face.

"The taxi's already outside."

She faced me a fraction of a second longer, the suitcase at her feet, her arms and legs crossed. *Go on, say it, say it, ask her!* I was paralyzed in body and mind, and nothing at all issued from my mouth. It was too late. Why was I defeated in advance? Was I possibly afraid of being confronted with something I didn't want to see? Or was I afraid the truth would destroy us definitively? Talking about her visit to your house meant opening the sluice gates and letting the "Teresa matter" come flooding in.

"Well, then, good-bye and good luck." I took a sip from my teacup, looking at her raised eyebrows, her tense lips, her ironic half smile. This unpleasant expression, which she assumed deliberately, communicated both resentment and indifference.

"Ciao, Daniel," she said, and she was off.

I heard the echo of her heels and then the front door closing.

I got up. My legs were heavy. I felt sorry for her, for us. Beneath the armor of her meticulous appearance, I saw that she was trapped, the same as me. There was no going back. Gracia had entered your house, and the fact that she hadn't mentioned her visit was of a piece with her earlier betrayal.

I'd reached a point where it was impossible for me to go in any direction at all. A dead end. I should have expected something would happen. You had taught me that: when you wait patiently, soon something moves in the darkness.

33.
EMILIA

I woke up with my hands pressed between my legs.

My nightshirt was pulled up around my waist. I released my hands and with my fingers brushed the inside of my thighs. I was surprised at how smooth and soft they were. How warm. I turned over on one side and squeezed my legs together. The air was dense and mild, as if an invisible sludge had filled the room. I moved my pelvis forward, then back, while at the same time pressing my legs together harder. The friction of the sheets kindled my senses.

I could hear my agitated breathing.

I felt myself swallowed up by a whirlpool that began at the base of my spine and spread out in concentric waves. It shook my stomach, my spinal cord, my shoulders, my fingertips. And then it disappeared.

I heard my heart pounding in the darkness. I rolled onto my back and lay still in the bed. My whole being was suspended, expectant.

I wanted to continue. But the back-and-forth movement of my hips and the pressure of my thighs weren't enough to reproduce the short-lived spasm that had taken me by storm, and that I wasn't capable of giving up.

But I didn't know how to get there again.

Beyond my window, seamless darkness dominated the night. I got up and turned on the lamp. Its light bathed the disordered sheets, the books on the floor, the faded flowers on the walls. The room had become a world with only two dimensions. The mirror above the desk observed me curiously. I unbuttoned my nightshirt and saw the reflection of my smooth belly. My navel, my pelvis, my hips, and my little breasts. I stayed where I was, unmoving, enjoying my body's obstinate, defiant presence. I tilted my head back and felt a slight dizziness. A breeze slipped in through the badly closed window. In the mirror, my skin had started to gleam. A light had come on under its surface. I contemplated my round face, the thick eyebrows that seemed to cut it in two, and I closed my eyelids to imagine high cheekbones emerging from that insipid roundness, and naughty lips uttering provocative words. I thought about Daniel. I imagined him gazing at the light shining from my body. His face, which I only then realized I'd never looked at long and hard, was an abstraction containing, at that moment, all possibilities.

The idea of his presence, crouched on the other side of the darkness, aroused my senses again. Before his eyes, now, I grasped my rosy breasts and squeezed them, making my nipples harden. I sat on the edge of the bed and closed my eyes. I was entirely present, yet interconnected with the devious smiles of the streetwalkers, with hands clasping each other, with the clocks whose perpetual ticking marked out the passage of time, with Daniel, watching me from the shadows. I turned off the light and stretched out at full length on the bed. "You have nothing to fear," I whispered. "Nothing to fear." I pulled up my knees and spread my legs apart. I reached out a hand. I was wet. I gently moved my fingers around and then raised them to my nose. A penetrating smell. I touched myself again. Everything was there. My middle finger, moving. The waves, surging up and then receding. I ran my hand over my stomach. It was covered with sweat. The heat it gave off enveloped my fingers, my palm. In the darkness, everything lacked shape and purpose. There was no more speech, no more sense. My breasts swelled, my body throbbed. I touched myself again, with a rhythmic movement, deep and intense. I imagined Daniel, a prisoner of the darkness, longing to participate in my rite. I needed to reach the place where I'd never been before, but which I could perceive with ever-increasing clarity. It was like remembering something I'd never experienced.

I accelerated the rhythm of my fingers. I spread my legs wider and raised my hips. A little protuberance had grown while I touched it, and it seemed to set off the spasms. The current became so powerful that I felt like crying. There was no turning back. I was there, all there, and sounds I'd never heard before were coming out of my mouth. The wave swept through my body, throwing it into convulsions. I no longer knew where or who I was. One spasm after another. And then a final, single spasm that split me open.

The subsiding urgency and the warm liquid running down my legs left my body exhausted.

My tears welled up slowly. They mingled with my perspiration. I got between the sheets. A great calmness came over me, as if my body had fallen asleep in its innermost cavities. I closed my eyes.

I woke up, shaken by a dream.

A young eagle flies over a swimming pool where a woman's naked body is floating; scorched grass, and hills gazing down drowsily; horrible stillness; children with shaved heads, barefoot children, children ghoulishly eyeing the corpse; and far-off sirens, filling the air with their tragic prophecy.

I got up abruptly, the image of the dead woman still sticking to my eyes. I went out onto the roof. Dawn was breaking. A few stars remained in the sky. My body felt weightless, like the body of a stranger. How had my body been transported from the known and familiar world to that ferocious, magical trance? That was how I'd imagined the sexual act: an attack of dementia, a savage, defiant irruption into a world where silence once had reigned. The cold and familiar silence I'd inhabited for so long.

34 · HORACIO

Pérez's chauffeur usually dropped Julián off at our apartment before six o'clock on Sunday evenings. But on that February day, it was already eight, and the boy still wasn't home. Vera had a ruined cake waiting for him, the kind she used to make when she was running out of energy and inspiration.

"We have to call up and find out what's going on," I said.

I made this point insistently several more times, but Vera, who was on her feet and leaning against the wall that faced the door, kept answering, without much conviction, "He'll be here."

She was smoking one cigarette after another. She'd taken the ashtray and placed it on the floor beside her. With her eyes fastened on the door, she kept flicking off her ashes, which fell everywhere but the ashtray. At eight-thirty, she poured herself some whiskey. She took a long swig, coughed, and wiped her mouth on her shirtsleeve. Not long afterward, she poured herself another. Before long she was going around in circles, moving things from one location to another. Eventually, she dropped onto the couch, exhausted. I poured myself some whiskey too. I found Vera's desperation unbearable. We drank in silence, absorbed in an exasperating wait for something we knew wasn't going to happen.

"You can't let him do this to you, Vera."

"Well, what I did to him wasn't so admirable, either," she replied.

"That's different."

"What's different about it? I hurt him, he's hurting me."

"But he can't involve Julián."

"He can do whatever he feels like doing."

It was our first quarrel, a cruel quarrel, in which each of us tried to wound the other.

Vera accused me of being self-centered. She said that her whole life revolved around mine, around my aspirations, my needs, my moods, and as a result she'd turned into a frustrated, bored woman. She was shouting, her voice shrill and disagreeable. When my turn came, I reproached her for the difficulties I was having in supporting her and her son. The alcohol set our nerves on edge, and we said hurtful things. The argument went on past midnight.

I woke up in a sweat, gasping for air. I went into the bedroom. Vera was asleep on the bed, lying on top of the comforter. I embraced her. I kissed her sleeping eyes, her mouth, her hair, and we awaited the dawn in each other's arms. While we were waiting, I thought about the enormous potential for destruction that adversity has. Love abides in the lovers' ability to resist that potential together.

Just before dawn, we opened the window curtains. The streetlights were withdrawing into themselves before the approaching sun. At seven o'clock, Vera called Pérez. The maid answered, a woman Vera didn't know. She told Vera that Mr. Pérez was sleeping. So was the boy. We called dozens of times during the course of the day, and the maid answered every time. Mr. Pérez and his son had just gone out, they were having lunch, they were napping, they couldn't, they weren't, no and no, until Vera lost patience and started yelling at her. By the time they hung up, Vera was shaking and weeping. She lay down on the bed, covered herself with the comforter, and didn't leave the room again. At intervals I went in to her and asked her to eat something, to drink something, to look at me, but it was no use.

It pained me to leave her in that defenseless state, but I had no alternative. I proposed that, after I got home from work, we should go to Pérez's house together, the house that had been hers until a few months ago, but she rejected the idea. She told me she'd be all right; she even got up, made herself some tea and toast, and sat down at the table in her silk robe to have breakfast. Her mouth had hardly any color. Her features had become sharper. Her skin looked as though it were covered with cracked paint. There's nothing at all beautiful or grand about sorrow. It's a mean, evil beast that distorts and ruins everything.

After shutting the door and leaving Vera behind, I wondered how I'd gotten to where I found myself. Was this what real life was like? Until then, I had—in spite of my travels and my various romances—always remained in the same place. A place I knew well, a place whose timeworn and familiar borders had put me to sleep. While I walked on the street, I looked at the faces of the other men who were hurrying to work. Had any of them had the opportunity to sit down and examine his life, he would have chosen never to move beyond the zones he considered safe and comfortable.

But I was already on the other side.

Pérez had decided that Julián would live in his house when school began. Vera and Pérez had one telephone conversation, and he was implacable. His mind was made up, and there was no possibility of Vera's standing in his way. If she tried it, he would accuse her in court of desertion. Two days a week after Julián's classes, and every other weekend, Sergio, the chauffeur, brought him to our apartment. The whole situation—roles, schedules—had been reversed. Vera sank into a sadness that was broken only on the occasions when Julián was visiting, or when we both got drunk, which happened more and more frequently. Without Julián to accompany her, she went on far fewer walks. She barely left the apartment. I urged her to see her women friends, but the world she and Pérez had shared was closed to her now. Vera was twenty-two when she married him, and all her friendships—except for a woman she'd known since they were schoolgirls together—gravitated around Pérez. More than once, I found her sitting in the dark, her long, slender body sprawled on the sofa in the living room. When I saw her, I couldn't help feeling desire for her, but there was no way that our bodies were going to come together and even less that we'd talk about it. She seemed wholly absorbed by a secret and malignant plan. Often I'd go to a café or bar after work and write for a while before going home. The idea of facing her discouragement irritated me more and more. However—and this was the sad paradox—all these ups and downs had unleashed a flood of new poems, more precise, more accomplished than any I'd ever written before. In three weeks, I had enough new work to add to the poems Vera and I had selected earlier, and I was finally ready to send them off to *SUR*. I asked Vera to come with me to the post office, just to get her out of the apartment. She put on an aqua-colored dress with mid-length sleeves, she stepped into high heels, she threw a white stole around her neck, and we went out. Her bloom and her beauty, which had dazzled me since the first time she came into my sight, returned to her as naturally as to a young animal in early spring, when it leaves the refuge where it spent the winter. Once again, I felt a mixture of pleasure and excitement at the way both men and women looked at Vera as she passed. She was aware of the impression she made and not at all indifferent to it. On the contrary, those stares seemed to invigorate her. That night we had an amorous encounter the likes of which we hadn't known for a long while.

Vera started getting up at the same time I did, and when I returned in the evening, I'd find her writing. As soon as

I came through the door, she'd hide the pages that had kept her so busy, and then she'd refuse to talk about them.

On the days when Julián was there, I'd try to get home early, and we'd have dinner before Sergio came to pick him up.

In the course of one of those dinners, Julián told us that on his second visit to the observatory up on Cerro Calán, he'd met a girl. He knew neither her name nor how old she was; he spurned questions on such matters, which paled before the immense fact of what he felt for her.

"Anyway, I'll be ten this year," he said, while out on the street the impatient Sergio blew his horn again.

In the following weeks, Julián talked about nothing but that girl and the stars. Her name was Augustine, she was French, and she worked in the observatory. She had to be at least twenty-five.

Once Julián's new situation had become the norm and Vera's depression was for the most part in the past, we settled into a routine of everyday life made up of little things about which we rarely agreed. Vera was accustomed to having servants and incapable of resolving the simplest domestic situations. She spent most of her time reading or working on her enigmatic stories, while her clothes and other things were scattered everywhere, waiting for someone to pick them up and put them where they belonged. For her part, she accused me of being obsessive and maniacal, and above all of not allowing her to make my apartment into her real home. Harassed by my insistence on tidiness and order, she felt like a stranger there.

The daily quarrels began to reveal to each of us aspects of the other that tended to cancel out the bedazzlement we'd felt in the beginning.

Nearly a month had passed since I'd sent my poems to *SUR*, but I'd received no reply. Every day when I woke up, I would hustle down the stairs in my building to get the mail, and every day I'd go back upstairs empty-handed. I couldn't stand for Vera to ask me questions about that. Nor could I bear her optimism, which was so categorical it came to sound artificial.

I was filled with doubts: about my poetic talent, about my vocation, and as a consequence, about the meaning of everything. My frustration grew, and I made Vera feel its weight.

One night, while we were sitting at the table, listening to the girls laughing in the nightclub down the street, I discovered that I didn't have very much to talk about with Vera. It had been at precisely those moments, when the day was ending and we were having a glass of wine, that our conversations had been the most animated.

"Did you go out today?" I inquired.

And as I was asking the question, I realized that there was in my voice a note of impatience, even of resentment. I remembered our two trips and those six nights together. The desire, the longing to enter the other's head and heart, the curiosity, the long walks when we never stopped talking or asking each other questions, the passionate surrender, the falling asleep in exhaustion, and the waking up with the same avidity, the same boundless interest in the other. Perhaps things had to be this way. That intensity was exclusively attached to beginnings, and all beginnings were fated, by their very nature, to be left behind. All at once, I understood people who are always starting over, looking for that exultant energy that comes from the prospect of a new love.

The mere fact of harboring such sentiments made me feel guilty. I had deprived Vera of her former life, of the security that Pérez could give her, I had separated her from Julián, and now I was yearning for the absurd, for the impossible. But perhaps what tortured me most was the idea that Vera probably thought the same thing, and that her recent depression had resulted not only from Julián's absence, but also from dark musings like my own.

35·
DANIEL

Our dinner was a week away, and we still had an infinite number of details to take care of. Emilia was enjoying organizing the whole thing with her new cell phone. Her neighbors had offered to help us. One of them was a lawyer and the other a painter. They often gave big dinner parties in their vast apartment, and they had no end of contacts that turned out to be useful to us. During our meetings in the hospital, Emilia and I exchanged information and resolved pending matters while you, from deep in your sleep, gave us your approval. As she talked to me about this or that, I would look hard at her, and then I'd shift my eyes to you. At which point Emilia would say, "Hey, you're not listening!" And I'd just smile, unable to explain my feelings to her. But day after day, a new clarity was coming into her eyes. The wind that bent her in half before was now blowing in her favor.

On one of those afternoons, as we were leaving the hospital, I suggested that we pay a visit to your house. I'd considered the idea previously, but I didn't get around to extending the invitation until after Gracia left for Lima.

Emilia was already on her bicycle when I made her my proposition. She took one foot off the pedal, and with both hands on the handlebars, she said, "There's nothing in the world I want more than that."

She spoke without theatricality. She was wearing a knee-length checked skirt and one of her white shirts. We walked along, Emilia pushing her bicycle and me at her side. It was a Friday, in the late afternoon. The drivers, immobilized in endless lines, were honking their horns impatiently, and yet, as we walked, we found ourselves on our own island.

When we got to your house, Arthur and Charly came out to meet us. They jumped and spun around, knocking each other down, all excited. After asking me their names, Emilia squatted down on her heels and called them. Both dogs ran to her, and when they were in front of her, with their long pink tongues dangling from their mouths, she stroked their necks and spoke to them in French, which the dogs seemed delighted to hear.

"I had a dog. Its name was Étoile. And yes, I know what you're thinking. I love dogs. Étoile used to sleep at my feet."

Followed by Arthur and Charly, we went around the house to your study. The bright green ferns had grown during the winter. When spring came, the corners were overgrown with poppies and marigolds, reviving the landscape you used to wait for all winter long.

"It's gorgeous," Emilia said admiringly.

I opened the door and invited her in. I'd talked with María, and she'd agreed to keep coming to clean the house once a week. When I opened the curtains, the evening light fell on your desk. Emilia remained standing for a good while, her arms hanging at her sides, her nearly flat chest rising and falling under her shirt. I noticed that she was staring at the photograph of you defying the camera lens and dancing the twist.

"Don't expect me to talk much, Daniel," Emilia said. "I think putting words to moments like this is like sticking a pin in a butterfly."

"I don't expect anything, Emilia. Seriously. Would you like a cup of tea?"

"Don't you have something stronger?" As she spoke these words, she seemed to regret them.

I smiled and said, "Of course. Wait here. I'll go over to my house and be back in a couple of minutes."

I'd pointed out my house from the sidewalk, and Emilia had gazed at it with that attention all her own, focusing all her senses. She asked me no questions. My marriage was a subject we didn't discuss. Even though I trusted Emilia's judgment, talking to her about our problems would have meant giving them a definite form, and it would have been tantamount to entering the territory of decision making, for which I was not yet prepared. Moreover, mentioning Gracia would let reality, with its cold halo, into the space that Emilia and I had constructed, and which was still too fragile to resist it.

Soon I returned with a bottle of champagne, two glasses, slices of toasted bread and Serrano ham, and *queso fresco* with oregano and olive oil.

We stood in front of your photo and drank a toast to your health. To ours too. I sat in the armchair while Emilia, her glass in her hand, went around looking attentively at everything, lingering over some details, such as the collection of postcards you've pinned to a wall, or your mugs from *Libération* and the Writers Guild of America, placed against the window and filled with pencils. But what most attracted her attention were the little paper figures, each one in its marked wooden box, the tree ornaments you and your son Julián had made one Christmas in the remote past, and which—like so many other things—you didn't like to talk about.

While she moved around, I observed her. Emilia's beauty wasn't obvious, but once you discovered it, you couldn't stop appreciating it. Her long neck, her delicate bones, her so white skin, and above all, the smoothness of her every movement, as if her body were immersed in some kind of liquid. She probably noticed I was looking at her, but she bore my scrutiny stoically. What was it in her that so fascinated me? Her never having been touched distinguished her from the rest in a mysterious way. There was also the suffering that she carried around inside her. She looked at me and smiled. Her face took on the appearance of a sunflower. After a few minutes, however, she retreated back into herself, wrapped up in her own arms. The light that was opening her up had quickly gone out. She gulped down the rest of her champagne and held out her glass for more. I filled it, and she, without looking at me, went back to her researches. I felt an urge to laugh at the daring and determined way she'd taken to drinking, like a woman of the world. She moved back and forth. That smile was one of her gifts, but then her gaze would stray to something, and she'd fall into one of her characteristic states of total absorption.

"They're in alphabetical order," she observed, staring attentively at your library.

I turned on your desk lamp. Its golden light filtered the air.

"Can I take one out and look at it?" She passed a finger over the spine of one of your books.

"Of course," I said.

She pulled out the volume she'd spotted and sat in the red metal chair where you usually piled up the books you were through with. They'd lie there for a while, waiting to be returned to their place on the shelves.

"It's a collection of stories," she said, barely raising her eyes from the page. "I didn't know about this edition. It was printed in Buenos Aires by a publishing house that had a very brief life. There are a couple of stories in here I've never seen. And I thought I knew her complete works!" She perused the book for a good while, and then she handed it to me. Her eyes were glistening.

It was a small hardcover volume bound in sand-colored linen. Your name and the title, *The Slow Grace of Cats or Plants*, were printed on the cover in maroon letters. In a square, in bas-relief, there was an engraving by Wifredo Lam, from his series *Fata Morgana*, the one showing a woman in profile, her torso nude, her hair caught up in a constellation of stars.

"It's valuable," I said. "It could be useful for your thesis."

"My thesis has hit a wall. Do you remember what I told you about Horacio Infante?"

"Of course."

"A few days ago I got an email from him, responding to the many I've sent his way. He says he's writing a letter in which he'll explain 'everything' to me, and soon he'll be in a position to send it. I'm dying of curiosity to know what he has to say. What do you think that 'everything' can mean?" Without waiting for my answer she went on: "I've continued my researches. The most interesting thing is that several of Vera's allusions to Infante's poems were actually made before he published them. You get it? That means that Infante was quoting from Vera's work too. There's something in this, Daniel, I'm sure of it. Something that can change the whole story. Vera's story *and* Infante's story—I know it, I know it." She held out her glass for me to fill once again.

"You haven't eaten anything, Emilia."

"Listen, Daniel," she said, ignoring my words. She drank half the contents of her glass in one gulp and then clicked her tongue in annoyance.

"What?" I said. I noticed that alcohol and lack of solid food were starting to have an effect on her. Her cheeks were aflame. She made several passes with the palm of her hand over her nose, rubbing it red.

"Do you still think that someone or something caused Vera's fall?"

"Absolutely."

I was tempted to tell her about my conversation with the hobo. In anybody's eyes, the information that Gracia might have entered your house made her the prime suspect. But was she, really? What passed between you that morning? Those were questions that came back to me again and again. But I didn't say anything. Maybe I never would.

"All right, it so happens that a few days ago, I remembered, clearly, the conversation I'd heard between Vera and Horacio at that luncheon," Emilia said, interrupting my meditations.

"I'm listening."

"Horacio told her she was putting him in a difficult position. I don't remember her answer, but I know Horacio reacted to it by striking his palm with his fist. That I remember well. I swear, there was violence in his gesture, Daniel. Today it doesn't seem to me to be absolutely impossible that he paid her a visit, as he had in fact announced that he would. I'm not saying he pushed her, no. But something might have happened between them, something that upset Vera and made her fall." Emilia's face took on the expression of a little girl pleased with herself. "They had unfinished business to settle. They hadn't been able to talk about it at the luncheon, which is why Horacio insisted on seeing her before he left Santiago. What do you think?"

"Well, at least it doesn't sound totally out of the question," I said, while trying to make all the pieces fit. "But Infante wasn't in Chile when it happened, and the evidence isn't convincing enough to persuade the police to question him."

"I'll write to Infante again," she said. She thought for a minute, got up, took a few turns around the study, and then fixed her eyes on the piles of paper littering your desk. "What did you say was the name of the psychiatrist Vera met in a café the week before her fall?"

"Calderón. Álvaro Calderón. Why?"

"Here's an article by him," Emilia remarked, brandishing about ten pages held together by a paper clip. On the cover page I read, *Three Women in Tres Álamos* by Álvaro Calderón.

Emilia looked over the pages for a few minutes. Then she said, "Vera was there. In that prison camp."

"Not possible."

"It's on the first page: "Tania Calderón, Cecilia Usón, and Vera Sigall were arrested in a police raid on the night of August 5, 1975, together with forty professors from the University of Chile."

"She never mentioned that to me," I said, shaken; then, in a whisper, I added, "Not that I ever asked her about what she'd done under the dictatorship." I felt a sudden rush of sadness and guilt for not having investigated your life more thoroughly.

I'd often had an urge to do just that, but you didn't like talking about yourself. We shared the days as if the time for the big questions was always ahead of us. In a future that, all at once, vanished.

Emilia sat next to me on the couch, and we started to read the article. It was an exhaustive account of what happened on the night of the raid and during the two weeks that followed it in the Tres Álamos detention center, where eight women shared four bunks in a single room. Of the three women who were arrested that night, only you came out alive. Cecilia Usón's fate was uncertain; the last person who offered information about her claimed to have seen her being taken away, handcuffed and blindfolded, to some other site. Tania Calderón was Álvaro's aunt. She died as a consequence of the torture she'd been subjected to. You and she slept in the same bunk. Tania was a philology professor, and the two of you became friends. Except for you, all the women who survived the camp testified to what had happened during those weeks. The reasons for your detention did not appear in Álvaro Calderón's account.

We finished reading it and then remained silent for a long time.

"Vera talks a lot about memory in her writing," Emilia said. "She always refers to it as something her characters try to escape from. And can't. She's even got a story called 'The Cell.' It's the cell her character, Gina, is a captive in—the cell of memories."

"The man wanted Vera to talk to him about Tania Calderón. He wanted to hear about the nights when they shared the same bunk."

"And Vera didn't want to remember. Or couldn't. It was too painful for her."

Emilia got up from the couch, took a few steps over to the window, and stood there looking out. It was getting dark in the garden. The dogs lay unmoving on the lawn, looking like stone statues. The evening had turned a steely blue, like an aquarium in which we were floating, each on our own waves.

Without turning around, Emilia asked me, "Daniel, do you think you ever really got to know her?"

"I'm not sure. There are so many secrets, so many hidden areas."

"In one of her stories she talks about a pair of sisters, Siamese twins. One of them tells the story during a night of insomnia, while her twin lies sleeping next to her, their heads close together. At some point the idea of killing her sister crosses the narrator's mind. The idea of getting rid of the other being who lives in her body, knowing that if she does so, she'll die with her."

"You think this story has some connection to Tania Calderón?"

"They slept in the same bed. Tania died. She was murdered. Something inside Vera must have died with Tania, but at the same time that death remained a part of her, attached like a Siamese twin's head," Emilia said. Her voice was breaking.

"My God!" I saw you lying in your hospital bed, and I felt an unspeakable sadness. "She's so alone. So alone," I said, and I couldn't go on talking.

Emilia put out her hand and touched my face. She laid her palm against my cheek, maybe measuring the degree of heat it could transfer to her hand. *Human warmth*, I said to myself. Something she was barely acquainted with.

"Can you put your arms around me?" she murmured, without moving.

Her limbs were stiff and cold, her eyes open and staring, like the eyes of a porcelain doll. Her resistance was so great that I had a hard time adapting my body to hers and making us fit comfortably together. She shut her eyes tight, she pursed her lips, and her breathing became agitated. I could sense her increasing rigidity. I was afraid for her, afraid of the effect such an immense effort might have on her nervous system. There was something heroic in that titanic performance, and her heroism rubbed off on me. Suddenly, she began to tremble. Convulsions rocked her.

"Don't let me go," she begged.

Emilia pressed one of her temples with the tip of her index finger, as if she were trying to adjust something inside her head. Her eyelashes whisked the air as they closed over her eyes. Little by little, her body was growing warmer. She lay in my arms, exhausted and unmoving. Outside the dogs were barking, exchanging some of their standard woofs of mutual acknowledgment.

"Where is she, Daniel? Where? Where is she?"

36.
EMILIA

I woke up in total confusion. Only after several seconds had passed did I remember that it had got too late the night before for me to go home on my bicycle, and Daniel had suggested I sleep in his studio. I also remembered his embrace, my convulsions, and the detonation in my brain. Followed by a great calm.

I got up furtively and dressed. There were piles of papers, receipts, and books on Daniel's desk. I also spotted a lettering guide template, an instrument used by the architects of olden days, and when I was a little girl by my father as well, in his drawings of constellations. The walls were covered with paintings, architectural drawings, and photographs. A black stone the size of the palm of my hand caught my attention. On the surface of the stone, drawn with silver threads, there were concentric circles that resembled a spiral. It was smooth and glossy. It was cold.

There was a shelf with photographs of Gracia. She was a magnificent woman. The look in her eyes, however, was uncommonly severe. Also the determination on her face. A hint of irony offered a glimpse of her intelligence.

I grabbed my bag and went out into the hall. Bookshelves covered one wall from floor to ceiling, while modern artworks hung on the opposite wall. I was curious about the rest of the house. But I walked to the front door and stepped outside. I was afraid the life Daniel lived with his wife would hurt me.

I found my bicycle propped up against a stone bench in the garden. I inhaled the sweetness of the Spanish jasmines and of the irrigated grass, which was beginning to impregnate everything.

I got on my bicycle and pedaled downhill. I needed to drive off my confusion, to find some minimum clarity that could calm me down.

When I was at the door of my building, the cell phone in my bag began to ring.

It was Daniel's voice: "I had thought we might have breakfast together."

I said nothing.

"Are you there?"

"Yes, yes. I'm sure you would have fixed me a delicious breakfast."

"That was my plan."

I fell silent again, and then he said, "It was incredible that you let me put my arms around you."

"Don't say anything more, Daniel."

"I know. Butterflies, pins. Do you have enough food to

make yourself a good breakfast? You hardly ate anything last night."

"Thanks to you, my refrigerator looks like a supermarket," I said, laughing.

"Then we'll see each other this afternoon. They're putting up the tent today, and I'd like to be there. Are you all right?"

"Of course I am."

In spite of my fears, the idea of seeing him filled me with happiness. I hadn't anticipated that this would happen, but Daniel had taken up residence in my heart. And it didn't hurt. However, I was afraid that—after what had happened—our actions would take on a new range of meanings I wouldn't know how to decipher. I thought about my body, and I could see only its margins, only its outline, like a pencil drawing. I remembered my girlfriends and the way they examined, criticized, and tried to change their shapes. Their bodies were the matter they used to construct their existence. A material they could mold as they wished, training it, adorning it, and even having it trimmed in the operating room. And I thought that unlike the cultures of yesteryear, whose duality consisted in opposing the spirit to the body, my girlfriends' duality—and my own, each in its own way—consisted in opposing our bodies to our existence.

On the roof terrace, the Transatlantic was sailing through the city's blue fog. On the previous day, I'd had the chairs and tables installed, along with the long bar that Daniel had designed and sent off to be built, and which now presided over the center of the space. It was a surprise sure to make him happy, I thought.

When I put the cell phone back in my bag, I noticed it contained the volume of stories I'd found in Vera's library: *The Slow Grace of Cats or Plants*. I felt a kind of hot flash. Daniel must have put the book in my bag. I remembered his embrace again and thought about the extraordinary fact that it had occurred.

I prepared a cup of coffee and two slices of buttered toast and consumed it all in a hurry, standing up in the kitchen. Then I went out to do my produce deliveries. By a lucky chance, there were only two orders that day. When I returned, Don José was rolling himself a cigarette. He fingered his mustache and said, "I'm thinking about giving you a raise, kiddo."

I don't know what had incited his generosity. He also gave me two pots of geraniums and asked his daughter Amparo to help me carry them. We put the geraniums next to the bougainvillea and the jasmines. As soon as she left, I looked through my various collections of Vera Sigall's stories, searching for the one about the Siamese twins. But I didn't have it. It was part of a volume that had often been republished, but which I hadn't brought with me. I remembered the collection Daniel had put in my bag, got it out, and opened it. The first story, which gave the volume its title, was one of her earliest ones, and Vera had won a prize for it. I was curious to read it, maybe because it was about a couple who both work in the same scientific field. Like my parents.

. . .

Gustavo Noriega is a mathematics professor and researcher at the University of Chile. His specialized area is the study of semi-local rings. His wife, Helena Bale, is also a math teacher. She works at a high school. Gustavo and Helena have two children, twelve-year-old Gustavito and ten-year-old Serena, and they live in a quiet part of the Providencia neighborhood. Gustavo is a man "so little inclined to frivolous words that when by accident they appear in his mouth, they get mixed up on his lips." As for Helena, "what he finds most moving about her is the way her left ear, smaller and pinker than the other one, becomes visible after a movement of her head." Gustavo and Helena received their degrees from the university together and were among the best students in their graduating class. Moreover, both of them are outstanding chess players and have won a great many tournaments. They got married because they were tired of having sex on the backseat of Gustavo's Fiat 600. "They like to challenge each other and to resolve equations whose variable can be as abstract or intangible as the sparkle in a piece of glass."

Gustavo's drama is his deep conviction that the world has not done him justice. His professional invisibility weighs on him so heavily it gives him the impression that "Gustavo Noriega doesn't exist. Reality is a purely social construction," he says to himself.

With the goal of gaining recognition, he has invested a large part of his life in resolving sequences of mathematical formulas. After discharging his university-related duties, he shuts himself up for long hours in the attic of his house. "He imagines the numbers and signs coming to life, like the awakening of a great bird that spreads its wings above the banality of the world." The multifarious vicissitudes and obligations of everyday life overwhelm him. They diminish him. Even though the sequences continue to evade his grasp, he knows that eventually they'll provide him with a way out of ordinariness. He goes out and wanders around aimlessly, imagining that from such devotion as his there must arise "a hidden key, the master key that will open the lock of understanding."

One Sunday evening, while his wife and children are in the garden, Gustavo leaves the house to go on one of his customary promenades. He walks down Pedro de Valdivia Avenue, under the oriental plane trees, whose shade calms him. He's worked all day long, and once again he's run into the same wall, the one that separates him from the "elect." But he has no intention of giving in. Surrender is for him a kind of death. The sun's already setting when he returns home, and Helena is preparing dinner "with that solidity all her own, which transports him back to his childhood." He goes up to his attic room and sees the equation at once, written on a sheet of paper lying on his desk. It's just a change of variables, a scratch in his last calculations, and nevertheless, it opens a road that had been off limits to him. He's overcome with a feverish energy. "He feels a silvery, sonorous happiness, which resonates in the silence of his room." That night he doesn't go down to dinner. He returns to the bedroom at dawn. Helena is asleep. When she feels his presence, she moves her body against his. "The future that appears before him devours the past unhappiness, the pettiness, the bad luck."

That Monday Gustavo teaches his class at the university and then returns to his attic. The house is silent. The children and Helena are at their respective schools. Through Gustavo's window, the leaves transmit a cool, uplifting sound. But there's a question that keeps on coming up, a question he's tried to repress.

How did Helena arrive at that equation? How is it possible that she, always preoccupied with the children and the smallest details of their existence, could have had time for a thought process elaborate enough to reach that defining conclusion? At the customary hour, distant sounds announce her arrival home. He pricks up his ears. He hears her going up and down the stairs, performing her domestic chores. In the middle of the afternoon, Gustavo goes down to the kitchen. The children are having their milk and chocolate, while Helena is stuffing laundry into the washing machine. They greet each other with a kiss on the cheek. Helena seems busier than usual. Gustavo can't look her in the eye.

The following week, after he comes home from his Saturday walk, Gustavo goes to his desk and finds a new equation, which once again opens up vistas for him that he's never imagined. That night, when Helena's already asleep, he takes her by the shoulders, turns her toward him, and makes love to her. She gives herself to him as she's never done before. In the course of the following weeks, her messages continue to appear, one after the other. Marginal notes, comments that adjust his direction and put him on the right track. After reading and studying them, Gustavo holds them in his hands for a long time. He longs to toss them in the trash and blot out any trace of the mute brilliance that his wife keeps laying before him, and which, he knows, will change his destiny. But then, unable to replace thought with action, he relegates them to the back of his drawer, among the many other forgotten, useless papers he's been accumulating over the years. Even so, Helena's notes seem to speak to him from their hiding place, and on more than one night, their obstinate presence wakes him with a start, "as if, instead of mere sheets of paper, what he was holding captive in that drawer was a living being that would devour him in the end."

Each note from Helena is followed by wordless sex. In the morning, however, Gustavo is unable to meet his wife's eyes. In the afternoon, he watches her from his window as she steps barefoot into the garden and, while smoking a cigarette, waters the corners the irrigation system can't reach; or he watches her from the corner of his eye while she serves dinner and chats with her children about the events of the day. His feelings about his wife have grown confused. He feels grateful to her, he admires her, but he's also afraid of what she's got hidden inside her head. Her genius has opened up a path for itself, stealthily, "like a panther or a game animal." He's also begun to feel an obsessive desire for his wife, a thirst that won't let him rest and is only barely slaked when they make love.

Two months later, Gustavo Noriega submits the results of his researches to the *Bulletin of the American Mathematical Society* and waits in anguish for a response. He's aware of the significance of what he's done, but accustomed as he is to being disrespected by his colleagues, he finds it difficult to imagine that recognition will finally come his way. One Friday morning, he receives the reply. It's a manila envelope. Helena finds it in the mailbox before going to work.

The recognition is immediate. He must travel as soon as possible to the AMS headquarters in Providence, Rhode Island, to present his research.

Helena and the children accompany him to the airport. They tell him good-bye at the doors of the government migration office. He's bought a new suit that confers an aura of seriousness. The pupils of his eyes now have a steely gleam. His smile is genuine, but it hides a touch of fear, a hint of sadness. He and Helena have never spoken about her equations. He's carrying in his briefcase the pages she's been leaving on his desk over the course of the past two months. "Gustavo is aware that the sham is harmless as long as it remains invisible. But if it comes to light, or if it fails, then all that will remain is the sham itself, in its pathetic nakedness."

The man who's waiting for him in the airport in Providence is at least a head taller than he is. He has the appearance of a dandy, with lively, intelligent eyes, and they welcome Gustavo confidently. He introduces himself as Joe Robinson, and he's none other than the society's president. Before they leave the airport, Gustavo asks him to wait a minute. He goes in the men's restroom, takes the pages out of his briefcase, and dumps them into the toilet.

"He looks at the pieces of paper as they fall, with the slow grace of cats or plants. A whitish layer covers the bottom. He's able to make out some traces of Helena's writing, firm and yet spontaneous, as if they'd been put down on paper with the urgency of a revelation. He pulls the flush chain, runs a finger under his shirt collar, and goes out to where the affable Joe Robinson is waiting for him, holding firmly in his hands the splendid future of the real Gustavo Noriega."

I read the final paragraph in thrall to a strange emotion. Vera, through her protagonist, had revealed the essence of the human soul, and though gazing upon it with contempt and irony, had redeemed it.

37·
HORACIO

Three months after Julián confessed to us his love for the young French woman, the letter I'd been eagerly awaiting for so long—from *SUR*, the literary magazine—arrived in the mail. It was a cold morning in May, the seventeenth, to be precise. I went downstairs, as I did every day, to get the mail. I was no longer feeling the anxiety I'd felt before. Now I was waiting with more restraint, without great expectations, but also without giving up hope. I didn't even bother to open the envelope before I ran back up the stairs.

"Vera, Vera!" I shouted as I entered the apartment door.

Vera had woken up early, practically at dawn, and she was reading, lying on the olive-green couch with a blanket over her feet. A few weeks previously, she'd begun working as a proofreader for the daily newspaper *El Mercurio*, and she'd submerged herself fully in her new job. She didn't want to tell me how she got it, and the idea that it was Pérez who had recommended her wouldn't stop torturing me. I tried to get her to tell me, but she answered me the same way she always did when I was striving to make pieces of her stories fit with concrete facts: "Anecdotes, anecdotes. They aren't important." She said it haughtily, as if in her world, where she lived on the heights of abstraction, such trivialities were an insult, and her tone made me feel wretched and vulgar for grilling her.

She heard my voice and jumped up. Her coppery hair shone in the morning light. The expectations aroused in me by the letter I was holding, even though I didn't know what it contained, made me see Vera in all her beauty and generosity.

"What is it, what's happening?"

I handed her the letter. "Open it," I told her.

"Do you really want me to?" she asked, stroking my cheek with one hand.

"Yes, my love," I assured her, and I kissed her fingers.

"First I'll fix us some coffee." She disappeared into the kitchen with the envelope in her hand. "And meanwhile, you can shave and make yourself handsome."

We sat at the table, and Vera opened the envelope. She was wearing her white silk robe with the blue scallop trim. She'd gathered her hair in a ponytail that displayed her long, smooth neck. She'd set the table with care: the linen placemats I'd bought years before on a trip to the Far East, the embroidered napkins, the doily with blue lozenges covering the basket of toast. It was the first time she'd done anything of the sort. She took the letter out of the envelope and read it in silence. With my hands on my knees, I watched her. Little by little, a smile emerged and lit up her face.

"Come on, let's go, tell me," I begged her impatiently.

"You did it, my love." She reached across the table and handed me the letter. Her fingers grazed mine tenderly.

The letter was written by Victoria Ocampo. In it she told me that my poems exhibited a perfect harmony between expression and substance. She also mentioned the peculiar syntax of the verses and how it made the words acquire new meanings. The poems would appear in the issue of the magazine currently being printed, she announced, and she promised to send me a copy soon. I raised my head. Vera was looking at me with misty eyes.

"You did it, my love," she said again.

She was so emotional that I got up from my chair and embraced her. Vera had accompanied me throughout all my strivings, and the triumph belonged to both of us. The sounds of morning began to reach us from the street.

We lived the following weeks in a state of exaltation but also of serenity. We knew that to be published in that review was to enter the antechamber of a myriad of possibilities. We were floating in a sort of beneficent suspension, in a warm and unambiguous plasma. Victoria Ocampo's letter had given me back my sense of worth, and this made me able to love Vera again. There's nothing more destructive to love than self-contempt.

An event that took me by surprise added to our felicity. *El Mercurio* would soon publish one of Vera's stories. Plucking up her courage, she had walked into the managing editor's office one morning, repressed her fears, and said, "I've written a story. Are you interested in publishing it?"

No doubt intrigued by her beauty, the editor asked her to take a seat. He'd never seen her before, and he wanted to know what area she worked in. Vera described the minor position she held, but even so, the editor agreed to take a look at the text she'd brought. After several minutes, he raised his eyes from the manuscript and said, "Who did you copy this story from?"

"Nobody. It's mine."

"Did you by chance translate it?"

"No," Vera replied.

I can imagine her upright posture, her implacable eyes.

"Then I'm going to publish it."

A few weeks later, he called her into his office. "Your story has caused quite a stir," he told her. "Everyone's been asking me why you're not one of our reporters. This is a man's world, but I have no doubt you've got the guts to stand up to it."

The articles she was assigned to write were mostly of a social nature, and so she seldom did any reporting out in the field. In any case, however, she wrote her pieces with dedication, granting each of them a character all its own. She had a unique way of looking at details that others passed over without noticing. Vera devoted too much time to them, minor as they were, but seeing her so contented was priceless, and it justified her determination. Above all, her new employment, along with entertaining her, provided us with the modicum of financial security we needed. One evening, Vera arrived home loaded down with bags. She'd gone shopping, and she had spent a goodly part of her month's salary on new outfits. From then on, she began to dress in white. She liked to wear a white blouse and skirt with a brown leather belt that emphasized her slender waist. She abandoned her high heels—unnecessary for so tall a woman—and let her hair fall loose to her shoulders. When she went out in the morning, she looked like a young girl ready to live life. I imagined that all this must be just another of her mood shifts, which I'd one way or another grown used to. But even so, in some part of my consciousness I knew that Vera had changed. The times were changing too. And the idea simultaneously excited and disturbed me.

Two months later, returning from the Foreign Ministry one evening, I found an envelope with the *SUR* letterhead in my mailbox. It was a copy of the issue we'd been waiting for, the one that contained my poems. Vera hadn't come home yet. I took a few turns around the apartment, made myself a cup of tea, and after calming down, opened the manila envelope and took out the magazine. There it was, the well-known arrow, pointing south. Between the names of Teilhard de Chardin, who wrote about happiness, and Alberto Girri, who had a piece on sorrow, the cover of the magazine announced my verses, and inside, there was this headline: "Horacio Infante, a new American voice." As soon as I glanced at my work, I realized that something had happened. The poems, spread out over six pages, weren't arranged in the order in which

I'd submitted them. I felt angry. No one had the right to do anything like that without consulting me beforehand. Not even Victoria Ocampo herself. I didn't know that the worst was yet to come.

I started to read. I could recognize the sentences, the words, and their ultimate meaning, but not their spirit. Someone had taken hold of my poetry, broken it down, and then put it back together, breathing into it the breath of another world. I struck the table with my fist, hard enough to sting my knuckles. I read through the poems once again. In many of them, the changes didn't seem very substantial at first. A word or two, the order of a sentence. However, the interventions were radical, and they gave my verses a force they had previously lacked. They transformed them into something superior. I read them again and then again, and with each of those readings, the poems looked stranger to me. Every one of them had cost me months of toil, I knew why and how each word had reached its final position, I knew them as well as I knew my own body. And what was there wasn't mine. I paced around and around my minuscule living room. I hid the magazine in a drawer in my closet and went out. I didn't want Vera to find me there when she came home.

A tepid wind was blowing. I walked to the center of town. By the time I reached the cathedral, it had begun to rain. The streets were empty of pedestrians. I went into a bar on Santo Domingo Street. The place was an elongated room that until a short time before had been a barber shop; I'd had my hair cut there a few times. The traces of its former life (white tiled floor, two barber chairs in the middle of the room) gave the bar an innovative but unconvincing air. A couple of guys were throwing darts at a board. A man stood at the bar, smoking a cigar that gave off a thick, heavy smell. I sat down in front of the bartender and ordered whiskey. What happened after that is part of the routine for any man who's floored by some event in his life and goes to a bar for the purpose of intoxication. It was still raining when I left. I hadn't brought an umbrella. I put on my hat, thrust my hands into the pockets of my raincoat, and proceeded through the deserted streets with my head bowed and a dull heaviness in my brain. Trees and the doors of buildings, streaked by the rain, emerged under every streetlight. It took me several minutes to open the big door downstairs. The time was past midnight. I climbed up the stairs. Inside the apartment I found Vera, still dressed, sleeping on the couch. She was lying face up under the lamp's circle of light. On her lap was the book she must have been reading when she fell asleep. I had a horrible feeling of guilt. I couldn't just leave Vera without warning—she didn't deserve that. The rain was beating, loud and clear, against the windows. I tripped on the shoes Vera had left on the floor and lost my balance. As I tried to regain it, one of my hands knocked over the reading lamp that stood next to the couch. Its glass shade broke into a thousand pieces. Vera awoke with a start. Her erect torso made her look like a sphinx.

"What happened?" she asked.

"The lamp fell over," I said, beginning to pick up the pieces scattered all over the floor. The wind was rattling the windowpanes. "Don't get up. You might step on broken glass."

"Are you drunk?" she asked me.

"No," I answered, still gathering shards.

"What happened?"

"Nothing."

I wasn't capable of speaking to her about the magazine, about the poems, about my feeling that what I was experiencing was impossible, about my longing to awaken from a bad dream. The whole world, including Vera, looked threatening to me now. There was no rational explanation for what had occurred. Someone had adulterated my poems, had twisted their nature and made them better. Someone had violated my privacy. Who? Why? I'd gone over such questions from every possible angle during the previous hours without getting anywhere; but what had indeed been growing—apart from my dismay—while I racked my brain was the certainty of my coming failure. A flash of lightning lit up the window.

All of a sudden, I knew. It was the surrender in her eyes, her imploring expression, her smothered silence. She had her feet pulled up and covered by a blanket, and she was looking at me without blinking. I was still on my feet in front of her, with various pieces of broken glass in one open hand, and for a moment I had an urge to close my fist.

"It was you, right?" I went on talking without waiting for an answer. "Why, Vera? Why did you do that?" I shouted.

Vera covered her upper body with the blanket. Not far away, a thunderclap resounded. "They're your poems, Horacio."

"They are not. And you know it."

"I only edited them. That's the editor's job. Any editor would have done the same. Think about all the changes Pound made to *The Waste Land*, or the work Fitzgerald's editor did on *Tender Is the Night*—he straightened it out! I'm not saying he made all the right decisions, but nobody questioned what he'd done, because that was his job."

"Could you please stop talking?" I yelled.

I turned around, went into the kitchen, and threw the broken glass into the trash can. Never before had I felt the tingling, the energy that was surging into my chest and suffocating me, and which I could assuage only with a blow, or with several blows, or with Vera's pain. I thought about what a fragile border separates men who are decent from those who aren't. Some pieces of glass were stuck in my palm, and thin lines of blood ran over it. It was raining harder than ever, and my faith in the rest of humankind was all used up.

"Horacio." Vera was speaking to me from the kitchen doorway. "It was my secret gift. I thought helping you get what you wanted so much would make you love me more."

We quarreled till dawn. We smoked and paced around the living room. Whenever the discussion appeared to be over and we were about to fall down in exhaustion, the anger would come charging back again. I'd rejoin the battle, repeating the same arguments: she had violated me, she'd taken away the single thing that was most important in my life, she'd destroyed me. The poems that had so dazzled the editors at *SUR*, the ones that had broken the ring of silence surrounding all my previous submissions, the ones that had earned me such an overblown and auspicious headline, the ones that were going to open doors for me and bring me the kind of recognition I couldn't even imagine—those poems weren't mine. I intended to write to Victoria Ocampo and tell her the truth, I said. That was when Vera got up and told me I was wrong, that I shouldn't do such a thing, that if I did I'd ruin everything, I'd ruin us, that those poems were mine, mine, mine.

The rain stopped before dawn. With swollen eyes, Vera went into the bedroom and lay down without closing the door. On the other side of the living room window, a dense fog was erasing everything terrestrial, everything human. My apartment was floating in the midst of a gray world. I experienced a peculiar sensation of weightlessness, as if I had gone out of my body and I was looking down from a great height on a man who barely moved, like a dying person. I fell asleep on the couch and woke up a few hours later, feeling physically battered. Vera was still sleeping. I made myself some strong coffee, sat at the dining room table, and wrote the note I would send that very day to the magazine, explaining what had happened. It was the only bit of dignity remaining to me. I was like a man who falls out of a comfortable blindness into painfully bright light. I put the letter in my briefcase, next to the magazine, and went outside, where the morning hustle and bustle had begun.

38.
DANIEL

On the eve of Gracia's return, I couldn't go to sleep. Until then, I'd managed to ward off the pointy questions stabbing at me.

Worn down by insomnia, I reconstructed what had happened during the past few months, trying to find the backbone that supported those apparently unconnected events. I was convinced that the answer was to be found in the details, in actions or moments that appear irrelevant, and which you used to say life and literature were composed of. The facts were simple. Gracia had seen Teresa and me going into your house that Sunday evening, the day before your fall, and the following morning she, Gracia, had visited you for the first time.

The point was that those events, which can be stated so clearly, were finely interwoven in a slim, tight braid of deceit. My wife, the same woman with whom I'd shared an important part of my life, had kept a secret existence hidden inside her. But isn't it always like that, after all? To what degree are we really capable of knowing someone else? There's always some inscrutable zone, a space where the most abject feelings dwell, a dark territory often invisible to our own eyes, because should we see it, the delicate framework we've built over the course of our lives would all at once come crashing down.

These thoughts didn't resolve my questions, however. One obvious answer stood out among the others. Informing on me to the detective—even if she'd taken into consideration the possibility that I myself had already told him—was her way of taking revenge. One betrayal for another. Both brutal. But there was something more. My adultery was cruel, but there was nonetheless an element in her treachery that made it darker and more intricate.

I remembered that Sunday night, how I'd left Teresa and returned home, pretending I was just back from my trip to Los Peumos. I remembered Gracia's sleeping face, the half-open curtain giving a glimpse of our garden, the night-blue light, the lilies on the chest of drawers, their sickly scent. I also remembered thinking I saw, for a moment, Gracia's eyes, open and looking at me. However, when I spoke to her she rolled over and faced the wall, and I imagined that her slow, even breathing meant she was still asleep. After seeing me with Teresa that night, how many horrible thoughts must have gone through her mind, how much anger and pain. The next morning, I got up earlier than usual. Gracia was in front of the bathroom mirror, putting on her gold earrings, the ones I'd given her for her last birthday. I seized her from behind and wrapped my arms around her waist. She tensed up and brusquely freed herself from me. Without taking her eyes off the mirror, she asked me how my trip had been. Inhibited by her reaction, I gave some meaningless answer and brushed my teeth over the other sink.

"You can tell me about it tonight. I have to pay a couple of bills online before I leave," she said, giving her hair a few final brushstrokes.

I remember hearing a brooding ferocity in her voice and seeing a contained nervousness in her movements. I attributed both signs to my sensitive, guilty state of mind and dismissed them as unimportant.

As I went out for my morning jog, I saw Gracia sitting in front of the computer. She held her torso perfectly erect, which heightened the graceful angle made by her waist and her lower body and showed to great advantage the curve of her hips. She looked at me without taking her hands off the keyboard. Her expression, despite its coldness, contained a mixture of impatience and pity. I thought I could even read what she was thinking: *How much longer will I complain about the way my carefully constructed dreams keep receding? How long before I finally come to terms with reality?* And how mistaken I was! Maybe that was the exact moment when she decided to challenge you.

Gracia had always considered you with distrust and anger, and although you tried more than once to enter into some sort of contact with her, she remained firm in her decision to ignore you. She'd been in your house only once. I'd forgotten my cell phone, and there was some urgent banking matter she needed to resolve with me. I remember her avid curiosity as she took everything in, and then she left.

The only reason that could explain her determination to cross your threshold that morning was that she wanted to challenge you. The fact that I'd been in your house with my lover made you, in her eyes, an accomplice in my betrayal. Maybe she even saw you as inspiring it, promoting it. But what did she mean to do?

All at once, I saw everything clearly. Gracia went to your house. She was upset when she got there. After seeing me with Teresa the previous evening, she hadn't slept all night, and the harder she'd tried, the more her nerves had betrayed her. She surely entered by the kitchen door. She knew it was always unlocked for me, a fact that seemed unacceptably intimate to her. You must have heard something, and maybe you called down from upstairs, "Is that you, Daniel?"; and probably—it was what you always did—you started talking to me right away, as if the conversation had begun long before, or was the remnant of an unfinished dialogue; it's even possible that you mentioned, from the upper floor, something about my visit the previous day, mine and Teresa's; nor is it implausible that Gracia, dismayed by your words, and above all by what she was doing, didn't answer you but walked farther into the house, silently, without any clear idea of what she was doing in your home, or of what, at that moment, she hoped to accomplish there. Maybe the encounter took place when you appeared, looking down from the upper floor, and she looked up from below and saw you as serious and threatening. I don't discard the possibility that Gracia, with her fists clenched and her arms folded over her stomach, insulted you and accused you of the harm she knew you'd done to our marriage. She probably blamed you for all our problems, including those that preceded you, the ones that had always been with us. She was desperately looking for someone to blame for everything she hadn't been able to resolve or understand. Yes. As far as Gracia was concerned, you were always the culprit, and the knowledge that she could foist her own responsibility for things off on you gave her, without her realizing it, a fragile but effective equilibrium. While she was talking to you, the tone of her voice probably kept rising, and she probably kept shouting as she climbed the stairs. I couldn't imagine her laying hands on you and making you stumble and fall. Not that. Because that would have entailed seeing Gracia as a more violent woman than I was ready to admit, or to bear.

There was something else. That scenario made me indirectly responsible for your fall. If my conjectures were right, Gracia's actions had been motivated by jealousy, jealousy not altogether unfounded. Your home was my secret world; it was not only the refuge where you and I shared our days, it was also the place where, with your approval, I'd brought my lover.

I got up from the bed in my studio and went out into the garden. It was a night without stars, endless, made of a solid, oppressive material. The scent of the flowers suffocated me. I needed to talk to somebody, to share the thoughts that were choking me. I couldn't get out of my head the idea that Gracia and I were responsible for what had happened to you. I'd never before felt so confused, so boxed in. Should I talk to the detective? Give him the background so he could question you? Accuse my own wife? An acidic laugh rose from my throat, poisoning the air.

I went inside and poured myself some whiskey. I turned off all the lights, sat on the living room sofa, and waited for Gracia.

I didn't fall asleep until almost dawn, and when Gracia arrived in the morning, I was still lying on the sofa. She opened the curtains, and the sound of her brisk movements woke me up. I was in time to see her with open arms, holding the ends of both curtains, like a crucified Jesus or a supplicant soul, her muscles finely toned at the gym, her slender gold bracelets sparkling in the early morning light.

"What are you doing here?" she asked, grabbing the suitcase she'd leaned against the wall.

"I was waiting for you," I said, sitting up.

I knew my appearance must have been deplorable, I knew I was presenting the image Gracia detested most: the look of a man who'd chosen to remain on the margins while the world and its concerns proceeded on their way. I swept my disheveled hair out of my eyes and looked at her. She didn't turn away.

"We have to talk, Gracia."

"I'm exhausted. I hardly slept, the flight from Lima was horrible, it left at two in the morning."

"I'll make coffee. I haven't slept much either."

"So I see." She left the dining room and went upstairs.

I stepped into the kitchen and set about making coffee. I trusted Gracia would come when I called her. We couldn't keep on pretending. The moment had come for us to face each other, she carrying her guilt on her back and I carrying mine. After a while, she came down. I was sitting at the kitchen table, waiting for her. She'd put on a pair of jeans and a white T-shirt that let her erect nipples show through.

"Here I am," she said, catching up her loose hair and knotting it at the back of her neck. A second later, it was free again, cascading down onto her shoulders. She remained immobile for a moment, her eyes fixed on the dishwasher. Then she slowly lifted her head and looked at me with an expression of contempt that made me flinch. She sat on a chair across from me and took a pack of cigarettes out of her jeans pocket.

"You've started smoking again," I commented.

She gave me an ironic smile, letting me understand that I'd succumbed to vices much more serious than hers. She lit a cigarette, got up, and went in search of the ashtrays, which for some time had been abandoned in one of the kitchen drawers. She took out an ashtray, the biggest one, and defiantly placed it on the table. When she got up, I'd figured she'd notice the jars of chestnut puree and mushrooms in vinegar I'd prepared for the Transatlantic dinner and put on the shelves, but if she did, she made no comment.

"It's just for a few days," she said, sitting down.

A dark and vigilant silence settled over the kitchen. In my nocturnal meditations, I'd never stopped thinking about how I would confront her.

"I'm listening," she said, crossing one leg over the other. She'd broken the silence and taken control, however precariously.

The only possibility of dealing with a situation like that was to charge it head-on.

"Gracia, you went into Vera's house that morning. What happened there?"

I looked straight at her; I needed to examine her every gesture, her every inflection. My senses were all on alert. Something was approaching. I froze in place, body and soul, to absorb it.

"How do you know that?" She leaned forward. The cigarette between her fingers trembled almost imperceptibly. Gracia had been able to control her expression, also her voice, but not her body.

"Someone saw you." My voice sounded sharp and abrupt.

"And may I know who this 'someone' is?"

"You don't know him."

"A stranger," she said, her eyes fastened on the table.

"In a way, yes, a stranger."

"And this stranger accuses me of entering Vera's house." I couldn't see the expression in her eyes, but her temples were visibly pulsing.

"He's not accusing you of anything, he's just a witness."

She raised her head and said, "And you believe him."

"I don't see why I shouldn't."

"And if I told you I wasn't ever there, would you believe me too?"

"No," I replied curtly.

A slight tremor in her chin told me that my refusal to believe her words had been a blow to her. My disbelief was the final betrayal, and it definitively broke the bond that had united us. She got up from her chair and went over to the window. One hand held her cigarette, the other hooked her belt. Her back was to me, and her slender figure seemed to be surrounded by a halo of light.

"That wasn't the only question you wanted to ask me, was it?" she asked me from the window, without turning around.

"Of course not. There are other things."

"Things like, you have a girlfriend," she said, still with her back to me.

"Had."

"Ah, I see. It seems that everything's very simple for you. 'Had,' you say without batting an eyelid, and that's supposed to be it? As if having a girlfriend were the most natural thing in the world."

I watched the battle that was going on inside her. She wasn't going to yell at me or lose control, as she had on other occasions. Nor was she going to cry. She looked at her cigarette ash, which was about to fall to the floor, as though she'd forgotten it was there.

"It isn't. It's not simple, and I'm ashamed of it."

"What if I tell you I did see you and your girlfriend go into her house the day before, I did go over to Vera's house the next morning, and..."

"And what, Gracia? And what?"

"And I rang her bell and no one came, and I waited a minute or two, and I thought about going in through the back door, the one that's always open for you, but then I just gave up, got in my car, and drove away."

"So that's how things went?"

"And afterward you called me and told me what had happened."

"And?"

"And I was afraid."

"Afraid of what?"

"Afraid you'd think what you're thinking now. Don't take me for a fool."

"And that was why you told the detective about my girlfriend and our visit the night before?"

"You can't play games with me, Daniel, because I'm going to win every time. Every time."

I never imagined the day would come when Gracia and I would speak to each other like that. It was the type of dialogue we'd hear when we watched movies, holding hands and eating popcorn, and it belonged to another world, to other people, to people who did one another harm, who lived in private wars that consumed their lives. But not us. Because we always imagined we were inhabiting a particular and unique territory, while the others, those outside, wallowed in their ignorance, their boredom, their meanness. Reality, I thought, doesn't become real until it kicks down the door and comes in. When all is said and done, we're made of the same stuff as the people we're looking down on so haughtily and disdainfully. Our island had been only a mirage. These thoughts saddened me, and I couldn't go on arguing with her anymore. What finally defeated me was that Gracia's version and the vagrant's differed on an essential point. According to him, Gracia had entered the house. According to her, she hadn't gone any further than ringing the doorbell. If Gracia was lying, it was because something shameful had happened inside the house.

The battle was lost, for both her and me. Now we were alone. In silence, I took my cup and put it in the dishwasher. When I sat down again, I noticed that the lilies had managed to disperse their yellow pollen as far as the surface of the wooden table.

"Say something," Gracia said.

The air we were sharing had grown heavier.

"I don't know what to tell you."

I sat back in my chair. Everything started to get farther away. As if I were looking through a porthole in an outward-bound ship, heading for the open sea. Gracia stayed far behind, she and her bracelets, which jangled in the silence as she lit another cigarette. Her aspirations and her utopias, which had never been mine, were far behind me now. I was out of her circle, I'd jumped over to the other side.

I would never know the truth about what happened in your house. Gracia's version would clash with the beggar's in my consciousness until one of them, for some reason—new evidence, or renewed conviction—imposed itself on the other.

39·
EMILIA

It was early when Daniel called me. Vera's heart had stopped at daybreak. "She went off into her dreams," I heard him say.

I imagined that last heartbeat, the same as the others, and then she was gone. She was gone. She was gone.

I was standing up, leaning against the wall of my room, and my legs buckled. Before seeing Vera unconscious in the hospital, I'd met her only once. And yet, grief for her struck me with great force, like gunfire inside my body. Why did it hurt so much?

I said it aloud: "Why does it hurt so much?"

We both remained silent. On a neighboring roof, pigeons were beak-fighting over a piece of bread. Their stark combat offended me.

After a few seconds I asked, "Where is she?" I heard Daniel sigh on the other end of the line.

I imagined one of those anonymous places called morgues, where naked corpses are stored. The impassive metal surface, the white sheet. A blast of cold air, like something from an icehouse, penetrated between my bones and my skin.

"What time did it happen? Was anyone with her? Are you sure she didn't suffer? Tell me, tell me," I begged him.

I needed to protect myself from death by immobilizing it with concrete facts and details.

"I'll tell you everything."

We stopped talking again. Silence was a hollow where neither of us was safe, but it was also our only way of expressing what we felt.

I wanted to evoke Vera's presence, but my memories of her were almost all imaginary. I saw myself holding her arm and walking at a steady pace. To where? We passed a yellow hill, near the sea, and then a square, the main square in Grenoble; Vera clasping my hand in one hand and her black umbrella in the other; Jérôme disappearing around a street corner; far off, the sound of church bells, the rain; Vera's umbrella opening.

I stayed fixed on that last image, afraid to leave it and enter pain.

"Are you there?" Daniel asked me.

"Yes, I'm here."

The sound of an ambulance siren burst in through the window. Loud and clear.

We agreed to meet an hour later at the hospital. I put on a white shirt and a black skirt. The cold was still imprisoned inside me. When I went out, the white tents, awaiting the evening's dinner party, were flapping without discretion in the morning breeze.

We walked toward each other in the hospital corridor. He kept his reddened eyes on me. When we were almost face to face, he stopped right in front of me, his arms hanging down in a gesture of defeat, as if the entire responsibility for what had happened to Vera had now landed on top of him. He closed his eyes and pressed his lips together, maybe holding back a sob, and then I put my arms around him and he let his head drop onto mine.

His body was pulsating and trembling.

We stayed like that, each clinging to the other. For the first time I was experiencing an intimacy in which the other person's body heat, instead of hurting me, felt indispensable.

We went into Vera's room. Although her eyes were closed and her face was empty of all expression, her presence was intense. Beside her, her life in those past months remained intact: her photographs, the jars of cream we used to lubricate her parched skin, and the Peruvian lilies I'd brought her the day before, now exhaling the oppressive air of death.

Daniel moved the bag of saline solution and sat down on the bed next to her. He stroked her gray hair. "And now what?" he asked in a whisper.

He closed his eyes, but the tears escaped between his eyelids. I went out into the corridor. I couldn't bear his sorrow. After a while I went back in, and Daniel was standing at the window, looking out. I went over to him and took his hand.

And there we were, Daniel and I, united in a way neither of us could assess at that moment.

"What are you thinking?" he asked.

I raised his hand and mine, together. "Vera brought us here. Now we have to go on."

I remembered the creaking of the white tents, like the sails of a ship about to set out.

"With everything?" he asked.

"Yes, with everything."

"I don't think I can do it, Emilia."

"Sure you can," I said, remembering the words that Jérôme had spoken a century ago. "Sure you can," I repeated.

40.
DANIEL

I was still a teenager when I realized how naive it was to try to make sense of events by labeling them "coincidences." Things happened in a certain manner, and the attempt to find a hidden design in them was a trivial and mendacious way of conferring significance on the banalities of life. But I couldn't deny the fact that you had left us at dawn on the day when our Transatlantic was to set sail. I suddenly understood the need—a human need, after all—to give meaning to what wounds us, to muffle the pain, to place misfortune in a larger dimension than ourselves. I wanted to believe Emilia was right, and the only possible interpretation—assuming one existed—was that since we were ready to weigh anchor, you had finally allowed yourself to rest. However, despite those thoughts, I wasn't able to go ahead with the dinner that evening. I had harbored, in some part of my consciousness, the illusion that you would wake up one day. I hadn't ever been able to imagine your death. I felt you were immortal. You were force, will, determination. And as in your story about the

Siamese twins, when you left you took the dream with you. The Transatlantic didn't make sense anymore. Maybe I'd conceived it for you, so that from the depths of your silence you could see me embarked on a dream. I don't know. The only thing I wanted to do now was to close my eyes. So that you couldn't escape me. I needed silence. There was no way I could be among all those people. I was unable to go on. Emilia and I argued for the first time. I pulled my cell phone out of my pocket to set the wholesale dismantling process in motion, but she caught my wrist and took the phone out of my hand.

"I'll do it," she said. "I understand you can't do it, but I can. Everything is practically ready. Now it's just a question of finishing up."

"But it's my project, and I don't want to go on with it," I said, almost shouting. When the dispute began, we'd stepped out of your room, and now we were in the corridor.

"It's mine too," she said firmly.

I didn't have the strength to keep on arguing. Emilia went into your room, and I stayed outside in the corridor, dazed and leaning against the wall. A second later, she walked out again with her bag slung over her shoulder.

"I'll do it for both of us," she said, and walked down the hall toward the elevator.

41.
EMILIA

Juan and Francisco were waiting for me, nervous and overcome.

Before Daniel decided not to go ahead with the dinner, he'd called them to report what had happened, and without hesitation they'd offered to take care of the final preparations.

Despite the boldness I'd shown in front of Daniel, I felt lost and alone, as if I'd been abandoned on some bleak plateau. Hours had passed since they'd taken Vera to the mortuary chamber, but Daniel had decided to spend the night in the hospital. He wanted to be near her.

"How's your friend?" Juan asked me.

Juan and Francisco had never met Vera, or Daniel either, but they knew that my life revolved around them.

"He doesn't want to be separated from Vera," I said, and my voice broke.

"Don't worry, we've made a lot of progress," Francisco said. "Look, the rest of the tables have been set up."

Only then did I notice the tables arranged around the terrace and the white tablecloths rippling in the breeze. The chairs—all different, but all simple in form—came from various antique dealers. On the big wooden table that Daniel had designed stood three blue-trimmed china vases, overflowing with geraniums and roses.

Flowers that represented life and death.

The two youngsters we'd hired to help Daniel with the last details of the dinner soon appeared. Daniel had prepared practically everything the previous day, and they could finish what he had left to do. Which is what they did. In the meantime, Francisco, Juan, and I undertook the final tasks. During what was left of the afternoon, the rest of the flowers arrived, along with the dinner services and the candelabras. An army of people was moving about in the mist before my eyes.

I made a quick dash to my room and put on the outfit I'd bought for the occasion in a secondhand clothing store. It was a sand-colored gauze dress, its material haphazardly printed here and there with scattered flowers. I also opened my computer and wrote to Jérôme, telling him about Vera's passing. It was the third email I'd sent him since receiving his letter. The first was blank, and the second, sent a week later, told him I was doing well. And asked him not to worry about me. Jérôme, for his part, had started sending me emails again, lots of them, in which he recounted to me the insignificant mishaps that had constituted our lives. It was hard for me to understand why he was doing that. He never talked about his lady friend, but on the other hand he never told me he'd broken up with her. I read his messages quickly, intent on keeping his words from hurting me or making my imagination go in directions I'd be sorry for later.

Juan and I started to receive the first guests at nine o'clock. As soon as they arrived, they asked for Daniel. Juan, with his baronial manners, explained that a problem had arisen. He spoke in a low voice, addressing one guest at a time, taking each of them into his confidence, letting it be understood that Daniel was attending to important matters and that they should feel privileged to have received his invitation, even though he was unable to be with them.

My body moved, reacted, and spoke, but I wasn't there. Now and then, I felt I was drowning. I couldn't help seeing the sinister fluttering of death behind every gesture, behind each musical cadence, behind the dozens of candles and their sparkling light. And nevertheless, as the night slipped away and the dishes Daniel had prepared with such care followed one after another, at once simple and splendid, his dream was becoming reality.

But he wasn't there to see it.

Every now and then in our nonstop bustling, I would run into Juan or Francisco, and they must have seen how bereft I was, because they would step back and look at me, shut their eyes for a second, sigh, and then continue on their way.

Except for Mrs. Espinoza, who came escorted by Efraín, the library's gardener, all those people were strangers to me. They presented a Santiago that the restricted perimeters of my comings and goings had not allowed me to discover. Slender, sun-bronzed women with long hair who walked around the terrace in between courses with their cigarettes in their hands, exhaling the smoke into the night as if they expected something from it; men who clapped one another on the back and charged from one subject to another without lingering on any. The moon winked, and the Transatlantic sailed deeper into the night. I kept moving from one side to another. Serving, clearing, agreeing, and thanking, while my eyes were turned inside, looking at Daniel.

At a certain point, a man tapped on his glass and halted all the conversations. A robust candle illuminated his face. He was slim, with straight hair, and he called to mind a polo champion, or a landowner who had spent a good period of time exposed to the benevolent Mediterranean sun. At his side, a woman with very white skin squirmed anxiously in place. The man spoke about Daniel. I don't remember his words. But I do remember that Daniel's absence made him get bigger and bigger, until he turned into a sort of hero. The hero who is off in some remote place, fighting a battle. Which was in fact the case.

It was at that moment, while the man's words were shattering the night, that I slipped away to my room and called him.

"Hello," he said.

"What are you doing?" I asked.

"Vera wanted to be cremated," he said, without answering my question.

"We'll see about all that tomorrow," I said, speaking in the gentle cadences one uses with troubled children. "How do you feel?"

"Lots of people came. Reporters everywhere. The story's going to be in all the papers tomorrow."

"Are you still at the hospital?"

"I'm very tired," he replied. He was broadcasting on his own frequency. He didn't ask about the dinner. Everything that went beyond the circle of death had ceased to exist for him.

"Don't pull away from me," I said, my voice breaking. "You're all I have, Daniel." Outside the music started up again, and the cruise ship continued its party voyage.

In the midst of this sadness, I had the sensation that we were falling, Daniel and I, tumbling through a corridor of silence. Maybe it was the same place Vera was moving toward at that very moment. I thought that there must be a point where life and death met, and that it must be the point of highest awareness. It had to be seized so that later, when the immediacy of the loss would have faded, its significance might be deciphered. I wanted to shout at him, "Listen to me, listen to me!" I wanted to embrace him, to feel his warmth, to unite my body with his in this journey we were making to immutable serenity.

"I'm here," Daniel said. "I'm here," he repeated.

. . .

After everyone was gone, Juan and Francisco stayed up on the terrace with me. They were afraid to leave me alone. The evening, according to them, had been quite a success.

"Nobody wanted to leave, I thought we'd have to be here till dawn," said Francisco. "Did you hear what they were saying about the food? They were thrilled. What a shame your friend Daniel couldn't have heard all that praise with his own ears."

They talked at length, and their voices pacified me. I wasn't really aware of what had happened, but I believed their words. We had done it. And it was sad that Daniel didn't know.

When I was alone again, I called him.

As soon as he heard my voice, he said, "I'm practically there. Here's your door. Now I'm coming up the stairs."

A few minutes later, he was standing in front of me. We hugged each other. I felt a kind of liberation, but at the same time I knew I was trapped. My sadness got mixed up with the pressing need to feel Daniel's living body. The candles were dying, their flickering flames projecting their shadows onto the tables and onto the black depths of the night. Without a word, we went into my room. But it was another room, another time, and I—perhaps—another woman, the one who sat on the edge of the bed and waited.

Lips were on my breasts, on the palms of my hands, on my stomach, on my shoulders, between my legs, until

Daniel pushed hard, groaned, rolled his eyes back, and collapsed on top of me like an untied sack whose contents have spilled onto the floor. I was struck by the knowledge that I could generate such abandon, and then such surrender. Warm liquid seeped down my thighs.

That day left two dead: Vera and my affliction.

42.
DANIEL

We'd brought up the subject only once, you and I. You mentioned it when you were making a pisco sour in the kitchen, with your back to me and your face turned away. You wanted to be cremated, you said, and your ashes thrown into the sea. However, since I wasn't a family member, I needed a document that testified to your wishes. The day after you died, Emilia and I went into your house, and for the first time, using the key you gave me, I opened your strongbox. As you'd told me, it contained a great many papers. Among them we found your son Julián's birth and death certificates, together with a photograph of him taken at the Nice Observatory. It was the first time I'd ever seen a picture of your son. I was struck by the force of his black eyes and the fragile look of his long, thin body.

"This is incredible! My parents worked there," Emilia said in a hushed voice. "Before I was born."

She looked at the photo for a long time and then turned it over. The names of some stars were written on the back.

"Apparently Julián inherited his mother's interest in the stars," I said.

"Or maybe it was the reverse, and the boy's interest aroused Vera's," Emilia suggested.

Besides Julián's documents and photograph, we found the certificates of your marriage to and divorce from your only husband, Manuel Pérez. His name and story had appeared alongside yours in that morning's papers. In fact, with amazing speed, your name landed on the pages of newspapers all over the world. People had already come forward to declare that you should have been given the National Prize for Literature, and prominent academics, domestic and foreign, regretted that you'd never received a Nobel.

Among the documents, we found a gray folder with several poems written in your unmistakable hand. Emilia stopped to read them, sitting on the edge of your bed. As she was doing so, she struck the pages with her fingers.

"Is something wrong?" I asked.

"These are Horacio Infante's poems. The ones that made him famous."

"So why are they here?"

"Because it was Vera who wrote them." Her voice sounded agitated.

"What are you saying?" I asked, incredulous.

"Do you remember my investigations, the ones that got me nowhere?"

I nodded.

"I had started getting suspicious, but this is practically proof. There's no doubt that Vera was the author of these poems."

"Are you sure?"

"They're in Vera's handwriting, and they're much different from the ones Horacio had published before, and also from the ones that followed. Infinitely superior."

Emilia looked again at the pages in her hand and then went on: "Many years later, Horacio published three short poetry collections that recaptured the special quality of these poems and made him a shining star again. Maybe Vera wrote those collections too. Maybe their long, long friendship included a pact, by which Vera made a gift of her poetic genius to Horacio."

"But if she'd published the poems in her own name, the acclaim Horacio received would have gone to her."

"Along with the countless prizes, the readings all over the world, the grants from American and European foundations—everything that allows Infante to live his comfortable, colorful life," Emilia added.

"Exactly."

"But maybe that wasn't what Vera aspired to. Horacio's poetry, or Vera's"—she clarified—"remarkable as it may be, not only has a simplicity her work lacks, it also represents something she wanted to escape from. Vera was always investigating the boundaries of words, even though she set no store by innovation in itself. She says so in her interviews. She didn't give many, but she emphasized this point in all of them."

"Yes, I remember she used to say you didn't need talent to write a text without the letter *e*, or without commas, or without whatever else, and you didn't need it to write an incomprehensible text either."

Emilia laughed and went on talking enthusiastically. "Sure! That sounds so much like her. Vera was looking for a truer freedom, the freedom to discover that you're creatively free. And the result is a demanding body of work, filled with labyrinths and meanings."

"That's why she leaves the reader uneasy, in a way. Anxious."

"Right. I think the poems she wrote for Horacio were a diversion for her. They flowed from her easily, and she didn't consider them worth much."

I asked her if she wanted to keep the poems, but she said no, she could see them later, and now we should try to find what we were looking for. She got up from the bed, and as she was putting the papers back in the strongbox, she said, "Daniel, Horacio was asking Vera for these manuscripts at that luncheon. They're the only evidence of the truth. Yes, yes, I'm sure, he must have known of their existence. That morning, Horacio was looking for these papers."

"It's possible."

A few hours earlier, Detective Álvarez, informed of your death, had called me on my cell phone. It had been weeks since I'd heard from him. He offered me his condolences and informed me that his superiors had ordered the case closed owing to lack of evidence to confirm my suspicions. That didn't mean it couldn't be reopened later, in the event that some new evidence was presented, but for now the situation was that the case was closed, and there was nothing he could do about it. My thoughts turned to Gracia. I had an urge to tell Emilia about my conversation with the bum and the conclusions I'd arrived at, but I didn't do it. Maybe I never would. If in fact Gracia was somehow involved in your fall, destroying her life, accusing her to the police, wasn't what you would have wanted.

"There's a story!" Emilia exclaimed. "One of Vera's stories—it explains everything. It's about a couple who are both mathematicians. Yes. Now I see it so clearly, Daniel. It's incredible."

Emilia summarized for me the tale of the mathematician whose wife discovers the formulas he's spent a lifetime searching for.

"I remember one of the last sentences in the story," Emilia said. "It's when the mathematician looks at the pages where his wife has written out the sequences and understands that she possesses something he'll never be able even to glimpse."

We kept on looking, and among the bank statements we found a certificate you'd signed in front of a notary, declaring your desire to be cremated. We also discovered your will. It was plain and precise, like everything that annoyed you and got shoved into a corner. It was dated a year previously. You left me all your possessions, including the house and the manuscripts to be found in it, and a sum of money that you kept in a Swiss bank. You commended Charly and Arthur to my care. This testament of yours finished me off.

We'd been sucked up in a whirlwind of activity since dawn, and it hadn't ever let us go. We'd lost the sense of time and of ourselves. But now that we had the document we needed in our hands and the course of events was determined, our grief came down on us again, with all its black weight, its black smell, its sooty black touch.

Now you're in the ocean. The boatman brought us out to the open sea and asked us to sit down facing the shore. A strip of golden sand lay in the distance. If we threw your ashes toward the horizon, he advised us, the wind would carry them away. And so we did. Nevertheless, at the moment when we turned over the urn and released its contents, a sudden breeze came up and blew some of your ashes back on us, and they stuck to our hands and our faces. We looked at each other in distress. It was as if death had stretched out its gray claws to take us too. We washed ourselves with salty water. And all at once, we burst out laughing. The boatman gazed at us without curiosity from the other end of his little vessel. Our laughter expressed a thousand things, among them how deep the bond between us had become. Emilia took from her skirt pocket a piece of paper, folded in half, and threw that into the sea too. I didn't ask her what it contained.

Maybe it was something she would have liked to say to you, a secret she wanted to send off with you across the open water. Or maybe she told you about us. I very much longed to know what she was feeling, to know what was the meaning, for her, of what had happened between us on the night of the Transatlantic dinner party. In the distance, a flock of birds zoomed across our field of vision. I touched her mouth with my fingertips, and she smiled sadly. When we returned to land, the sun was setting behind us. Emilia wore a tortoiseshell headband that gleamed in the last rays of sunlight. Our boat was moving toward the shore over the serene blue of the sea like a small prehistoric animal.

43.
HORACIO

Human nature, for all its puniness, can bend even the most ironclad resolutions. I wasn't the only person who had read the last issue of *SUR*, and in the following days I received no end of compliments. It had been a week since I'd written Victoria Ocampo the letter that was still in my briefcase, along with the magazine. And from there, from its hiding place, that letter emanated a putrid odor. If someone offered me congratulations, someone who had never read my poems and didn't know the magazine but who had heard so-and-so or what's-his-name talking about me, a peculiar venom would circulate in my veins, a venom that was surely visible in my cynical smile, in the affable, enthusiastic way I received the words of encouragement, in the false humility that aroused warm feelings and instigated fresh praises. A venom that began to transform me into somebody else.

Vera and I hardly saw each other, and if we did, we didn't speak a word. I'd gone back to sleeping on the olive-green couch, as I'd done in the days when Julián lived with us. I would leave early, while she was still sleeping, and after work, without stopping in at home, I'd make my way to the darts bar, sit on a stool, and order a whiskey. Sometimes four or five whiskeys. My intention was to leave the bar drunk, retard the flow of venom, and return to my apartment as late as possible so that I wouldn't have to look at Vera's face. More than once, I opened the bedroom door and gazed at her body as she lay between the sheets, barely illuminated by the light that filtered in from the living room. The desire I felt for her hadn't diminished one iota; it had even grown stronger. I loved her and hated her at the same time. I needed her and despised her. I admired her and envied her. Yes, I envied her. I envied her the gift she had, which allowed her to see what I would never be able even to glimpse. The something that would transform a fairly good text into an extraordinary one. And it wasn't only Vera's brilliant way with words; it was something much deeper, something I didn't have so much as a clue how to go about looking for.

Visual, muscular, and *emotional* were the words Einstein used to explain the origins of his particular way of thinking. Never before had I understood what he was referring to. Knowledge and the products of reason, for example mathematics and physics, were his supports, but his genius came from someplace else. A place Vera knew well.

One night in the bar, while observing the everyday scene—the bartender and his juggling act, the bottles behind his back, the wall-to-wall mirror reflecting the smoky barroom—I pulled the magazine out of my briefcase for the first time. As I read the poems, sitting on the same stool I sat on every day, I felt once again the feelings I'd had on that fateful evening, but cushioned this time by the effects of alcohol and the passing days. I read them several times, and all of a sudden I found myself declaiming them aloud. Three women were conversing at a table near the bar, two guys a few stools down from me were drinking alone, and a group of office workers were playing darts. The women were the first to break off their chatter and fix their eyes on me. They were around forty, and they appeared to be women of the world. One of them, despite looking slightly timeworn, was even attractive. Her gaze incited my courage, and I raised my voice. Then came the two solitary guys, and within a few minutes everyone in the bar, including the bartender and a girl who was washing glasses in a corner, had ceased all other activity and was listening to me attentively. The man I had been until then wouldn't have been able to do it. His reserved nature and a heightened sense of the ridiculous would have prevented him. But that guy with the still-young face reflected in the mirror behind the bar, the one projecting his voice and gesticulating like an amateur actor—that wasn't me.

A few days later, when I got home to the apartment, I could see from the hall that Vera still had the bedroom light on. That morning I'd received a letter from Nascimento Publishing. They were interested in publishing my work, but first they needed me to send them my next project. The problem was I didn't have any project. Maybe that was what I resented most. Vera had robbed me of my future.

On the rare occasions when we talked, I'd asked her again why she'd done it, and her line of argument remained immutable: her meddling with my poems had been superficial, and she'd done it for love.

"Horacio." I heard her calling me from the bedroom.

My nerves were numb with alcohol. I took off my jacket, draped it over a chair in the dining room, and went into the bedroom. Vera was in bed with her knees up and a notebook propped on her thighs. Her large and unusually pale mouth projected anxiety. I could smell her, her scent that had always excited my senses, but this time it hurt. She looked tired.

"Next month they're going to have a Francisco Matto retrospective, and they've offered to send me to Montevideo to interview him."

She was looking at me with a mixture of pity and impatience.

"Sounds like a good idea," I declared.

She shook her shoulders, as if something had fallen on them and she wanted its weight off her.

"You don't mind if I take a trip?" she asked.

"Why ask me that? It's your life," I said, with intentional disdain.

"Then I'm leaving Friday."

Her words sounded sharp and precise, like the darts when they hit the bull's-eye. The beastly feelings I'd been harboring all those weeks filled the room so completely that I had trouble breathing. I needed to get out of there.

"Good night," I said.

I woke up in torment. The room was lit by the first bluish lights of dawn. I opened the window to a tepid wind. The threat of rain was hovering in the air again. I went into the bedroom. Vera was sleeping face down. I yanked the blanket off her body. She didn't move. I penetrated her without even looking her in the face. She buried her head in the pillow. I heard her moan.

The night before she left, I got home even later than usual. There was a plate of dinner, now cold, on the table. Two red candles were guttering in their chandelier, and in the amber vase—as a rule empty—was a bunch of red roses. This made me furious. Vera's efforts seemed to be designed to transfer guilt, so that in the end she'd wind up looking like the conciliatory, charitable soul, the victim. But at the same time, I couldn't help appreciating them and noting the desperation they communicated.

The morning of her departure, I was sitting at the table, drinking my cup of black coffee and reading an office document when she appeared in the living room. Rain drummed on the windows. It had also been raining on the day when the magazine came in the mail and changed our lives. She leaned in the bedroom doorway and stayed there. I looked at her out of the corner of my eye and returned to my document. She was wearing her silk robe, and she'd gathered her hair into a ponytail. She had deep rings under her eyes, and her pale skin seemed even more delicate. A ray of sunlight passed through the half-open curtains and traced a line on the floor.

"After Montevideo, I'm going to Buenos Aires for a few

days. The newspaper has some other stories they want me to do. I'll be staying with a couple of Chilean friends." Her voice had turned a little hoarse, as though worn down from cigarette smoke.

"For how long?" I asked, without raising my eyes.

"Two weeks," she said, and remained in the same place, without moving, waiting for something to happen. "Will you be all right?"

"Of course I'll be all right." My words sounded caustic.

Two pigeons landed on the windowsill with their noise like rusty cans and then vanished. I listened awhile to the silence that had fallen. It wasn't only the absence of sound. There was something else in that silence, as if it wished to communicate something about itself and us.

"Look at me," she said.

I took a sip of coffee with my eyes fixed on the document.

"See you soon, then," she said. She took two hesitant steps toward the line of light and then turned around and disappeared behind the bedroom door.

When I finished my coffee, I picked up my briefcase and, without telling her good-bye, left the building.

That scene came back to me insistently over the course of the following weeks, like a line that you know is important to the development of the poem, but you can't figure out why. I remembered the noise of the pigeons on the windowsill, Vera's fragile, stoic presence leaning in the doorway, her hoarse voice, the silence that had fallen on us, with all its multiple significance. It had been one of those moments that at first seem slight, unremarkable, moments that can nevertheless change the destiny of those who live them. What would have happened if, instead of staying stubbornly focused on my reading, I had looked at her? Or if, when I saw her step toward the beam of light, I'd taken her hand?

Essential but useless questions. I hadn't done anything to hold on to Vera, and now she was far away.

A few days before the full two weeks were up, I got a letter from her telling me she was extending her stay. She didn't know for how long. The newspaper was delighted with the articles she'd been sending them, and the editor had given her permission to remain as long as she thought necessary. It was a bland, formal missive.

One Saturday evening, while ordering the papers on the desk Vera had occupied since her arrival in the apartment, I found a gray folder. I opened it and discovered my poems and the corrections Vera had made to them. There were also the cardboard figures she'd made to decorate the Christmas tree. For a moment I thought about going out onto the landing and throwing all that into the incinerator. But instead I took the poems Vera had rewritten out of the folder and started to read them. Some were verses I hadn't even considered when we chose the ones to send to *SUR*, but those too, like the others, had been transformed in her hands.

The street was silent and still. The lights of the building across from mine were floating in the dusk. I closed my eyes and the poems appeared, with their images and cadences, like a landscape I'd known in my childhood and kept in the background of my memory. Then I knew that in spite of how many words, verses, or whatever Vera had altered, those poems were still mine. They bore the imprint of my feelings, which were neither better nor worse than hers, but different, and my own. And that was something that nothing and no one could refute. Nobody would remember the events the way I remembered them; nobody, even though in similar circumstances, would experience my feelings, my joys and my sorrows. Vera's work had only stripped my poems of what stopped the reader from seeing their essence.

I wasn't certain that these revelations, which came with ambiguous clarity, were authentic. But I needed to emerge from the darkness, and I clung to them like a true believer clinging to a supreme truth.

Something unprecedented was taking shape in me. And for it to happen, I'd needed to die a little, I'd needed to pass through that no-man's-land where there's no life, no air, no hope. That's the nature of beginnings, and only in that instant did I understand it.

Part THREE

44.
EMILIA

The day after we threw Vera's ashes into the ocean, Daniel left his house.

In the first weeks, we'd spend the day on my rooftop and at night he'd go back to the hotel room he'd taken. However, before long he practically stopped going back there. One afternoon we went to the hotel; he paid the bill, picked up his suitcase, and moved in with me. A few days later, we collected Charly and Arthur. Even though Daniel had been going to Vera's house every day to walk and feed them, we both thought it was obvious that they should come and live with us.

With Daniel, I experienced a new freedom, as if I'd been filled with air. Everything that had remained in silence now found a way of expressing itself. They were sensations and images difficult to formulate, and because of that all the more deeply rooted, for no thought could destroy their mystery.

To tell the truth, I wasn't thinking.

Everything was suspended. Daniel's life, mine, and that possible future together that neither of us would bring up. He didn't go into details about his separation, nor did I ask him for any.

In the morning he'd get up early and go for a jog. When I woke up, he'd be back already, having bought fresh bread, made coffee, and squeezed some oranges. After breakfast, I did my produce deliveries, and then I'd head for the Bombal Library. Daniel had countless meetings to go to. The comments on our recently inaugurated Transatlantic in magazines and newspapers left nothing to be desired. But the most important thing was that Daniel was encouraged enough to request a loan from the bank to buy the site on the cliffside. Going forward, he wanted to build the real Transatlantic.

After a few weeks, I already knew that Daniel slipped a hand under his pillow when he slept, that he woke up several times a night, that along with cooking he took a secret pleasure in the act of cleaning up, that he shaved every other day, that when he woke up his hair was damp with nocturnal perspiration, and that his skin brought back from his dreams the smell of wet earth. We never stopped talking. Even the most insignificant detail about the other interested us.

On one of those mornings, Daniel found Infante's letter in the mailbox. I'd sent him an email the day after Vera's death and he had replied, obviously shaken. He'd gone on to announce that within a few days, he would send me the text he'd promised. He asked me to read it calmly and not to judge him until I'd reached the end.

What Daniel brought upstairs was a big envelope containing a typed manuscript with a handwritten note from Infante on the first page:

Emilia:

When Vera fell down those stairs, I knew she would never come back to us, and I knew that our story, if I didn't reconstruct it as soon as possible, would be buried with our old bones forever. And so I've spent the past few months working on that task. For Vera, for us.

But only some weeks ago, amid delirious memories of her, did I finally realize that you would be the recipient of this account, that the reader I was talking to was you. I kept on writing, even though I was assailed by doubt at every turn. Everything that until then had seemed essential turned out to be superficial, and what I had previously rejected now appeared immensely important. I address these words to you in fear. Perhaps I should have spoken sooner, much sooner, or perhaps I should have kept my mouth shut. I actually don't know. Now you're the one who will have to decide the fate of the truths you'll find here. Because in the end, all this is nothing more than my clumsy, belated attempt at expiation. If that's in any way possible.

Horacio

After reading the letter, I put the manuscript under my pillow and went out to make my produce deliveries.

I felt a great sense of worry and foreboding.

I had a premonition about that manuscript. I knew that reading it was going to disrupt my life, one way or another.

That I'd never be in the same place again. When I got back to my apartment, I made myself some tea, sat out on the terrace, and opened the manuscript. It was a sunny morning. There was a fresh, benevolent breeze.

> *It was the summer of 1951, and I was thirty-three years old. For the past thirteen, I'd lived in various cities, but mostly in Geneva, working for the High Commissioner for Refugees, in whose offices I occupied a minor position. My return was a response—according to the official story—to my mother's plaintive letters, wherein she detailed the multiple infirmities that could, any day, snatch her away to the grave. But the truth is, I was returning home chock-full of anticipation and plans, which included renting a cabin facing the ocean and dedicating myself completely to poetry, or meeting an attractive, intelligent compatriot to share the rest of my life with. From a distance, Chile had turned into the place where all the dark corners of my existence would be filled with light. The Promised Land, the Paradise Lost...*

I kept reading, and by the time Daniel came home that evening, I'd read more than half. While trying to process what Infante had written, I tried for the first time to cook something for Daniel, following the instructions for a pasta recipe I'd found on the Internet.

A new Vera had emerged in Infante's words. A woman of flesh and blood, but a woman who at the same time opened up new mysteries. Try as he might, Infante hadn't ever managed to pierce the shell she lived inside, which made her inaccessible for everyone, maybe even for herself.

We sat on the terrace and ate the pasta, followed by an arugula salad with warm slices of pear and parmesan cheese shavings that Daniel prepared. I told him about my confirmed suspicions. And about the discovery I'd made, and how it had been halfway corroborated by the manuscripts in the strongbox and was now a reality. That was Horacio's great secret. The cross he'd carried all those years. I also described to Daniel a few of the episodes in the manuscript. I told him about Vera's fortitude in confronting prejudice because of her Jewish origins. About the meeting in the snow in New York, which was in one of Vera's novels and Infante's poems. I talked about Vera's son Julián and the obsessive love she'd lavished upon him.

After dinner, Daniel lit a few candles, and their fragile light shone on the place I was occupying, the armchair on the terrace.

Soon I went back to my reading, with Arthur lying by my side.

I was sailing on an ocean. I wanted to get a look at its floor, at the scrap scattered down there, at the substratum that underlay the vast, ungraspable, and somehow artificial sea constituted by Infante's words. I'd read a stretch and stop and wonder, why did he send me this long manuscript? What sense did it make that I should be the repository of secrets, things kept in confidence for so many years?

There had to be something more.

It was late in the night when I got into the bed I shared with Daniel and nestled against his body. The person who was there, clutching his shoulders, wasn't me, but then again it was. He wrapped both his legs around one of mine and kept on sleeping.

I wondered if that was how people felt when they said they were happy.

When I woke up, Daniel was almost finished dressing and about to leave. He had a meeting with an investor who'd shown some interest in joining him in the Transatlantic adventure. Daniel had dressed himself with care. A blue-and-white-striped shirt and a well-ironed pair of black trousers. His hair was damp and combed back. His facial features showed in all their splendor, naked and firm. He raised his eyes and met mine as they were watching him. He took my hand and explored my palm with his fingertips.

I had isolated myself from everything, imagining that my own interior silence would be where I'd find real life. Now I was learning that I could go there and come back, and that this entering and exiting, this in and out, was a kind of freedom.

"You've never looked at me like that, Emilia."

"Like how?" I knew what he meant. For the first time, I had got a glimpse of his disturbing beauty. And I felt neither rejection nor fear. Because what I knew was still there, under that male carapace.

"Like this." He focused his pupils on the bridge of his nose, making himself look cross-eyed. We both laughed. A tingling sensation ran up and down my spine.

After Daniel left, I took a bath.

I felt the weight of the water on my skin. I stretched out one leg, as though disentangling a ball of wool. My arms too, which I made circles in the air with, like two blades of a lazy fan. My breasts, two little animals, poked out into the semidarkness. When I pressed them, my nipples opened their eyelids. I submerged my head and listened to the hum. In the silence, someone or something was being born.

How could I feel so good if, for the first time, I was going forward without any certainties, without the boundaries that had protected me?

Daniel had left a tray on the kitchen table with everything laid out for my breakfast. I sat on the terrace under the white canopy and continued reading Infante's manuscript.

45·
HORACIO

Vera never came back to my apartment. She made the announcement in a letter she sent me from Buenos Aires. After her return to Santiago, she said, she'd stay for a few days with a woman friend, a newspaper colleague, as long as she would need to find an apartment for herself and Julián. Pérez had consented to let Julián move in with her. Within a few weeks, Vera had conceived and organized a new life that didn't include me. At that moment, I understood the true magnitude of my loss. From the very beginning, we had kept up a long conversation with many dimensions, and now Vera had turned her back on me, leaving me in that wasteland to talk to a stranger who was theoretically myself but with whom I didn't know how to communicate.

What came after that is part of the official history. Vera continued to work at the newspaper, and after a while she published her first collection of stories, which found unanimous acceptance among the critics. Four years later, she published her first novel, in which the individual prose and unique style that would eventually turn her into a cult author were already in place. I for my part remained firmly seated inside the train Vera had put me on. A few years after publishing a couple of poetry collections that hadn't had much of an impact, using the manuscripts of the other poems of mine I'd found in Vera's gray folder and then copied, I put together a book that Arnaldo Orfila himself, the director of the Economic Culture Fund, was delighted to publish. That book would nourish my life, literally and figuratively, from then on. Once you lie, I'd discovered, you're turned into someone else, and that other, high on his comfortable promontory of inventions, can't stop himself anymore, he doesn't remember how to turn back.

As the years passed, I wrote other collections of poetry. Many of them were received with enthusiasm, but none had the brilliance of the one Vera had worked on. That was a gift I never let go of, afraid that someday someone, perhaps even Vera herself, would snatch it away from me. I lived in terror of that moment. In time, the demon, which in the beginning had appeared before me in the form of frustration, anger, shame, and self-contempt, gradually became distilled and turned wholly into fear. How many times did I wish Vera were dead. I read every one of her novels, seeking out trails that would lead me to the poems, afraid that someone else would take the same path and discover the truth. I often found such trails, and I lived in a state of dread until the reviews of Vera's book ran out. But then the translations would come, and I knew shrewd academics all over the world would be scrutinizing her work, and there was a good chance one of them might find Ariadne's thread, the thread hidden among the letters and leading to me. To my sham, to my big lie.

I obsessively recalled the words Thoreau had written in his journal: "The youth gets together his materials to build a bridge to the moon, or, perchance, a palace or temple on the earth, and, at length, the middle-aged man concludes to build a woodshed with them." The modest hut where his soul resides and in which, every day, he has no choice but to look his littleness in the face. All my life, I'd tried to fight against Thoreau's prophecy, and in a certain way I'd succeeded. I'd built stately stairways and temples, castles and gardens. Except that the original materials he'd mentioned were in my case false, and they ended up crumbling inside me. How many times, over the course of those many years, did I run the whole gamut of my arguments again, seeking to justify myself? Arguments that piled up like an alcoholic's empty bottles in a corner of the kitchen.

When Vera went into a coma, I thought that at last I'd be able to relax, without the fear that had gnawed away at my life for more than forty years. However, one night, a few days after her accident, I woke up with the air blocked in my throat. I was drowning in my own impotence, the kind that comes when you know nobody's going to change anything and you should expect nothing, and beneath your old skin humiliation and uselessness are roaring. Then I started writing. It was a solitary, futile exercise.

Until, some time later, I came to know that I was doing it for you, Emilia, and that I had to go all the way to the end.

46.
EMILIA

It was the first time that Infante had addressed me in his manuscript.

I raised my eyes. An ancient brown light, heavy with dust, covered the vastness of the sky. I had my legs curled up under me on the chair, and they were getting cramps. I put the manuscript aside and took a few turns around the roof. I watered the red geraniums Don José had given me. The hibiscus too, and the jasmines I sometimes saw opening in the night. The bougainvillea had started to climb the western wall of the roof terrace, covering it with its vibrant purple color. Arthur and Charly followed me from one side to the other, wagging their always happy tails. Then I checked my computer for emails. Jérôme had gone back to writing me. He'd been shaken by the news of Vera's death. He wanted to know how I was and what my plans were. When would I return to Grenoble?

I went back to the chair and resumed my reading. Infante's manuscript aroused confused feelings in me. There was a structure underneath his words that wasn't related to the facts or the details. And that somehow tied them all together.

47. HORACIO

Pérez died seven years later as a result of a liver deficiency. During those years, I'd spoken to Vera only a couple of times, and I'd never seen her again. It was a cold autumn morning, and in the General Cemetery of Santiago, the avenues leading to the graves were covered with dried leaves, which crunched underfoot as the procession passed. There were countless heartfelt speeches by family members, friends, and important personages, including an ex-president who talked about Pérez's work in saving thousands of Jews from the extermination camps; this speech caused more than a little throat clearing, as if those episodes in Pérez's life were unworthy of being told. Vera, dressed in strict mourning, stood off to the side with Julián and looked straight ahead, her eyes lost in the depths of the gray morning light. The air was so cold that it felt like a rain of needles piercing our skin. I made as though to approach Vera and her son, but she stopped me with an almost imperceptible movement of her head. Her breath formed clouds of mist. It was obvious that leaving Pérez for another man had resulted in her banishment from the world he'd introduced her to. In fact—as I learned much later—she never received so much as a cent of Pérez's fortune, and his family even prevented any part of Julián's inheritance from going to her. At the time of his father's death, Julián was sixteen, a slender, long-limbed boy whose demeanor retained the same rectitude and control he'd exhibited when he was a child. Under thick eyebrows, his black eyes had an unreal, neonlike gleam. His hair, also black, fell over his forehead, an area where all his force and self-assurance were concentrated. Standing beside Vera and several inches taller than she, Julián listened attentively to the words that were being dedicated to his father. Every now and then he took his mother's arm, closed his eyes for a second, and kissed her head, which was covered by a black scarf. Behind them, on top of a cupola, a sculptured Madonna raised her arms heavenward; her marble head was bowed, her eyelids were closed, and her palms open, dangling defeated from her wrists. At the end of the ceremony, Julián came up to me, holding out his hand in greeting the way he'd done that first time, when he and Vera arrived at my apartment.

"I'm very sorry I wasn't able to tell you good-bye," he said. His words took me aback.

It seemed to me extraordinary, to say the least, that he remembered me, but what surprised me most of all was how amiable he was. I had imagined that child would hate me for the rest of his life as the person responsible for the destruction of the protected world he'd been born into. I gripped his hand forcibly, trying to transmit the feelings that were overwhelming me and the immense affection I hadn't realized I felt for him.

"I still live in the same place," I said. "I'd love for you to visit me. We could take up our long conversations again. I'm certain you don't remember them, but I assure you, they were very enjoyable."

"I remember them perfectly, sir," he declared.

"You can call me Horacio," I said, and I handed him my card. "Call me at this number whenever you want. I would be honored to have you in my home."

"I'll do that," he said, and he turned his eyes toward Vera, who was standing in front of the Madonna with the extended arms and looking at us with a sad expression on her face.

Julián waited almost a year to call me. He spoke in whispers, and I imagined he was hiding the call from his mother, but that didn't stop me from inviting him to come for tea the following Saturday. He arrived right on time, carrying a box of chocolates. When we finished drinking our tea, we went out for a walk in the heart of the city. Julián tried quite frankly to show me that the years hadn't transformed him into an empty-headed teenager. He spoke to me of his reading and his knowledge of astronomy, asked about my books, and also talked about the column I wrote for the Sunday edition of *El Mercurio*; according to him, his mother read those pieces with great attention.

I had long since given up imagining her. In fact, I'd removed her as far as possible from my thoughts. The idea of her was accompanied by a sensation of loss and, more than anything else, by a perception of my own insignificance. Nevertheless, I couldn't help getting jittery at the notion that she read my columns, that she was out there somewhere, and that from time to time she thought about me.

Our meetings, Julián's and mine, continued throughout that year, 1964, and the next. He had chosen me, taken me by the hand, and drawn me to him. I wasn't able to understand his reasons, but I made sure to respond to his appeal as best I could. Part of that effort involved not milking him for information about Vera or her relationship with Pérez. I never even asked him whether his mother knew about his visits to me. Even so, as time passed, Julián gradually revealed certain things. For example, that Pérez, long before I appeared on the scene, had withdrawn into himself and the various infirmities he suffered from. Julián had adored and admired his father, but that devotion, and the fact that Pérez was already a middle-aged man when his son was born, had never allowed the boy to have a truly close relationship with him.

One day while we were walking back from a performance of *Turandot* in the Municipal Theater, I mentioned Augustine, the young Frenchwoman who had worked at the observatory.

"I still see her," he said with a smile. His shoulders looked narrow under the huge tweed jacket that must have belonged to his father.

There wasn't much traffic, and a gentle calm hung over the trees lining the sidewalk.

"Thanks to her, I've had access to the observatory all these years."

"And you still like her?" I asked, moved by an unhealthy curiosity.

"She's a mature woman," he said gravely.

Right then I would have liked to tell him a few home truths about the women I'd known, but the fact that his mother had been one of them held me back. Julián was a seventeen-year-old boy, but his formal bearing and the way he expressed his ideas made him seem much older. At his side, I could feel the effect he produced on women of all ages—like his mother's effect on men—and I wouldn't have been surprised to hear that this Augustine felt attracted to him.

The following year, Julián enrolled in the University of Chile to study astronomy. We'd had many conversations by then, and I had repeatedly told him that after completing his degree, he should leave the country, get to know the world, maybe acquire some practical experience in a European observatory. I was a great believer in insularity as a malady you would do best to recover from quickly if you didn't want it to turn into a credo.

When I expressed these concerns to Julián, I was also, without saying so, talking about myself. I'd spent too many years coming and going between my apartment and the Foreign Ministry, attending the social functions (they bored me rigid) connected to my work, beginning and ending affairs that led nowhere, and now it was time to emigrate. Despite the fame I'd achieved through my work, which was published by important houses and appeared in Spanish-language periodicals, for some reason, perhaps my shyness or my inability to develop a sense of belonging, I'd never joined the city's intellectual circles. On the street, I'd often run into Santiago del Campo, who would very chivalrously salute me by tipping his hat. On other occasions I'd come across Claudio Giaconi, whom I'd met in El Negro Bueno, but my relations with that group of intellectuals never went beyond such fortuitous and insubstantial encounters.

I activated my former contacts at the United Nations, and in February 1965 I moved to Paris to work on a project that involved African immigrants from the colonies.

When the time had come for our farewells, I'd invited Julián to a bar for the first time. He'd passed his eighteenth birthday. We both made an effort not to fall into sentimentality; the endeavor caused long periods of silence, which we tried to dodge with the aid of our glasses.

In accordance with his gentlemanly affect, Julián sat up very straight. He stoically resisted the onslaught of the alcohol. His eyes were fixed on the table, and at regular intervals he ran his hand over it. I had an urge to embrace him.

Toward the end of the evening, when I was ready to pay our tab, I asked him about Vera. It was the first time I'd ever done that. He frowned and then said, "I think... despite the years...I think she still misses you." He looked off to one side and stroked his chin.

"And I miss her," I said.

Julián looked at me with a questioning expression, as if asking me, "Well?" To which, after another silence, I responded by taking a sip of my whiskey.

We left the bar and walked together to the apartment on Providencia Avenue where he lived with his mother. The streetlights lit up the sidewalks lazily, and the darkness of the night imprisoned us.

The metal grille in front of the building where they lived opened onto a paved garden that surrounded three low structures composed of simple, straight lines, typical of the architectural style of those years.

"That's our apartment," Julián said, pointing to a lighted window in the middle of the rear building. The light was yellow and dim.

In the foggy depths of my alcohol-soaked mind, I imagined Vera's living room, her papers on the floor, the ashtray spilling over with half-smoked cigarettes, the books scattered here and there. Vera and her world, Vera and her mysteries, which I'd never managed to unravel.

We said good-bye with a firm handshake followed by an embrace. I was carrying in my jacket pocket a copy of *Admonitions*, my first book of poems, which had never been republished. I'd inscribed it with a dedication that I asked Julián to read after I left. Julián entered and stayed on the other side of the grille while I walked away. I turned around, and he was still there. He was looking at the sky behind my back.

• • •

I met Rocío at the Chilean ambassador's residence in Paris. She'd been educated in a school run by French nuns, she was thirty-two, and she worked in a great fashion house. A few months later, we got engaged and set our wedding date. We were married in Santiago, complying with all the social demands of her large, conservative family, and then we went back to Paris. Our only daughter, Patricia, was born there on December 14, 1966. The marriage lasted five years. Rocío returned to Chile with the little girl, and I stayed in Paris.

During that time, invitations for me to give poetry readings were multiplying, arriving from every part of the world, but after Rocío and Patricia left, my life was a solitary one, deprived of genuine affection. When Julián announced that he was coming to live in France, I was overjoyed. Through an important French astronomer who had worked in Chile, he'd got himself accepted for an internship in the Nice Observatory, on the summit of Mont Gros.

On the very day of his arrival, I invited him to my apartment on rue Saint-Étienne-du-Mont. Julián was thirty years old by that time, and despite his tall stature, he projected an image of vulnerability. He coughed a good deal, his complexion gave off a pallid glow, and his hands were long and white, like hands in a Pre-Raphaelite painting. We sat in the living room of my home, and while we drank our tea, we looked out my little windows and watched the snow fall on Paris. The fire in the chimney sent up spirals of sparks like golden veils. I couldn't share with him my memory of the first time his mother and I met in New York, and how it was snowing then too. The same muffled silence in the streets, the same stillness, the sense of time suspended as the fragile snow came down. I did, however, find the nerve to ask him about her. He told me she'd bought a house on the slopes of San Cristóbal Hill, where she'd isolated herself even further from the world. She was still writing for the newspaper and working, as always, on a novel. Julián admired her strength, her beauty, and above all, the particular way of life she'd chosen. I asked him, cautiously, if she was involved in any romantic relationship.

"She never lacks suitors. They're always circling around her, trying to get closer in all sorts of ways, from the most pedestrian to the most intricate. But she seems to have contempt for them just because they court her."

In order to cover up the emotions his words set off in me, I offered him a little glass of cognac.

I recalled Vera's face, her slanted eyes, her pouting mouth, the malicious expression of someone who understands it all but isn't going to give herself the trouble of explaining it to you, a pout full of the smugness and sadness of one who knows she'll always stand apart. I had seen all this, I'd loved it, and I'd let it get away. The spirit of the savage days that followed Vera's departure came back to me and filled the room with the dust of desolation, so much so that I had to rise from the chair, open the window wide, and breathe deep. Julián asked me what was going on. I lied and told him the smoke from the chimney, even though it was imperceptible, always choked me.

The darkness came on fast. The burning logs crackled, throwing up embers that bounced off the metal screen. He told me he'd suffered a relapse, his pulmonary malady had flared up again, and even though he felt capable of meeting any challenge, he hadn't completely recovered yet. It was then that I told myself I'd do anything at all for Julián, including, if necessary (without knowing at that moment how far I'd have to go to keep the promise I was making myself), stepping over his mother.

Julián continued to visit me. On the weekends, he'd stay in a modest but charming hotel near my apartment. We used to wander around the Saint-Germain quarter, conversing about his studies, about his new life in the observatory, about history, astronomy, art, and architecture (the main dome of the Nice Observatory was designed by Gustave Eiffel), and then I'd take him to a brasserie where we would remain, drinking until the wee hours of the morning. We went to operas and plays. Every visit left me wanting to spend more time with him. His sensitivity amazed me. With his attentive gaze, he'd point out things to me in Paris—hidden corners, special scenes—that I'd never noticed before, even though I imagined I knew the city very well. I remember the day we went to 8 boulevard de Grenelle to see the plaque that commemorates the 13,152 Jews who were taken from their homes on July 16 and 17, 1942, brought to the stadium known as the Vélodrome d'Hiver (Winter Velodrome), and sent by train to Auschwitz to be exterminated. Julián ran his fingers over the letters. Then we turned and walked away, he with his hands in his pockets and his head bowed down. I wondered how much he knew about his mother's history.

One Saturday afternoon in the middle of April the following year, I was just about ready to go out when my doorbell rang. I was neither accustomed to receiving unannounced visits nor fond of doing so. However, the sound of Julián's voice over the intercom brought me, as always, great joy.

"Can I come up?" he asked.

I took off my jacket and waited for him with the door open while he climbed the three flights of stairs to my apartment. I invited him inside and offered him a cup of tea, which he refused. He also didn't want to sit down or let go of the coat he was holding against his chest with both arms.

"So what's happening?" I asked.

"I'm in love with a married woman," he said without preamble, fastening his eyes on the darkened window. His face contracted, achieving an even greater degree of seriousness and circumspection.

He lit a cigarette, threw the match into the ashtray, and took a few deep, utterly uneasy drags. He shot me a quick glance, trying to make out my reaction.

"Sit down," I told him. And he obeyed me. I noticed that he was working hard to maintain his concentration. His eyes shifted from one side to the other, and he looked confused.

"And that's not all," he said, standing up restlessly. He leaned against the window and blew rapid lungfuls of smoke toward the street. "She's pregnant."

"Pregnant?" I asked stupidly.

"Pregnant with my baby, which she's going to have with her husband."

"You'll have to explain that," I said. "I don't understand anything."

"He's accepted the child. It will be theirs. Apparently they've had some problems in that regard, I don't really know what, but the thing is, they're going to have the baby together." He shook his hand in the air, as if trying to erase his last words. "She wants me to disappear from her life and the child's life. It will have her husband's name, grow up with him, and never know I'm its father."

His speech was labored and broken, and he was having trouble breathing. Maybe his lungs were bad again, maybe he was getting sicker. He shouldn't smoke, I thought.

I went over to him and put my hand on his shoulder. I thought about Vera and about what she would have wished me to say to her son in those circumstances, but the truth was, I'd never known her well enough to be capable of interpreting her will. And now her son was before me, overcome by a sorrow he couldn't hide, and I was trying without success to find something meaningful to say to him. Then all at once, I knew what I had to do. That woman couldn't snatch his baby away from him that way. Julián had to fight for his child, and I would help him.

"She's an astronomer and she works in the observatory. Her name is Pilar." His black eyes got darker, and his voice took on a deeper resonance. "Pilar," he repeated, as if he were talking to himself.

48.
EMILIA

A weight inside my chest stopped me from breathing. I flung Infante's manuscript away, and its pages scattered. The evening breeze picked up some of them and carried them to the farthest corners of the terrace. Julián's words reached me across time. The past, contained in my mother's name, was collapsing on top of me.

If Julián was the man who'd impregnated my mother, Vera and I were united by ties of blood.

I raised my eyes. The city was covered with gray gauze.

I'd always known that my father wasn't my father. The knowledge had brought with it its own sorrows, its humiliations and disappointments, until in the end it came to rest under the shade of a tree. Maybe my father's way—firm and at the same time totally without histrionics—of exercising his fatherhood was the reason why my eagerness to discover the identity of my biological father was practically nonexistent. That was a question whose answer I preferred not to know, because it seemed to involve betraying my father.

I got up from the armchair where I'd spent the last couple of hours, absorbed in my reading, and walked to the edge of the terrace, which looked down over the city.

In the sky, the evening airplanes were taking flight, while on the sidewalks people were walking up and down, brushing shoulders, transmitting to one another their animal smell, their sweat, their urine, inhaling the others' pestilence through their nostrils. Excrement, dampness, decay, secretions. I felt nauseous. My disease was stalking me again.

And attacking me on my weakest flank: memories.

I saw my past rise up like a big wave. So far I'd always succeeded in dodging that great wall of water, whose consequences it was now impossible for me to predict. I brought both my hands to my chest. When I was a little girl, I used to feel my wrists and the sides of my neck, looking for my pulse, trying to find the living being that remained encapsulated in my skin, inside the body I detested. If I had closed off my body from the world, I'd done so not to protect what it contained, but to avoid any form of physical contact whatsoever with my father, who I knew wasn't my father. When I was a child, I used to like to watch him. With his Viking's stature, his intensely blue eyes—so different from my mother's and mine—and that absent expression, which lit up only when he was looking at his stars, or at me. The love we felt for each other filled me with joy, but also with torment. I was afraid that if I took shelter in his arms, maybe I'd never be able to get free of them. Like one of those enchanted forests where the trees reach out their twisty branches to catch children, who then get lost and wander the wooded paths.

49.
DANIEL

Emilia was out on the roof terrace, sleeping in the armchair with her knees drawn up against her belly. I went to her, sat beside her, and stroked her hair. She opened her eyes.

"Are you all right?" I asked. She nodded and closed them again. I covered her with a blanket and got ready to prepare our evening meal. I'd brought some eggplants to make lasagna. Earlier in the afternoon, I'd passed by Gracia's house. I needed to recover some of my architecture books and the hard drive where I'd saved the plans for the construction of the Transatlantic. We'd agreed by text message that she wouldn't be there when I arrived, but Gracia had broken the agreement.

News of the Transatlantic dinner had spread to all the corners of the city. The most diverse and contradictory rumors were circulating. That I'd run off with a teenager, that I was living in the suburbs, that I'd taken a cooking course in Paris, that I'd gone into partnership with Alex Atala, that I'd turned into a hermit. Gracia was waiting for me in the living room, standing in front of the window. She was wearing a summery, cream-colored dress and holding a lighted cigarette between the index and middle finger of one hand, palm up. Only a couple of months had passed since I'd moved out, and yet I couldn't remember the details of our life together—how she smelled when she woke up, or the sound of her footsteps when she came home at night. The years I'd spent with her felt like a part of me that had atrophied or died.

I figured forgetfulness was an evolutionary trait humans had developed in order to survive. I looked around and saw the many objects that had been witnesses to our life together—the blue-and-yellow Gertrud Arndt carpet, the Akari lamp, the paintings and sculptures we'd gradually acquired over time—and I felt no sense of ownership. They were nothing but the carcass of a dead fruit.

Although I could have stopped her, I decided to answer every one of her questions. Unsaid words had destroyed our marriage, and I was determined to avoid them no longer. Emilia wasn't a teenager, nor had I run off with her; I was living across from Bustamante Park, and for the moment didn't need to take any more of my things; I'd decided to buy the cliffside site I planned to build my restaurant on; I'd applied and received approval for a loan. Gracia looked at me with suspicion and then half closed her eyes, as if she were being forced to listen to a lot of nonsense. Her questions went on for some time, while behind her silhouette the garden's luxuriant green—and between the leaves, a piece of the sky—showed through the window. I set my gaze on that abiding fragment of sky, seeking the equilibrium that Gracia's interrogation was threatening to overturn. In the end, many of her questions remained unanswered, and they revealed to me the precariousness of the situation our breakup had left me in. The format of the world I was sharing with Emilia didn't fit within the three-dimensional parameters Gracia and I had used to measure our life.

Gracia lit her third cigarette. She'd listened to me with controlled calm, but now her emotions began to betray her. She kept running her hand through her chestnut-brown hair, and her eyes, unable to settle on anything, shifted restlessly from one side to another.

"What's her name?" she asked, pressing her lips together in a grimace that showed the first traces time was starting to leave on her face.

I'd never paid attention to our difference in age, nor had it seemed important. But now, all of a sudden, it was obvious. Not only because of those first signs, but also because I was the one sailing away and she the one remaining, with the firmness and resignation time uses to harden us.

Emilia's name came between us, like a dense, definitive mass.

I was deep in thought when Emilia appeared in the kitchen.

"Smells great," she said, peering over my shoulder. Her hair grazed my neck. I turned around and looked at her.

Her round face, divided by the line of her dark bangs, had the simplicity and force of a good drawing.

"Did you sleep well?"

"I didn't sleep."

"So what were you doing?"

"I was thinking."

"Something has happened, right?"

She jumped up on one of the work surfaces in the kitchen and sighed. The exhaled air lifted her bangs. She crossed her feet at the ankles and started swinging her legs. She was wearing a pair of white sandals and a green dress I didn't recognize. She'd been gradually leaving behind her checked skirts and her boots, changing her look, making it lighter, more feminine, without losing that air she had of spinning around in a different orbit.

"Yes," she whispered.

"Want to tell me about it?" I asked. I washed my hands and dried them on my apron and turned off the oven, after making sure the lasagna had turned properly golden.

"While we're eating," she said. "I'm hungry."

Emilia had come into my life so intensely that I'd started to fear the days when she wouldn't be with me. It was strange to think that when our relationship had barely begun, but in some part of me I knew that Emilia, maybe not right away, but someday, would leave.

We sat out on the roof, and Emilia ate heartily. A good sign. But she didn't start talking until we'd finished our dessert.

"When things weren't going well, my father used to say, 'I know a planet where there is a certain red-faced gentleman. He has never smelled a flower. He has never looked at a star. He has never loved anyone.' Do you understand?" she asked, wrinkling her nose, a gesture I'd learned to identify with certain of her moods.

"More or less," I replied. But she went on, without trying to explain.

"Once and only once, my father let me spend an entire night with him in the observatory. It was a special night, because the next day was my twelfth birthday. We went up together to the dome that housed the Schmidt telescope, a gigantic telescope more than ten meters long. That night, instead of the usual cold, a current of fresh, almost pleasant air was coming in through the slit. After a while, my father told me he was going to look for a photographic plate. He left the platform and disappeared through the door. His name is Christian. Christian Husson. I've never mentioned him to you, have I?"

I shook my head, and she went on: "After he went away, the silence became absolute again. The immensity of the sky produced a terrible sensation of loneliness in me. I started singing sotto voce. But I shut up right away, because I realized that my father had left me on purpose. He wanted me to perceive that silence, because it was a silence that made you feel alive. Me, facing the sky, me, facing the universe and its mysteries, from the depths of my littleness. It was a lesson in humility and fortitude, both at the same time. I understood it and remained still, looking out through the slit, listening beyond the tinnitus of silence to the distant sounds of the night birds, and—nearer—to my palms rubbing together. Until he returned.

"That night I slept in one of the beds that had been set up in the corridor so the observers could take rest breaks. I'd already fallen asleep when my father asked me in my ear, 'You heard, didn't you?' and I told him yes, I'd heard."

Emilia was trembling. I brought my chair close to hers and hugged her.

"Christian's not my father," she whispered. "I've always known it, and it never mattered to me until now."

It wasn't until the following morning, while we were making breakfast, that Emilia told me what she'd read in Infante's manuscript. She told me without making a fuss. Julián was her biological father, which meant she was the granddaughter of Vera Sigall.

"Sigall, Sigall, Sigall," she repeated, again and again. "It sounds like *cigale*, French for 'cicada.' *S* as in singing, ceaseless, sunshine. And *l* as in labyrinth."

50.
HORACIO

So now you know. I can't imagine what you must be feeling, Emilia. I remember our walk through the Père-Lachaise Cemetery, when you told me your father wasn't your father. Those were the exact words you used. You also said that even though there were no blood ties between you, you were both made out of the same stuff. Throughout these past days, that declaration of yours has given me the stamina to go on. You knew that somewhere in this world there must be a man who carried your same genes, but you also knew that what bound you to your father was solid and deep. That was what your words transmitted to me.

I remember the day when you came up after one of my readings at the university with a copy of *Admonitions* for me to sign, and the excitement I felt when I heard your name. You had the same black eyes as Julián, the same sobriety in your gestures. Maybe, without my realizing it, that was the moment when the road we've traveled together began to take shape. Now that I'd met you, I couldn't let you go, and although I also couldn't just come out point-blank and reveal the truth to you, at least I could try to interest you in your grandmother's work.

You must remember the only time you and Vera were together, in my daughter Patricia's house. It was a moment I'd been looking forward to for a long time, getting the two of you side by side. I knew Vera would be instantly fascinated by you, which turned out to be the case. I don't know if you remember how many times she mentioned the impression she had that she'd met you before. I would have loved to tell her the truth, but I'd kept the word I'd given Julián all those years ago, and I wasn't about to break it then. Vera couldn't know, but she knew. Something inside her pushed her toward you.

To bring her face-to-face, in the sunset of her life, with the granddaughter she never knew she had was a secret way of thanking her. In my memory, the whole garden is abloom with the callas that Vera brought that day, which is, of course, a fantasy. I also remember the tension my secret charged you with, the two of you. It was a meeting that seemed to be taking place outside of time.

And only two days later, she would fall down those damned stairs. How could we have known? And yet I can't get over a feeling of guilt, Emilia. For not having pushed you harder. I let things happen at their own rhythm, and it took you some time to feel the necessity of traveling to Chile. I always thought you'd do it as soon as I mentioned the invaluable material Vera had donated to the Bombal Library. Some reason I don't know was holding you back. And I was waiting for the moment to arrive. But it arrived very late. And I'm sorry for that. You don't know how sorry I am. You must be wondering why now, when Vera's ashes have been scattered over the sea. What right do I have to reveal a truth that neither of your parents revealed? I imagine how upset they both must have been when they saw you getting deeper into Vera's work and closer to the secret they'd kept for so many years. They saw the past coming closer, and they knew that sooner or later it would turn their lives upside down, like the images inside a camera obscura.

So you're going to wonder, "How can this man be so arrogant as to disregard my parents' wishes and throw out revelations nobody asked him for?" And I must confess, I have no answer to that. Maybe it's because I myself see the black gleam of death coming closer, and I need to do something meaningful before it reaches me.

You're also going to wonder, "And I, what am I supposed to do with all this? What do I care about the guilt and the unsettled accounts of an old man on the point of exiting the scene?" I don't know, Emilia, I don't know. And I beg your pardon for that, because I've kept on writing all the same, and in a few days this manuscript will be in your hands.

I never had a chance to tell Julián that he ought to fight for you, because before long his cough started getting worse and worse. Obviously, his health had deteriorated in the course of the past months, and he'd barely had strength enough to last as long as he had.

I proposed that he should stay in my apartment until he felt better, but he rejected my offer. He did accept, however, a glass of cognac, and he downed it in one gulp with his eyes on the dark street outside.

I saw the apartment on Mosqueto Street, the lighted reading lamp with the glass shade, and Vera and me, sitting at the dining room table after dinner, she drinking one last glass of wine and me smoking a cigar. The image was so vivid it gave me a start. The Greeks described it, long ago: memory anchors itself in places in order to survive. In loci that the soul creates to store its mementos. And there was the image of little Julián, lying on the rug at our feet, concentrating on drawing up some equations in which, instead of numbers, he used suns, stars, satellites, and planets.

I remembered Julián's mature expression when he told us that his equations would solve all the world's problems.

"All of them," he asserted with conviction.

"I'm sure you'll be able to solve them," said Vera. Her voice vibrated, as if affected by an emotion she was trying to silence.

Julián had on sand-colored pajamas with an embroidered shield, like something worn by a miniature Hollywood heartthrob. We looked at each other, and Vera smiled. One of her broad smiles, a young woman's smile, full of teeth and pink, fresh gums. For an instant, we both believed Julián's words.

More than twenty years had passed since then, and the man in front of me, the child, his stars and his illusions, were about to depart. I could sense it. Yes. I sensed that

Julián, in the not very distant future, would be leaving this world. He went back to Nice that same night, and that was the last time I saw him.

We talked on the telephone several times during the following weeks, and in one of those conversations, he told me he'd seen Pilar one last time. He spoke kindly of her. In spite of the frustration and sorrow that losing her and losing you caused him, he was incapable of hating her, incapable of letting his anger spill out over his love. Your mother had insisted that if he desired you to have a life, he had to give you up. It was the only way, and that implied that he should never tell anyone what had happened. The curtain had to come down completely, and the lights had to go out. Forever. At the end of our telephone conversation, he said, "Although it must surely seem strange to you, Horacio, I'm going to keep the promise I made to her. You'll be the only person who knows this secret."

He sounded tired. His words, instead of being projected outward, seemed to remain at the bottom of his throat.

"I'm not even going to tell my mother. She'd set off around the world to find her granddaughter. I guarantee it. I've given Pilar my word, and now I need yours," he concluded.

And I gave it to him.

"Maybe Pilar's right," he said. "And this may be our child's only chance of being happy."

Julián died of an asthma attack in the middle of the night, four months after that conversation. I traveled to

Chile with his remains, while Vera made arrangements for his funeral.

We buried him on September 5, 1977, in the General Cemetery in Santiago, next to his father. It had rained steadily harder during the night, leaving a trail of flowers and leaves on the pathways. Many of Julián's former comrades were there, professors and friends, and about thirty people who offered Vera their condolences, which she received from the faraway depths of her sorrow. That morning I'd picked her up at her house in the Pedro de Valdivia Norte neighborhood, and during the drive she'd questioned me about Julián.

"Was he happy, Horacio?" she asked several times.

I was struck by her asking me that question. "What shall I do with this peace that slips in through the cracks, smothering me, and which you others call happiness?" she'd written in one of her novels. And I, bound by my promise, couldn't tell her that Julián had loved and lost. Nor could I tell her that in a few weeks, you would arrive in this world.

51.
EMILIA

That was where Infante's manuscript stopped.

In a note on the last page, he told me again that I could do what I wished with what he'd written. He said that he felt relieved of a great weight. Now that he was old, he could grant himself the privilege of getting rid of everything. The privilege of casting off, of letting himself be carried along through the ups and downs of the brief stretch of life remaining to him. He had nothing more to lose or to gain from the world outside. Everything that was gestating or dying was inside of him. And at last, stripped of its secrets after so many years, his being was at rest.

I felt angry. He was now strolling calmly through the streets of Paris, satisfied with himself, free of his ghosts, while I, in the heat of a Santiago summer, was doing battle with them. Ghosts that penetrated into the most remote corners of my life. Until then, the man who had fathered me had been nothing more than a concept. An idea that didn't change the order of things in any way. Christian had constituted my world. He was real, and so was the love we had for each other. Nevertheless, now, no matter how hard I tried to think that nothing had changed, I knew that everything had changed.

But in what way, I couldn't see.

In this tangle of sentiments, the notion of Vera Sigall as my grandmother appeared. The image that surged up before my eyes was a train station where I'd been hundreds of times, but where everything it contained—the platforms, the rails, the big clock with its gilt hands—had taken on a new and fantastic life. The platform wasn't a platform anymore, and the clock wasn't an instrument for measuring time.

Daniel found me that afternoon as he'd found me the day before, sitting on the terrace with Infante's manuscript in my hands.

Ever since the bank approved his loan, things had been moving fast. Together, we'd gone over the plans for the building on the cliffside countless times. It was to be a wood and glass cube that would float on the edge of the earth, a transparent planet ready to fall into the sea. We didn't talk about the future. But I could see in his eyes that I wouldn't be excluded from his. Sometimes, while we were looking at the computer together, he'd hug me tight and kiss my cheeks and my mouth, as though surprised that I was there.

"I finished reading the manuscript," I said when he sat down beside me.

A fresh breeze cooled the burning air a little. Above San Cristóbal Hill, the evening star looked like a bit of shiny paper stuck on a glass background.

"And?"

"Julián died a few months before I was born. He never even knew that I was a girl."

He put his arm around my shoulders, and I rested my head on his chest.

Some bougainvillea flowers had succumbed to the late afternoon heat and fallen exhausted onto the cement of the terrace.

"Daniel, I have to tell you something," I said, sitting up straight.

His body tensed up. He was wearing a pair of light-colored jeans and a mandarin-orange shirt that made his pupils gleam. "Let me talk first," he said.

He pressed his lips together as if he'd just made a decision.

"All right."

"You know what's in Vera's will."

I nodded.

"Well, everything is yours, Emilia. Her house, her manuscripts, the rights to her books, everything. It's only right. I've spoken to her lawyer, and the process isn't very complicated. I can explain it to you later. But the important thing is that you can live here. It's a lovely house. I could help you modernize it a little. It won't take long."

"Are you serious?" I raised my head and laughed. "Gracia would be my neighbor."

"Gracia hates that house. She's going to sell it as soon as she can. Seriously, Emilia, I can't stop thinking that Vera passed away without knowing who you are. And although

I've never believed that anything exists after death, I feel it's important that you should live there."

"That I should gather up her spirit."

"I don't know, something like that. That you should sort things out, that you shouldn't let what's left of her die, the part no one else will ever be able to see. Only you can do that."

"Sounds like too grand a project for me."

"There's no hurry. You can take your time."

Behind the faint evening light, which was in retreat, the stars appeared. Every one of them in its proper place. A sky whose equilibrium had been broken. If I tried with all my might, if I had enough nerve to do what was necessary, maybe I could put it back together.

"Daniel," I said, and his muscles went on the alert again. "Maybe, as you say, I should gather up the threads that bind me to Vera. But first I have to speak to my father and gather up my own threads. Do you understand what I mean?"

I took his hand and squeezed it, and he raised it to his mouth. My whole body shivered.

"I'm not sure."

"I'd like to go back to Grenoble. Just for a while."

He looked at the clouds that were spreading out above the treetops, the buildings, the new constructions, and the hills.

"Would you come with me?" I asked him.

A slight tremor ran over his face, as when a breeze takes the leaves of a tree by surprise.

"If you have to go back and gather up the threads you're talking about, it would be better for you to do that alone."

That "alone," barely stressed, remained suspended in the silence. I moved closer to him, and he put his arms around me.

"When do you want to leave?" he whispered.

"After you take me to see the cliff," I said.

"It's a deal," he said, and I hid my face on his chest.

I longed for his touch every minute of the day. And yet I couldn't stay there. It was as if, when I woke up, my body had been split away from me. My senses were marching along on their own, alert, steady, while my being, still disoriented, ran after them without ever catching up. I was obliged to make everything fit together somehow. And to do that, I had to look into my father's eyes.

52.
DANIEL

We'd slept badly the past few nights, and as soon as we turned onto the highway, Emilia fell asleep. The air coming in through the car's half-open side window tousled her dark bangs.

Where I'd lived until then had been miles away from the place where life went on for other people. I longed to cross that distance, but I had no earthly idea how to begin. You had shown me part of the way. But when all was said and done, as in a relay race, it was Emilia who'd grabbed me by the neck and exposed me to the light.

The plains, the deserted hills, Emilia breathing beside me—everything was penetrating me now. How many times, while I watched her watering the plants, washing clothes, helping me carefully and clumsily to prepare our dinner, had I asked myself, "What is it? What is it you're showing me, Emilia?" Maybe it was something that couldn't be translated into a logical thought or enunciated in words. Or maybe Emilia had put a mirror in front of me, and for the first time, what I'd seen hadn't produced in me a feeling of alienation or defeat. I felt afraid. Afraid of what might happen after Emilia left.

We'd spent every minute of those last days together. Feverish, agitated days. When we woke up, she'd press herself against my body and I'd press mine against hers, as if we were afraid to fall into a well from the threshold that separated sleep from waking.

We exited the highway and turned onto the dirt road. I kept one hand on the steering wheel and passed the fingers of the other over her sleeping face. We were about to arrive.

"Look," I said, indicating the stretch of white earth refracting the intense sunlight. She ran her hands over her face and sat up.

"Daniel," she stammered. "This is incredible."

"Wait till we get there," I said with a smile.

I parked the car, and we walked the two hundred meters that separated us from the cliff. Emilia was wearing jeans and a pair of white sneakers that were soon covered with dirt. She walked along, steadily observing the place we'd talked so much about. And while we walked, careful not to trip over stones, our eyes met expectantly. We stopped on the edge of the cliff. Down below, a giant mirror rested on top of the sea.

With a branch we found on the side of the path, I traced the outline of the proposed construction on the dry earth. Emilia helped me, pacing out the distances. The seagulls passed lazily overhead, occasionally uttering their rude and strident cries.

"One, two, three. This makes three meters," she said, and I marked the point where the next line had to begin.

After an hour, we were able to move from space to space, look out over the terraces, open doors, go over the kitchen with its stainless steel tables and its work surfaces, sit down in the middle of the dining room, and gaze at the magnificent and peaceful expanse of the ocean. Emilia knew the plans well. She lingered in each large room for a good while, stepping to the windows and the corners and then suggesting something, some small change I wrote down in the red notebook she'd given me, the one I made my colored-pencil drawings in. We'd brought a picnic lunch, which we ate without much appetite, sitting on the rough, dry earth.

The time passed too quickly, and although neither of us named it, the weight of her departure the following day sank down on us. After eating, Emilia walked a few meters away and squatted down to urinate, facing the sea.

Our return trip was long and silent. Emilia didn't sleep but kept staring blankly out her side window, as if she wanted to find herself in the reflection there. The automobile silently devoured the kilometers of black and silvery land while the day closed behind our backs.

For a moment, I thought about telling her that I finally had proof that Gracia was in your house that morning. But then I gave up the idea.

I had obtained that proof the day before. I'd needed to pick up some papers the bank required, and thinking that Gracia wouldn't be home, I'd shown up there around eleven in the morning. To my great surprise, she was working at her desk and came in to tell me hello. She looked well. She'd even made a few changes, including installing the Akari lamp in a glassed-in corner of the hall, where the outside light made it look quite impressive. It was when I complimented her on this move that, without realizing what she was doing she revealed the truth. "It was you who gave Vera hers, wasn't it?" she asked me. I'd given you an Akari lamp for your last birthday, only a few months previously. The single time Gracia had been in your house, it had been only for a few minutes, and at least two years ago. There was but one way she could have known about your lamp. I had an urge to shout at her, to accuse her, to destroy her. But I kept quiet. The same way I was doing now. I thought maybe the truth was too raw, and if I drew it into the light, it would bring nothing but destruction.

Back on the roof terrace, we ate fried sweet potatoes and grilled salmon with herbs. Soon after that, we went to bed. We were exhausted. Nevertheless, I was unable to go to sleep. I lay awake, picturing Emilia bounding from room to room with the sky for background, her slender legs, the distant clamor of the seagulls. Then I thought that happiness and sorrow went together, and that we couldn't know in advance when one of the two would get the upper hand.

53·
EMILIA

I woke up before the sun rose behind the mountains.

Daniel was still asleep. I'd packed my suitcase the day before, the same suitcase I'd arrived with.

I went out onto the terrace and watered the geraniums. Also the bougainvilleas, which—without the light to bring out their best—looked faded and tired. The streetlights were still lit. I sat on the bench that Daniel had installed on the east side of the terrace and draped a blanket over my shoulders. A fingernail of sun appeared behind the mountains.

I remembered the night when my father brought me to the Schmidt telescope and I learned to know the silence of the celestial vault. That morning, we watched the sun rise together. It looked so cleansed, so renewed, that I remember thinking it must have come from another country. When I told him that, he laughed and said, "Emilia, I don't know where that little head of yours is going to take you."

I missed his laugh, the way he always found the right words.

I heard the sound of a distant helicopter. It came closer and closer until it filled the dawn silence, and then it disappeared eastward. I saw Daniel coming toward me, still half asleep, in his striped pajamas.

"Hold me," I said to him.

He helped me up and put his arms around me. I felt the warmth of his hands on my back and his moist breath in my ears.

"Are you sure you don't want to come with me?" I murmured.

I knew it was already very late for that, but it was a question I'd asked him countless times during those days, and his answer was always the same. I had to go alone, talk to my father, tie up all the loose ends. Then I could come back, and we'd build the Transatlantic together.

We sat on the bench, still holding on to each other. The sun had completely risen above the mountain range.

"I've got a present for you," he said.

He wrapped me in the blanket I had on my shoulders and disappeared behind the door of the bedroom. A few seconds later, he appeared again. He'd put on a sweater over his pajamas, and he had his hands hidden behind his back.

"It's for you."

It was the stone I'd seen on his desk. The smooth, black stone with the silver threads.

"Vera gave it to me. It was Julián's."

We remained silent. It was a vivid silence, behind which could be heard the first warbles of the birds and the sound of the engines moving through the city. I took the stone in my hands. It was cold. A tiny silver seal was embedded in the back. When I looked at it closely, I discovered that it was a *J* entwined with a *P*.

In the evening, Juan and Francisco came to say good-bye.

They brought me a white case with everything necessary for an overnight flight: moisturizing cream, a toothbrush and toothpaste, a sleeping mask, and earplugs.

"We figured you weren't traveling in business class," said Juan with a roguish smile.

Daniel opened a bottle of champagne, and we drank a toast to the new Transatlantic, the one we'd open one day, facing the sea.

They accompanied us to the main door of the building, and we said our farewells on the sidewalk. I embraced Francisco and then Juan. Except for Daniel, they were the first people I'd ever hugged. I felt a wave of gratitude. Unexpected and powerful. I told Charly and Arthur good-bye and promised to return soon.

When we were already in the airport, a few minutes before I entered the migration office, Daniel told me, "Take your time. I'm not in a hurry."

He took my face in his hands and looked me in the eyes, with that clear, direct gaze that let you see inside him. It was hard for me to speak. The words *love, longing, promise* had been turned into containers too small for the magnitude of my feelings. We stayed on our feet, caught up in that contact, which crystallized the moments we'd spent together.

• • •

While the purring airplane was taking me home, I remembered my flight out, how I'd imagined from high up in the air the placid texture of the sea below and recalled the fear it used to instill in me when I was a child. Back then, I'd thought that maybe all things had a second dimension. A hidden dimension I'd never seen. Now I couldn't stop being surprised at the premonitory nature of that thought. But I also knew that there were so many things in me, apart from the ones I'd seen, that were still lying silent.

I reached into my bag, took out the stone Daniel had given me, and held it against my cheek. He was in that touch, and so were Vera and Julián. That was when I knew I would write our story. Vera's and Horacio's, Daniel's and mine, and how they'd intertwined until they arrived at this moment. I could also include Horacio's text. He'd told me in his letter that I could do whatever I wanted with the manuscript. Writing the story would be a way of uniting myself with Vera, of bringing to light what had remained in darkness. In the same way that my father discovered his dead stars when they got closer to the sun.

That precise instant, I thought—the stone cool against my cheek, the peaks of the mountains uniting me with the oceans, with Vera's remains, with the waves breaking far offshore and my mother's head rising up from among them, all those things that seemed to be in the distance, but which in reality were part of me—that precise instant would be the end.

THANKS

To Sebastián Edwards for the poems and his love. To Isabel Siklodi for her confidence in me. To Pablo Simonetti for his generosity. To Benjamin Moser for his biography of Clarice Lispector, whose life is interwoven in this novel with Vera Sigall's and my own. To Marian Pollas for her account of the nocturnal excursions with her father to the Schmidt telescope. To Felipe Assadi for explaining to me the architectural details that preoccupy Daniel. To my editor Andrea Viu for her professionalism and her friendship.

CARLA GUELFENBEIN is the author of five novels and several short stories, which have appeared in magazines and anthologies. Her work has been translated into fourteen languages. In 2015 *Contigo en la distancia* won the prestigious Alfaguara Prize. Before becoming a writer, Guelfenbein studied biology at Essex University and graphic design at St. Martin's School of Art in London. In her home country of Chile, she worked as an art director for BBDO and as a fashion editor at *Elle*.

JOHN CULLEN is the translator of may books from Spanish, French, German, and Italian, including Philippe Claudel's *Brodeck*, Juli Zeh's *Decompression*, Kamel Daoud's *The Meursault Investigation*, and David Trueba's *Blitz*. He lives in upstate New York.